UNFINISHED
BUSINESS

ALSO BY J. A. JANCE

ALI REYNOLDS MYSTERIES

JOANNA BRADY MYSTERIES

J. A. JANCE

UNFINISHED BUSINESS

AN ALI REYNOLDS MYSTERY

Pocket Books

New York　London　Toronto　Sydney　New Delhi

Pocket Books
An Imprint of Simon & Schuster, Inc.
1230 Avenue of the Americas
New York, NY 10020

This book is a work of fiction. Any references to historical events, real people, or real places are used fictitiously. Other names, characters, places, and events are products of the author's imagination, and any resemblance to actual events or places or persons, living or dead, is entirely coincidental.

First Pocket Books paperback edition June 2022

POCKET and colophon are registered trademarks of Simon & Schuster, Inc.

For information about special discounts for bulk purchases, please contact Simon & Schuster Special Sales at 1-866-506-1949 or business@simonandschuster.com.

The Simon & Schuster Speakers Bureau can bring authors to your live event. For more information or to book an event, contact the Simon & Schuster Speakers Bureau at 1-866-248-3049 or visit our website at www.simonspeakers.com.

Interior design by Erika R. Genova

Manufactured in the United States of America

10   9   8   7   6   5   4   3   2   1

ISBN 978-1-9821-3112-8
ISBN 978-1-9821-3113-5 (ebook)

For CSJ and Michael S. Bowl on!

|PROLOGUE|

BUTTE, MONTANA

— October 1981 —

An icy wind blew in from the west, and Broomy McCluskey, age fifteen, huddled in the moon-cast shadow on the far side of the shed, shivering—whether from the chill or anticipation—and waiting for the light in the kitchen to come on, signaling that his mother was about to send her mutt, Rocco, out to do his business. Broomy flexed the fingers of his right hand, feeling the unfamiliar weight of the brass knuckles and wondered if, when the time came, he would have nerve enough to go through with it.

Another blast of cold air ripped through the night. The first snow of the winter was supposed to fall by morning, and a good snowstorm was exactly what Broomy needed. Still, he shivered again, wishing he'd brought his jacket along. Had he done so, however, one or more of his drinking buddies might have noticed he wasn't just going outside to take a leak. It wasn't a huge worry, though. As far as he could tell, by the time he left, everyone was far too soused to notice much of anything.

The party was supposed to be nothing more than a last-minute kegger, held at Tony's house because his parents were out of town for a week. Broomy, having raided one of his dad's secret stashes of booze, had crashed the party, ensuring his welcome by adding a couple of fifths of tequila to the mix. He might have been the youngest guest at this underage gathering, but the tequila he brought along made him a very welcome one. He had pretended to swill down shots right along with everybody else, but by the time his buddies started passing out, Broomy was still stone-cold sober.

After making his excuses, he left the party by way of the back door and went straight to Tony's aging GMC pickup. He chose that vehicle for two reasons: Everyone knew that Tony always left his keys in the ignition and the brass knuckles he had inherited from his cousin in the glove box. Broomy had no problem maneuvering the vehicle out of the driveway. He might have been too young to have a license, but he had his learner's permit, and his dad had been teaching him how to drive a stick shift. His big worry now was that a cop might spot him coming or going, so Broomy made sure he didn't exceed the speed limit or do anything at all that might attract unwelcome notice.

At last the kitchen light came on. The back door opened, and Rocco sprinted down the steps and into the yard. As the door slammed shut behind him, Rocco stopped for a moment and stood still, sniffing the air. That's when Broomy let out a low whistle. He didn't care for his mother much, but he did like her dog. Without so much as a bark, Rocco galloped straight to the shed and stood there with his tail wagging while Broomy pulled a hunk of jerky out of his pocket. Rather than giving it to the dog immediately, Broomy opened the door to the shed and tossed the jerky inside. When Rocco leaped in to retrieve it, Broomy shut the door behind him.

Then he waited again. Minutes later, Ida Mae McCluskey, now wearing her long flannel nightgown, appeared on the back porch. "Rocco," she called. "Where the hell are you? It's cold out here."

Broomy knew from experience that the dog hated being locked in the shed. Rocco was scratching on the door and whining, and when the door didn't open, he started to bark, just as Broomy hoped he would. Stepping back into the shadows, Broomy peered around the corner and watched Ida Mae make her moonlit way across the yard, still calling for the dog, who was barking frantically by this time, hoping to be let out.

Tense with anticipation, Broomy stood still and held his breath, remembering what Tony had told him about the brass knuckles. "If you hit someone with these hard enough, right at the base of the skull, they'll be dead as a doornail, and there won't be no blood neither." That's what Broomy was counting on—no blood.

As his mother approached the door, Broomy sneaked around the far side of the shed so he'd be able to surprise her from behind.

"How the hell did you get yourself stuck in there, you stupid dog?" Ida Mae muttered as she reached to wrench open the door. "Come on, now. I'm freezing my ass off."

Those were Ida Mae's last words. Before her hand touched the knob, Broomy aimed a powerful punch at the base of her skull. He heard a sharp crack as the brass knuckles connected with skin and bone. His mother crumpled to the ground and lay there moaning. There wasn't a moment to lose. Afraid she might start making noises or calling for help, Broomy bent down and picked her up. It wasn't hard. Two years of weight lifting with the JV wrestling squad paid off in that moment. At this point Broomy could regularly bench-press a hundred fifty pounds, and his mother didn't weigh nearly that much.

He slung her over his shoulder in a fireman's carry and hurried back toward the truck he'd left parked on the side of German Gulch Road, just beyond their drive. Halfway to the truck, Broomy felt a warm gush of moisture as urine flowed down over the front of his shirt and pants. That's when he knew she was gone. Probably the very act of slinging her over his shoulder had been enough to finish her off. Now that his mother was dead, Broomy assumed he would have felt something, but he didn't. He was mostly annoyed that he was so wet, because it really was cold as hell.

Back at the truck, he hoisted her over the tailgate and dropped her into the bed of the pickup. Then he headed for what he hoped would be Ida Mae's final resting place. All around Butte there were low spots where brackish, mineral-laced mine-water runoff spilled into the earth and formed shallow ponds. Anaconda, doing its best to keep kids and wildlife from coming into contact with the contaminated water, had built chain-link fences and padlocked gates around most of the ponds, not that the gates were impervious. As kids, Broomy and his pals would use a bolt cutter to slice through the chains so they could come and go at will. When they were done wading, they'd wire the chain back together in a fashion that made it appear to the casual observer that the padlock and chain were still intact. Earlier that night, before

Tony had come to pick him up, Broomy had smuggled his dad's bolt cutter and a roll of baling wire out of the shed and hidden them away in some brush near the end of the drive. With his mother loaded into the pickup, Broomy retrieved both those items and headed out.

The pond he had in mind was less than two miles from the house and down half a mile of rocky dirt road. At the gate he made short work of the chain. Once the gate was open, he went to retrieve his mother's body from the bed of the pickup. Before lifting her out, he took hold of her cold left hand, wrenched off her wedding ring, and stuffed it in his pants pocket. Then he picked Ida Mae up and carried her to the edge of the pond, where he heaved her into the water. He couldn't throw her very far, and the pond wasn't especially deep—only a couple of feet—but it was deep enough. Standing in the moonlight, Harvey "Broomy" McCluskey caught one last glimpse of his mother's pallid face as her still body slipped beneath the surface of the water.

"Go to hell, you bitch," he muttered under his breath. "Go to hell, and good riddance."

|CHAPTER 1|

MONROE, WASHINGTON

— May 2017 —

Mateo Vega lay on his narrow, metal-framed cot with his hands behind his head and stared up at the blank ceiling. He knew every hairline crack and blemish in the dingy paint. He knew which of the three hundred–plus CMUs, the concrete masonry units, that made up the three solid walls of his eight-by-ten cage had faint remnants of graffiti scratched indelibly into their rough surfaces by hopeless souls marking time. He'd been in this cell for eight of the past sixteen years, but tomorrow, finally, he'd be out.

"So tomorrow's the big day, then?" Pop said from his cot on the far side of the cell. Pop's given name was Henry Mansfield Johnson, but no one called him that. He was a wiry Black man, a gay one as well, who had murdered his former partner and the partner's new lover sometime back in the eighties. Pop was the first to admit that his double homicide had been a cold-blooded crime, with plenty of premeditation thrown into the bargain. Somewhere along the way during his lengthy incarceration, he'd had his come-to-Jesus moment. Based on what he'd read in a now well-thumbed Bible, his sins were forgiven and his soul was saved. That was fine as far as the spiritual world was concerned. In the real world, however, nothing had changed, and Pop was determined to serve out his two life sentences with as much humility and grace as he could muster.

Mateo and Pop had been cellmates for five years now and friends for most of that, primarily because they both were outsiders. They kept their noses clean and steered clear of trouble. Neither of them was a lifetime criminal with a long, diverse rap sheet that started with juvenile offenses and escalated from there. They were in prison for similar crimes—the murder of a previous lover. There was one major difference between them, however: Pop accepted full responsibility for what he had done. Mateo did not. At his public defender's urging, he had entered a guilty plea to second-degree murder, but ever since he'd steadfastly maintained his innocence.

His final parole hearing, his tenth, had taken place six weeks earlier. They'd approved his request, but it had taken from then until now for the Department of Corrections to finally get its act together and issue his discharge papers. Evidently it took that long to cross all the *t*'s and dot all the *i*'s.

"According to what I've been told," Mateo responded finally, "I'm supposed to be on my way by eleven tomorrow morning."

That was how their leisurely conversations went. With nothing but time between them, the reply to a question might come five to ten minutes after it had been asked.

"What's the first thing you're gonna do?"

"Find a taco truck," Mateo answered, "preferably one where they make their tacos with shredded beef as opposed to mystery meat."

Food in the Monroe Correctional Facility was, generally speaking, bad news, but what was purported to be Mexican food scraped the very bottom of the barrel.

Pop laughed. "If it was me, I'd head straight for the Central District and hook me up with some of Ezell's Famous Chicken—if they's still in business, that is," he added. Another long pause followed. "Then what?" Pop asked.

For someone like Pop, doing life without parole, the idea of getting out of prison was an impossible dream, and hearing about someone else's upcoming release was like listening to a fairy tale. Knowing that was the case, Mateo was glad to humor him.

"Find a place to live."

"How you gonna pay for it?"

"Work."

"Doing what?"

Mateo shrugged. "I don't know. Maybe I'll be a day laborer for now. I bet there are still groups of guys hanging out by Home Depot and Lowe's looking for work."

"I hear they's almost unionized these days," Pop told him. "Some guy organizes it all, and then he takes a cut of what everyone makes."

"Figures," Mateo muttered under his breath.

"Knowin' you," Pop said encouragingly, "I think you'll be jus' fine."

"What I'm really going to do," Mateo added determinedly after another long pause, "is find the son of a bitch who really killed Emily Tarrant."

"You bet," Pop agreed with a grin, "you and O.J. How do you think that's gonna turn out for you?"

Mateo didn't answer. The conversation ended then, and another long silence fell between them, as much silence as there ever was in the perpetual din of the cellblock. And in that silence, Mateo lay there thinking.

No matter how many years crept by, Mateo remembered the conversation with his public defender almost verbatim. It had occurred in an interview room deep in the bowels of Seattle's King County Jail. All the interview rooms looked exactly alike, as did all the corridors leading to and from Mateo's cell. During the interview his hands had been attached to the table with a pair of cuffs. His suit-clad public defender's hands had been free to wave in the air when he wasn't prying dirt from under seemingly pristine nails.

"It's a good deal," Arthur Harris had assured him. "Emily Tarrant died of manual strangulation. She was sexually assaulted before her body was thrown into a blackberry bush just up the bluff from the beach. The state is willing to let you plead guilty to second-degree murder. With a sentence of sixteen years to life, you'll most likely be out in eight. By then you'll only be in your early thirties. You'll still have your whole life ahead of you."

At the time Arthur Harris must have been somewhere in his sixties, and no doubt those words came easily to him. For Mateo, age twenty-two, eight years in prison could just as well have been forever.

"How can I plead guilty to something I didn't do?" Mateo had objected.

"They have your DNA," Arthur replied.

"They have somebody else's DNA, too," Mateo

countered. "Emily and I went to a beach in Edmonds. She was drinking and flirting with everybody in sight. Later on I caught her down by the water making out with one of the guys she'd been hanging with. I punched the guy in the nose, and then I dragged her kicking and screaming back through the party to my car. I thought we were headed home, but when I stopped at the first stop sign, she jumped out and took off running. That's where she was the last time I saw her, hotfooting it down the road. I said the hell with her, drove home, and got into bed. In other words, the last time I saw her, she was still alive. I got home, I went to sleep by myself. The next day, when she didn't come home, I reported her missing."

"Which amounts to your having no alibi, since you claim you lost your phone at the party," the lawyer suggested.

"I did lose my phone at the party," Mateo insisted. "It must have fallen out in the sand, or maybe someone stole it. But what about the lie-detector test I took? I passed it fair and square, didn't I?"

Harris remained unmoved. "Lie-detector results aren't admissible in court. DNA is, and with that conveniently misplaced phone, the cops can't trace your movements. Being home by yourself means you have zero alibi. And there was bruising on your hands."

"Of course there was," Mateo agreed. "Like I already told you, I punched a guy in the nose."

"Be that as it may," Arthur intoned, "in my opinion, if you go to trial on a charge of first-degree homicide, you're really rolling the dice. With sexual assault thrown into the mix, there's a good chance you could end up getting life without parole."

"Like I said, Emily and I had consensual sex before the party, but when I left, she was mad as hell and still very much alive."

"Physical evidence suggests that what happened to Emily Tarrant was not consensual," Harris countered, "but it's your call. The plea deal is on the table—take it or leave it. If we go to court, though, I think there's a good chance you'll end up with a whole lot more than sixteen years."

If Mateo had asked, his folks probably would have helped, but he was used to being on his own. He had made his way through school on scholarships and by working nights at Pizza Hut. During his junior and senior years, he'd had to resort to student loans. He was pretty sure the interest on those was going to keep on growing even if he ended up going to prison. Not wanting to add in a mountain of legal fees, he'd settled for a public defender. Unfortunately, he realized much later, you get what you pay for.

In the stark silence of the interview room, Mateo did the math. Serving eight years of a sixteen-year sentence would be better than risking a life sentence by going to court. After all, Mateo's paternal grandfather had been ninety-three when he died. Even so, Mateo still wouldn't go for it. When he came before the judge to enter his plea, he looked the man in the eye and pronounced the words "Not guilty."

For the next ten months, Mateo languished in a cell in the King County Jail awaiting trial. The longer he waited, the more hopeless things seemed. Would a jury ever overlook the DNA evidence and return a verdict of not guilty? More and more, the answer to that seemed to be, "Not likely." Finally, two weeks before his scheduled trial date, Mateo cratered and called Harris at his office.

"I'll take the deal," Mateo told him.

Two weeks later, in a King County courtroom, Mateo Vega had stood up and pled guilty to second-degree murder in the death of Emily Tarrant. The sexual-assault charge had somehow disappeared from the mix. He was sentenced to sixteen years to life, with a year credited for time served in the King County Jail while awaiting trial. After that he was shipped off to the Monroe Correctional Facility, where, one by one, the years inched past. By the time his first parole hearing came along in 2009, he had a new public defender—a woman this time, Alisha Goodson.

"All you have to do is accept responsibility and say you're sorry," she explained to him. "Your record here is squeaky clean. If you express remorse, they'll let you out first time at bat."

Mateo took some of her advice but not all of it. "I'm sorry Emily Tarrant is dead," he told the parole board when it came his turn to speak, "but I didn't do it."

Emily's mother, Abigail, was right there in the hearing room, watching and listening to every word. She stiffened visibly when Mateo spoke. When it was her turn, she told the board she was still devastated and that her life had been forever changed by the death of her daughter at such a tender age. Mateo had caught Emily cheating on him only that one time at the party, although he had no doubt there'd been plenty of others he didn't know about. But according to Mrs. Tarrant, her beloved Emily was as pure as the driven snow. And that's when Mateo's dream of being paroled after eight years went out the window.

The same thing happened year after year, and year after year, as Mateo refused to accept responsibility and parole was denied—one hearing after another. Finally, in year sixteen, for Mateo's final parole-board hearing, Mrs. Tarrant didn't show up. Although no one mentioned it, Mateo guessed that she must have passed away between hearings. That was when they finally agreed to let him go—without even bothering to ask the responsibility question.

A little over a month later, Mateo awakened early on the morning he was due to be a free man. Still in handcuffs, he was escorted to the property division, where an attendant gifted him with an ill-fitting set of cast-off clothing. Had the clothing he'd surrendered years earlier still existed, it wouldn't have fit the thirty-eight-year-old man he was now. Next a clerk returned his property—his 1994 class ring from Yakima High School and a faded wallet that contained sixty-three bucks in cash, along with an out-of-date driver's license, an expired Visa card, a no-longer-valid proof of insurance, and a scrap of paper listing the phone numbers for several of his family members. After that he was given a check that contained the outstanding amount from his commissary account and what remained of his accrued wages—an average of five bucks a day—earned from working first in the laundry and later in the library. Most of the inmates sent all their earnings directly to their commissary account, but Mateo had banked close to half of his, and the check amounted to almost sixteen hundred dollars.

At that point he expected to be escorted straight to the sally port. Instead, much to his surprise, he was taken to the warden's office.

Mateo had been there once before. Years earlier he'd happened to be in the prison library when the computer system crashed. The librarian, Mrs. Ancell, was mid-meltdown and on the phone to some long-distance tech support when Mateo asked if he could help. He had just graduated from the University of Washington with a degree in computer science and had started working his first job with a company called Video Games International when he ended up in prison.

Mrs. Ancell, totally unable to understand a word of what the remotely located tech guy was saying, had handed the phone over to Mateo. The technician's mangled English-language skills had made it challenging for Mateo to understand him as well, but he grasped enough that he'd been able to create a work-around and reboot the system. Out of gratitude Mrs. Ancell had sung his praises to the warden and lobbied for him to be given a certificate of appreciation, which had been handed over in person by the warden himself. Up until then Mateo had worked mostly in the prison's laundry facility or handled mess-hall duties. From then on he was assigned to work in the library. Yes, prison might have been the wrong place to be, and a prison library was probably even wronger—if there was such a word. But in that moment, it was both the right place and the right time, because over the years working in the library had proved to be a huge benefit.

From that moment on, Mrs. Ancell had taken a personal interest in Mateo. She located textbooks and articles that had enabled him to advance his studies in computer science. His disciplined self-improvement program might not have earned any additional degrees, but it had allowed him to accumulate a good deal of practical knowledge and to keep up-to-date with what was going on in the fast-moving tech world. Then, in those final weeks leading up to his release, Mrs. Ancell had allowed him to go online in search of possible rooms to rent. He found one south of Seattle in Renton, where, with the remainder of the money in his prison account plus his accumulated wages, he'd have enough to cover the first and last month's rent. Anything extra, along with the sixty-three bucks found in his wallet, meant he'd be able to buy some food prior to receiving his first paycheck.

Seated in the bare-bones waiting room outside the warden's private office, Mateo began to fret and wonder as the time ticked closer to the prison van's scheduled departure. What was the holdup? Had some kind of glitch developed that would mean he wasn't being released after all? Finally the door opened, and Warden Pierce beckoned him inside.

"Come in," he said with a welcoming smile and an outstretched hand. "I understand you're leaving us today."

A handshake was way more than Mateo had expected. "I believe so," he said.

Warden Pierce motioned him into a chair. "I'm sure Mrs. Ancell is going to miss you," he said. "From what I hear, you've been a great help to her."

"She's a good lady," Mateo replied. Saying more than that seemed unwise.

"I asked you to drop by because I have something for you," Warden Pierce said. He opened a desk drawer, removed an envelope, and reached across the desk to hand it to Mateo. Looking down at the envelope, Mateo recognized his mother's stilted handwriting, but the letter wasn't addressed to him. It was addressed to Warden Pierce and bore a postmark that was only a week old. The words "PERSONAL AND CONFIDENTIAL" were prominently displayed just beneath the stamp.

"It's open," the warden said with a smile. "You're welcome to look inside."

So Mateo did. He found a piece of lined paper that had most likely been torn out of a grandchild's spiral notebook. The words written there were brief and to the point.

> Mateo Vega is my son. Since I no longer live in my own home, I'm unable to offer him a place to stay upon his release. Would you please pass this along to him so he'll have some funds available to find a place to live and food to eat?
>
> Sincerely,
> Olivia Vega

Mateo unfolded what he recognized to be a postal money order and was astonished to see that it was written to him in the amount of one thousand dollars. He studied it for a long moment and had to swallow the lump in his throat before he could speak again.

"My mother isn't rich," he said gruffly. "How could she afford to send this to me, and why would she?"

"I suppose the answer to both questions would be that she loves you very much," Warden Pierce suggested.

Mateo looked up at the man. Inmates generally regarded Pierce as a thin-skinned hard-ass, someone worthy of fear and loathing. Yet as the two men sat there together, with Warden Pierce gazing kindly at Mateo across an expanse of wooden desk, Mateo came to the blinding conclusion that there was an essential kindness to the warden that no one had ever noticed or mentioned.

Pierce glanced down at the top of several pieces of paper in a file folder that lay open on his desk. "It says here that you want to be dropped off in Seattle, but wouldn't you be better off back home in Yakima? The cost of living there would be far less, and maybe you could start out by staying with one of your relatives."

In a family of eight kids, Mateo had been the baby, born when both of his parents, Joaquin and Olivia, were in their forties. While the older kids had been growing up, the family had lived in straitened circumstances, and there had been no question about the older kids being able to go on to college. His sisters had all married straight out of high school, and after graduating from Yakima High, Mateo's three brothers had gone to work in the orchards like their father. By the time Mateo came along, his father had been promoted several times over, eventually landing as the foreman of an orchard operation where he'd once been a mere laborer, a situation that offered him employer-provided housing. In addition, Mateo's mother had gotten a job working in the high school cafeteria. With his parents having a much-improved income situation and far fewer mouths to feed, Mateo's childhood circumstances were far different from those of his brothers and sisters.

Joaquin, determined that Mateo do something besides follow in the footsteps of his older siblings, had encouraged him to focus on his studies. As a result Mateo had earned top grades and ended up with a sizable academic scholarship to the University of Washington.

Naturally his brothers and sisters had resented everything about this and weren't shy about letting Mateo know exactly how they felt. They ragged on him about being lazy and thinking he was too good to work in the orchards the way everybody else had. They called him a crybaby and a spoiled brat, among other things, and when he went off to Seattle to enroll in the U Dub, they'd been united in saying so long and don't come back anytime soon.

During the years Mateo had been locked up, his mother had developed diabetes and could no longer work. Then, when his father was killed on the job by a freak lightning strike, not only did Olivia lose her husband and her primary means of support, she no longer had a place to call home. She now lived with her oldest granddaughter, helping look after five of her great-grandchildren in order to earn her keep.

At the time of Joaquin's death, Mateo had applied for and been granted a temporary release to attend his father's funeral. Of course, he would have had to go to the service in handcuffs accompanied by a guard, but he'd been looking forward to attending. Then, the day before the funeral, a letter arrived from his oldest brother, Eddie, saying that his presence at the funeral would be a disruption, adding that it would be best for all concerned if Mateo simply stayed away.

So when Warden Pierce suggested that perhaps Mateo would be better off going home to Yakima, a whole turmoil of thoughts and emotions raced through Mateo's mind and heart. "No," he said at last. "I can't go back home to Yakima. It just wouldn't work."

"All right, then," Warden Pierce said. "Suit yourself." He stood up. "On your way, Mateo. Take care of yourself. With any kind of luck, I hope I won't see you back here ever again."

"Yes, sir," Mateo replied. "I hope so, too."

In the prison yard, Mateo was loaded into a van and driven to Seattle as part of a van network known as "the Chain" that shuttled prisoners back and forth between jails, courthouses, and prisons inside the state of Washington. The van dropped him off on the sidewalk outside the sally port's entrance to the King County Jail. He found a taco truck, Jorge's Tacos, parked on Yesler next to City Hall Park, and gorged himself on three tacos and a luscious homemade tamale. Then he set out for Renton on foot.

It was May. The air was cool and clean. After being locked up for so long, he enjoyed walking. His future landlord wouldn't be off work until after five, and there was no sense in arriving early. As Mateo headed south from downtown, he was shocked to see the homeless encampments along the way—the derelict but clearly occupied campers parked here and there along the street, the tents erected under overpasses, and pan-handlers begging at almost every street corner. Seattle hadn't looked like this before, or if it had, Mateo didn't remember it.

At one point he spied a check-cashing store. Once inside, he turned his mother's money order and the check the property clerk had issued him into actual cash. As the clerk counted out the bills into his waiting hand, Mateo couldn't help but wonder how his mother had come by that much money. He was pretty sure it was something his brothers and sisters knew nothing about.

He put enough money to cover his first and last

months' rent in his wallet. Then, outside the store, he located a bench and sat down long enough to stow the rest under the insole of his ill-fitting shoes.

It was close to six, and his feet were killing him by the time he finally arrived at the address he'd been given—a ramshackle house at the end of Northwest Sixth Street. The place was a wreck, with a collection of half-dismantled cars parked in the driveway and a sagging porch propped up on one corner by a strategically placed stack of concrete blocks. The other houses on that same stretch were well maintained with manicured, fenced-in yards. This one was clearly a teardown awaiting a change in the real-estate market, when investing in new construction in the neighborhood would once more be profitable.

Mateo was seated on the front porch examining the oozing blisters on his heels when Randy Wasson, his soon-to-be landlord, arrived at five forty-five, driving up in a rattletrap Ford pickup that might have seen better days, but unlike the rusted hulks clogging the driveway, still ran. Mateo would learn later that the man worked as a mechanic at a nearby Jiffy Lube. Unfortunately, Randy's interest in automobile mechanics didn't extend to his own fleet of derelict vehicles.

"You must be Mateo," Randy said, sauntering up the cracked and weedy front walkway.

Mateo slipped his ill-fitting shoes back on and winced as he stood up to greet the man. Randy looked back toward the street. "No car?" he asked.

Mateo had owned his own car a long time ago, but once he went to jail, his dad had taken it home to Yakima, where it had been passed down to one of his many nephews—who, according to his mother, had wrecked it in short order.

"Nope," he answered. "I'm on foot."

"So how'd you get here? Bus? Uber?" Randy asked.

"I walked," Mateo replied.

"From downtown Seattle?"

Mateo nodded.

"So no furniture, then?" Randy asked.

"Not so far."

"All right," Randy told him. "There's a bed in each of the bedrooms, but not much else. I can spare you some sheets, a pillow, and a couple of blankets. I live in the basement. There are three bedrooms upstairs. The next roomer is due to show up tomorrow, so you get first choice. The three of you share the kitchen, living room, and bathroom. Everybody takes care of his own food and cleans up his own mess. Does that work for you?"

"Sounds fair," Mateo agreed.

"Not much luggage, I see," Randy ventured.

Mateo had been up front with Randy, letting him know that he was being let out of prison on parole. There was no point in lying about it and having it turn into a big screwup later.

"Nope," Mateo said. "What you see is what you get."

"You're in luck," Randy said. "There's a St. Vincent de Paul store right here in the neighborhood, through those trees and just over an eight-foot sound-barrier fence." He nodded toward a grove of second-growth trees that separated the weedy backyard at the end of the cul-de-sac from the commercial businesses on Rainier Avenue South. "You can probably pick up some duds there on the cheap and maybe some furniture, too. If you find something, I'll be glad to haul it home in my truck. Come on. Let me show you around."

Given his choice of either an east-facing room or a

west-facing room, Mateo settled for east. It was still cool in May, but he was pretty sure the house didn't have air-conditioning and probably not much insulation either. With summer coming on, he'd be better off dealing with morning sun than afternoon heat.

———

The next day Mateo took Randy's advice and made his way to the massive thrift store that was almost next door. His older brothers and sisters had been forced to wear secondhand clothing while they were growing up—that was something else they had against him—but this was Mateo's first venture inside one of those establishments. And he was surprised by what he found there. In the furniture section, he located a small dresser and an easy chair, along with a nightstand and lamp, all for a total outlay of eighty-eight dollars. He paid for those and had them set aside to be picked up later with Randy's truck. In housewares he gathered up a couple of pots and pans, some plates and bowls, some silverware, and two glasses. In the clothing department, he found three pairs of pants, several shirts, and two pairs of shoes—including a pair of almost new work boots—that actually fit him. The total for all that was just over a hundred bucks.

Pleased with his purchases and clothing in hand, he was on his way out of the store when he spotted a HELP WANTED sign in the front window. It turned out they were looking for someone to work the loading dock, accepting donations. Mateo didn't think twice about filling out an application. A job that was within easy walking distance was far preferable to dragging his ass all over town looking for casual-laborer work at the nearest Home Depot. Two days later he was hired.

Three days out of the slammer, Mateo Vega had a

place to live and a job. Yes, it wasn't the kind of job he'd dreamed of back when he was going for his degree in computer science, but Mateo wasn't proud, and he wasn't picky either. Working on a loading dock was a hell of a lot better than having no job at all. Once he had a bus pass and could find a nearby public library, he'd get on one of the library computers and start sending out résumés. There had to be better jobs out there somewhere, and he planned to find one. Once he did, he'd devote himself to doing exactly what he'd told Pop he intended to do—find the guy responsible for killing Emily Tarrant.

|CHAPTER 2|

COTTONWOOD, ARIZONA

— April 2018 —

Ali Reynolds sat at her desk in High Noon Enterprises' corporate office and tried to keep from nodding off over her computer keyboard. It was just after the first of the month. She might have held the title of CFO in the cybersecurity company she and her husband, B. Simpson, owned, but she really functioned as a glorified bookkeeper most of the time. While B. was busy doing the globetrotting glad-handing necessary to maintain good relations with established customers and bring in new ones, Ali generally stayed put in Arizona, keeping the lights on and the bills paid.

B. had flown out of Phoenix on Sunday afternoon to get to Helsinki in time for a Monday-afternoon meeting, which, she realized, glancing at her watch, was probably over by now. After B. left, Ali had planned on going to bed early in preparation for tackling two equally complex tasks today—paying the monthly bills on the one hand and sending out the monthly billings on the other. Yes, both of those operations were computerized, but they nevertheless required human oversight—preferably alert human oversight. Right that moment Ali was definitely not at her best.

Her plan for an early bedtime had been derailed by news from her son, Chris, saying that her daughter-in-law, Athena, had just gone into labor a week earlier than expected. Rather than hitting the sack at a decent hour, she had followed her son and daughter-in-law to the hospital in Prescott, where she had taken charge of their twins, Colin and Colleen. She had hung out in the waiting room with them while Chris and Athena were otherwise occupied. Ali's new grandson, Logan James Reynolds, had finally made his reluctant entrance into the world via an unplanned cesarean at 3:10 in the morning. With Chris planning to stay on at the hospital, Ali took the older kids back home to Sedona with her. After she got the two of them situated in the guest room, it had been close to 5:30 before Ali was able to hit the sack. Her grandkids, left in the care of Ali's majordomo, Alonzo Rivera, were still fast asleep when she dragged herself out of bed. Not on spring break, Ali staggered off to work a little past 9:00.

She had arrived at the office bleary-eyed and weary but not empty-handed. Thanks to Alonzo's early-morning efforts, she had shown up at work with a tray full of freshly made cupcakes sporting appropriately bright blue frosting. With the cupcakes receiving rave reviews in the break room, Ali had retreated to her office and gone to work. By midafternoon she was struggling to stay awake when the front-desk receptionist, Shirley Malone, stomped into her office.

"I just came from the bank," she announced. She tossed what appeared to be a check into the air, letting it slide the last few inches across the smooth surface of Ali's desk. "Guess what?" she added. "It bounced."

The check was still in motion when Ali spotted the bright red words stamped across the front: INSUFFICIENT FUNDS. She didn't need to read the signature to know what it said: Harvey McCluskey, their egregiously dead-beat tenant.

Several years earlier the landlord of the office com-plex where High Noon was located had run into finan-cial difficulties. Ali and B. had been able to purchase the property at a bargain-basement price. After doing exten-sive remodeling, they'd rented out the office spaces that High Noon didn't currently need. Yes, having rental income was a boost to the bottom line, but the problems of finding suitable tenants, overseeing maintenance issues, and collecting the rent had been added to Ali's ever-growing list of responsibilities.

McCluskey, who billed himself as a real-estate con-sultant, occupied a one-man office at the far end of the complex. Initially Ali had assumed he was in real-estate sales. Over time she had learned that he actually worked as a home inspector. A recent conversation with Chris and Athena had revealed that McCluskey had done a home inspection for friends of theirs and had failed to turn up serious termite damage that would have killed the deal. Now the new owners were stuck with exten-sive repairs they could ill afford to do, and the fine print in the contract they'd signed with McCluskey meant he was off the hook.

McCluskey was consistently a slow pay when it came to rent. The check he'd given Shirley earlier that morn-ing had been meant to cover the previous two months' worth of rent, which were both now in arrears, along with the one for April that had been due on the first of the month.

"What now?" Shirley asked. "Can't we just put a padlock on the door and shut him out?"

"Unfortunately, no," Ali told her. "We have to write up a five-day eviction notice and hand deliver it. The notice must be dated and needs to include the exact name and address of the tenant's unit and the reason for the notice—failure to pay rent—along with the exact amount of rent due, including any late fees. It must advise him that he has five days from his receipt of the notice to pay up or we start eviction proceedings. Once you finish typing the letter, bring it here for my signature."

"Okay," Shirley said, getting to her feet, "I'm on it, but just so you know, McCluskey isn't in his office right now. As I was leaving the bank, I noticed his truck parked in front of the Cowpoke Bar and Grill over on Main Street."

"Then we'll deliver it to him there," Ali responded.

Shirley paused in the doorway. "We?" she inquired with a puzzled look on her face.

Ali nodded. "Yes, we, as in you and I. We'll need to be able to document that we actually served him notice. I'll hand it over to him while you take the video."

"Gotcha," Shirley replied with a grin. "I can hardly wait. I'll have that letter typed up in a jif."

"Once we deliver it," Ali added, "I'm going home. After spending most of last night at the hospital, I'm beat."

While Shirley headed for her desk and computer, Ali went back into the lab in search of Stuart Ramey, B.'s right-hand man at High Noon Enterprises. Because of all the electronic equipment humming away, the areas of the building occupied by banks of CPUs had to be kept several degrees cooler than the office spaces. It might have been pushing the eighty-degree mark outside the building, but in the lab both Stu and Cami Lee, the company's primary tech crew, were decked out in sweatshirts. The third key member of High Noon's staff, Lance Tucker, was covering the night shift this week and would come on duty as the others went home.

"I'm calling it a day and taking off early," Ali informed Stu when, noticing her presence hovering in the background, he glanced away from the oversize monitor mounted on the wall in front of him.

"Did you get a chance to look at any of those job applications?" he asked.

Months earlier High Noon had prevented an attempted corporate coup—an inside job—that might have put one of their best customers, Swiss-based A&D Pharmaceuticals, out of business had the plot not been stopped in its tracks. The whole matter had been handled with utmost discretion and without any law-enforcement involvement. Since then Albert Gunther, the partner left in charge of A&D and the main beneficiary of High Noon's work, had been lavish in praise of their efforts even though he was sketchy when it came to providing details. As a result there'd been a major expansion of High Noon's customer base—including the potential new client B. was currently pursuing in Helsinki.

Naturally, the increase in business called for an increase in personnel. When word they were hiring got out, High Noon had been overwhelmed with unsolicited applications and résumés. The ones on Ali's desk awaiting perusal by both Ali and B. were the ones that'd made it past Stu's initial scrutiny. Each of those was accompanied by a background-check dossier created by Stu's pet artificial intelligence, affectionately referred to as Frigg. When provided with a name and date of birth, Frigg would search public records and the world of social media for any and all material on the applicant in question, including school-age indiscretions, sports participation, teenage pregnancies, unpaid income taxes, and DUIs. Frigg simply accumulated the material without providing any opinions. She delivered information only. Value judgments on what she unearthed had to be supplied by the human element involved.

Stu had dropped a stack of file folders containing both the applications and the dossiers on Ali's desk sometime Friday morning, and that's where they remained. She hadn't had time to lay hands on any of the material either Friday or today.

"Not yet," she said in answer to Stu's question. "I'll do my best to get after those applications tomorrow, but right now Shirley and I need to run an errand. I wanted you to know that we'll be locking up and closing the security shutters early. If anyone needs to come inside, you'll have to buzz them in."

"Got it," Stu said. "See you tomorrow."

Ali returned to her office and cleared her desk. She sat for a moment, studying the application files. At the last minute, and on the off chance that she might get her second wind later in the evening, she grabbed the files and stuffed them in the side pocket of her voluminous purse. She was about to shut down her computer when Shirley popped into the room, waving a sheet of paper in the air.

"Here's my first-ever eviction notice, all typed up and ready to sign," she announced. "You may want to read through it and make sure I didn't leave anything out."

Ali turned off the computer and then quickly scanned through the letter. Not surprisingly, everything was in order. After scrawling her signature at the bottom, Ali took a close-up photo of the document before sealing it in a blank envelope and addressing the missive with the clearly handwritten words "Harvey McCluskey."

"It looks fine to me," she told Shirley, "so let's saddle up and go track down our bad boy. With any kind of luck, he's still at the bar."

"Do you want me to ask Cami if she'll come watch the front?" Shirley asked.

"Nope," Ali replied. "We're locking up for the day. Once we finish serving our five-day notice, we're both taking the rest of the afternoon off."

A few minutes later, they pulled in to the parking lot of the Cowpoke, where Harvey's aging, steel-gray Chevy Silverado occupied one and a half spaces marked COM-PACT directly outside the front door.

Figures, Ali muttered silently to herself. *Other people's rules don't apply to Mr. McCluskey, but at least he's still here.*

Ali knew she and Shirley would be better off confronting the man in a public place rather than tracking him down at home, something she could easily have done had it become necessary.

The town of Cottonwood, Arizona, contains any number of respectable bars and cocktail lounges, but the notorious Cowpoke wasn't one of them. It had a reputation for hosting regular bar fights in which contentious customers whacked one another over the head with cue sticks or whatever other weapons came readily to hand. Local EMTs laughingly referred to the Cowpoke as Concussion Junction for that very reason.

Coming into the bar's darkened interior from bright afternoon sunlight, Ali and Shirley had to pause just inside to get their bearings and allow their eyes to readjust. The place reeked of stale spilled beer and a long history of greasy food. As Ali walked across the floor, the soles of her shoes stuck to the grimy surface. Most of the illumination came from a series of neon signs posted on the walls in place of artwork. They provided some light, but not enough to expose the accumulated dirt lurking in cracks and crevices.

Once Ali could see again, she noted that although it was still too early for happy hour, the dim room was already fairly crowded. McCluskey was seated at the bar. A half-empty pint of beer along with an empty shot glass sat on the counter in front of him. He was hunched so far forward on the barstool that his shirttail had pulled out, leaving an unnerving three inches of flabby, lavender-tinted flesh showing between the bottom of his shirt and his belt line.

"There he is," Ali said as she turned her iPhone's camera to Record and passed the device to Shirley. "I'll do the talking. You're in charge of video recording."

She made straight for the bar, with Shirley following behind.

"Mr. McCluskey?" Ali said.

"Yeah, I am," he muttered, slowly straightening up and turning to face her. "Who's asking?"

Harvey McCluskey had probably been a good-looking dude in his younger days, but that was over. He still had a silvery mane, but his ruddy complexion and the thickness of his nose both spoke of someone who drank more than was good for him. Over time his figure had definitely gone to seed. The only vestige of what might have been his salad days was the hint of a gold chain peeking out from under the open collar of an incredibly loud Hawaiian shirt.

In her days as a newscaster in L.A., Ali had seen plenty of his type—the bigger the jackass, the heavier the gold chain. The fact that her deadbeat tenant was wearing one of those wasn't a mark in his favor.

"I am," Ali told him firmly, holding out the envelope.

Beer in hand, McCluskey peered first at Ali and then at the envelope, but he made no move to take it from her. "What's this?" he wanted to know.

"It's your five-day eviction notice," she told him. "As of today your rent is three months in arrears, and not for the first time either. You have five days to pay up in full, or High Noon will begin eviction proceedings."

"Eviction? How can that be?" he demanded, pointing an accusatory finger in Shirley's direction. "I gave that broad over there a check just this morning." Then, noting the camera, he added menacingly, "What the hell do you think you're doing? Turn that damned thing off!"

Ali didn't back away, and Shirley didn't stop filming, but by now every eye in the place was focused on them. Ali was still holding out the envelope, and McCluskey was still refusing to touch it.

"Yes, you gave her a check," Ali agreed. "It bounced."

She didn't bother lowering her voice. She didn't care if all of Harvey's drinking buddies knew he was a worthless lout. Chances were they already did.

"By the way," she added, "I've included our bank's charge for a dishonored check in among late fees. You'll find the total amount due laid out inside. As I said, final payment must be in our hands and clear the bank no later than Friday, four days from now."

"You can take your five-day notice and shove it," McCluskey said, laying his hand on his chest as if to ward off a sudden attack of indigestion.

With that, he started to turn back to the bar, but Ali was too fast for him. In a deft maneuver, she slipped the envelope into his shirt pocket and gave it a quick pat. "I already did," she told him with a smile. "Shove it, that is."

Several of McCluskey's barstool neighbors guffawed at that.

Moments later Ali and Shirley were back outside in blinding sunlight.

"Did you get it?" Ali asked.

"Every bit of it," Shirley replied. "For a minute there, I was afraid he was going to take a swing at you."

"So was I," Ali said darkly, "but if he had, Harvey McCluskey would be going to court for a lot more than just a simple eviction hearing."

|CHAPTER 3|

COTTONWOOD, ARIZONA

The whole time that incredible bitch of a Reynolds woman was reading Harvey McCluskey the riot act and threatening him with eviction, he'd sat there burning with fury. The only thing that kept him from outright decking her was being able to touch his chest and feel the icons he wore under his shirt, dangling on his gold chain.

Harvey might have been hearing Ali Reynolds's words, but all the while the face he'd seen had belonged to his mother. Ida Mae McCluskey had been the same kind of arrogant harpy. Once she went off on either Leo, Harvey's dad, or on Harvey himself, there had always been absolute hell to pay.

Harvey's physical body remained in the Cowpoke Bar and Grill in Cottonwood, Arizona, during her tirade, but his soul and heart were transported back in time to Butte, Montana, and to the day when, at age seven, he had suffered his first public humiliation at his mother's hands. They'd gone to the drugstore in town. While his mother was back at the pharmacy counter picking up a prescription, she left her son unsupervised and sitting alone at the fountain to finish his root-beer float. When it was gone, Harvey had climbed down from the tall stool and meandered around the store on his own for a few minutes before his mother returned to collect him.

By the time they stepped outside, Harvey had two pilfered candy bars from the counter on the far end of the fountain—a PayDay and a Snickers—along with a bag of peanuts, all of them concealed in the pockets of his jacket. Once sprawled in the backseat, and thinking his mother wouldn't be any the wiser, Harvey had stealthily opened the bag of peanuts and slid one of the salty treats into his mouth. That's when she suddenly slammed on the brakes. "What the hell are you eating, boy?" she demanded.

At the time he'd had no idea how she knew what he was doing. Now he understood that she'd probably caught sight of him in the rearview mirror. However she figured it out, she had him dead to rights.

"Just a peanut," he said. "I found it in my pocket."

Ida Mae wasn't fooled in the least. "Like hell you did," she muttered.

Harvey was aware that his mother was careful not to use bad words like that at church or around other people they knew, but when they were alone at home or in the car, Ida Mae's cuss words buzzed through the air like swarms of angry hornets.

Moments later the car was parked on the shoulder of the road. Ida Mae got out of the driver's seat, slammed open the back passenger door, and dragged Harvey from the station wagon. Seconds later she turned his pockets inside out and tossed the two stolen candy bars onto the ground. As for the remainder of the peanuts? She emptied them from the bag and then mashed them to pieces in the dirt with the sole of her shoe.

"Did you steal these?" she demanded.

When Harvey said nothing in reply, Ida Mae slapped him hard across the face. "I'm speaking to you, young man!" she railed. "When I ask you a question, I expect an answer. Did you or did you not steal these?"

Harvey's face hurt like crazy. Despite his best efforts, tears started to flow. "Yes, ma'am," he muttered finally.

"Get back in the car," she barked at him. "Now!"

Harvey did as he was told. His face ached, but he resisted the urge to touch it. Moments later his mother was in the driver's seat again. Instead of going home to their double-wide off German Gulch Road, she executed an immediate U-turn and headed back into town.

"Where are we going?"

"Shut up," Ida Mae said.

Apparently they were returning to the drugstore. When they got out of the car, Ida Mae grabbed Harvey by his shirt collar and frog-marched him into the store. Mr. Wilcox, the owner, was also the pharmacist. In order to find him, they had to go to the very back of the store, as whoever was there—customers and employees alike—watched their every move.

"Why, yes, Mrs. McCluskey," Mr. Wilcox said pleasantly when he noticed Harvey and his mother standing there. "Will there be something else?"

She pulled the two candy bars and the remains of the peanut bag out of her pocket and slammed them down onto the counter. "Tell him," she ordered Harvey. "Tell Mr. Wilcox exactly what you did."

Harvey hesitated for a moment. Instantly his mother's fingers dug sharply into his shoulder, and she gave him a fierce shake. "Tell him," she commanded again.

"I stole them," Harvey admitted in a tiny whisper. "I hid them in my jacket pockets."

A bemused Mr. Wilcox, looking as though he were doing his best not to smile, glanced first at Ida Mae and then back at her son.

"You mean you took them without paying for them?" he asked after a pause.

Harvey nodded.

"Do you have any money to pay for them now?"

Harvey shook his head.

"What do you suppose we should do about that?" Mr. Wilcox asked.

Harvey shrugged.

Mr. Wilcox appeared to be considering the problem. "Well," he said at last, "I suppose you could work it off. Do you know how to use a broom?"

Harvey nodded.

Mr. Wilcox turned and disappeared into a back room, returning a moment later with a huge push broom that he handed over to Harvey.

"Supposing you spend the next half hour sweeping the sidewalk on this side of the block," Mr. Wilcox suggested, "and we'll call it even. Fair enough?"

Harvey nodded again.

"All right, then," Mr. Wilcox said. "I'm setting my stopwatch. I'll come let you know when your time is up. Perhaps your mother would like to take a seat at the fountain and have a cup of coffee while you're doing that."

Lugging the heavy broom, Harvey scurried back to the front of the store. Thankfully, Ida Mae didn't follow him outside. The broom was nearly twice as tall as he was, making it unwieldy and difficult to use. Except for a few cigarette butts, there wasn't much dirt on the sidewalk, but Harvey swept it diligently anyway. The sun was hot on his face. He was sweating and puffing as he worked. It seemed like he'd been sweeping forever when a trio of girls from school showed up. The three of them were inseparable. They were mean and spiteful and liked to lord it over everyone else because their daddies were bigwigs with Anaconda, and they lived in large houses in the nicest part of town. Rhonda Ward, the ringleader, zeroed in on the hapless Harvey. "What are you doing?" she wanted to know.

"I'm sweeping," he muttered.

"But why?"

"It's none of your business. Leave me alone."

Rhonda turned back to her pals. "From now on maybe that's what we should call him," she said, pointing in his direction. "We'll call him Broomy—Broomy McCluskey."

Pretty soon the name caught on, and everyone at school started calling him Broomy. The moniker stuck until after he graduated from high school and was able to join the army.

But that day, even with the girls taunting him, he continued to sweep, all the while burning with indignation. Ida Mae was the cause of this. Here he was, sweeping to pay for candy bars that had already been returned and for peanuts he hadn't even gotten to eat. The injustice of it really rankled, and having the girls jeering at him and shaming him made it that much worse.

Two weeks later, after school, Harvey used the pocketknife his dad had given him for Christmas to slash both tires on Rhonda's bicycle. He got even with her, but he didn't really hate her for calling him names. The person he hated more than anyone in the world was his mother.

After Ali Reynolds left, Harvey removed the envelope from his shirt pocket. Without opening it, he set it down on the counter in front of him and sat there in silence, staring at it. He had no idea how much time passed before Joe, the bartender, roused him from his reverie.

"Hey, Harve," Joe said, placing an icy cocktail glass on the counter in front of him. "Pull yourself out of your doldrums and drink up. This one's on the house."

Harvey studied the contents in the brimming glass. These days he mostly drank beer and shots as opposed to fancy cocktails, and he didn't recognize this one right off the bat.

"What is it?" he asked.

"Vodka, Galliano, and orange juice," a grinning Joe told him. "Otherwise known as a Harvey Wallbanger, but tonight only, for happy hour, we're calling them Harvey Ballbangers, and I'm selling them for a buck apiece."

The bartender seemed to think this was the greatest stand-up joke ever, and everybody who'd been on the scene during the earlier confrontation seemed to agree. It was downright hilarious to all concerned—to everyone, that is, except Harvey himself.

"I'll have me a Ballbanger," one of his barstool neighbors said.

"I believe I'll have two," someone else added.

As Joe hustled off to mix their drinks, Harvey picked up the glass and downed his without pausing, swallowing it in one long gulp. As a serious case of brain freeze spread from his nose to his forehead, Harvey had someone else to hate besides his mother—Ali goddamned Reynolds.

|CHAPTER 4|

SEDONA, ARIZONA

With the Harvey McCluskey problem handled for the time being, Ali set off on her half-hour commute from Cottonwood back home to Sedona. While she'd been in the Cowpoke, two texts had come in, first one from B. followed by a second from Chris:

> On my way to bed now. Meetings today went well. They should sign on the dotted line. Will meet with another prospective client tomorrow morning. I'll give you a call during the day when you're in the office. Get some sleep. After being up all night, I'll bet you're bushed. Chris sent a picture of Logan. Cute, but I'm glad they'll be the ones taking him home and not us.

You've got that right, Ali thought with a laugh. Next up was the one from Chris.

> Athena and Logan seem to be doing fine. Should be released tomorrow or the next day. I collected the

twins from Alonzo. We'll be staying with friends here in
Prescott until they get out. Good thing it's spring break.

Much as Ali loved Colin and Colleen, she couldn't
help but feel a bit of relief at being excused from grandmother duty for the remainder of the evening. B. was
right. She was bone tired. As the adrenaline rush from
her confrontation with Harvey McCluskey faded, so did
she. She was driving along listening to the Broadway
cast recording of *Man of La Mancha* when a phone call
came in from Alonzo. Since he seldom called her during
work hours, Ali was immediately concerned that something was amiss, and she wasn't wrong.

"What's up?" she asked.

"Your mother's here," Alonzo answered, speaking in
a hushed voice as though worried about possibly being
overheard. "She didn't say anything, but she's clearly
upset. And she came equipped with a suitcase. Fortunately, I had already done the sheets in the guest room,
so I put her things in there. I offered her tea, but she
asked for a gin and tonic, so I gave her one of those. She
and Bella are sitting together in the library."

Ali was totally bewildered. Her mother had shown
up unannounced and uninvited and was planning on
spending the night? How come? And if she was so upset
that she was soaking up comfort from B. and Ali's rescued dachshund, Bella, Edie Larson had to be beyond
upset. She wasn't someone who naturally gravitated to
dogs or cats, either one. As for indulging in a daytime
cocktail? That was unheard of, especially at four o'clock
in the afternoon. Everything about Edie Larson's unexpected visit was completely out of character.

"No hint about what's wrong?" Ali asked.

"None whatsoever," Alonzo replied.

"All right, then," Ali said. "Thanks for the heads-up."

She spent the next fifteen miles trying to imagine what was going on and gearing up to deal with it. Her folks were well into their eighties now. Since they were both slowing down, there was a good chance whatever was wrong had to do with some kind of health issue. That was a scary prospect, but thanks to Alonzo's call Ali at least had a little time to prepare herself for whatever was coming her way rather than walking in on it cold.

Entering the house through the garage door that led to the kitchen, she noticed that Bella didn't come racing to meet her as she usually did. Even so, that was hardly surprising. Soon after Bella had become part of their household, Ali had noticed that whenever someone was dealing with any kind of emotional distress, the dog stuck to that person like glue.

"Library?" Ali asked Alonzo as she walked by.

He nodded in reply.

Ali found her mother dozing in one of the easy chairs in the library with Bella curled in her lap and one hand resting on the dog's long back. When Bella raised her head and wagged her tail in response to Ali's arrival, Edie shook herself awake. The haggard expression on her face took Ali's breath away.

"Hey, Mom," Ali said, in a voice filled with concern. "Is something wrong?"

"You have no idea," Edie said.

"Tell me," Ali urged.

Edie emitted a heavy sigh. "It's your father," she said at last. "He threw me out of our apartment and says he wants a divorce." Once the D-word escaped her lips, Edie Larson dissolved into a storm of tears.

"A divorce?" Ali repeated the word, more for her own benefit rather than her mother's. She had expected bad news, but certainly not *this* kind of bad news, especially in view of the fact that her folks had recently celebrated their sixty-fifth wedding anniversary with a big party at their retirement community, Sedona Shadows. That shindig had occurred a bare two months earlier, and now her father was ready to call it quits? Ali took a seat in the easy chair opposite her mother's and sat in silence, waiting for Edie to regain control.

"Betsy said I could stay with her," her mother continued eventually, once she had quieted enough to be able to speak. "But she has a one-bedroom unit with only a foldout couch. That would just kill my back. Since I didn't know where else to go, I came here. I hope you don't mind."

Betsy was Betsy Peterson, Athena's grandmother, who had sold her home in Minnesota and moved to Sedona to be closer to Athena and Chris. With encouragement from Bob and Edie, Betsy, too, had moved into Sedona Shadows, where the two great-grandmothers, thrown together by family ties, had morphed into the best of friends.

"Of course I don't mind," Ali assured her. "You're welcome to stay as long as you need to, but tell me. What on earth is going on?"

"I've officially canceled your father's driving privileges," Edie admitted, "and he hit the roof. I've never in my life seen him as furious as he was this afternoon. I was afraid he was going to put his fist through the drywall."

Ali was stunned. Her father had always been a gentle giant of a man—patient and unflappable. Around town Bob Larson was known as someone who loved his neighbor as himself. For decades needy folks in the community, ones living on the edge for whatever reason, had been astonished to have Bob show up outside with his aged Bronco loaded down with whatever was needed most, be it food, clothing, or firewood. As far as Ali knew, he had never once raised a hand in anger to anyone, and most especially not to her mother, who he often said was the love of his life.

"Maybe you should start at the beginning," Ali suggested. "Tell me what happened?"

Edie took a deep breath. "It's been building for a while now," she confessed, "but today is when it all came to a head."

It? Ali wondered. She was completely in the dark and had no idea what her mother could possibly mean. "*What* came to a head?" she asked.

"You know how Dad likes to spend his mornings down at Nick's, tinkering on the Bronco?" Edie asked.

Ali nodded. When her folks had first moved to Sedona Shadows, their unit had been assigned only one parking place. They'd decided that Edie's Buick would take that and the Bronco would be farmed out somewhere else. For several years now, the Bronco had been garaged in a back bay of Nick's Auto Care, a mile or so away from their retirement home. The owner, Nick Ryder, and Bob were old friends, and Nick made it clear that Bob was welcome to drop by and hang out whenever he wanted. Not only that, Bob was allowed free access to Nick's superb collection of tools in the event the urge to tinker became overwhelming.

Nick's place was close enough to Sedona Shadows that in good weather Bob could walk there on his own, getting what he liked to call his "daily constitutional." In bad weather—either too cold or too hot—Edie dropped him off and picked him up. And Ali knew that her mother was right. Bob Larson was never happier than he was when he was hanging out in the garage and messing around with his Bronco. It was a social milieu that allowed him to shoot the breeze with his pals. People like Harvey McCluskey hung out at dive bars. People like Bob Larson hung out at Nick's.

"So what happened?" Ali prodded.

"This morning, while it was still cool, Bobby decided to walk to Nick's on his own. We both knew it would be too hot for him to walk home later, so I was waiting for him to call and say he was ready to be picked up. Instead he showed up not only in a squad car but in handcuffs."

"Are you kidding me?" An unbelieving Ali demanded. "The cops brought him home?"

For a moment she expected her mother to dissolve into tears once more, but after a momentary pause Edie stiffened her shoulders, nodded, and resumed her story. "Yes, the cops," she repeated. "It's a wonder they didn't arrest him and throw him in jail. If the responding officer hadn't been someone who knows us through Chris and Athena, I'd be bailing your father out of the hoosegow about now."

Edie's roundabout way of telling the story left Ali dying a thousand deaths. She wanted her mother to get on with it in a more straightforward fashion. Unfortunately, she knew Edie was far too fragile right that minute to deal with any kind of interference. Difficult as it was, Ali had to stifle her impatience and simply wait it out.

"According to Nick, Bobby had been working on the Bronco earlier, doing something that required him to start the engine," Edie continued. "So Nick brought him the keys from his office. Then, while Nick was occupied with a customer, Bobby simply got in the Bronco and drove off. Nick didn't think that much of it at the time. He assumed Bob had taken the Bronco out for a test drive. Instead of doing that or coming home, Bobby drove to the Sugarloaf, barged into the kitchen, and started raising Cain with the cook and demanding to know what the hell the guy was doing in *his* kitchen. If Derek or Elena had been there, it wouldn't have been a problem. But they were in Phoenix today, shopping for a new stove, and the guy who was subbing in the kitchen didn't know Dad from Adam's off ox. The cook was the one who called the cops."

Husband and wife Derek and Elena Hoffman were the couple who had bought the Sugarloaf Café several years earlier when Bob and Edie had retired.

"That nice Officer Hernandez—his wife teaches with Chris and Athena—was the one who responded to the call, and he's the officer who brought Bobby home, through the front lobby and down the hallway to our unit. Since it was noontime, and people were heading to the dining room for lunch, everybody and their uncle saw exactly what was going on. I wanted to go through the floor. I've never been so embarrassed in my life."

"What about Dad?" Ali asked.

"He was all kinds of upset, still insisting that complete strangers had taken over his restaurant and he wanted them out of there. I was able to talk him down enough that Officer Hernandez took off the cuffs, and things seemed okay for a while. He had worn himself out so completely that he ended up falling asleep right there in his recliner. Officer Hernandez had given me the keys to the Bronco, so while your father was asleep, I called Nick, and the two of us went over to the Sugarloaf to retrieve the Bronco. Nick generally keeps the keys in his office so he can move the Bronco around as needed and start it from time to time to keep the battery from going dead, but I told him that from now on, Bobby is no longer allowed to drive. And when I came back home, after Bobby woke up, I gave him the same message in no uncertain terms. Just to make sure he understood I wasn't kidding, I took his driver's license out of his wallet and cut it to pieces."

"You actually cut up his driver's license?"

"I most certainly did," Edie declared, "and that's when he came completely unglued. He yelled and cussed at me something fierce, which you and I both know is not at all like him. And that's when he told me he wanted a divorce. He said since I still had the Buick, I was the one who needed to move out, so he could stay on at the Shadows, where he'd at least have access to a bus. Not knowing what else to do, I packed a bag and left," Edie finished lamely, "and here I am."

For a moment Ali was too thunderstruck to respond. The idea that her mother had unwittingly inserted a pair of scissors, a potentially dangerous weapon, into that volatile situation was utterly terrifying. That was bad enough in and of itself, but for her father to have forgotten that they no longer owned a restaurant that hadn't been theirs for years now . . .

Ali took a deep breath. "You said earlier that all of this has been coming on for a while. What did you mean by that?"

"Bobby just hasn't been himself for the past few months," Edie replied. "He's been moody and unpredictable, but up to now it's been handleable. I mean, between the two of us we've been able to cope."

Ali realized that last statement about her parents' ability to cope was absolutely true. During family gatherings around Christmas, Ali had noticed that her father wasn't exactly himself. He'd been far less sociable than in the past. He had planted himself in front of the nearest television set and mostly stayed there rather than interacting with others. He'd been grumpy and morose a lot of the time, barking at the twins, who up until that time could do no wrong.

Ali felt a sudden stab of guilt. Although she had noticed the subtle changes in her father's behavior, she'd been too preoccupied with her own life and times to pay that much attention. She had waved off every separate occurrence, attributing each one to nothing more or less than her father's having a bad day.

Now, however, an element of anger merged with that initial sense of guilt. If her father's situation had been building for a number of months, why the hell hadn't her mother mentioned it? But without having to voice the question aloud, Ali already knew the answer. Bob and Edie Larson were both very private people—independent and determinedly self-reliant. They didn't go around airing their dirty laundry in public. And in Edie Larson's book, admitting something was amiss at home was tantamount to admitting failure.

But with her mother sitting there awaiting some kind of response, Ali ended up offering the least offensive comment she could think of.

"Have you taken him to a doctor to be checked out?" she asked.

Edie shrugged her shoulders. "What good would that

do?" she replied helplessly. "I've googled Alzheimer's and dementia. There's nothing to be done. There aren't going to be any miracle cures or any happy endings. It's just the way things are."

Alonzo appeared in the doorway right then. "Excuse me," he said, "but dinner's ready."

"I'm not hungry," Edie stated at once.

"With everything that was going on with Dad, did you happen to eat any lunch today?" Ali asked.

"Well, no," Edie allowed, "I guess I didn't, but I don't want to be any trouble."

"It's no trouble, and dinner's nothing fancy," Alonzo told her with a smile. "It's just leftover tamale casserole and a green salad."

"Considering what you've been through today," Ali told her mother, "Alonzo's tamale casserole will be just what the doctor ordered. Now, scoot, Bella," Ali added. "Off with you. We're going to go eat."

Getting the message, the dog abandoned her perch, and Ali helped her mother to her feet. To say that night's dinnertime conversation between mother and daughter was strained would be a gross understatement. Luckily, halfway through the meal a text came in from Chris and with it a photo of Colleen and Colin sitting side by side with baby Logan tucked between them. The picture offered a welcome change of subject and focus.

They had almost finished eating when Edie's phone rang. "It's your father," she told Ali, glancing at the screen before answering. "Hello, Bobby," she said, switching the phone to speaker. "How are things?"

"Where are you, and when are you coming home?" Bob Larson wanted to know. He didn't sound angry or out of sorts. He sounded somewhat anxious, but other than that his voice seemed normal.

"I stopped by to see Ali," Edie replied. "Chris just sent her a photo of Logan and the twins."

"How's Athena doing?" Bob asked. "Having a cesarean isn't to be sneezed at, but I hope you'll be home soon. I've been waiting for you to show up before heading for the dining room. If you don't hurry, we'll miss out."

"Don't worry," Edie assured him at once. "I'll be there in a few minutes. I'm leaving right now."

While Edie hurried off to the guest room to collect her goods, a mystified Ali remained seated at the table. Her father remembered exactly who Athena was and that she'd recently given birth by way of a C-section, but had he forgotten that he'd told his wife he wanted a divorce and ordered her out of the house? How could he be completely lucid and rational one minute and completely off the charts the next? How was that even possible?

When Edie returned, she was ready to head out.

"Are you sure you should go home after what happened earlier?" Ali asked.

"I don't have a choice," her mother responded simply. "All those years ago, when I promised 'in sickness and in health,' I truly meant it."

A moment later she was gone.

|CHAPTER 5|

RENTON, WASHINGTON

Mateo added another blanket to the top of his covers and then turned the fan on full blast before crawling back into bed. Not that he needed the fan to cool things off. It was April after all, and temperatures in and around Seattle barely limped into the fifties on a daily basis. No, he used the fan as white noise to block out the constant squabbling and the roaring television volume. His latest housemates were a pair of argumentative drunks, and their never-ending wrangling went on for hours. Staying up all night didn't bother either of them because they weren't working. Of the three, Mateo was the only one with a job, which meant he had to be up and out early.

Still, drunk or not, slovenly or not, these guys were a big improvement on the last pair, both of whom had been convicted felons. Since Mateo was on parole and wasn't supposed to associate with felons, he'd been terrified that word would somehow get back to his parole officer. Fortunately for him, both of the undesirables had reneged on paying their rent, and Randy had sent them packing. The drunks were drunks and very annoying, but at least they didn't constitute the kind of parole violation that could have sent Mateo back inside.

Now, with the fan muting the racket, he lay with his hands behind his head, stared up at the dimly lit ceiling, and considered the state of his life. He'd been out of prison for eleven months at this point, but he had made very little progress in rebuilding his life. Yes, he still had his loading-dock job at the thrift store next door. St. Vincent's didn't necessarily pay much, but you couldn't beat the commute. And the job came with some surprising side benefits.

Because Mateo was on the loading dock and in charge of the drop-off location for donations, he was also in charge of the first sort. This meant that he saw stuff coming in before it ever made it inside, to say nothing of onto the sales floor. When items came in that he wanted, he was able to put them aside and then wheel and deal when it came to setting the price. In fact, that was how he had scored the fan last summer before it got really hot outside. He'd bought it for five bucks. By positioning it in his open window, it had kept him cool as a cucumber all through the latter part of July and the middle of August, when a ninety-degree heat wave had settled over the city and stayed on for the better part of a month.

He continued to be astonished by the stuff people just threw away. Someone had tossed an old MacBook Air into their rubbish heap. Mateo had found the computer but no power cord. He bought the computer for ten bucks and then paid another twenty-five online for a used power cord. When he finally was able to boot up the computer, he discovered that the previous owners hadn't bothered to wipe it before throwing it away. Mateo had no interest in whoever had tossed the computer, so he had returned it to its factory setting and started over, including installing any number of updates before he could make the damned thing work. Not doing required updates was probably the reason the original owner had chucked it in the first place, but eventually Mateo was able to get it going.

By then, having lived in the place and paid his rent on time for five months in a row, Mateo had become one of Randy Wasson's longest and most dependable tenants. As a bonus Randy had given Mateo the Wi-Fi code that allowed him to sign on from home, but only on the condition that he not share the password with anyone else. Considering the caliber of his fellow roomers, that promise was easy to keep.

The fact that Mateo had saved so much of his meager wages while he was in prison made a huge difference in his quality of life once he was out. Even before his first thrift-store paycheck, he was able to buy groceries and a bus pass and could treat himself to the occasional Burger King or TacoTime lunch. When that first paycheck finally did show up, he didn't dare leave any money lying around in his room. Instead he went to a bank, and after keeping back enough to live on, he created an actual savings account and got himself a prepaid, refillable Visa card he could use in place of cash. One of the first things he did with the Visa and then every month thereafter was log on to the prison's commissary system and make a fifty-dollar deposit into Pop's account. His friendship with his former cellmate had seen Mateo through some very tough times, and sending Pop a little something each month was Mateo's way of repaying that debt. But he didn't bother with sending along any messages. He knew something about Pop Johnson that no one else inside the Monroe Correctional Facility knew—he had no living relatives on the outside, or friends either for that matter. Sending the money itself was message enough. Nothing more needed to be said.

Prior to getting his cast-off computer up and running, Mateo had made good use of the computers at the Renton Public Library. When he asked Randy where the nearest library was located, his landlord had looked at Mateo as though he were off his rocker.

"The library?" he asked in dismay. "You want to go to the library? What the hell for?"

"To use the computers," Mateo had told him.

"I thought libraries had books," Randy said. "I didn't know they had computers." But in the end, he'd located the address. "It's quite a ways from here," Randy said, presenting Mateo with a printout of a MapQuest map.

In actual fact it wasn't all that far—a little over a mile. "Thanks, man," Mateo had told Randy. "I've got this. I can walk."

And so he did. He loved being able to walk somewhere with a purpose—like going to work or the library. It beat walking empty-headed laps around a prison rec yard just to get a meager bit of outdoor exercise.

The first time Mateo arrived at the Renton Public Library on Mill Avenue, he was enchanted. The building had been constructed over the Cedar River, and seeing it for the first time took his breath away. He stepped inside and located an unused computer. Once he settled down in front of it and, for the first time, logged in to the e-mail account Mrs. Ancell had helped him create, he felt as though he was finally free, and although Renton was a long way from Yakima, he also felt a sense of homecoming.

IT work was what Mateo had studied in college, and he was determined to somehow work his way back into that field. It was why he'd continued to study on his own the whole time he was incarcerated, and many of the advanced materials Mrs. Ancell had obtained for him over the years had come to him through the magic of interlibrary loans. Warden Pierce probably would have had a fit if he'd known that the prison librarian had allowed Mateo to search out the books he wanted by using her desktop computer. Once he located the titles he needed, she'd been the one who actually ordered them, but he was familiar with the process.

The first time he tried to do an interlibrary loan on his own, however, he ran into a major stumbling block. In order to request a title, he had to supply his library-card number, and of course he didn't have one of those. He went up to the desk and filled out the form, including his name and address. When he handed it over to the clerk, however, she told him, "I'll need to have proof of residence."

"How do I do that?" he asked.

"A current driver's license, voter ID, or even your name on a utility bill would work," he was told. Unfortunately, Mateo could produce none of those. Randy wasn't especially keen on paying taxes to the IRS on any of the money he earned renting out rooms, so his tenants paid their rent in cash—with no receipts and zero paperwork. Nobody's name was on a lease, much less on a utility bill. Voter ID? As a convicted felon, you could forget about that. And although Mateo still carried around that long-expired driver's license, that wouldn't have worked either.

So he didn't manage to request any interlibrary loans that night, but he didn't walk out of the library empty-handed either. In addition to helping Mateo find technical materials for himself, Mrs. Ancell had introduced him to the world of science fiction. In the lobby of the library, he found shelves lined with books being sold by friends of the library. Among them was a fat volume of Isaac Asimov's short stories. That night, when his fellow renters turned on the TV set and started bickering over what to watch, Mateo had something else to do.

But that fruitless trip to the library had launched him off on something else—a quest to get his driver's license—although not because he wanted to drive. Without either a car or insurance, that was out of the question. He wanted a driver's license so he could obtain a library card.

The next week he took a bus to the nearest Department of Licensing, grabbed a number, and waited in place for the better part of an hour before being called to the counter. The fact that he was able to pull out his long-expired license and hand it over to the surly clerk carried no weight whatsoever. He was told he needed to start the process over from scratch, including showing up with a birth certificate and then taking both the written and driving exams. In addition, for the driving exam, he was told he would need to provide his own vehicle.

Presented with two monumental obstacles, Mateo decided to tackle what he considered to be the easier one first. By then he had managed to buy a cheap phone, as opposed to a smart one, a phone that, like his Visa card, didn't come with a pricey contract and could be refilled with minutes as required. Armed with that and the scrap of paper from his wallet that listed family phone numbers, he dialed the one for his mother, but she didn't answer. "The number you have dialed is no longer in service. Please check the number and dial again," a computerized female voice told him.

When calling on the phone didn't work, Mateo sat down and wrote his mom a long letter, thanking her for her help, telling her where he was living and that he had found work. At the very end of the letter, he asked if she could please send him a copy of his birth certificate. A week and a half after he'd mailed the letter, it came back to him, unopened, with the words "RETURN TO SENDER" scrawled in ink across his mother's name on the envelope. He didn't know who had returned his letter, but the handwriting definitely wasn't Olivia Vega's.

Unwilling to give up, Mateo returned to that very old list of phone numbers. Two of the numbers were answered by people who clearly weren't family members. With the only remaining number belonging to Eddie, his oldest brother—the one who'd given him orders not to come to their father's funeral—Mateo took a deep breath to steel himself before dialing the number.

"*Hola.*"

Mateo knew at once it was Eddie. That was how he always answered the phone.

"Hey, Eduardo," he said, not bothering with any niceties. "Mateo here. I've lost Mom's phone number. Can you tell me how to get in touch with her?"

"Why don't you go straight to hell?" Eddie replied. "Don't you think Mom has enough on her plate right now without having to deal with you?" Then he hung up. Mateo was left holding a dead phone to his ear and wearing a hole in his heart. The parole board might have decided he'd paid his debt to society, but obviously his family disagreed.

Some people would've just given up then, but not Mateo. He went through the cumbersome process of obtaining a copy of his birth certificate through official channels in Yakima. That took close to two weeks, and a week after that, with the help of Randy's borrowed pickup truck, Mateo had his newly minted driver's license in hand.

And all the way along, he spent his online time at the library searching down and perusing every tech magazine he could lay hands on. Technical advances were proceeding at such exponential rates that by the time a book was published, the material was often already obsolete, so the techniques mentioned in the magazines were far more current than what was available in books.

When Mateo wasn't pursuing the most up-to-date technical information, he devoted a good deal of time to searching out everything he could locate on the death of Emily Tarrant. The first item he found was an obituary in the *Seattle Times* online edition concerning the death of Emily's mother, Abigail Marie Tarrant, who had passed away from natural causes in January. No wonder she hadn't attended his final parole hearing. The article mentioned that she'd been preceded in death by her husband, Matthew, and her beloved daughter, Emily Anne. In lieu of flowers, donations were suggested to the Emily Tarrant Memorial Scholarship fund at the University of Washington.

So Emily was still being remembered and memorialized, while the guy who'd presumably murdered her had been ground to dust under the heel of the so-called justice system. Mateo was able to find plenty of coverage about both the murder and his subsequent conviction. There wasn't a peep anywhere about his being released from prison sixteen years later, and as far as Mateo was concerned, that was just as well.

The other thing he didn't find in the articles was any hint at all about who might have been the real killer. It seemed likely that eventually he would have to find help in that regard, probably by hiring a private detective, but doing that cost money—more money than he could earn at St. Vincent de Paul's. That meant he needed a better job. So he gave up the Emily Tarrant searches in favor of focusing on job searches and sending out résumés, both of which he'd been doing for months now to no avail.

When the paperwork called for personal references, he always used Maribeth Ancell and his boss at St. Vincent's, Raymond Dougherty. Those obviously weren't doing the job, however, since he had sent out dozens of résumés without getting so much as a single callback. He was never invited in for an interview, even for the lowly coder jobs for which he was overqualified.

Lulled by white noise from the fan, Mateo fell asleep. When he awakened the next morning, he turned off the fan and discovered that the house was blissfully quiet. He used the electric pot in his room to heat water for instant coffee and then settled down in front of his computer to do some online research. These days the workstation in his bedroom consisted of a small wooden desk and a rolling chair he'd scored from a pile of abandoned office furniture left on the loading dock. The whole thing had cost him forty bucks—twenty for the chair and twenty for the desk.

That morning, while scanning through an article on trendsetters in the world of computer science, Mateo was stunned to spot a familiar name— B. Simpson. The article stated that Mr. Simpson and his Arizona-based company, High Noon Enterprises, had won international renown for being on the cutting edge in cybersecurity.

Mateo sat frozen, staring at the name on the screen for the better part of a minute. Mr. Simpson had been the co-owner of Video Games International, the company Mateo had gone to work for shortly after graduating from college. Mateo had met the man once, but that was it. His immediate supervisor at VGI was a guy named Stuart Ramey. Stuart had been nice enough in a weird sort of way.

Once the cops had placed Mateo under arrest, he had used a jail telephone to let Stuart know that due to a "pressing personal matter" he would be unable to return to work. Calling being arrested for murder a "pressing personal matter" was a lot like putting lipstick on a pig, and considering the amount of coverage the case had received in local media outlets, Stuart probably knew the truth about his situation anyway. After his parole, on the off chance that they might consider taking him back, Mateo had looked for Video Games International, but it had vanished completely, most likely gobbled up by a larger corporate entity of some kind.

When Mateo's fingers were once again capable of keyboard movement, he googled High Noon Enterprises. Several articles came up. High Noon Enterprises was a closely held corporation operating out of a small Arizona town called Cottonwood. Several articles mentioned that the previous fall, people from High Noon had been involved in saving the life of a man named Francis Gillespie, the archbishop of the Phoenix Diocese. And there, in one of those articles, Mateo saw another familiar name—Stuart Ramey.

Mateo could barely believe it! Stuart was still working for B.? With his heart beating fast in his chest, Mateo wondered if there was even the remotest chance that Stu would be willing to give him a reference. Probably not, he realized a moment later. They had worked together briefly seventeen years earlier—before Mateo's homicide conviction, before he'd spent sixteen long years sitting in a cell.

No, Mateo told himself despairingly. *Don't be stupid. That's not going to happen. Don't even ask.*

But later that day on the loading dock, Mateo couldn't get Stuart Ramey out of his head, and sometime in the afternoon he made up his mind. It couldn't hurt to ask. What was the worst that could happen to him?

When he got home, everyone else was out and the house was still quiet. In his room with the door closed behind him, Mateo located the phone number and dialed.

"High Noon Enterprises," a woman's voice answered. "How can I help you?"

Mateo had to swallow hard before he could answer. "I'd like to speak to Stuart Ramey," he said.

"Who may I say is calling?"

"My name's Mateo Vega," he hedged. "I don't know if he'll remember me, but a long time ago I used to work for him."

"One moment, please, and I'll put you through," the woman said.

She went away, leaving Mateo waiting on the phone. It seemed like a very long time before anyone else came on the line, but that was probably because Mateo was holding his breath.

|CHAPTER 6|

COTTONWOOD, ARIZONA

By the time Harvey finally left the bar, he was three sheets to the wind, but when he drove back to the office, it was late enough that everyone else had left the business park. There was one car parked at the High Noon end of the building, and the van the janitors used to come and go was sitting out front. He waved at one of the custodians as he shambled into his office. He had opted out of using the cleaning service for two reasons: number one, he didn't want to pay for it, and number two, he didn't want anyone to know he was spending his nights in the office. It turned out that the manager of the apartment complex where he'd been living had been much less forgiving in terms of back rent than the people at High Noon had been, and when it came time to choose between keeping the apartment or keeping the office, he'd chosen the latter.

Originally, he'd thought about bringing in a cot of some kind, but it turned out there was no place out of sight to store one. Instead Harvey had opted for a blow-up mattress, one that came complete with a hand-held compressor. Once he let the air out of it in the morning, he could roll it up and store it in one of several empty file drawers. Getting up from that every morning wasn't easy, but that cushion of air underneath was a hell of a lot easier on his back than sleeping on a concrete floor with only the thinnest layer of commercial-grade carpet on top.

That night, having had far too many of Joe's special "beverage of the evening," Harvey was fortunate to have made it from the bar back to the office without getting a DUI. And once inside he had a hell of a time removing the mattress from the drawer and hooking it up to the compressor. When he finally flopped down on the mattress, the room went spinning out of control.

"Yup, Harvey old man," he mumbled aloud to himself. "You're drunk as a skunk this time, so don't forget to set the alarm."

Turning on the alarm on his phone wasn't any easier than running the compressor, but eventually he got the job done. He had a home inspection to do early the next morning, and he didn't want to miss it. This was with a real-estate agent who was willing to pay up front and in cash as long as he gave her clients the news they wanted to hear about the house they were trying to buy. Agents who got bad news weren't nearly as eager to pay up, and if Harvey could manage to find a few more of those this week, he might be able to catch up on his back rent after all.

Once the alarm was set, he lay there staring at the ceiling above him, hazily lit by the lights in the parking lot outside. Not surprisingly, once again the room began to spin.

Damn Joe and his goddamned Harvey Wallbangers. From now on he'd be sticking to beer.

Sometime overnight he dreamed about his mother. Most people would have regarded the dream as a nightmare, but not Harvey. With the scene now lit by a full moon, he saw her body disappear under the surface of the dark water. During the daytime hours the water had an iridescent glow from all the chemicals in it, but at night the water had always been jet-black.

The dream was enough to awaken him, and he needed to take a piss. Unfortunately, that meant getting up off the floor and trudging down the hallway to the restroom two doors away. Once on his mattress again, he couldn't go back to sleep, because, as it had for all these years, that night and the days that followed Ida Mae's death returned to him in minute detail as though they had happened hours ago rather than decades.

In the dream, as vividly as in real life, he had once again watched Ida Mae's face slip beneath the surface of the water, and he had awakened then with the memory alive and well inside his brain. He remembered clearly how once he'd cut off a length of wire to refasten the gate, he'd tossed both the bolt cutter and the remaining wire into the water beside her. After closing the gate behind him, he drove back to Tony's place. Once at the house, he parked the truck in the same spot where he'd found it. He used an outside hose to rinse off the brass knuckles before drying them and returning them to Tony's glove box. Then he used a stray piece of paper napkin from the floor to wipe down the glove box's latch, the gearshift, the steering wheel, and the driver's-side door handles. Next, knowing he still reeked of urine, Broomy stripped off his clothing and sprayed it down with frigid water from the same outside hose. By then snowflakes were falling thick and fast. Freezing cold, he tiptoed into the house, lugging his sodden clothing. He hung his shirt and pants over the showerhead to dry out and returned to the living room.

By then the beer and tequila had done their work and the party had broken up. Twenty or so people had been on hand to begin with, but in Broomy's absence most of them had gone home. Only the drunkest of the bunch remained, passed out cold in the living room. Tony himself had retired to the privacy of his own room. With Broomy's teeth chattering and his body quaking from the cold, he pulled his letterman jacket tightly around himself and took the last remaining spot in the room, a broken-down recliner situated in one corner. Eventually the warmth of the room, combined with mental and physical exhaustion, lulled him to sleep.

"So what happened to you, Broomy boy?" one of the older boys asked jeeringly as he shook Harvey awake the next morning. "Did you have to go outside and barf your guts out? Are those your wet clothes that were hanging in the shower?"

"I guess," Broomy admitted sheepishly as he tried to sit up.

Tony appeared in the background, looking hungover as hell but carrying a cup of coffee. "You'd better get dressed so I can take you home," he said. "I just saw something on the news. There's a lot of police activity over on German Gulch Road. They're saying a woman has been reported missing. I'm not sure, but it looked to me like where they're parked is just up the road from your place."

Broomy's heart went to his throat. "Someone's missing?" he asked shakily, hoping he appeared to be as startled by the news as everyone else.

Tony nodded. "Get dressed. I put your clothes in the dryer. They should be almost dry by now."

Broomy's pants and shirt were warm but still slightly damp as he put them on. Outside, a good two inches of snow that hadn't been there the night before covered the landscape. As they piled into the GMC, Broomy worried that Tony might notice it was parked in a slightly different position from the way he'd left it, but he said nothing, and Broomy didn't either.

As they approached the McCluskey place on German Gulch Road, they were stopped by a roadblock made up of a collection of law-enforcement vehicles and media vans. A uniformed deputy from the Silver Bow Sheriff's Department flagged them down.

"Sorry," he said, "there's been an incident. You can't go any farther."

"What kind of incident?" Broomy asked. He didn't have to try to make his voice sound frantic. It came out that way of its own accord. "That's my house over there," he added, pointing at the double-wide. "What's going on? What's happened?"

"What's your name, son?" the deputy asked.

"Harvey, Harvey McCluskey."

"Hang tight here for a minute," the deputy told him. "Let me go check with my sergeant. I'll be right back."

As the deputy walked over to his patrol car, Broomy clambered out of the truck.

"Do you want me to hang around?" Tony asked.

"Nah," Broomy said. "Just go. No telling how long this is going to take, and there's no sense in your being caught up in it."

Tony did as he was told, executing a U-turn and leaving the way he'd come while Broomy stood on the shoulder of the road waiting for the deputy to return. The sun was up now, and the thin layer of snow was already starting to melt. Suddenly, out of nowhere, Rocco appeared. The dog raced straight for Broomy and then, at the last moment, launched himself into the air, landing in Broomy's arms.

Fortunately for Broomy, video footage from one of the local television stations happened to capture the dog racing into the frame and making that leap. For a long moment, they stood like that, Broomy holding the dog, his face buried in Rocco's thick winter coat. As far as television viewers were concerned, that heartbreaking moment spoke volumes about the devastating scene. Here was the missing woman's bereaved teenage son, caught forever in the act of seeking consolation from his tragic loss in the comfort of his mother's dog. And no one who saw that touching news clip ever questioned whether or not the boy was as grief-stricken as he appeared, nor did they think it remotely possible he might be responsible for whatever had befallen his mother.

The viewers were all completely wrong about that, of course, but it didn't really matter.

Eventually the deputy returned, accompanied by a guy in a suit who introduced himself as Detective Manning. "You're Harvey McCluskey?" he asked.

"Yes, sir," Broomy replied. "Like I told the deputy, that's my house over there. What's going on?"

"We're dealing with a missing person," Detective Manning answered.

"What missing person?" Broomy insisted. "Is my mother okay?"

"If you don't mind, I'd like to take you back to the department and ask you a few questions."

"How can I answer questions if I don't even know what happened?"

Which is how Broomy McCluskey ended up in a sheriff's department interview room early in the morning after murdering his mother the previous night. Even now, all these years later, Harvey could remember almost every word uttered in that interview. But right that minute, Joe's Wallbangers hit home again, and Harvey was out like a light.

When the alarm went off a few hours later, the dream was still fresh in his mind. Struggling to get up off the floor was hell. Once he'd deflated the mattress and stowed the pillow and bedroll in their proper file drawers, Harvey headed to the gym, to shower rather than work out. Thanks to the smoking-hot deal he'd gotten on a gym membership at the first of the year, he was still able to maintain a modicum of personal hygiene. But the reality was, he wouldn't be able to afford the gym much longer either.

Still hungover but presentable now, he grabbed a quick breakfast at a hole-in-the-wall diner and then headed for Black Canyon City. Today's home inspection couldn't come at a better time. It probably wouldn't pay enough to get Harvey out of the hole on his rent, but it would tide him over for a day or two, and that was the best he could hope for.

|CHAPTER 7|

SEDONA, ARIZONA

Ali's plan to go to sleep early the night before had been a complete fail—not that she hadn't tried. After the disturbing conversation with her mother, she *had* gone to bed early, but not to sleep. She'd tossed and turned so much that Bella had eventually been obliged to leave her customary spot on Ali's side of the bed and retreat to B.'s pillow for the remainder of the night.

Ali, for her part, had given up. Getting out of bed, she took to her computer and composed a long e-mail to B., telling him about everything that was going on with her folks. He called her at ten past seven the next morning, waking her out of what was finally a sound sleep.

"What terrible news," he said when she answered. "How are you doing?"

"Better now," she said groggily. "It took me forever to fall asleep."

"Sorry I woke you, then," he apologized. "As late as you sent that e-mail, I should have just let you sleep, but once I go into a meeting I won't be available for several hours."

"It's okay," she said. "My alarm would have gone off in a few minutes anyway."

"How's your mother doing?"

"You know her. She's all about 'We'll handle this on our own, thank you very much.'"

"That's Edie Larson, all right," B. agreed, "but it's going to be tough on everybody. From what you said, it sounds like your dad's lucid one minute and totally out of it the next. That's going to create some very rough waters for your mom to navigate."

"Not just Mom," Ali said. "What about Colin? He thinks the world of his papa. The first time Dad blows up at him, it'll break the boy's heart."

"Let Edie know we'll do whatever needs doing," B. assured her. "All she has to do is ask."

Ali had to laugh. "That's going to be the first major stumbling block," she pointed out. "Knowing my mother, getting her to ask for help will be like pulling teeth. In order to know what's really going on, we'll need to become first-rate mind readers."

"The only way to know what's what will be to spend more time with both of them," B. suggested.

"Right," Ali allowed, "but if Mom figures out we're hovering, that'll blow up in our faces, too. In other words, heads we lose, tails we lose."

"Exactly," B. said. "So for the time being, we all practice tightrope walking. But you still haven't given me a straight answer about how you're doing."

Ali had to think about that for a moment before she could reply. "Not so hot, I guess," she admitted at last. "How could all this have been going on and gotten so serious without my having the slightest idea it was happening? How could I not notice? When it comes to being a good daughter, this counts as a massive fail for me."

"My guess is your mom has been going to great lengths to make sure nobody noticed. In that regard, the driver's license blowup that resulted in Bob throwing her out of the house did us a real favor, because it's a wake-up call for everyone," B. said. "As this unfolds, we're all going to start encountering different kinds of new normals. After each succeeding crisis, Bob and Edie will eventually be on a different plateau, and so will we. The problem is, each of those will be a little worse than the one before—not only for them but for the rest of us, too. All we can do at the moment is be more present in their lives—and in our grandkids' lives, too, for that matter," he added bleakly. "What this has brought home to me is the reality that time is precious for all of us, and we need to make every moment count."

"You're right about that," Ali murmured after a moment. "You're a good man, B. Simpson—a very good man."

"Thanks," B. said. "I'll have to go soon because my meeting starts in ten, but what's on your agenda today?"

"I have to tackle that pile of job applications," Ali said. "Stu has done a first sort on them, and Frigg has compiled dossiers on each remaining applicant. You know Frigg. She doesn't do anything halfway, so she's accumulated massive amounts of material on each one. I'll scan through all of it and see if anything jumps out at me. By the time you get home on Friday, we should have the remaining applicants winnowed down to the top four or five. We'll schedule each of them to come in for a face-to-face interview with you and Stu, but you're the one who'll be making the final call."

"Fair enough," B. agreed. "I'd best get going now. I'm

out in the parking lot, but for a meeting like this I'm better off turning up slightly early than slightly late."

"Good luck," she told him, "and keep me posted."

Once off the phone, Ali pulled on her robe and went to the kitchen in search of coffee.

"I noticed your mom didn't stay over after all," Alonzo said as Ali slipped into her accustomed place at the breakfast nook.

Alonzo, a retired submariner, was in charge of running the Simpson/Reynolds household, but he also functioned in a very real way as Ali's personal assistant. Since whatever was happening with her folks was going to affect Ali's life, it would no doubt affect Alonzo's as well, so she took the time to bring him up-to-date on exactly what the deal was with Bob and Edie Larson.

When she finished, Alonzo nodded knowingly. "My grandparents went through something like this when I was a kid," he said. "Nobody ever diagnosed my grandfather's condition as Alzheimer's, dementia, or whatever. Or if they did, no one ever told me about it, but it was tough, especially on my nana. I remember coming home from school one day and finding her sitting on the couch crying. I asked her what was wrong. 'Sometimes life is hard, *dulce nieto*,' she told me. 'Sometimes life is very hard.' That's all she ever said to me about it. My grandfather was sick for years. I never heard her complain about the situation, but I saw how taking care of him wore her down. She died only a few months after he did. So if there's anything you need me to do to help out, just let me know."

"Thank you, Alonzo," Ali told him. "You're very kind, and I really appreciate it."

"Now, what would you like for breakfast?"

"Hard-boiled eggs, I think, along with toast and some

bacon," she told him. "If I'm going to make it through this day on the amount of sleep I got the last two nights, I'd better have some protein in my system."

Ali went back to the bedroom to shower and dress. By the time she emerged again, breakfast was on the table. She left the house on Manzanita Hills Drive a good half an hour after her usual departure time. On her way, she called Shirley to let her know she was en route. There was very little traffic, and she used part of her half-hour commute time to call Chris.

"How are things?" Ali asked when her son answered. Prior to having Siri dial his number, she'd already decided that with twins and a newborn to look after, Chris and Athena had enough going on in their lives at the moment without the further complication of knowing what was happening concerning Ali's parents. To that end she was determined to edit that bit of information out of the conversation.

"Athena's great, but Logan had some breathing issues overnight," Chris replied. "That means the doctors want to keep them one more day. Hopefully we'll be homeward bound tomorrow sometime. Right now the twins and I are having breakfast."

"Is there anything you need me to do, anything at all?"

"No, Mom," he replied. "Thanks for offering, but we've got this."

Ali couldn't help smiling. Two months prior to the birth of her son, Ali's first husband and Chris's father, Dean Reynolds, had died of glioblastoma. Left as a very young widow with a newborn, Ali had raised Chris mostly as a single mom, and yet he'd turned out to be this terrific human being, one who was a great husband, an even better dad, and as far as she knew an excellent teacher as well. What more could she have asked?

"Okay, then," she said. "I'll let you go."

Driving along, Ali was tempted to call her mother, just to check on her. After all, in terms of loving care, Ali owed her big. Edie Larson had been there for her in every way when she'd brought Chris home from the hospital. Ali had no idea how she and Chris would have survived those first challenging months on their own if her mom hadn't been there helping. Now Ali desperately wanted to return that favor, but she worried that if she showed too much of a sudden interest in what was going on with her folks, her mother would bristle. So instead of calling her mom, Ali resorted to calling Edie's best friend and co-great-grandmother, Betsy Peterson.

"I just found out about what's been happening," Ali said when Betsy answered.

"So Edie finally got around to spilling the beans, did she?" Betsy returned. "I've been telling her for months that she needed to bring you and B. up to date on Bob's condition."

Focused on the word "months," Ali felt a lump form in her throat. *This has been going on that long?* she thought.

"Word's out now," Ali replied after a moment. "As you may have noticed, my mother has quite a stubborn streak."

"You don't say," Betsy said with a laugh.

"That's why I'm calling," Ali continued. "Just because my mom needs help doesn't mean she'll break down and ask for it. I'm hoping to use you as a backstop for keeping an eye on things."

"In other words, you want me to be your spy?"

It seemed best to be straight up about all this. "Exactly," Ali admitted. "So what *has* been going on?"

Betsy paused as though reluctant to reveal any telling details, but finally she did. "There have apparently been a couple of incidents of . . . well . . . shoving."

"You mean Dad actually pushed her?"

"Yes," Betsy responded, "during one of his angry outbursts."

Ali was dismayed. The idea that things had deteriorated to the point of physical violence was nothing short of shocking.

"Sometimes he doesn't know who she is," Betsy continued. "Other times he'll be his old self and sharp as a tack. Most of the time he refuses to go to the dining room because he doesn't want to eat with 'all those strangers,' although he's known most of the people who live here for years. That means, of course, that your mom isn't able to socialize nearly as much as she used to or needs to either. Not only that, she has to cart his food and dishes to and from their unit. She'll give him his meds, and he'll pretend to take them, but later on he'll spit them out. She's found the pills hidden behind the cushion of his chair or buried under leftovers when she goes to clean his plate."

Betsy fell silent, as if feeling she'd said more than she should have. As far as medications were concerned, Ali knew that her father had been on high-blood-pressure meds for years and also something for his prostate, and probably more besides. One thing was certain, however— taking any prescribed medication on an intermittent basis was not a good idea. At this point Ali was feeling more alarmed than ever, but she didn't want to let on for fear of spooking this invaluable resource into silence.

After a very long pause, Betsy resumed. "I've been trying to tell Edie that she shouldn't try to handle all this on her own, but I haven't been able to make the slightest headway. She's been so deep in denial that everything I say falls on deaf ears."

"She probably won't listen to me either," Ali said, "but with your help at least I'll have a better idea of what's really going on and whether there's a crisis looming."

"Well, then," Betsy said, "you can count on me to keep an eye out and report in if something untoward happens. It's the least I can do, but tell me, have you heard anything from the kids?"

"I just got off the phone with Chris," Ali told her. "Logan evidently experienced breathing difficulties overnight. That means the doctors are keeping both Athena and the baby for another day, but they should be home tomorrow."

"They're keeping her overnight for a second night? That's mighty big of them," Betsy sniffed. "The very idea that they'd kick a woman out the day after having a C-section is ridiculous."

The same thought had occurred to Ali, but she had filtered that nugget of medical Monday-morning quarterbacking out of her conversation with Chris. In the background of the call, Ali heard what sounded like a doorbell ringing.

"I need to answer that," Betsy said quickly, "but you just go on about your business, Ali. As I said, if I spot anything amiss with your folks, I'll call you on the double."

"Thank you so much," Ali told her. "I really appreciate it."

Ali drove on, but with a less troubled heart. The situation with her parents was seemingly much worse than she had suspected, but with Betsy's help Ali would at least have access to information that hadn't been spun out of all recognition by Edie Larson's determination to keep their difficulties to herself. Right that moment it was the best Ali could hope for. By the time she arrived in Cottonwood, however, she knew she had to put personal concerns aside for the time being in order to concentrate on work.

"Have we heard from Harvey McCluskey?" Ali asked Shirley as she entered the office.

"Nope," Shirley answered, "not a word."

"That's par for the course," Ali replied. "Based on previous experience, I'm guessing he'll wait until the last minute."

Once inside her office, Ali set worries about her late-paying tenant aside in favor of tackling the stack of applications, résumés, and Frigg-created dossiers, each of which contained massive amounts of information.

During Ali's senior year in high school, she and her best friend, Irene Holzer, had found themselves in the principal's office for attempting to promote a senior ditch day in protest of the sudden and what they felt to be unwarranted midyear dismissal of the school's beloved football coach. Ali had found out years later that the dismissal had been absolutely justified, although the grubby details of Coach Majors's illegal gambling activities were never made public. At the time, though, sitting in the office and waiting to be read the riot act, Ali remembered Reenie saying something to the effect that the infraction would probably end up as a black mark in what kids back then referred to as their "permanent record." Later Ali had come to realize that the whole idea of a permanent record was nothing but a convenient fiction used to trick kids into toeing the line.

Now, however, with the advent of social media, the idea of having a permanent record had become all too real. As Ali sorted through the résumés and dossiers, what turned out to be permanent records on each of the applicants gradually emerged, and that wasn't necessarily a good thing. If you happened to be looking for a job with a cyber-security firm, for instance, maybe posting videos of yourself playing volleyball on a nude beach in California wasn't such a good idea. And maybe showing Facebook montages featuring you and your pals toking up at high school pot parties wasn't a great strategy either. Smoking pot might or might not have been illegal in that locale at the time, but what fellow partygoers seemed to consider hilarious antics didn't demonstrate the presence of much common sense, and at High Noon common sense counted for everything. The pot smoker had graduated from college with honors but not without picking up a pair of DUIs along the way. And then there was the young woman who had posted a spiteful after-Christmas rant saying that since her grandparents' political leanings disagreed with hers, she was writing them out of her life forever.

All three of those applicants had outstanding academic records and top-notch GPAs, but the kinds of grandstanding and irresponsible behaviors they exhibited in private made them all no-gos in Ali's mind. High Noon was a small company that operated as a well-oiled machine, primarily because the people involved dealt with one another on the basis of goodwill and mutual respect. Given that, was it a great idea to bring people on board who were not the least bit ashamed of posting their histories of bad behavior on the Internet? How would people like that conduct themselves on a daily basis with fellow employees and customers alike? Ali dropped all three applications into the discard heap.

She was still up to her eyeteeth in the process when Shirley tapped on her door. "Gus Robbins, the security installer, is here," she said.

The High Noon campus had all kinds of outdoor

security cameras, and High Noon's interior space had even more. Recently, however, several of the tenants in other parts of the compound had asked for additional interior surveillance. Leaseholders were responsible for whatever systems they wished to install inside their individual office spaces, but it was up to High Noon to provide protection for the common areas, including lobbies, hallways, and restrooms.

To that end Ali had taken it upon herself to go looking for the right product and vendor. She wanted something more subtle than the eye-in-the-sky look preferred by retail establishments, so she'd chosen a newly designed system that operated on a Wi-Fi arrangement and consisted of a small camera located inside an innocuous-looking plastic cube. Placed on a wall next to an interior door in a corridor, it was capable of delivering high-def motion-activated videos of the entire length of the hallway. A few keystrokes on the controlling keyboard allowed the operator to move the focus up or down the hallway as needed.

"Wasn't he supposed to be here earlier?" Ali asked.

Shirley nodded. "He was due this morning."

"Better late than never, I suppose," Ali said. "Send him in, and ask Cami to please join us."

Gus Robbins wasn't especially impressive. He turned out to be a very young guy sporting freckles and a puny effort at a goatee. He seemed nervous and ill at ease, and the uniform he wore didn't do much to convince Ali he was a knowledgeable professional. When Cami showed up, he looked wary. As Ali explained to Gus that he would be working with Cami regarding any glitches or hiccups in the program, the poor guy looked downright terrified. Once they went off to work on the security installation, however, Ali returned to the job-applicant issue.

By four o'clock in the afternoon, she was finally finished, but she was also suffering a severe eyestrain headache. As she cleared her desk in preparation for going home, a frowning Stu Ramey appeared in her doorway. He stepped inside her office, closing the door behind him, and took a seat in one of her visitor chairs. As he sat down, he slid a single piece of paper across the table in her direction.

"What's this?" Ali asked, picking it up.

"A letter of recommendation," he answered. "My writing skills aren't always the best, and I wanted you to take a look at it before I send it along."

> *To Whom It May Concern:*
>
> *A number of years ago, I was Mateo Vega's immediate supervisor when he was employed by Video Games International. He came to the company shortly after graduating from the University of Washington with a degree in computer science.*
>
> *I found him to be a dependable worker and a quick study when it came to learning new skills. I think you'll find him to be a valuable addition to your team.*
>
> *Regards,*
> *Stuart Ramey*

Ali looked up from the paper with a puzzled frown on her face. "It's a good letter," she said, handing it back. "But Video Games International? That was a long time ago."

Stu nodded. "A very long time ago," he agreed, "sixteen years at least."

"So why send out a letter of recommendation for

someone who hasn't worked with you for more than a decade and a half? Wouldn't he be better off with a recommendation from a more recent employer?"

Shifting in his seat, Stu looked uncomfortable. "Mateo called me earlier and asked," he told her. "If you don't want me to send it out with High Noon's name attached, I can delete it."

"I don't understand," Ali said. "Why would I think it necessary for you to remove High Noon's name?"

Stu sighed. "It's a long story," he said. "Like I said in the letter, Mateo came to VGI right after he graduated from the U Dub. He was all the things I mentioned—dependable, bright, and a good worker. He seemed like a great guy, but then one Monday a couple of months after he came to work for us, he didn't show up on the job. And he didn't call in either. It was several days later before I finally heard from him. He called to say he was dealing with a personal matter and wouldn't be coming back to work."

After a pause Stu continued. "Eventually I learned that he'd been involved in an altercation of some kind with his girlfriend over that weekend, and she ended up dead. This happened at about the same time the whole thing at VGI blew sky-high and B. and I ended up coming back home to Arizona. I never heard anything more about how things turned out with Mateo until he called this afternoon. He told me he didn't kill the girl but that he accepted a plea deal, from first-degree murder down to second, in order to avoid a possible life sentence. He was let out on parole in May of last year after serving sixteen years of a sixteen-to-life term. According to him he's spent the last year trying to get a job in the IT world, but no one will give him a chance."

"How did he know where to find you?" Ali asked.

"He said he saw B.'s name and High Noon Enterprises mentioned in that scientific trendsetter article from last month. He did some googling, found High Noon, and learned that I was working here. He called this afternoon on the off chance that maybe I'd be willing to give him a letter of reference."

"Which you've already written," Ali observed.

Stu nodded. "Mateo was a bright kid," he said. "Not in Lance Tucker's league, of course, but still very smart. I hate to think of him wasting his whole life working on the loading dock at some charity thrift shop. It sounds to me as though he's paid his debt to society and is trying to get his life back on track. If I can give him a helping hand after all these years, why not?"

Ali couldn't help thinking about that angry young woman hoping to work for them who was busy ghosting her grandparents.

"Why not indeed?" she agreed. "And there's no need to delete High Noon's name from the letter. It sounds like this is someone who could use a second chance, and having our name on the letter of reference might give him more of a boost."

"Thanks, Ali," Stu said, rising to his feet. "I'll send it off, then."

"Wait," Ali told him. "Before you go, take these." She handed him the file folder containing the paperwork on the four remaining applicants. "These are the four who made the next cut. Give them to Cami. She's the only one who knows B.'s schedule backward and forward. Tell her to work with these folks and make travel arrangements for them to come in for interviews."

"Will do," Stu said. "Are you heading out?"

Ali nodded. "Yes, I am. It's been a very long couple of days, and I'm in desperate need of some beauty sleep."

|CHAPTER 8|

OAK CREEK VILLAGE, ARIZONA

As Stuart Ramey headed back to Oak Creek Village that evening, he was feeling decidedly uneasy. Yes, he'd written that letter of recommendation for Mateo. Given Stu's own personal history, how could he do otherwise? He had been in desperate straits and living in a homeless shelter when B. Simpson had reached out and offered him not only a lifeline, he'd offered him a life.

Stu tended to take what people said to him at face value, and he was beginning to understand that wasn't always wise. What if Mateo's story turned out to be different from what he'd let on? What if he *hadn't* been wrongly accused and was indeed a killer? And then there was the problem with his credentials. In the letter, Stu had said Mateo had been a hard worker, and that was certainly true—back then.

VGI had been at the very top of the heap in the video-game world. As a consequence they had often been targeted by hackers attempting to steal their intellectual property. Stu had been tasked with the job of fending off those attacks, and Mateo had been hired to assist him in doing just that. But if computer science had more than reinvented itself in the past seventeen years, so had hacking—perhaps even more so. What if an employer hired Mateo based on Stu's written recommendation only to discover that his work skills and knowledge were hopelessly out of date? Yes, Stu maybe owed Mateo a hand up, but what did he owe those potential employers?

Halfway between Cottonwood and Oak Creek Village, Stu called his AI, Frigg.

"Good afternoon, Stuart," the computerized voice greeted him cheerfully. "I hope you had a pleasant day."

"I did, but I need your help," he said.

"Of course," Frigg answered. "How can I be of service?"

"Earlier today I wrote a letter of recommendation for someone who years ago used to work for Mr. Simpson at a previous company, Video Games International. The guy's name is Mateo Vega. According to him, he spent sixteen years in prison in Washington State after pleading guilty to a charge of second-degree murder. I'd like you to find out everything you can about him."

"What kind of dossier do you prefer?" Frigg asked. "Complete or ordinary?"

The last was code. "Complete" meant Frigg would make use of all possible sources, including ones that were not necessarily open to public scrutiny and could be accessed only through some of the AI's more creative hacking techniques. Having been created to function as the virtual handmaiden to a would-be serial killer, Frigg had cut her teeth gaining access to all kinds of unauthorized material. "Ordinary" meant she would utilize only sources of information readily available to the general public. In terms of situations where law enforcement might be involved and where the information had to stand up in court as admissible evidence, "ordinary" was the order of the day. Fortunately, that wasn't the case here.

"Complete," Stu specified.

"Very well. I'll get right on it."

And she did. By the time Stu got home and made himself a bologna sandwich, Frigg had put her eight hundred CPUs to work and rounded up a mountain of material. As he sat down in front of his wall of monitors with both the sandwich and a Diet Coke set out on a TV tray, Stu was grateful Cami Lee couldn't see what he was doing. She continued to wage open warfare in an effort to wean him off his preferred diet of what Cami called "junk" food rather than "real" food.

"What do you have for me, Frigg?" he asked. Other people might have had Siri or Alexa answering their various questions. Stuart Ramey had Frigg.

"Bio first?" Frigg asked.

"Please."

"Mr. Vega, born in Yakima, Washington, in 1979, is the youngest of eight children born to Olivia Ortega Vega and Joaquin Manuel Vega. Do you require the names of each of his siblings?"

"Not necessary," Stu said, "but please call him Mateo."

"Very well. Mateo graduated as salutatorian of his class at Yakima High School, won an academic scholarship to the University of Washington, and is the first and only member of his family to attend and graduate from a four-year college."

"Yes, the U Dub," Stu replied.

"That would be the University of Washington?" Frigg asked, seemingly puzzled by the terminology.

There was still a good deal of English-language jargon that eluded the AI.

"Dub is shorthand for W," Stu explained. "It's what people in Seattle call the University of Washington."

"All right, then," Frigg said agreeably. "The U Dub it is." Then she continued. "All seven of Mateo's siblings still survive. His father is deceased. Joaquin died while Mateo was incarcerated at the Monroe Correctional Facility in Monroe, Washington. Mr. Mateo was granted leave to attend his father's funeral services, but that leave was rescinded when Mateo received a letter from his eldest brother, Eduardo, saying that Mateo's presence at their father's funeral would be a distraction."

Stu let out a long sigh. Once again Frigg had managed to hack her way into a penal institution's records system to gain access to an inmate's personal correspondence. Fortunately, none of this information would need to show up in a court of law. Stu had asked for a complete dossier; that's exactly what he was getting.

"That's interesting," Stu said. "Sounds as though there's some bad blood inside the family."

"I'm sorry," Frigg interjected, "I don't have any information regarding Mateo's blood type."

"Never mind," Stu said. "Go on."

"In 2002 Mateo pled guilty to second-degree homicide in the death of his former girlfriend, Emily Anne Tarrant. He was sentenced to sixteen years in prison. He appeared before the parole board ten times prior to his being released last May. I have transcripts from each of those hearings. Would you care to read them in their entirety?"

"Just summarize."

"Although he entered a guilty plea prior to being sent to prison, during each of his parole-board appearances Mateo insisted he had done so not because he killed her but because his public defender said that accepting a plea agreement would result in a lesser sentence. Had he been convicted of first-degree homicide, he might have received life in prison."

Stu nodded. That was all in line with what Mateo had told him on the phone earlier.

"What's he been doing since his release?"

"Living as a renter in a house purported to be a single-family dwelling in the city of Renton south of Seattle. His landlord's name is Randy Wasson. Mateo works at a nearby establishment called St. Vincent de Paul's, which is evidently a charity thrift shop of some kind. At the time he left the prison, he was issued a check in the amount of one thousand six hundred dollars due from wages earned while working inside the prison."

"What kind of work?"

"Primarily in the prison library, where he served as an assistant to the librarian, a Mrs. Maribeth Ancell. She was responsible for giving him an achievement award due to his being able to solve some difficulty with the computer system inside the library."

"That figures," Stu said. "That's what he was trained to do. He has an undergraduate degree in computer science."

"And Mrs. Ancell does not," Frigg replied. "She has a B.A. in English and a master's degree in library science.

That's what makes her preferred choices in reading material so interesting."

"What do you mean?"

"She has an extensive record of interlibrary loans, dating back twelve years or more. Much of the borrowed material—textbooks and the like—had to do primarily with science and technology. Some of what she borrowed appear to be dissertations on computer science available only through various university library systems."

Suddenly Stu sat bolt upright. "Wait, you're saying the librarian was checking out and presumably reading multiple dissertations on computer science?"

"That's how it would appear," Frigg replied. "That would include computer science, computer engineering, cybersecurity, and similar topics."

"Let me ask you this, has she continued to request those kinds of materials since last May by any chance?"

"No," Frigg answered, "not at all. Mrs. Ancell's last request for material through an interlibrary loan occurred in April of last year. However, I have learned that Mateo is now in possession of a library card for the King County Library System, and those kinds of interlibrary loan requests are common in *his* borrowing history."

Stu felt downright jubilant. Mateo's knowledge of all things computer-related wasn't seventeen years out of date. He'd been studying on his own the whole time he was in prison, but even with updated skills, he was now stuck working on a loading dock because of his record—thanks to a stint in prison for something he claimed he hadn't done.

In advance of High Noon's current hiring spree, Stu had asked Frigg to create five separate fictional computer networks and lace each of them with a separate known hack. Because Stu loved watching professional bowling and sorting out the physics of each roll of the ball, he'd given the individual hacks names similar to those used as lane oil patterns in professional bowling tournaments: Badger, Wolf, Shark, Scorpion, and Cheetah, with the last one being by far the most difficult.

All those hoping to make the second cut in the hiring process had been given copies of the material and told they were required to locate, identify, and disable each of the hacks. Frigg, of course, had kept track of the amount of time each applicant had worked on the individual problems. Only those who succeeded in finding and successfully countering three or more of the test cases remained in the final group of applicants Stu passed along to Ali, and not one of them had scored a five. Most had managed two or three. One had hit four. If Stu was correct in his assessment of what Mateo Vega had on the ball and what he'd been studying while he was locked up in prison, there was a good chance he might be able to ace that same set of tests.

"Frigg," Stu said, "do you still have copies of those sample hack problems we sent to High Noon's job applicants?"

"Of course," Frigg answered, sounding a bit miffed, as though she couldn't believe Stu could be so simple minded as to think she'd discarded something so valuable.

"Please send working copies of all five to my High Noon address," he said.

"Anything else?"

"Go ahead and send along the materials on Mateo's arrest and conviction. I'll look over those at my leisure. In the meantime, Frigg, thank you. You've been a huge help."

"You're welcome," Frigg replied. "Have a good night. Sleep well."

|CHAPTER 9|

On her drive home that afternoon, when Ali drove past Sedona Shadows, she was tempted to do a surprise drop-in visit at her folks' place, but mindful of being accused of hovering, she went straight home instead. She was dressed in shorts and a tank top and having a pre-dinner glass of merlot when B. called. It may have been early morning where he was, but he was wide awake and downright jubilant.

"Nailed another one," he announced. "It's not finalized, because the lawyers have yet to draw up the participation agreement, but Helsinki is a previously untapped market for us, and we may pick up another account or two along the way. How are things with you?"

Ali told him about her conversation with Betsy Peterson and about bringing her in as a source of backdoor information on what was going on with Bob and Edie. She also told him about her preliminary sort through the job applicants. Only at the end of the conversation did she tell him about Stu having written that letter of recommendation for Mateo Vega.

"Why would Mateo be asking Stu for a letter of

recommendation after all this time?" B. asked. "Wouldn't it be better for him to have those from more recent employers?"

"That's what I thought, but it's because he hasn't been working," Ali explained. "He's been in prison for murdering his girlfriend."

"Murder?" B. echoed. "Are you kidding?" Then, after a pause, he continued. "Oh, wait," he said. "Now it's coming back to me, but only vaguely. She died after some kind of beach party. I guess I knew Mateo had been arrested for that, but I don't remember ever hearing that he'd been convicted. How long was he locked up?"

"Sixteen years," Ali said. "At least that's what I think Stu told me. And he wasn't convicted. He took a plea bargain in hopes of receiving a lighter sentence, but he claims he didn't actually do the crime."

"I remember Mateo," B. continued after a thoughtful pause. "Bright kid and eager to work. The problem is, when that was going on, the situation with Clarice and me was going down the tubes. I wasn't really paying close attention."

Clarice was B.'s first wife, and Ali knew that his divorce and the dissolution of Video Games International had occurred at almost the same time. No wonder he'd been too preoccupied with his own affairs to pay attention to Mateo Vega's.

"If Mateo's been in prison this long," B. continued, "he'll be decades behind in terms of what's happening in today's IT world. It was nice of Stu to write the letter, and if Mateo had asked me for one, I probably would have done the same thing. Not that it's going to do much good. I doubt that anyone will be willing to hire him. His skill set will be so far out of date that he'll never catch up."

When Alonzo appeared a few minutes later to say that dinner was ready, Ali ended the call. She went to bed that night at the impossibly early hour of eight thirty and slept straight through until six the next morning.

She hadn't just been tired the night before—she'd been dog tired, but on Thursday morning she was more than ready to be up and at 'em.

Chris called while Ali was still eating breakfast to say that the doctor had just been by doing rounds and that Athena and Logan would be released within the next couple of hours. "If you want to stop by for a little while this evening," he added, "that would be fine."

"How about if I ask Alonzo to whip up a tuna casserole so I can bring that along?" Ali said. "A big dish of that would feed your household for a day or so."

"Sounds great," Chris agreed. "Cooking isn't one of my strong suits."

On her way to Cottonwood, Ali decided to disregard her own anti-hovering advice. At the last moment, she turned off the highway and pulled in to the parking lot at Sedona Shadows. Her excuse, of course, was to give everyone the news about Athena and Logan's expected homecoming.

Ali found Betsy and Edie in the dining room finishing their breakfasts, and she was glad to see that Betsy had prevailed on Edie to venture out of the unit. Ali's father, however, was nowhere in sight.

"Chris called a few minutes ago," Ali said quickly as she approached their table. "I wanted to let you both know that the doctor is releasing Athena later this morning and they'll be home here in Sedona probably by early afternoon in case you want to drop by and meet your new great-grandson."

Betsy clapped her hands in delight. Edie frowned. "I'm not sure Bob will want to go," she said, "and I don't want to leave him here alone."

A look of disappointment flashed across Betsy's face, and Ali understood why. Betsy didn't drive. If Edie wasn't going, neither was Betsy.

This is the first new normal, Ali thought. If her mom was afraid to leave her husband on his own for the short time it would take to peek in on her new great-grandson, it was clear Edie would only become more and more isolated in the future. So would Ali's father, for that matter.

"Look," Ali said, "check with Chris and then let me know when it would be convenient for you to drop by. If you can give me enough advance warning, I can leave work early and stay with Dad while you're gone."

Before Edie could raise another objection, Ali glanced at her watch and then jumped to her feet. "Oops," she said. "I'd better get going or I'll be late."

Ali arrived at the High Noon campus a little after nine. Since she didn't punch a time clock, concern about arriving late to work as an excuse for her abrupt departure from Sedona Shadows had been entirely bogus. But that also meant she was clear to show up and mind her dad while her mother and Betsy went to visit the new baby. It would give Edie a small break, and it would provide Ali with a firsthand glimpse into how things really stood with her folks, but for right now her focus was on High Noon.

Cami turned up in her office shortly after Ali settled in. "I've got the flight arrangements made for the applicants," she reported. "I have them coming in on separate days—one on Friday of next week and one each on Monday, Tuesday, and Wednesday of the following week."

"Good enough," Ali said. "How about the security-camera issue?"

Cami made a face. "That kid didn't know his ass from a hole in the ground, and we didn't finish up last night, even with me having to explain how the job should be done. He's coming in later today to finish. With any luck our system should be up and running by tonight."

"Good," Ali said, glancing at her ringing phone and seeing Betsy Peterson's name show up on caller ID. "Thanks, Cami."

Ali picked up the call.

"I'm glad my playing the poor-widow card guilted your mom into taking me to meet little Logan later today," Betsy said. "Edie and I are due to be at the kids' house right around three. She'll probably call in a few minutes to let you know. FYI, I think she set the time for three because that's usually when your dad takes an afternoon nap."

That figures, Ali thought. *If Dad's asleep, there's that much less opportunity for our having any meaningful interaction.*

"I'll be there," Ali said.

"Don't let her know I already told you," Betsy added. "If Edie finds out we've established this back channel, she'll hit the roof."

Ali laughed. "Right," she said, "mum's the word."

She had just turned back to her computer when her mother called. "Betsy wants to go meet Logan this afternoon," Edie Larson said. "Would you mind stopping by to stay with Dad for a bit?"

"Not a problem," Ali said without revealing that she'd already received an advance warning from Betsy. "What time?"

"Around two thirty?"

"Sure," Ali said. "I'll be there."

A few minutes later, she ventured into the computer lab and found the place in a state of high alert. A coordinated cyberattack, most likely from China, was wreaking havoc with Internet providers and servers worldwide. Several of High Noon's top clients had been targeted. So far no successful incursions had been discovered, and Cami, Lance, and Stu were determined to keep it that way. Not wanting to disrupt their focused concentration, Ali retreated to her nontechnical part of the building and kept her head down by tending to paperwork, balancing the corporate checkbook, and generally staying out of everyone's way.

At two that afternoon, her heart filled with misgivings, Ali headed for Sedona Shadows. As Edie prepared to leave the unit, she was as skittish as a new mother leaving her child with a babysitter for the first time.

"Bobby usually has a snack of some kind when he first wakes up from his nap," she told her daughter. "There's some angel food cake in the fridge and some butterscotch pudding as well. After his snack he generally watches TV. He likes Major League Baseball best, but I don't know if there are any games on today."

"Don't worry, Mom," Ali said. "Dad and I will figure it out."

"And if he's upset or if he doesn't know who you are . . ." Edie's voice faded, and she left the sentence unfinished. She stood in the doorway of the unit, purse in hand, as if reluctant to leave.

"Just go," Ali urged. "We'll be fine."

Betsy appeared in the corridor behind Edie. "Ali's right, you know," she said. "They really will be fine. Now, come on. We don't want to be late."

"We won't be long," Edie said, "not more than an hour or so."

"Take however long you need," Ali said, "and be sure to bring back some photos."

Once Betsy and Edie departed, Ali settled into what was generally considered to be her mother's chair in the tiny space that passed for the unit's living room. As she waited for her father to awaken, she hauled the iPad out of her purse and began listening to the latest Daniel Silva novel. She'd given up on her self-imposed force-feeding of classics for the moment in favor of reading straight-out old-fashioned thrillers. She'd been there only fifteen minutes or so when she heard a thumping noise from the bedroom. Moments later her father appeared in the doorway. He stood there for a moment, leaning on a cane—something Ali hadn't seen him use before—and stared at his daughter.

"Who are you?" he demanded. "And what are you doing in my house?"

Edie had hinted about this, and Ali had tried to prepare herself for the possibility that her father might not recognize her. Still, when it happened, it felt as if a bucket of ice water had splashed across her body. Given the circumstances, Ali decided her best bet would be to sidestep the question rather than provoke some kind of direct confrontation. Since Bob Larson didn't appear to realize Ali was his daughter, there was no point in her claiming Edie was her mom.

"Edie had to go out for a while," Ali answered noncommittally. "She asked me to look in on you until she gets back."

"I'm perfectly capable of looking after myself," Bob muttered gruffly, dropping into his chair. "I don't need looking after."

"Of course you don't," Ali agreed, "but can I get you something? I believe there's angel food cake and maybe some butterscotch pudding in the fridge."

"I like both," Bob said.

"Would you like some of each?"

"Please," he said, giving Ali a wink. "But don't tell my mother," he added. "She doesn't approve of my eating snacks just before dinner."

Fighting back tears, Ali fled to the small kitchenette on the far side of the room. Her father's parents had been dead long before Ali arrived on the scene. No doubt Bob was confusing his wife's disapproval with that of his deceased mother.

Ali took her time cutting the cake and dishing up the pudding, using those few extra moments to pull herself together. She noticed a serving tray on the counter and guessed that was probably there so Bob could eat in his chair rather than having to move to the table.

By the time she delivered the promised snack Ali had a tightly controlled smile glued to her face. "Here you are," she said.

He looked up at her and frowned. "Who did you say you are again?" he asked. "You look familiar, but I just can't come up with the name."

"Ali," she said. "My name is Ali, short for Alison."

"Pretty name," he said thoughtfully, taking a bite of angel food cake. "Very pretty. Do you live around here?"

"In town."

After that a long silence fell over the room. Ali had no idea what to say. "Where's Edie again?" Bob asked finally.

"She needed to run some errands. I believe she and her friend Betsy were going to stop by to see Chris and Athena and their new baby."

"Oh, yes, the baby. What's his name again?"

Ali had to swallow the lump in her throat before she could answer. "Logan," she murmured. "I believe his name is Logan James."

"That's a strange one. I don't think I've ever met anyone named Logan before. Have you?"

"I don't believe I have," Ali said.

Another long silence followed. Ali felt as though her heart would explode. How could she sit here talking with her father who looked at her as though she were a complete stranger? And how could her mother have managed to keep her husband's downward spiral so completely under wraps? And if this was hard on Ali, how much harder must it be for her mother! Having your husband of sixty-some years confuse you with his mother had to be emotionally devastating.

Desperate for something to fill the silence, Ali picked up the remote. "Would you like to watch TV?" she asked.

"Sure," Bob said agreeably. "But not the news. I don't like the news anymore. Most of the time, I don't know what any of those kids are talking about."

Wielding the remote, Ali was unable to find a baseball game. They ended up watching a rerun episode of *Star Trek: Voyager*. Bob watched with seemingly avid interest. Ali didn't hear a word of it. She was lost in thought.

Betsy and Edie returned about four fifteen. They'd

been gone only an hour and a half, but as far as Ali was concerned, it felt like forever.

"How are things?" Edie asked anxiously.

Her question was addressed to Ali, but Bob was the one who answered. "Things are fine," he said. "Why wouldn't they be? When's dinner?"

Betsy insisted on hauling out her phone and showing off a flock of photos. Out of politeness, Ali lingered long enough to look at them, but as soon as she could do so, she fled.

And cried all the way home.

|CHAPTER 10|

BLACK CANYON CITY, ARIZONA

Harvey was elated. The home inspection had gone better than he'd expected. He'd looked around and told the young couple exactly what they wanted to hear: that the roof was probably good for another five years. It wasn't. Anyone with a brain could see that the shingles were ready to give up the ghost. Harvey had told them the water heater would last a couple more years at least. That wasn't true either. It was already beyond its expected lifetime. There were cracks in the foundation that hinted there might be problems with the slab, but he told them that was no big deal. When the inspection was over, the buyers were relieved to have heard such good news. As for their real-estate agent? Cynthia Waller was overjoyed. She met up with Harvey on his way back to Sedona and handed him a six-hundred-dollar cash bonus over and above what he'd receive once the sale closed in escrow. In Cynthia's book a top-grade home inspection called for some extra monetary emoluments.

As he drove north on I-17 with some cash in his

pocket, Harvey's thoughts drifted back to the past. Detective Manning had been nice enough the day he told Harvey that his mother had gone missing. He told Broomy that at five o'clock in the morning his father, Leo, had placed a call to 911 to report that his wife was nowhere to be found. When he discovered she'd never come to bed, he went looking for both her and her dog, who was also among the missing. There was snow on the ground by then, but no sign of footsteps leaving the house. Leo had called for the dog and had eventually located the animal shut up in the shed, but there was no trace of his wife anywhere and no sign of a struggle either. Search and Rescue had been called in, but so far they, too, had been unable to locate the missing woman.

"Mind if I take a look at your arms and hands?" Detective Manning asked.

Broomy dutifully rolled up his sleeves and held both arms out for inspection. He guessed that the cop was looking to see if he'd been in some kind of physical confrontation. He had, but the brass knuckles meant that his fingers were clear of any signs of bruising, and the fact that he had struck down his mother from behind with no advance warning meant there were zero scratches to be found on his arms and no bloodstains, either.

"So where were you last night?" a seemingly satisfied Manning asked finally.

"A party," Broomy replied.

"What kind of party?"

"Do I have to say?"

The detective nodded. "You'd better."

"I don't want to get anyone in trouble."

"Why? What was it, a kegger?"

Broomy nodded reluctantly.

"Where?"

"At my friend Tony's house."

"Tony who?"

"Tony DeLuca. His folks are out of town this week."

"And you were there all night?"

Broomy nodded again.

"From when to when?"

"From about eight or so until just a little while ago. Tony saw something about this on TV and gave me a ride home."

"I'll need the names of the guys at the party."

"Like I said, I don't want to get anybody in trouble."

"Look," Manning said, "I'm not planning to bust anyone for underage drinking. I need some way to verify your whereabouts at the time your mother went missing."

"You mean like I need an alibi or something?"

Manning nodded. "Exactly like an alibi. Our K-9 unit was able to track your mother's steps from the house to the shed. After that she simply vanishes. That means there's a good chance we're dealing with foul play here, rather than just a simple disappearance. That's why we need to know where everyone associated with the household was and what they were doing at the time she disappeared. Do you know where your father was?"

"No, sir," he said.

Broomy knew exactly where his father would have been—drunk as a skunk in the bedroom. He'd already been a long way down that road when Tony came by to pick Broomy up earlier in the evening. Knowing that Tony's dad was friends with several city cops, Broomy worried about throwing him and the other guys at the party under the bus, but he needed an alibi in the worst way, and giving out their names was his only option. After another bit of hemming and hawing, Broomy reeled off several names, including those of the guys who'd been fast asleep in the living room once he returned to Tony's house.

"Is that all?" Broomy asked as the detective finished jotting down the information.

Manning shook his head. "Not exactly," he said. "Tell me about your folks."

"What about them?"

"Do they get along?"

Broomy shrugged his shoulders. "I guess," he said. "I mean, they argue sometimes like people do, but they get along most of the time."

As long as Dad gave the bitch everything she wanted, Broomy thought, but he didn't say that aloud.

"Was there any kind of disagreement yesterday?" Manning asked. "Anything that stands out?"

When Tony had come by to pick Broomy up, Ida Mae had been screeching at Dad and calling him a drunken bum, but that wasn't anything unusual—more like a daily occurrence. His dad went to work every day, brought home his paycheck and a few bottles of booze here and there, and what did he get for his trouble? A bitching-out more often than not. And that was something Broomy simply couldn't understand. Why the hell did his father put up with Ida Mae? Why didn't he just tell her to go to hell?

"Nothing that stands out," Broomy answered.

"What about the marriage?" Manning asked. "Any hints that it might have been in trouble?"

"You mean like a divorce or something?"

Manning nodded.

"Never!" Broomy declared. "My parents are Catholic."

And that was the truth. No matter how bad things got between them, neither Leo nor Ida Mae would ever have considered filing for a divorce. With any kind of luck and with his mother gone, maybe now Broomy's father would be able to find someone who actually gave a damn about him.

"What about money problems?" Manning asked.

Broomy shook his head. "Not that I know of," he said. "I mean, they always seemed to have enough."

That was an outright lie. According to his mother, there was never enough money to go around. However much there was, she always wanted more.

"All right, then," Manning said, shutting down the recorder. "I guess that's it."

"So I can go now?" Broomy asked. "I can go home?"

"Probably not," Manning said. "Your house is currently designated as a crime scene. Is there somewhere else you could stay?"

"Where's my dad?"

"He's currently a person of interest in your mother's disappearance. Detectives are speaking to him at the moment, and I have no idea when that process will come to an end. When that happens, however, I doubt he'll be allowed to go back to your home either."

"Where's Rocco?"

"With no one at the residence to take care of him, we've handed him over to Animal Control for the time being. He'll be looked after. You don't need to worry about him. They won't put him down or anything. When you're able to return home, he'll be able to go with you."

Broomy considered his very short list of options. "I guess I could stay with Tony," he suggested.

"Fair enough," Manning said, pushing back in his chair. "I'll have one of our deputies give you a lift."

It was three whole weeks before Broomy, his dad, and Rocco were allowed to return home. By then his father had lost twenty pounds and looked like a dead man walking. Surprisingly enough, he'd quit drinking. For Leo McCluskey booze was a thing of the past. Instead he sat at the chipped Formica kitchen table drinking endless cups of coffee and wondering aloud how in the world the cops could suspect that he'd done something to his Ida Mae.

Somehow Broomy hadn't tumbled to the idea that his father would be the prime suspect in his mother's disappearance. He'd just assumed that Leo would be as relieved as he was to have her gone, but that wasn't the case. Leo was utterly devastated. Three weeks later Broomy came home from school to find the house empty. When he discovered that the door to his father's gun cabinet had been left unlocked and open, on a hunch he went looking in the shed.

There, at the foot of the workbench stool, Broomy McCluskey found his father's body. Leo had used his shotgun to blow his brains out. The weapon lay on the floor beside him, mere inches from his hand. Broomy was so shocked by the blood and gore that he almost threw up on the spot. Close to fainting, he staggered over to lean on the workbench to keep from falling. And that's when he saw it. On the workbench was a note scrawled in Leo McCluskey's distinctive hand.

> *I loved my wife. Whatever happened to her, I didn't do it.*
>
> *Leo Ray McCluskey*

Understanding the significance of what was essentially a deathbed denial, Broomy had the presence of mind to pocket the note. He took it into the house, placed it in one of his father's ashtrays, and set it on fire. Only when he had flushed the ashes down the toilet did he pick up the phone and call 911.

"You've got to send someone!" he shouted into the phone. "I think my dad just committed suicide!"

And that was pretty much the end of the investigation into whatever had happened to Ida Mae McCluskey. Her case remained on the books as an open missing-persons case rather than a homicide, but in reality it was essentially closed. After his father's funeral, Broomy's situation in town was forever changed. He was now the poor kid whose father had murdered his mother. Tony DeLuca's folks, Candace and Oscar, were good people. When it became clear that Broomy had nowhere to go, they stepped up and offered to take in not only Broomy but also Rocco. They looked after him all through high school, treating him as if he were a second son as opposed to a foster child. They helped oversee the sale of the place on German Gulch Road and made sure the paltry proceeds were held in trust for Broomy until he came of age. They were the ones who attended his high school graduation, saw him off when he joined the army, and welcomed him home with a party when he returned to Butte on leave after finishing basic training. Broomy was struck by the stark differences between Ida Mae McCluskey and Mrs. DeLuca. If Ida Mae had been half the woman Candace DeLuca was, she wouldn't have died to begin with.

Eight years later all of what had happened back then was mostly forgotten. The name Broomy had disappeared from the conscious memories of everyone except for a few high school classmates. Thanks to the United States government, the boy once known as Broomy was referred to by his birth name, Harvey. Having attained the rank of staff sergeant, he was still in the army and stationed in Wiesbaden, Germany, when he was summoned to his commanding officer's presence and told he should wait for a phone call.

When it came in, the man on the line identified himself as none other than that long-ago detective Ray Manning, only now he was Sheriff Ray Manning.

"I'm calling with some difficult news," he told Harvey. "After all these years, we've found and identified your mother's remains."

"You have?" Harvey stammered. This was news he had never expected or wanted to hear. "Where?"

"With Anaconda mostly shut down, the EPA has come in to clean up the hazardous waste the company left behind," Sheriff Manning explained. "When they drained one of the standing mine-water ponds near where you used to live, we found human remains. We identified your mother's body through dental records."

For a time Harvey was too overcome to speak. "What happened to her?" he managed finally.

"The medical examiner determined that she died from a blow to the back of the neck. A vertebra at the top of her spine had been broken in several places," Manning told him. "We're now treating her death as a homicide, but given there's only ever been one suspect . . ."

Harvey's hand went to his chest and to his mother's wedding ring, which he wore every day, hidden under his uniform and dangling from the gold chain he'd given himself as a high school graduation present.

"My dad, you mean?" he asked.

"Exactly," Manning replied. "As far as our investigation is concerned, the case is closed. Now that the ME is ready to release the remains, we need to know what your wishes are."

"Do I have to decide about a funeral?"

"Yes."

"I don't know what to tell you," Harvey began. "I'm in the army and stationed in Germany right now."

Since the call had come in on his commanding officer's phone, Colonel Glenn had been listening in on the entire conversation. At that point he held up his hand. "Not to worry, son," he said. "I'll see to it that you get home for your mother's funeral. You have my word on that."

Harvey's trip down memory lane ended as he pulled in to the parking lot at the Cowpoke. He went inside and took his customary stool at the bar, glad to be out of his complicated past and back in the straightforward present.

"What'll it be?" Joe asked.

"I'll have a beer," Harvey said, "a Coors draft and an order of chicken wings."

"No hair of the dog?" Joe wanted to know.

"Not on your life," Harvey answered. "Learned my lesson. From here on out, I'm sticking with beer."

|CHAPTER 11|

RENTON, WASHINGTON

Mateo Vega had been blown away by his late-afternoon phone conversation with Stuart Ramey. Stu had sounded just the way Mateo remembered him—slightly reticent and clearly uncomfortable having to speak on the phone. Stu had always seemed to be more at ease interacting via texts or e-mails than he was in spoken communication. At the end of the call, Stu hadn't come right out and said he'd write a letter of recommendation but said he'd at least consider it. That was such good news that when Mateo went to bed that night, he couldn't fall asleep.

He was still tossing and turning at eleven when he heard the ding on his computer announcing the arrival of an e-mail. Curious, Mateo scrambled over to his computer and was thrilled to see a message from Stuart Ramey. Mateo opened it immediately, read the message itself, and then opened the attached PDF. He read the words written there, and Mateo's eyes brimmed with tears. Stu had done exactly as he'd asked. He'd

mentioned Mateo's work skills and dependability without making any reference to or about the long pause
between his employment with VGI and now.

For the first time in a long time, Mateo felt the faint-
est glimmer of hope that things might be better. Maybe,
when he sent out another round of job applications, he'd
make it as far as the interview stage. That would count
as huge forward progress. He went to work on the loading dock the next morning with a happy heart.

Even so, it was unseasonably hot that day, and by the
time Mateo got home, he was beat. His first instinct was
to give up on his trip to the library that evening, but
because he had some books that needed to be returned
that day, he went immediately after work, without bothering to check his e-mail before he left. As a consequence he was seated at one of the library computers
when he discovered there were six new messages from
Stuart Ramey sitting in his in-box. He opened the first
one and read:

> Dear Mateo,
> As requested, I sent you a letter of recom-
> mendation. It occurred to me after I sent
> it, however, that I could probably write a
> more effective one if I had some idea of
> your current job-skill level.
>
> High Noon specializes in cybersecurity.
> When we're vetting applicants, we like
> to put them through their paces. I'm
> attaching simulated versions of five
> separate hacking problems High Noon
> has isolated and countered over the years.
> I'd like you to try your hand at these to

*see if you can identify each separate hack,
isolate it, and effectively counter it. We'll
be able to keep track of the amount of
time it takes for you to either solve the
problem or give up on it.*

*Because the files are too large to send
as a group, I'm sending each one separately.
Looking forward to hearing from you.*

Sincerely,
Stu

Mateo stared at the list. Each of the remaining
e-mails had a different subject line: Badger, Wolf, Shark,
Scorpion, and Cheetah. When he looked at Badger,
the number of megabytes in the file gave him second
thoughts about attempting to open that file or any of
them on a public computer. Instead he packed up his
goods and headed home.

As he walked along, Mateo felt a spring in his step.
The hard hours working on the loading dock were forgotten. Stuart had taken his request seriously and had
written the letter of recommendation, but he'd gone one
step further. He wanted to evaluate Mateo's current job-
skill level. If Mateo could manage to deliver the goods
on these hypothetical problems, maybe Stuart would be
willing to give him a second letter of recommendation,
one that was more in keeping with what was currently
out in the marketplace. That being the case, Mateo
couldn't wait to get started.

Back at the house, he put his latest thrift-shop trophy to work, blocking out the racket from his drunken
housemates by donning the pair of noise-canceling Bose
headphones that he'd purchased for a mere seven bucks.

They hadn't been functional when he brought them home, but all that was needed to fix them was a tiny bit of solder to repair a broken connection.

Slightly uneasy that someone would be keeping track of his times, Mateo started with the file called Badger. At first glance he was sure he'd be in over his head and that finding the required solutions would be virtually impossible. Except it wasn't. The materials Mrs. Ancell had obtained for him over the years and all the solitary reading he'd done meant he'd kept pace with what was going on in the tech world outside the Monroe Correctional Facility. That realization left him energized and focused. He opened each file in turn, working his way through them one at a time, in order of appearance, noting as he did so that each succeeding problem was more challenging than the preceding one. It was ten past three in the morning when he successfully completed isolating the hack named Cheetah and began working on countering it.

An hour later, after double-checking his work, Mateo e-mailed all five solution files back to Stu. Once they were sent, Mateo went to bed. He was exhausted, yes, but still far too elated to go to sleep. Stuart Ramey had given him a challenge, and he'd risen to it. Not only had he delivered, but Mateo also felt as though he might even have redeemed himself.

A few hours later he went to work on the loading dock without having slept a wink, but he worked all day with a happy heart and without a word of complaint either. The next time he sent out a job application, Mateo was pretty sure Stuart Ramey would have his back.

|CHAPTER 12|

SEDONA, ARIZONA

Ali and B. spent a long time on the phone that night. But though it was nighttime for her in Arizona, it was early morning for him. She longed for him to be there in person so she could lean on his shoulder while she spilled out her worries and concerns—the blind panic she felt about her father's mental and physical decline, to say nothing of the despair brought on by the fact that he had failed to recognize his own daughter.

B. waited for the storm of emotion to abate before he spoke, and when he did, his calm and measured responses were a balm to her soul.

"First thing is," B. said, "we all owe Betsy a huge debt of gratitude here. Without her insisting on getting your mom out of the house today, we'd still have no idea about the real state of affairs with your dad. From the sound of things, the situation is far more serious than anyone would have guessed. You're going to have to have a no-holds-barred talk with your mom. Going forward, your mother's proposed strategy of not taking

Bob to the doctor because she doesn't want to hear the diagnosis is simply not an option.

"I've spent some time on the phone today with a few of my Big Pharma contacts, folks who are very familiar with what's going on in terms of Alzheimer's research—not that we know for sure Alzheimer's is what we're dealing with as far as your dad is concerned. Obviously, there's no cure, not yet, but there are medications out there that may help deal with some of the symptoms and may even slow the progression of the disease. Without having a physician do a thorough evaluation and write prescriptions, however, those potentially helpful meds won't be available to him."

"But how do I get Mom to see reason here?" Ali asked.

"Ask her what Bob would want," B. replied, "not Bob as he is now but Bob as he's been for most of the more than sixty-five years they've been married. He wouldn't want your mom to be shouldering this burden alone. He wouldn't want her to risk actual physical harm, because at your mother's age even a minor shove could result in lasting damage."

B. paused before changing the subject slightly. "How did your dad seem? Was he angry? Upset?"

Ali thought about that for a time. "More melancholy than anything else," she admitted. "It's as though he's aware that something's wrong—that he's lost track of things—but doesn't know why or what to do about it either."

"He *has* lost track of something," B. asserted. "He's lost track of himself. He may realize that he has serious deficits, but not knowing what those deficits are or how to deal with them has to be terrifying. If there were medications available, that might make him feel better—relieve those symptoms and make him less sad—doesn't he deserve to have access to them? Wouldn't that be the

loving thing for your mom to do, for her to stop pretend-
ing nothing's wrong and face up to it instead?"

"You're right, but—" Ali began.

"There is no but," B. interjected. "Your mother's like
that frog swimming in a pot of gradually heating water.
The only way to fix it is to slap her with a bucket of cold
water. As her only child, you're the one who has to do it."

"Still . . ."

"There's one other thing you need to know," B. continued. "According to one study from Stanford, forty-one
percent of Alzheimer's caregivers die before the patient
does. Your mother's healthy right now, but she won't be for
long if we don't get her the help and respite she needs."

"So I have to talk to her."

"Yes," B. said, "and the sooner the better."

Ali was ready to change the subject. "When I left
the office this afternoon, it was all hands on deck
dealing with that coordinated cyberattack."

"I know," B. said. "Stu kept me updated. It was a pretty
big deal, but it looks as though every one of our customers
came through unscathed. Two of them were specifically
targeted, but our firewalls repelled the attackers. However, today's attack only underscored the fact that we
need more people. Cami tells me she's got the job applicants lined up to fly in for personal interviews late next
week and the week after. We've already got good people
on board, but it isn't a smart idea to overwork those we
have to death."

They talked a while longer after that. When Ali went
to bed, she worried for a time about how and when she'd
tackle her mother, but finally she fell asleep.

She woke up the next morning to find a text from B.
sitting on her phone.

> Don't like the idea of your having to handle all this
> on your own. I've rearranged some appointments. I'll
> be home this afternoon rather than tomorrow. Plane
> should land in Phoenix around three.

Ali breathed a sigh of relief. Over breakfast she gave Alonzo the news that there would be two for dinner. Then, with a much happier heart, she headed for the office in a timely fashion. She had barely put her purse away in a file drawer when Cami charged into the room and plunked her iPad down on Ali's desk. Peering at the device, Ali could tell she was looking at what appeared to be a still photo of a long corridor. A time stamp in the corner of the screen said "11:59:56 p.m., April 5, 2018." Ali pressed the arrow in the middle of the screen, and the still photograph became a video with blurry movements showing some distance away. There was no way to discern any features, since the figure was totally out of focus.

Ali looked up at Cami. "From the new security system?"

Cami nodded.

"Can you focus it better?"

Cami called up the flat-screen and tapped in a command. Suddenly the blurred shape reconfigured itself and was completely recognizable. A barefoot Harvey McCluskey, wearing only a T-shirt and sweats, disappeared into a restroom.

"Harvey McCluskey?" Ali asked unnecessarily. "What's he doing in the building at that hour of the night?"

"And more to the point," Cami added, "why isn't he dressed?"

"He's sleeping here?" Ali asked in dismay. "In his office?"

"That's how it looks."

High Noon had a zoning variance that allowed for sleeping arrangements inside their corporate offices, but that wasn't true for the other units in the Mingus Mountain Business Park complex. So not only was McCluskey violating the terms of his lease agreement by not paying rent, he was also using his office space as an unauthorized dwelling unit.

"How long do you think this has been going on?" Ali asked.

"Probably a lot longer than we'd like to think," Cami replied. "What say we go down and give him a surprise wake-up call?"

"What say indeed," Ali said, rising from her chair, "and I'll give him a piece of my mind while I'm at it."

The two women set out together, noticing as they went that McCluskey's Silverado was parked in his designated spot, next to the building. As they walked, their two shadows—one short and one tall—showed in sharp relief on the pavement. Seeing them together, Ali couldn't help but smile. Cami Lee was of Chinese extraction, and though her petite frame might have made her appear to be small and harmless, anyone who came to that conclusion would be dead wrong. Cami was a serious devotee of Krav Maga and could wipe the floor with people twice her size. With Cami along as Ali's backup, Harvey McCluskey would be smart to realize he was totally outgunned.

Cami was the one who pounded on the door to Harvey's office. The resemblance to a cop knock was hardly coincidental. "Anybody home?" she shouted.

Naturally, there was no reply. As landlord, Ali had a passkey that opened all the doors in the complex, one that allowed her access in case of emergencies. As far as she was concerned, this counted as an emergency.

"We're coming in, Mr. McCluskey," Ali announced.

When the door opened, a cloud of musky male cologne wafted through the air. Harvey himself was behind the desk, hurriedly trying to pull on his pants. A khaki-colored bedroll and a grungy pillow lay on an inflatable mattress on the floor next to the far wall.

"What the hell do you think you're doing?" he demanded. "You can't come barging in like you own the place."

"As it happens, I do own the place," Ali replied. "Not only that, this is a commercial building. It's a place for doing business, not a private residence."

Still in his stockinged feet, McCluskey rounded the desk and barreled in their direction as if preparing to take a swing at them. Next to Ali, Cami stiffened just as McCluskey seemed to change his mind about getting physical. He stopped, snorting like an enraged bull, as Cami calmly continued holding her iPad in a manner that Ali knew enabled her to record every moment of the confrontation.

"What are you going to do about it?" McCluskey bristled, sounding more like a recalcitrant kindergartner than an adult. "You can't evict me. My five days aren't up."

"True," Ali agreed, "they're not. I may not be able to start the eviction proceedings at this time, but I can sure as hell call the cops and have your sorry ass hauled out of here for violating the occupancy requirements in the building code. I'm here to advise you that we have a new surveillance system that notifies us of any unauthorized movements inside our buildings. If you happen to turn up in the building during overnight hours, be advised that law enforcement will be summoned." She turned to Cami. "Now, let's get out of here so Mr. McCluskey can finish getting dressed."

With that, Ali turned on her heel. She waited for Cami to pass before pulling the door shut behind them.

"If he'd followed through on that first blow, he would have been in for one hell of a surprise," Cami muttered darkly. "A swift kick to the balls would have had him crying like a baby."

Still pumped full of adrenaline, Ali laughed aloud at that. "I'm almost sorry it didn't come to that," she said.

Back in the office, she had barely settled in at her desk when Stuart came rushing into the office. "You're not going to believe it!" he exclaimed.

"Believe what?"

"Mateo got 'em all."

Ali was mystified. "All what?"

"Out of curiosity's sake, I sent him the hack-simulation problems we gave to the other applicants."

"The hacks with names that sound like they stepped out of a zoo?" Ali asked.

She meant her question as a joke, but Stu was in no mood for humor. "I sent them to him yesterday evening. I thought having a chance to assess his current skill level might make it possible for me to revise my letter of recommendation to something more applicable to today's market. According to Frigg, he started on the first simulation at six forty-five last night and mailed me all five completed solutions just after four o'clock this morning. He nailed all five of them, Ali, every last one! Believe me, none of our final-cut applicants did nearly that well."

"But if he's been in prison for sixteen years, how's that even possible?" Ali asked.

"I had Frigg do some digging through his prison records. While Mateo was there, he worked in the prison library. In her analysis Frigg discovered that the librarian had been supplying him with all kinds of technical materials that she borrowed from libraries across the country. What he had to work with was just theory, but the way he performed on these hacking problems was outstanding. Believe me, it takes real smarts to turn written tech theory into practice."

Ali was seated behind her desk. Stu was still standing in front of her, shifting uneasily from one foot to the other, like a kid being hauled before the principal.

"What are you saying, Stu?"

He took a deep breath before answering. "Look," he said, "Mateo's been out of prison for nearly a year. During that whole time, despite having a degree in computer science, he hasn't been able to land even so much as a simple coding job. But he's smart, Ali, really smart. He completed all the problems in less time than one of our official candidates took to solve one."

Ali sat for a moment, studying Stu's demeanor. He wasn't someone accustomed to dishing out effusive praise.

"Using the word 'official' to refer to our candidates would suggest you're of the opinion that there's an unofficial one," Ali observed. "Is that what you're thinking— that we should consider interviewing Mateo for one of our two openings?"

Stu gazed at his feet before he answered. "I know it's not standard operating procedure. . . ." he began.

"It's okay, Stu," Ali said. "Give Mateo a call and see if he's interested in flying down for an interview."

Stu looked thunderstruck. "Really? Are you sure?" he asked. "Don't you want to talk this over with B. first?"

"B. trusts your judgment, and so do I," Ali assured him. "If Mateo says yes, give Cami his contact information so she can set up his flight arrangements."

|CHAPTER 13|

COTTONWOOD, ARIZONA

Harvey was beyond furious as he peeled out of the parking lot later that morning. He'd looked for the telltale signs of surveillance equipment as he left the office, but he hadn't seen anything. Where the hell had that come from? And how dare that bitch walk in on him when he wasn't even dressed?

There'd been only one bathroom in the double-wide back in Butte. He'd been fourteen when his mother barged into the room moments after he'd stepped out of the shower. The lock on the door had broken years earlier and never been fixed.

"Mom," he said, quickly covering himself with his towel. "How about a little privacy?"

"I need an aspirin, and Mr. Hot Stuff thinks his privacy is more important? Well, get over yourself," she told him. "It's nothing I haven't seen before. Who the hell do you think changed your diapers when you were a bare-assed baby?"

She'd stomped out with her aspirin in hand, slamming the door shut behind her and leaving her son awash in humiliation. That was the last time Broomy showered at home. From then on he limited himself to showers at the school gym, or else he bummed them at friends' houses. But that had been a critical moment for him. Standing there dripping wet and holding his towel was when he made up his mind that one way or the other, Ida Mae had to go.

And this morning's events seemed eerily similar. The idea that Ali Reynolds could use a passkey and barge in on him with complete impunity was unacceptable. Just as he had with his mother, Harvey was going to make Ali Reynolds pay for her transgression—no matter how long it took.

|CHAPTER 14|

RENTON, WASHINGTON

Mateo was eating lunch in the break room when his phone rang. The number wasn't familiar. Fearing it might be a spam call, he almost didn't answer.

"Mateo?" Stu Ramey said when he answered. "How're you doing?"

At the sound of Stu's voice, Mateo's heart seemed to skip a beat. "Pretty well," he answered after a moment. "How are you?"

"Amazing results on those hacking problems," Stu said, "completely amazing."

Flushing with pleasure at the praise, Mateo fled the break room and hurried back to the loading dock.

"So I did all right?"

"You did more than all right. I'm impressed."

Mateo could barely believe what he was hearing. "I'm glad," he managed.

"So here's the deal," Stu continued. "We're looking to take on a couple of new hires, and I was wondering if you'd like to fly down for an official interview."

Mateo thought about the state of his finances. "When," he asked finally, "and how much would it cost?"

"It wouldn't cost you anything," Stu told him. "High Noon will pay your way. As for when, we need to hire someone now, so we'll have to conduct the interview as soon as possible. However, the exact timing isn't up to me. My colleague, Cami Lee, is in charge of scheduling the interviews. Would it be all right if I gave her your number so she could call you?"

Mateo looked at his watch. "My break is almost over," he said, "and I can't take personal calls out on the dock. Could you have her call me around four?"

"Will do," Stu said, "and I'm looking forward to seeing you again."

For a long time after the call, Mateo stood staring at the phone resting in the palm of his hand and marveling at what had just happened. How was this possible? How had his stumbling across B. Simpson's name in a magazine article led to this kind of result mere days later? Was it even real? Maybe he'd dreamed the whole thing up.

The two hours Mateo spent on the loading dock that afternoon were the longest he'd ever endured. Alive with hope and anticipation, he felt time slow to a crawl. He'd work his way through a box of donations and then glance at his watch, only to discover that almost no time had elapsed. Once he was finally able to punch out and head home, however, his phone rang before he made it past the sound-barrier wall.

"Mr. Vega?" an unfamiliar female voice inquired.

"Mateo," he answered, "yeah, that's me."

"My name's Camille Lee, but everybody calls me Cami. Congrats on solving those hacking problems, by the way. Scoring five out of five is awesome."

"Thank you," Mateo murmured.

"We'd like to schedule your interview as soon as possible. Is there a day next week that would be convenient for you?"

"I have to work during the week," Mateo said. "Is there any chance I could do it on a weekend?"

"Just a moment," Cami said.

She was off the line for a period of time. Mateo could hear conversation going back and forth, but he couldn't make out the words. He was too busy castigating himself. Why hadn't he just said he could come any day they wanted him to? The truth was, he didn't want to jeopardize the job he had now when he didn't already have another one lined up, and with jobs as scarce as they seemed to be . . .

Cami's voice came back on the phone. "I just found out B. is coming home a day early and is willing to make time for an interview over the weekend, so what about tomorrow? We could fly you down in the morning and back home to Seattle on Sunday afternoon. Would that work for you?"

Mateo could barely believe his ears. High Noon would fly him down for an interview tomorrow?

"Sure," he managed. "That would be great."

"What's your preferred airline?"

"What do you mean?"

"Which airline do you usually use?"

"I've never flown on an airplane in my life," he said.

"Never?"

"Not once."

"All right, then," Cami said. "I'm looking at the schedules right now. Alaska has an eight-fifteen a.m. flight that would have you in Phoenix around eleven thirty. Have you ever used Uber?"

"Never."

"What about car rentals?"

"I've never done one of those either."

Mateo heard what sounded like an exasperated sigh. "Just a sec," she said. Again he heard mumbled words in the background before Cami returned to the line.

"Okay," she said, "I'm guessing that renting a car will be a bit of a hassle, so Stu will pick you up at the airport and bring you back there. But since I'll be making your flight reservation, I'll need your name as it appears on your official photo ID."

"My driver's license, you mean?" Mateo asked, digging his wallet out of his pocket.

"I'm not sure a driver's license will work unless it's one of the enhanced ones."

"I think it is," Mateo replied. "I'm pretty sure I paid extra for that."

Once he had the card in his hand, he saw the word "ENHANCED" in all caps across the top of it. "Yes," he told Cami. "That's what it says here—enhanced."

"Okay, I'll need your full name as it appears there and also your date of birth."

"Juan Mateo Vega," he replied. "Born December second, 1979."

"All right. And will you be checking luggage or doing carry-on only?"

"For one day, carry-on should be plenty."

"All right," Cami said. "I'll get back to you once I've purchased the tickets. I'll need your e-mail address so I can send you the reservation info. And if you're not accustomed to traveling by plane, you'll need to be at the airport at least an hour and a half before your flight in order to clear security."

"Will do," Mateo said.

"Okay," Cami replied, concluding the call. "See you tomorrow."

Once Mateo was back at the house and still not quite believing what was happening, he stripped off his work clothes and jumped in the shower. He stood under the pounding water and marveled. He was flying to Arizona? He was actually going to do a job interview with B. Simpson? Was there a chance that after so much time he might be able to pick up the lost strand of his life? It all seemed way too good to be true. Maybe he was only dreaming. When he woke up, would everything vanish into thin air?

But it didn't. Forty-five minutes later, an e-mail arrived from Cami telling him that his airline reservation from Alaska Airlines should arrive at any moment and that when it did, he should go ahead and print his boarding pass if he could. If not, he'd have to do that at the airport in the morning.

When Randy got home that Friday afternoon, Mateo was waiting on the porch.

"Would you mind giving me a lift to the airport in the morning? I should probably be there around six thirty."

"The airport," Randy said. "Where you going?"

"Arizona," he said. "I've got a job interview."

"In Arizona? Hell, man, good for you, but bad for me. You're the best damned renter I've ever had."

|CHAPTER 15|

SEDONA, ARIZONA

For the second day in a row, Ali left the office at two o'clock in the afternoon and headed for Sedona Shadows. Her timing was deliberate. Theoretically this was when her father took his afternoon nap. If Ali was going to have any kind of meaningful health discussion with her mother, this was the time to do it.

And she wasn't wrong. The day before, her mother had been put together—makeup on, hair fixed, dressed to go out. Today when she opened the door, she looked a good ten years older. She appeared defeated and distraught. With her hair a mess. Without the benefit of makeup, her face looked drawn and haggard. Edie's greeting matched her appearance and wasn't especially welcoming.

"I didn't know you were stopping by," she grumbled. "Why didn't you call me?"

"Because I wanted a surprise visit," Ali told her.

Shaking her head, Edie reluctantly stepped aside and allowed Ali to enter.

"Your father's napping," Edie said.

Ali nodded. "I was counting on that. You're the one I wanted to talk to. This is serious, Mom. Yesterday when I was here, Dad had no idea who I was."

Edie bit her lip. "I was afraid of that," she said with a helpless shrug. "Some days are better than others, and mornings are better than afternoons and evenings, but there are times when he doesn't know who I am either."

"Look," Ali said, using her most take-charge tone of voice. "I understand why you've been keeping this a secret and covering for him, but the cat's out of the bag now, and clearly you need help."

"What do you expect me to do?" Edie asked. "Am I supposed to ship him off to one of those so-called memory homes?"

Ali shook her head. "I'm not suggesting anything of the kind. The two of you are settled in here—settled in and comfortable, right?"

Edie nodded.

"And even if Dad doesn't go to the dining room anymore, you can—and you should. You've made friends here, Mom, and friends are what you need right now. It's important for you to maintain connections to the outside world and not shut yourself away with him inside this unit."

Edie started to object. Waving aside the attempted interruption, Ali continued. "You can't make your whole life about him. He wouldn't want that, and if he were in his right mind at the moment, he'd be the first one to tell you to stop. What you both need is someone to come in every day—a home health worker/caretaker who can look after him and give you time to look after yourself. Dad needs nursing care. You need respite care."

When Ali stopped speaking, Edie said nothing. She kept her eyes averted, but Ali caught sight of a single tear dribbling slowly down one cheek.

"I understand why you've resisted the idea of going to a doctor on the grounds that there's no cure for all this," Ali resumed. "You're right about that. There is no cure, but B. and I talked about this. There are meds out now that have the potential of easing some of the symptoms and perhaps even slowing the progress of the disease. In order to access those medications, however, Dad's going to need to visit a doctor—a qualified geriatric physician or a neurologist so he can be properly evaluated. Once there's an actual diagnosis and we're told what, if any, therapeutics may be helpful, then we figure out the next step, and I do mean we. You're not in this alone, Mom. B. and I will help you. The kids will help you. Betsy will help you, but you're going to have to let us. That's the only way this is going to work."

Ali fell silent again. For a moment neither of them spoke. This time Edie broke the silence.

"In the mornings he seems to know who he is and realize that he's losing it. Later in the day, he has no idea that anything's wrong. By the time evenings roll around, he seems like a complete stranger," Edie said with a sigh. "The thing is, I don't want our problems to be a burden on you, Ali. I don't want to put anyone out."

"You're not being a burden," Ali insisted, reaching over and taking her mother's hand. "We love you, Mom, and we love him. The two of you have spent your whole lives looking out for the needs of others. Now it's time to let someone else look out for you."

A thumping noise from the bedroom alerted them to the fact that Bob Larson had awakened from his nap.

"He's up," Edie said quickly, laying a finger on her lips in a shushing gesture.

Ali understood. Edie wasn't yet ready to take the next step—not just now—and Ali didn't want to throw her mother under the bus.

"Hi, Dad," she said cheerfully when Bob appeared in the doorway. "Did you have a good nap?"

"Hey, Ali," he said after a moment as he tottered over to his recliner and settled into it. "Are you here to watch the game?"

Dutifully Edie reached for the remote. As she did so, mother and daughter exchanged a meaningful glance, and Ali nodded her understanding. No wonder her mother felt like she was riding an emotional roller coaster. She was.

A few minutes later, Ali took her leave. Preoccupied with the baseball game, her father barely noticed. This time Ali didn't cry as she drove home. She had done what she could by at least starting the process. She had broached the issues and opened the door for some very difficult discussions. She was helping her mother in the only way a daughter could—by asking questions and helping her parents search out answers.

That was the best she could do, and under the circumstances it was also all she could do.

|CHAPTER 16|

COTTONWOOD, ARIZONA

Harvey's anger simmered for the remainder of the day. He wanted to tear into Ali Reynolds and rip her apart, but he knew better. She and her husband were a big deal around here, and when bad things happened to big-deal kinds of people, important people, law enforcement climbed all over themselves trying to solve the crimes. When bad things happened to little people, the unimportant ones, cops didn't give much of a damn. Harvey McCluskey was living proof that was true.

Take that bitch of a prostitute whose body he'd left behind after a drunken night on the town in Munich. He'd gone there on a weekend pass with some of his buddies not long after returning from his mother's funeral. In a sleazy bar near Munich's central train station, he'd cut a likely-looking girl named Brigitta out of the herd, bought her a beer or two, and suggested they retreat to an equally sleazy nearby hotel, where he had willingly forked over her asking price. The problem was, Brigitta had turned out to be a bit too likely. Once she thought he was asleep, the conniving bitch had tried to roll him. Not cool. He strangled her on the spot. She was already naked, and he left her that way. She'd been wearing a bracelet and a pair of hoop earrings. He had stripped those all away. Then, after wrapping the body in the coat she'd been wearing, he flung her over his shoulder and carted her down the fire escape to the narrow alley behind the hotel. The street out front might have been alive with neon lights and drunken partygoers, but the alley itself was black as pitch. Harvey had to be careful where he stepped in order to avoid the human waste left behind. Three blocks away from the hotel, he pulled off the coat and dumped the naked body into an open dumpster, then found a homeless bum asleep a block farther on and wrapped Brigitta's coat around him.

Once in the army, Harvey had asked to be assigned to the military police. By then he'd learned a good deal about forensics and crime-scene investigation. He went back to the hotel room and cleaned it up. He used a pillowcase from the bed to wipe down every single surface in the room that might possibly contain his fingerprints—or hers either, for that matter. He gathered up the clothing she'd worn and stuffed that into her very large purse, which he smuggled out of the hotel under his jacket. Once outside, Harvey walked as far as the train station and took a cab to the Deutsches Museum. If the cabdriver wondered why this crazy American was going there when the museum was closed for the night, he didn't ask. When the cab drove out of sight, Harvey walked to the nearest bridge across the Isar.

It was still early winter, so the river had not yet frozen over. After removing all of Brigitta's IDs from her purse, he dumped both the purse and her clothing over the bridge rail. After that he stood there shivering and smoking a cigarette for the next ten minutes, giving the current a chance to do its work before tossing Brigitta's IDs and jewelry into the water as well. The only thing he held back was one of the golden hoop earrings. After all, he wanted something to remember her by.

A short time later, he flagged down another cab and rode back to the bar, where he met up with his pals and bragged to them about getting lucky. If any of them noticed the scratches on the backs of his hands, no one asked. Staff Sergeant McCluskey had a certain reputation on base, and his fellow soldiers had the good sense not to say anything that might get his nose out of joint.

The next day, Sunday, Harvey and his buddies boarded a train and returned to their base some two hundred miles away. From that distance it wasn't really possible for Harvey to monitor what was going on in Munich. He never knew when or even if Brigitta's body had been found, much less identified. On those occasions when German authorities suspected American soldiers of any wrongdoing, the MPs on post heard all about it. This time there was nothing—not one peep—and once he realized he'd gotten away with it scot-free, Brigitta's hoop joined Ida Mae's wedding ring on the chain Harvey wore around his neck.

Occasionally someone might summon up enough nerve to ask him about the chain he wore under his uniform. Harvey always had a ready answer for that. The wedding ring had belonged to his dear departed mother, who had been murdered long ago. As for the hoop? It came from a pair of earrings owned by his one true love, the high school sweetheart and fiancée who'd died in a horrific car wreck shortly after graduation. Once the unfortunate questioners heard the tragic answers to their inquiries, they were always hugely embarrassed and sorry they'd ever asked, and Harvey was always amused by that. He wondered what they would have thought if he'd told them the truth.

So Harvey had some real-life experience suggesting that unimportant people tended to disappear with hardly any notice. Well, if he couldn't go after Ali Reynolds directly, what about that little bitch who'd been there in his office with her. All the time Ali had been bitching him out, that black-haired vixen had been filming the entire proceedings on that pricey-looking iPad of hers.

Harvey knew Ali's sidekick worked for High Noon. He had no idea what High Noon did, nor did he care to find out. It was none of his business. What *was* his business was to track down Ali's pal. She was a tiny pissant of a thing, and he could probably strangle her single-handedly. First, however, he needed to find out exactly who she was and where she lived. He left the bar finally and returned to his office. Once inside, and knowing that Ali Reynolds would probably make good her threat to sic the cops on him, the first thing he did was to collect his bedding, haul it back outside, and stuff it under the canopy on his pickup. If he had to sleep in that for the time being, so be it.

While going in and out, Harvey quickly spotted the presence of a small electronic device that he'd never seen before. It was attached to the glass of the outside door, just beneath the push bar that opened it from the inside. A quick glance on his way past told Harvey that this had to be some newfangled kind of surveillance camera. He understood that if there were surveillance cameras inside the buildings, it was easy to assume that the parking lot was probably full of them as well, so he settled into the chair in his office and used the pair of binoculars he kept in his desk to surveil the parking lot through his outside window.

At ten past five, he saw his little black-haired target exit High Noon's front entrance and climb into a bright red Prius. He was out of the building in a flash, fast enough that her vehicle was still at the stoplight at the intersection of Business Park Way preparing to turn right onto 89A and head back into Cottonwood as Harvey pulled out of the office park. His pickup was tall enough that he could keep the Prius in view without having to be too close. When it pulled in to the parking lot of a nearby strip mall, he drove past, then made a U-turn a block and a half away. He returned in time to see his target grab a gym bag from the backseat of the Prius before heading inside one of the businesses in the mall. A slow swing through the parking lot revealed that the strip mall contained not one but three martial-arts studios. The one his black-haired Princess Prius had entered was marked KRAV MAGA.

Harvey had never heard of Krav Maga. He had no idea what it was, but if it was some kind of martial-arts deal she thought would help fend off an attack when Harvey McCluskey came calling, she would be sadly mistaken.

Harvey made another U-turn and located the last line of parking places at another strip mall. There, partially concealed behind a billboard, he settled in to wait. The only way for him to know precisely where Princess was going—since he didn't know her name, that's what he had decided to call her—was to follow her home, and that's exactly what he intended to do. Once he knew where she lived and who, if anyone, lived there with her, it would be time for him to make a plan, and devising plans to kill someone happened to be a skill set Harvey McCluskey had mastered long ago.

He waited patiently for over an hour and a half until she finally emerged from the gym. Once she got into the Prius and fired it up, he once again followed her at a discreet distance. It was dark by then, and that worked to his advantage. He knew it would be far more difficult for her to differentiate one vehicle from another based on headlights alone. She drove through town and then turned onto Cornville Road where there was much less traffic, and Harvey was forced to drop back.

Approaching the little burg of Cornville, Princess began signaling for a right-hand turn. He slowed to allow her to turn onto a dirt road and then took the first possible left, which supposedly led to the local post office. He turned in at the entrance to a storage facility, where he pulled over and was able to observe the Prius's movements on the far side of the highway. After traveling a short distance, the headlights turned right into a driveway. Moments later the vehicle seemed to come to a complete stop. After a pause of maybe a minute, what appeared to be a porch light flashed on, followed seconds later by several interior lights as well. Obviously she had entered a dwelling. After waiting a few minutes, Harvey followed, finding himself on a dusty dirt track named Tuff Cody Trail.

The house in question wasn't especially impressive. It appeared to be a small bungalow that probably dated back to sometime in the fifties. Two outdoor lights—one by the front door and one leading into the house from a carport—illuminated a small unfenced yard. The Prius, fully visible in the light from the back door, was parked under the carport. Harvey was delighted to note that it was the only vehicle on the property. If someone else lived there in addition to Princess, wouldn't there be a second vehicle parked at the house as well?

Not wanting to raise anyone's suspicions, Harvey didn't linger, but a plan was forming in his head. Cornville wasn't that big. He drove into town and located a store—the Cornville Mercantile—where he paid cash for a six-pack of Coors—bottles rather than cans—as well as a prepackaged sandwich. When the cashier offered him a receipt, he waved it aside and left it sitting on the counter. He didn't want to bring along any kind of damning paper trail.

He pulled in to an almost empty parking lot outside a closed tattoo parlor. The place didn't look upscale enough to have any kind of video surveillance, and that was exactly what Harvey wanted. He parked behind the darkened building and sat there, eating his sandwich, drinking his beer, and waiting for time to pass. He had picked up several napkins to go with his sandwich, and he used those to hold the bottles. He didn't want to leave behind any fingerprints, and when the bottles were empty, he wiped their spouts both inside and out. Leaving behind traces of DNA would have been worse than losing track of the cash receipt.

Once Harvey deemed it was late enough, he got out of the truck, walked over to a curb near the dumpsters, and began breaking the now-empty bottles. It was a challenging process because he still needed to use a napkin when handling the bottles. In order to achieve the exact effect he wanted, each one had to be broken in just the right way, without his getting cut up in the process. Finally, all six bottles in, he had a total of four perfectly jagged bottlenecks. Still careful not to touch the glass, he loaded them back into the cardboard six-pack case and headed for Tuff Cody.

It was close to midnight when Harvey parked just short of the house itself. It was dark both inside and out. Princess obviously wasn't much of a night owl. Harvey got out of his truck and left the door cracked open to avoid the sound of his closing it. Carrying the bottlenecks in the cardboard container, he approached the house by walking on the rough, gravelly shoulder of the road rather than the road itself in order to avoid leaving behind any visible footprints. There were no streetlights, but a partial moon glowed overhead. If there were dogs in the neighborhood, none of them barked.

It took only a few moments for him to position his broken bottlenecks behind all four of the Prius's tires, propping them between the rubber and the cement in a way that was bound to slice into the tires the moment the vehicle was put in reverse.

Mission accomplished, Harvey left the yard and then bailed on Cornville. He went straight back to the office park and pulled in to his designated spot, but he didn't venture inside the building. Instead he crawled into the shelter of the canopy, unrolled his bedroll and pillow, and slept there. Without the air mattress, however, it wasn't very comfortable. He still had the compressor, but lacking an available electrical outlet, he couldn't use it.

Harvey figured even Ali Reynolds would have a difficult time convincing the local cops that they should arrest some poor guy for sleeping in his own vehicle. With all the focus on surveillance, somebody would probably be watching if he had to crawl out of the bed of the truck overnight to take a leak behind his back tires. And if Ali Reynolds minded that . . . well, piss on her.

|CHAPTER 17|

RENTON, WASHINGTON

Having not slept at all the night before, Mateo went to bed that Friday night and slept like a rock—so hard in fact that he failed to hear his alarm and might have missed his plane if Randy hadn't come pounding on his door at 6:35, saying, "I thought you wanted to be at the airport by now."

The crowd at Sea-Tac wasn't as bad as Mateo had expected. Even so, the security line seemed to take forever. He had his boarding pass and ID in hand, so he was good on that score. Cami had sent him an e-mail explaining that his toiletries had to be in a clear quart-size plastic bag, and they were. Not that he had much along for an overnight stay—his toothpaste and a tube of hair oil. What she had failed to mention, however, was the allowable size. So although his nearly empty tube of Crest toothpaste couldn't have contained more than two ounces at the most, the tube itself was too large. It was confiscated and tossed into the trash.

Cami had also warned Mateo that there might or might not be food service on the plane, so once he was through security, he took her advice and bought himself a Burger King Whopper to take along. He had always imagined that flying in a plane would be luxurious. This was anything but. He was stuck in a middle seat near the back of the plane. On one side was a huge guy whose shoulders were inches wider than the back of his seat. On the other was a tattooed, pierced young woman with spiky pink hair who glowered at him as if daring him to speak to her.

He didn't. In fact, for the duration of the flight not one of his seatmates exchanged a word. But when the flight attendant came by to close the overhead luggage compartments and check for fastened seat belts, she left Mateo almost breathless. She looked so much like Emily Tarrant that the two of them might have been sisters. And that had been Emily's plan—to become a flight attendant once she had finished college.

What had happened that night outside Edmonds had destroyed both their lives. Emily died. She never got to finish college or be a flight attendant or marry or have kids. Mateo had finished college, but he hadn't married or had a family either. Emily had been his first serious girlfriend and his only serious girlfriend.

Now here he was with a chance—maybe his only chance—of getting his life back on track. But with Emily's look-alike pushing the beverage cart up and down the aisle, a sense of foreboding settled over him. Emily's brief appearance in Mateo's life had derailed his once-promising prospects, and maybe the unexpected appearance of Emily's look-alike was an omen that the same thing might happen again and that this whole trip to Arizona was an exercise in futility. Come Monday morning Mateo Vega would most likely be back working on the loading dock with no hope of ever finding anything better.

|CHAPTER 18|

CORNVILLE, ARIZONA

When Cami Lee's alarm went off that Saturday morning, she was tempted to ignore it, but she knew she couldn't. It was her turn to do the Saturday watch at the office. If a possible intrusion alert sounded for any of the networks under High Noon's protection, someone needed to be on hand to take immediate action.

Opening her eyes, though, she looked up at the sky-blue ceiling of her bedroom, and her heart did a little leap of joy that only got better once she was standing under the rain-bath showerhead in the spacious, glass-enclosed shower of her newly remodeled bathroom.

For a number of years after coming on board at High Noon, she'd lived happily in a studio apartment in Cottonwood. Unfortunately, the apartment complex was now under new management with a company that didn't respond readily to complaints regarding plumbing or electrical issues. The building had also previously been designated as nonsmoking. That was still supposedly true, but the rule was no longer enforced. Months earlier she had been expressing her dissatisfaction about her living conditions at the apartment complex in the break room at work when Shirley Malone had spoken up.

"On my way into the office this morning, I noticed that one of my neighbors in Cornville had a brand-new For Sale by Owner sign posted in her front yard. It's not a very big place and probably not in the best condition, but it would be bigger than a studio apartment, and the nearest neighbors are far enough away that even if they smoke like chimneys, it shouldn't bother you."

"How much?" Cami had asked.

"I have no idea."

Cami had driven out to Cornville that very afternoon. It turned out the words "not in the best condition" were a huge understatement. The house was built in the fifties, and its last occupant, a recently deceased eighty-nine-year-old widow, was a hoarder who'd lived there for thirty years. Her kids were attempting to unload the property, but none of the local real-estate agents had been willing to list the place without the widow's relatives doing a massive cleanup job beforehand.

The truth is, at this point in her life Camille Lee, despite being only in her mid-twenties, was in the enviable position that, whatever the asking price on the house, she could probably pay cash to buy it. Six months earlier the beloved grandfather she'd called "Papa" had passed away after a brief illness. Liu Wei Ling, known to his customers as Louie, was the longtime operator of a family-owned restaurant in San Francisco's Chinatown.

His was a dysfunctional family, where bad blood between parents and children went with the territory. Cami's grandparents had expected their daughter, Xiu, to grow up and take charge of the restaurant. Instead she had changed her name from Xiu to a more Americanized Sue and gone off to college. While there she met Cami's father, Cheng Lee, a foreign student from Taiwan, at an antiwar rally. With Cheng's student visa about to run out, the two had married, primarily in order for him to secure a green card. The thing was, once Cheng became a citizen, the couple had never taken the customary green-card marriage step of getting a divorce.

Both husband and wife were professors at Stanford—Cheng in computer science and Sue in French literature. They lived separate lives while at the same time inhabiting opposite ends of the same house. The only thing the two of them had in common was their daughter, Cami, and she'd been a bone of contention between her parents from the day she was born. While Cami was growing up, the only thing her parents had been able to agree upon about their daughter's future was the plan that she would ultimately become an academic of some kind.

The problem was, Cami had been no more interested in becoming a college professor than her mother had been in running the family's restaurant, and both parents had gone apoplectic when Cami took her two cum laude bachelor's degrees and went off to work for High Noon Enterprises in some godforsaken place called Cottonwood out in the wilds of Arizona.

Only after Cami left California did she discover that her grandfather had spent his lifetime working in the restaurant business because his own father had deemed him too stupid to go to college and become a doctor the way his older brother had. It came as a shock for Cami to learn that the stories her mother had told her about how much her grandfather loved the restaurant business hadn't been true at all.

When Papa died, Cami had of course attended the funeral. The restaurant had already been sold, and her parents were busy making arrangements for her widowed grandmother to come live with them. Knowing that sparks between Nainai and Sue would be flying early and often, Cami was grateful to have many miles of empty desert between her parents' home and hers.

A month after the funeral, a gentleman with a briefcase in hand had turned up outside the door of Cami's studio apartment. He was a claims adjustor for an insurance company. It seemed that on the occasion of Cami's birth her grandfather had taken out a twenty-pay life policy in the amount of two hundred fifty thousand dollars on his own life, naming his newborn granddaughter, Camille, as the sole beneficiary. The lawyer handling Liu Wei's estate had found the paid-up policy among his papers. Cami doubted that her mother had any knowledge of the policy's existence, and that was just as well, since she probably would have been offended—even more so if she'd suspected that her father had just paved the way for Cami to remain well off the beaten path her parents had charted for her.

So that day, when Cami went to see the house in Cornville, she knew going in that she had the wherewithal to buy it if she so desired. The woman trying to sell the place was reluctant to show it to anyone in its current condition, but eventually she succumbed to Cami's polite inquiries and seemingly genuine interest.

True, the place was an appalling mess. Aside from mounds of trash and filth, the house consisted of tiny closed-off spaces, with far too little lighting, far too much wood paneling, and an antique pink tile bathroom that had not aged well. The dingy windows were of the single-pane variety and were in grave danger of falling out of their frames.

But through all that, Cami Lee saw something else—a place that could be entirely her own, one that suited her own style and interests. She watched enough HGTV to know that the kind of remodeling she had in mind—opening up the spaces, getting rid of the paneling, replacing the windows, and upgrading the electrical service—would cost in the neighborhood of a hundred thousand dollars. She also knew that the comps in the area said houses there were going for right around two hundred thousand.

"How come you're selling the house yourself instead of using a real-estate agent?" she asked.

The woman shook her head. "No one's willing to take it in this condition—it's such a mess. I can't afford the kinds of repairs it will require, and even if I could, by the time I do all of that and pay closing costs, I'll barely walk away with anything."

Obviously none of those agents are fans of Flip or Flop, Cami thought, but that's not what she said.

"Tell you what," she told the woman. "I'm willing to pay a flat hundred thousand in cash as is with zero contingencies. If you'd like, I can give you a cashier's check today."

The woman had looked at her in utter astonishment. "As is?" she repeated. "You mean I wouldn't even have to clean out all the garbage and I'd still walk away with a hundred thousand dollars?"

"Exactly," Cami answered.

The woman's face brightened with relief. "Done," she said, and the two of them shook hands on the spot. It took longer than Cami expected to sort out the paperwork and the title and so forth, but ten days later the deal closed, and Cami took possession of the place on Tuff Cody Trail. It had taken three dumpsters, a keg of beer, and a whole flock of pizzas to empty out the house. Lance Tucker from work had rounded up some pals from his gym. They had turned up early one Saturday morning and made short work of the job. The woman selling the place hadn't wanted any of her mother's mounds of stuff, so there was no need to sort any of it. They carted it all out in wheelbarrows. By the end of the day, everything in the house was gone. When the work crew finished with the trash, they took down and hauled away all the paneling for good measure.

The following week, at Ali's recommendation, Cami had summoned Morgan Forester, the contractor who'd handled the remodeling of Ali's once-crumbling mid-century modern on Manzanita Hills Drive. Morgan had listened to Cami's wants and desires and had come up with a proposed budget that was well within her means. Forester brought in an architect to do the drawings, then he obtained the necessary permits and went to work.

Three months later Cami was living in her dream home. The quartz countertops and the kitchen cabinets had been customized to account for her less-than-average height. The open-concept design made for a large space that included a sitting area, a dining table, and a sparkling top-of-the-line kitchen. That area basked in the glow of a massive skylight that came with remotely operated blinds for those times when summer sunlight became too much of a good thing.

Three tiny bedrooms and one bath had been transformed into two of each—a master suite with a massive bath and a deluxe walk-in closet and a smaller bedroom, also with a bath, that held a combination desk and Murphy bed to serve as both guest space and private office.

Showered and dressed, Cami went to the kitchen and made herself a raspberry smoothie to take along in the car. She was due at work at eight, but preferring to arrive early, she left the house at seven fifteen.

As soon as she backed out of the driveway and started down Tuff Cody, Cami noticed that the car seemed to be pulling to one side. Suspecting a flat, she stopped short of the intersection with Cornville Road and got out to check. She had a flat tire, all right. Unfortunately, she had more than just one. All four tires were toast.

Realizing that the car would need to be flatbedded to a garage for repairs, Cami dialed the only tow-truck operator located in Cornville. Jim Baxter from Baxter's Garage was there within ten minutes. While she waited, Cami called Shirley, who was now her neighbor, and asked for a lift into town.

"I'll be right there as soon as I get dressed," Shirley said, "but how's it possible that you have four flats at once?"

"Beer bottles," Cami answered grimly. "I came back to the house and looked. There's debris from four beer bottles lying just behind where each tire would have been."

"Are you saying somebody did this on purpose?"

"Evidently."

"Why would they?" Shirley asked. "And when?"

"Sometime after I got home last night."

While the Prius headed for Discount Tires, Shirley dropped Cami off at the office.

"You're late," Lance Tucker said pointedly, glancing at the clock. It was eight fifteen.

"Someone wrecked my tires," she said. "I woke up to four flats."

"You're kidding."

"I wish I were. Somebody came into my carport last night and put broken beer bottles behind each of my tires. Shirley gave me a ride to work."

"Where's your car?"

"On its way to Discount Tires. The tires are shredded. I'll have to buy all new ones."

"Who did it?"

"No idea."

"Don't you have surveillance cameras set up?"

"Not yet," Cami admitted. "I hadn't quite gotten around to it."

"You'll have a system in place before the day is out," Lance told her. "Give me your house keys. I'll have it up and running by this afternoon."

"Thanks, Lance," she said, gratefully handing over her key ring. "I really appreciate it."

|CHAPTER 19|

COTTONWOOD, ARIZONA

When Harvey McCluskey woke up early that Saturday morning, not only was he freezing cold, he also had a crick in his neck and an aching back. Cottonwood might have been located in what's called high desert, but nighttime temperatures were surprisingly cold. Wanting to be up and out of the parking lot before occupants of the other offices and nearby assigned parking places arrived, he moved to the cab of his Silverado and drove out of the lot. A warm shower at his gym got his blood running again. After leaving the gym, he stopped by a gas station, where he picked up a cup of coffee and used their compressor to fill up his air mattress. He wouldn't be spending another night sleeping on the hard bed of the pickup. Then he headed for Cornville.

From the day he slashed Rhonda Ward's bicycle tires, he'd never forgotten the amazing sense of power that surged through his body when, hidden behind the hedge of a neighboring house, he watched Rhonda walk up to the bike rack, discover the damage, and race back into the school building in tears. She returned moments later with the principal in tow. They were still conferring when an invisible but triumphant Harvey slipped away from the scene.

This morning was his chance to relive that long-ago thrill. Twenty minutes later, with coffee in hand, he was parked on the shoulder of the road across from Tuff Cody Trail. If either the storage-unit facility or the post office had video surveillance—which he thought unlikely—he was too far away for them to pick up any details of his vehicle other than the fact that it was a pickup truck with a canopy on it.

He'd brought along the binoculars from his office and shoved them into his glove box. Now he pulled them out and sat with them resting on his lap. If anyone asked what he was doing, he would tell them he was a bird-watcher. That was true, he was a bird-watcher, with Princess Prius being the current bird in question.

He had thought about her all night long. She was a dark-haired little beauty—a bit on the exotic side—and seeing her reminded him of the stray hitchhiker he'd picked up years ago, somewhere along US-95 north of Vegas.

While Harvey was still in the army and wondering whether to stay or leave, one of his buddies, Patrick Duffy, had left the service and landed a terrific job working security at Caesars Palace. Lured by Duff's enthusiasm for the locale, Harvey had opted for Vegas as well, and he, too, had ended up working at Caesars.

For a while it was a great gig. Their immediate boss was a good ole boy who willingly turned a blind eye to someone having the occasional drink on the job or maybe slightly fudging on his time card. Unfortunately, a couple years in, all that changed. Someone put a woman named Margo De Angelo in charge of the department. The daughter of one of the big bosses, she was a bitch on wheels for sure. As the first-ever female to hold that position in a major casino, she was determined to make a name for herself, and she did.

First to go was Harvey's good-guy boss. Shortly thereafter Duff bailed as well, taking a job with a newly opened casino in Reno. He'd needed help moving, and Harvey had been happy to oblige. Back then he'd been driving a Toyota Tundra. He had traveled north with the bed of his pickup loaded down with as much of Duff's furniture as the truck would hold. After helping unload, Harvey was on his way back to Vegas and fuming because Witch Margo had cost him such a good friend, when just south of Beatty he'd spotted a lone, dark-haired girl hitchhiking along the highway. He'd stopped and offered her a ride.

She told him her name was Dawna Marie Giles. She was seventeen years old, came from Tonopah, and was heading to Vegas to meet up with her boyfriend. Her parents hated the guy's guts and had forbidden her to see him again. The parents got their wish on that score, because Dawna Marie never did see the boyfriend again. In fact, she never saw anybody. Harvey had made sure of that.

A few miles after picking her up, he'd turned off the highway onto a dirt road. Once Dawna Marie realized what was going on, she'd actually thrown herself out of his moving truck, but he'd caught up with her and knocked her silly. It had been a cold March day, and she'd been wearing leggings. He had used part of the leggings to tie her hands together. Then he'd thrown her facedown into the sand of a nearby wash, unzipped his pants, and did what needed doing, including wrapping his hands around her throat and squeezing the life out of her. She was wearing a ring of some kind—a class ring, he realized later. After pulling that off her finger and pocketing it to add to his trophy chain, he siphoned some gasoline out of his truck, splashed it on her, and set her body on fire.

All this had happened in broad daylight. By the time he made it back to the highway, the cloud of smoke seemed to be clearing and barely showed.

When someone at work asked about the scratches on his hands, he said it had happened when he was helping Duff clean weeds out of his new backyard. In the days that followed, Harvey had checked the news on a daily basis, but he never spotted any mention of what had happened to Dawna Marie Giles in either newspaper coverage or on TV. It seemed likely to him that even if someone had found Dawna Marie's body, what happened in Beatty wasn't newsworthy in Vegas.

If the local cops devoted much time or effort to investigating her homicide, they never came knocking on Harvey's door. Out in the middle of the desert like that, there'd been no surveillance footage to lead back to him and most likely no remaining fingerprint or DNA evidence either. Yes, Dawna Marie had been just another throwaway kid who nobody really gave a damn about. Harvey hoped the same would hold true for the Princess in the Prius.

As for Dawna Marie's class ring? He still had it, and he wore it every day as one of his trophies. While Harvey sat in his truck that morning, waiting and sipping his cooling coffee, he let his fingers touch each of them in turn, taking comfort in the reassuring presence of what he considered to be his good-luck charms.

At seven fifteen Harvey saw activity at the house on Tuff Cody Trail as the Prius backed out of the carport and then nosed its way north toward Cornville Road. Just short of the intersection, it pulled over onto the shoulder and stopped. Harvey could tell from the way the car moved that the broken beer bottles had done their job. All four tires were trashed.

Watching through his binoculars, he saw a frowning Princess climb out of the driver's seat and walk around the vehicle, surveying the damage as she pulled a cell phone from her pocket. She was clearly upset. Harvey wanted to see more, but he didn't dare risk moving any closer.

Surprisingly, a tow truck arrived in short order. Leaving the driver to load her Prius onto his flatbed, Princess hoofed it back to her house. He saw her standing outside the carport, where she seemed to be examining the debris left behind. Fat lot of good that would do her.

Minutes later another vehicle came down Tuff Cody. He recognized it as a Honda sedan that was usually parked near High Noon's portion of the complex. It stopped at the end of Princess's driveway. Once she climbed into the passenger seat, the Honda drove away.

"Show's over," Harvey said aloud, putting the binoculars away. He felt vaguely disappointed. It hadn't been quite as much fun as he'd hoped or expected. For now, though, it was time for him to go have a real breakfast and figure out his next move.

|CHAPTER 20|

SEDONA, ARIZONA

With B. at home and lying next to her in bed, Ali slept better than she had for days. Awakening late on Saturday morning, she was grateful that the only official event on that day's agenda was B.'s upcoming appointment with Mateo Vega, which, according to Stu, was due to happen at 3:00 p.m.

Venturing out of the bedroom, she located B. in the library with coffee in hand, a computer open on his lap, and Bella stretched out next to his thigh in his easy chair. "Morning, sunshine," he said. "Or should I say good afternoon?"

B.'s ability to negotiate time zones with no lingering aftereffects was always a source of wonder to her—wonder and envy.

"How long have you been up?" she asked.

B. glanced at his watch. "A couple of hours. Coffee?" he asked.

A thermal carafe and a cup and saucer sat on the coffee table in front of him.

"Sure," she said. "So what are you up to?"

"I'm reading through the dossier on Mateo Vega that Stu had Frigg prepare for us. If we're considering hiring an ex-con—"

"Another ex-con," Ali inserted with a smile. After all, Lance Tucker had been in a juvenile lockup before High Noon helped correct the miscarriage of justice that had put him there.

"Yes," B. agreed, "another ex-con."

Taking her coffee, Ali settled into her own chair. Bella stayed where she was. "What are you finding?"

"I've been reading the transcripts of the parole hearings," B. replied, "and Mateo's story remains consistent. He claims that he agreed to the plea deal on the advice of his public defender, who said that if they took the case to trial, there was a good chance Mateo would end up with a life sentence. Ever since that court appearance, however, he's maintained that he didn't commit the crime. He says that as he and Emily were leaving the party, she exited his vehicle, and he never saw her again.

"Frigg also provided copies of his prison correspondence," B. continued. "Initially there were letters from both his parents, but Mateo's father, Joaquin, died while Mateo was incarcerated. In their letters back and forth, he complains that law enforcement always focused on him and never bothered looking at anyone else."

"That's because it's always the boyfriend," Ali murmured.

"He was released last spring," B. continued. "As near as I can tell, he's kept his nose clean ever since. He got a job with a local thrift store within days of his release, and he's still working there. He obtained a Washington State driver's license but apparently doesn't own a vehicle. He also has a King County Library System card. The catalog of materials he's checked out not only since his release but also while in prison explains why he was able to ace our hack simulations. Back when he worked for us at VGI, people were trying to steal our intellectual property, and Stu was training Mateo to counter those folks. So whenever he was reading through technical material, he already knew what he needed to learn from it. And that laser focus has made a huge difference."

"It sounds to me as though, interview or not, you've pretty well already made up your mind," Ali suggested.

"I think I have," B. agreed after a long, thoughtful pause. "My whole life was in shambles when Mateo was arrested. I had just learned that my wife and my partner were carrying on an affair right under my nose. If I'd been thinking clearly back then, at the very least I could have seen that Mateo had better representation than he received at the hands of that public defender. Maybe the outcome would have been the same, who knows? But even if he's guilty, he's paid his debt to society, and he's evidently walking the straight and narrow now. The real injustice is that even though the guy is way smarter than the average bear, no one in Seattle will give him an opportunity to work at even the lowest entry-level job."

"And you think he deserves a break."

"I do," B. said with a nod, "a break and a second chance."

"What are you planning on offering him?"

"I'll start him out at about the same level of compensation we gave Cami when we hired her—probably a little more to account for inflation. I'll also give him a signing bonus to help offset his moving expenses."

"Sounds fair," Ali said. She reached for the carafe,

intent on pouring more coffee, but it was empty. "I'll go make more," she said, standing up and starting for the kitchen. "And I'll find out what's for breakfast."

"You're welcome to get more coffee, but we're skipping breakfast today, at least for right now," B. said. "I spoke to your mom a little while ago. We're due at Sedona Shadows at eleven to have an early lunch with your folks."

Ali sat back down. "We are?" she asked. "At Sedona Shadows? In the dining room?"

"That's what I suggested, and your mom agreed."

"But . . ." Ali began.

"I wanted to check something out," B. said, "to do an experiment, if you will. I think that when your dad's around you or Edie, he behaves one way. When he's around other people—me, for instance—he somehow puts on enough of a game face that we think he's okay. I suspect that's one of the reasons we've had no idea about how serious all this was becoming. Last year at the Halloween party and over the holidays, we had no clue anything out of the ordinary was going on. I want to see if that's still the case."

"All right, then," Ali conceded, not without some misgivings. "I'd best go get dressed."

"Oh," B. added as she headed back toward the bedroom. "I told the kids we'll stop by later on this afternoon, once the interview is over. Everybody else has met that new grandson of ours. I'm ready to make his acquaintance."

|CHAPTER 21|

PHOENIX, ARIZONA

When the pilot announced they were crossing over the Grand Canyon, Mateo wished he could see out the window, but his view was blocked by the bulky-shouldered man beside him. The flight seemed to last forever. Mateo was tall enough that his knees were crammed against the seat in front of him, and his occasional glimpses of the Emily Tarrant look-alike left him feeling half-sick. By the time the plane finally hit the tarmac in Phoenix, Mateo was a nervous wreck.

Because he was seated at the back of the plane, getting off took an incredibly long time. He made his way through the airport, following the signs. Cami had sent him an e-mail advising him that Stu would meet him in baggage claim. Since Mateo had already told her that he was traveling with carry-on only, that seemed strange, but he followed her directions to a tee and was relieved when, as the escalator reached ground level, Stu was right there waiting for him. He was older and more well groomed than Mateo remembered but definitely the same guy, with one major exception: When Mateo approached him, Stu reached out and shook his hand. Back in the day, handshaking had never been part of Stuart Ramey's MO.

"Come on, then," Stu urged. "Let's get going. Your meeting with B. is at three, but Cottonwood's about two hours from here, and we've got to make a stop along the way."

Stu led Mateo through first the terminal and then the parking garage, where he used a key fob to unlock the door of a Dodge Ram dual-cab pickup. The earlier version of Stuart Ramey hadn't owned a vehicle or driven one either. So far the changes in him seemed downright remarkable.

"Nice truck," Mateo said as he settled in and fastened his seat belt. As far as conversation went, that was the best he could manage. They exited the airport and had merged onto a freeway before either man spoke again.

"Have you ever been to Arizona?" Stu asked.

Of course not, Mateo thought. *Until today I've never been outside Washington State*. He shook his head. "I was hoping to catch a glimpse of the Grand Canyon when we flew over it, but I wasn't in a window seat."

"If you come to work for us, I'll take you there sometime," Stu offered. "It's not all that far from Cottonwood."

The only word in Stu's previous statement that stuck with Mateo was the first one—"if." What if he didn't get the job? What if this whole trip was for nothing? What if the only thing in his future was working on that loading dock?

A few miles farther on, as they prepared to exit

the freeway at a street called Camelback, Stu pointed toward a red mountain off to their right. "The street's named after Camelback Mountain off over there."

Looking out the passenger window, Mateo had to agree that the rocky outcropping looming in the distance really did resemble a camel's back.

"So where are we going?" he asked.

"We've got to pick up some supplies," Stu told him. "It's not the kind of thing that's readily available in Cottonwood, but it won't take long. The order should be ready for us. All I have to do is pay for it."

They stopped outside a strip mall in front of a store labeled Tech City. Mateo followed Stu inside, where they stopped at the customer-service desk. "I'm here to collect some stuff for Lance Tucker," Stu announced.

While the clerk went looking for their order, Mateo wandered off on his own. Eyeing the vast array of exotic electronic equipment on display, he felt like a little kid who had accidentally stumbled into Santa's workshop.

Minutes later they left the store with a dozen boxes, each containing what appeared to be a simple yard light. Reading the label on one of them, however, Mateo discovered that in addition to supplying illumination, each separate unit also contained a Wi-Fi-based surveillance camera, all of which operated by means of a solar battery pack. In other words, what would appear to be a simple wire-free yard-lighting system was actually a sophisticated surveillance network as well.

"What's all this for?" Mateo asked as he helped Stu load the boxes into the backseat of the truck.

"Some jerk put beer bottles behind each of the tires on Cami's car last night, and all of them were shredded when she tried to come to work this morning,"

Stu explained. "Lance wanted me to pick these up so he can install them later on today. That way if whoever did it shows up again, you can bet we'll have the goods on him."

"Lance is Cami's boyfriend?" Mateo asked as they merged back onto I-17 and headed north again.

"No, Lance Tucker is another guy who works with us. He's young, but he's a real brainiac."

"How many people work for High Noon altogether?" Mateo asked finally.

"Right now there are six—B. and his wife, Ali—"

"Wait, I thought B.'s wife's name started with a C— Claire, maybe?"

"Close," Stu replied. "Clarice was her name, but she's long gone. Ali Reynolds is B.'s second wife, and she's great. You've already met Cami on the phone. She's fine as long as you don't start singing the praises of fast food. She's a complete nutcase when it comes to healthy eating. Lance just graduated from UCLA. There's Shirley Malone—the older lady who's our receptionist—and then there's me."

"Only six?" Mateo asked in amazement. "That's all? I mean, from what I read, I thought High Noon was a big deal."

"High Noon is a big deal," Stu replied, "an international big deal at that, but in this business you don't have to have hundreds of employees to be effective."

Mateo sat thinking about that for some time, letting the words soak in while observing the changing landscape outside the window of the speeding pickup. There were communities strung here and there along the freeway, but most of what he saw was a vast empty desert, surrounded on all sides by looming mountains. There was desert around Yakima, too, but nothing like this.

"What are those tall, sticklike things called?" he asked. "They look like giant pitchforks."

"Saguaros," Stu explained, "a kind of cactus. In a few weeks, the tops will all have halos of white flowers on them. Later the flowers turn into fruit that local Native Americans use to make wine, but I've never tasted any of that."

As the elevation changed around them, moving higher and higher, the landscape changed too. Along the way Stu pointed out the various kinds of plants growing alongside the roadway—prickly pear and cholla with yellow flowers and groves of mesquite. As they traveled, Mateo felt his spirits rise. Being in open country like this made him feel as though he could breathe again. He'd gone straight from his prison cell to the confines of his rented room at Randy's. With the world literally opening up around him, he felt almost giddy. Was there a chance he could live here? What would it feel like to walk outside under this huge canopy of blue sky every single day and feel the sun all over his body?

Stu had gone on talking, explaining things about High Noon's customer base and the kinds of needs they had across the globe, but Mateo was too lost in his surroundings to pay much attention. By the time they turned off the freeway at a place called Camp Verde and headed west, they were in what appeared to be an area that was more grassland than desert.

Mateo was raised Catholic, but it had been years since he'd attended Mass. Now, as Stu's Dodge Ram headed toward another looming mountain range, Mateo found himself uttering a silent prayer that maybe this strip of highway really was the road to his future.

|CHAPTER 22|

SEDONA, ARIZONA

"That was certainly interesting," Ali said as she and B. pulled away from Sedona Shadows once lunch was over. "You were right," she continued. "Dad was almost like his old self. He really did put on a show, and according to Betsy it's been weeks since he's been willing to go to the dining room."

"Which is why we have to be there for your mom at every opportunity. This must be an emotional nightmare for her. From one minute to the next, she has no idea if she'll be sharing her unit with her husband of sixty-some years or with a man who regards her as a complete stranger. We need to help her see her way along the road ahead."

"I'm not sure even I want to see that road," Ali said, brushing away a tear, "not for her or for any of us."

B. reached over and took her hand. "I seem to remember someone telling me not so long ago that that's the cost of loving—knowing that eventually you'll have to lose."

"Not fair," Ali said.

"What's not fair?"

"Spouting my own words back at me," she replied.

"What goes around comes around," B. replied with a grin.

They arrived at the office in Cottonwood a whole hour before the scheduled meeting, and both B. and Ali retreated to their separate offices to catch up on things. Sorting through the mail, Ali noticed immediately that there was no sign of a payment of any kind from Harvey McCluskey.

"Time's up," she told herself under her breath. "Monday morning we start eviction proceedings."

By 3:00 p.m. B. and Ali were waiting in the break room when Stu ushered Mateo inside, then let himself out, closing the door behind him. B. took the newcomer's hand and shook it. "Welcome," he said. "Good to see you again, and this is my wife, Ali Reynolds."

As Ali shook hands with Mateo, she tried to assess the man. He was a handsome enough guy—tall, slender, with light brown skin and a hint of gray peeking through the thick black hair at his temples.

"Glad to meet you," Mateo murmured.

It was clear enough for Ali to see that he was nervous and had no idea what to expect. She was grateful when B. charged right ahead with putting Mateo out of his misery.

"I understand Stu's been giving you a guided tour."

"A short one," Mateo answered with a nod. "It's pretty amazing."

"Stu also tells us that you're interested in coming to work here."

The man's whole demeanor brightened. "Absolutely," he said.

B. slid a notepad across the table. Ali could tell that there was writing on it. Although she couldn't make it out, she was reasonably sure of what it said.

"This is what we're prepared to offer," B. said, "but you need to know in advance that there's some shift work involved because we need to have someone on-site at all times."

Mateo pulled the notepad close enough to read it. When he did so, his eyes widened. "You're offering me a job just like that, and you're willing to pay me this much?"

It was clear that he couldn't quite believe what he was seeing.

"Just like that," Ali said, stepping into the discussion. "Your performance on those hack simulations far outstripped everyone else's. Your work for B. at VGI years ago was entirely satisfactory, and although you've had some personal difficulties since then, we're of the opinion that you deserve a second chance."

What no one in the room expected right then was for Mateo Vega to break down in tears, but that's what he did. Finally, however, he gathered himself.

"Sorry," he said, "but I never expected—" He broke off, unable to continue. Then, after taking a deep breath, he added, "How soon would you want me to start?"

"How soon *can* you start?" B. asked. "I'm assuming you have things to take care of up in Seattle."

"Not really," Mateo replied. "I'm renting a room on a month-to-month basis. Everything I own came from a thrift store, and my boss knows I've been looking for another job for months. The only things I have outstanding are some books that need to be returned to the library, and I'm pretty sure Randy—my landlord—would return those if I ask."

"You're willing to come here with just the clothes you're wearing and what you have in your backpack?"

For the first time, Mateo grinned at them. "It's more than I had a year ago when I got out of prison. Oh, and that's another thing. You'll need to let my parole officer know where I've gone and why."

"I'm pretty sure we can handle that," B. said. "Just give me a name and address. Other than that? Welcome aboard."

"Thank you," Mateo said. "I can't wait to get started."

|CHAPTER 23|

COTTONWOOD, ARIZONA

Once the witch at Caesars Palace had driven Harvey out of his cushy security job, he'd gone to work selling real estate at a time when the housing industry in Vegas had been booming. Eventually he'd come to suspect that his boss, one of the name-brand real-estate agents in town, was playing loosey-goosey with her escrow accounts. Maybe it takes a crook to know one. Harvey had been smart enough to deactivate his real-estate license and get out of Dodge before the whole thing had imploded. Several of his former associates, including his boss, had actually gone to prison.

He'd landed in Prescott after finding employment at Bucky's, one of two casinos in town. Unfortunately, he'd arrived with a very real gambling addiction, something that had eventually cost him his job at Bucky's. Unemployed, he hit on the idea of setting himself up as a home inspector. He fudged his way through an online course and then breezed through the exam, having purchased the answers online for a mere hundred bucks.

There were plenty of pricy real-estate transactions going on in Sedona, but he couldn't afford to live there. That's how he ended up in Cottonwood. It was less expensive in terms of rental costs. Not only that, it was a short trip, up and over Mingus Mountain, to both Prescott and Bucky's.

For months, on the days when he wasn't working or hanging out at the Cowpoke, he was in Prescott at Bucky's—as a customer now rather than an employee. For a fairly long time, he'd had good luck playing poker and blackjack. His winning streak had come to an abrupt end at some point. In his subsequent losing streak, he'd dropped even more. Eventually Harvey was evicted from his apartment for not paying rent, and now the same thing was about to happen at his office.

He still had the Rolex he'd bought back during his salad days in Vegas. He could have sold that and covered his rent arrears with no problem, but he had no intention of doing so. His first plan had been to simply wait out the eviction process, then use the Rolex to bankroll his move to someplace else. He'd expected the process to take months, but if he could no longer sleep in the office, what was the point in hanging around?

So he spent much of Saturday at his soon-to-be-former office, sorting out what he would take with him. It became apparent there wasn't much. At the time he got tossed out of his apartment, he'd put everything he owned into a storage unit. Eventually he'd stopped paying the rent on that as well, and most of that stuff disappeared, too. The one thing he'd rescued from the storage unit was a banker's box full of keepsakes. As he picked through its contents, looking for one particular item, Harvey came face-to-face with the fact that at age fifty-two he didn't have much to show for his time on the planet.

His high school diploma was there, as was the pocketknife his father had given him during his very brief foray in Cub Scouts. It was the same knife he'd used to slash Rhonda Ward's bicycle tires all those years earlier. The collection included a worn Little League baseball glove, a pair of high school yearbooks, the first-place wrestling trophy he'd won at the state tournament his senior year at Butte High, and a shoebox holding an odd collection of photographs.

He'd kept no pictures of his mother, but there were several of his father as a young man and a few with Harvey and his father together. However, the ones taken the night of Harvey's high school graduation featured the beaming faces of the DeLucas standing in for his parents. There were photos of Harvey from his army days, including several of him proudly wearing his dress uniform, but most of those were faded color snapshots of Harvey and his MP pals hanging out and raising hell in beer gardens all over West Germany. Shuffling through the photos, he spent more time on those beer-garden gatherings than he did on any of the others, because he now counted the time he'd been in Germany as the best days of his life. Back then he'd still believed he had a future. Now he knew better.

Underneath the shoebox, he found what he was looking for—an unlabeled file folder containing two very different items. One was the picture of him and Marnie on their wedding day—a part of the standard wedding-chapel package from Caesars Palace. The other was Marnie's death certificate, dated two days later.

Marnie Richards was the closest Harvey had ever

come to falling in love. She was ten years younger than he was and had turned up in his life when she moved into the same apartment building where he lived, a none-too-classy low-rise on Eastern in Las Vegas. Good-looking and sweet, she was an LPN who worked at Sunrise Hospital and was in the process of divorcing an abusive husband. Her ex had assured her he'd be glad to deliver her furniture and household goods, and she was incredibly grateful for that—right up until he dumped everything she owned out of his truck and into the parking lot.

Coming home that day, Harvey had found Marnie struggling to lug her goods up the two flights of stairs that led to her apartment. He'd ridden to her rescue by knocking on doors and organizing a fire brigade of neighbors who finished the job in no time. That single act of kindness—something of a rarity as far as Harvey was concerned—turned him into a knight in shining armor in Marnie's eyes, and for a while he almost lived up to her vaunted opinion of him. Three months later she'd let her apartment go and moved into his. Three weeks after her divorce was final, they married.

Harvey had gotten an employee discount on the wedding itself, and they'd spent that first drunken night at Caesars Palace. But for the honeymoon he'd chosen the Grand Canyon, where he'd even sprung for the honeymoon suite at Bright Angel Lodge, and that's where it had all gone bad. He couldn't get it up that night—not at all! Marnie tried to be sweet about it—she laughed it off, told him it was no big deal and not to worry about it.

But Harvey McCluskey wasn't capable of laughing off humiliation. It wasn't just a big deal to him—it was a huge deal—and to his way of thinking, his inability to perform was all Marnie's fault. The next morning at breakfast, he had suggested they hike a ways down into the canyon, hoping they'd be able to get better pictures than the ones taken on the rim. She had objected at first, but eventually he won her over.

They were walking along, having a good time, when Marnie's shoe came untied. She was bent over retying it when he came up behind her and simply knocked into her with his hip. That's all there was to it. He hadn't really thought about it in advance. The opportunity presented itself, and he decided that being married was just too damned much trouble.

Caught completely off balance, Marnie tumbled over the edge. People above and below them on the trail heard her screaming "NO!" as she fell, but no one saw anything. Several people came running to where a dazed and grief-stricken Harvey stood staring over the edge. They joined forces to keep him from trying to follow her and hung around comforting him until the authorities arrived.

When Marnie's body was finally recovered, there were no defensive wounds or any sign of foul play. It had taken only a gentle shove on Harvey's part to send her to her death. He told the detectives that things had seemingly been fine until she had somehow lost her footing and tumbled into the abyss.

Had the cops dug deeper, they might have discovered there was a group life-insurance policy. Marnie hadn't gotten around to changing her name, but she had already changed the beneficiary arrangement on her insurance policy at work. Without looking into that, however, the cops had let Harvey go, and Marnie Richards's death was ruled accidental. When Harvey checked out of the hotel three days later, the man at the front desk expressed his profound sympathy for Harvey's terrible loss and comped his whole stay. As far as Harvey was concerned, that was a win.

When the medical examiner released her body, Marnie's personal effects—including her wedding ring—were turned over to Harvey. Since he was basically a cheap bastard, and since he'd already had his mother's perfectly good wedding ring readily at hand, he'd given that to Marnie, telling her how much it would mean to him if she would be willing to wear his dear departed mother's ring. With sparkling eyes, she'd told him she would be honored to do so.

Back home Harvey discovered that Marnie's tragic honeymoon death had been big news in Vegas, so people around him—even the witch at work—showered him with sympathy. He went to a jeweler and asked to have Marnie's name engraved on the wedding ring that already held his mother's name, and the guy hadn't batted an eye. When the engraving was done, the jeweler returned it to him with no charge, a shake of his head, and a solemn murmur: "So sorry for your loss."

During the time Harvey and Marnie were together, he had deep-sixed his gold chain, but once the engraving was done, he retrieved the chain from its hiding spot and returned the ring to its place of honor, only now it counted as a twofer. Along with the whore's hoop earring and Dawna's class ring, he was amassing quite a collection.

Everything else in the banker's box was expendable, but not the wedding picture and death certificate. He carefully slipped the file folder into the bottom of the gym bag he planned to take with him when he left Cottonwood in his rearview mirror. He loaded all the remaining bits and pieces of his life back into the box, put a lid on it, and carried it out to the truck. When Harvey disappeared, so would all those mementos he'd carried around with him for far too long. He was done with them now.

By noontime Harvey had hauled everything he intended to keep out of the office. The trash could stay where it was. Let someone else clean up his mess. Once the truck was loaded, however, he didn't take off right away. Instead he spent most of the afternoon keeping an eye on what was happening at High Noon's end of the complex. He noticed that for a Saturday afternoon things seemed to be quite busy. Several people came and went in the course of the day, but there was still no sign of the Prius—and the Princess in the Prius was now both his target and his primary concern.

Harvey had had no known connection to two of the women he'd killed, and that had made it easy for him to get away without being caught. In both his mother's murder and in Marnie's, he'd done an excellent job of covering his tracks, but Princess was a special problem because he did have a connection to her. She'd been there when Ali Reynolds had walked in on him in his office. Unfortunately, slashing her tires and serving notice that someone might be after her had probably been a bad idea on Harvey's part, but that didn't mean he'd changed his mind about going after her. He wanted her in the worst possible way, and for the same reason he'd murdered his mother. That was the price the little bitch would have to pay for witnessing Harvey's humiliation.

———

By late Saturday afternoon, he was parked just south of the post office in Cornville, armed with his binoculars and a newly purchased copy of *Birds of the American Southwest*. Had anyone asked, he was in full bird-watching mode, but rather than scanning the skies, he kept his binoculars trained on Princess's yard, where a trio of people—probably her coworkers from High Noon—were engaged in installing what looked like a network of yard lights. Increasing the illumination around her place was probably a direct reaction to the damaged-tire incident from the night before, but Harvey knew that increased lighting wasn't a magic wand that would protect Princess from what he had in mind.

The men had nearly finished their installation job by then and were in the process of loading tools back into a big Dodge Ram pickup when the Prius appeared, turned off into Princess's driveway, and parked in the carport. Princess herself got out of the vehicle, greeted the three men, and welcomed them into her home. As they all trooped into the house, Harvey had seen enough. The moment was at hand for him to go to work on his exit plan, because by the time the world realized Princess was gone, Harvey McCluskey would have disappeared as well.

Any number of sketchy people hung out at the Cowpoke. One of those happened to be a guy named Leonardo Bianchi, who referred to himself as "Big Dude" and claimed to be a retired mafioso out of Chicago. Leonardo was a braggart and a royal pain in the ass, especially when he'd had one too many. He liked to talk about the people he'd "rubbed out" on his way to the top and claimed he still had the connections to make things happen as needed. Most of his listeners simply regarded him as a blowhard, but Harvey suspected there was at least some truth buried underneath all the braggadocio. Not only that, on several occasions the Big Dude had expressed a more-than-passing interest in Harvey's treasured Rolex.

That night Harvey used the last of his home-inspection advance to ply Leonardo with drinks and a convoluted sob story. Harvey claimed he'd knocked up some girl—the daughter of a Prescott bigwig—who had told him she was eighteen. Unfortunately, she was only sixteen. Harvey said the father was after him, determined to get him charged with statutory rape. Not wanting to end up "back in the joint," Harvey told Bianchi he was in desperate need of a new identity and a way to disappear.

"Where you gonna go?" Leonardo asked.

"Baja, I think," Harvey told him. "I figure living like a bum on the beach in Mexico is better than being locked up in prison here in the States."

"That means you need papers," Leonardo guessed. "New name, new ID, new passport, and some running money."

Harvey nodded.

"That's going to cost you, you know."

Harvey nodded again.

"How much you got?"

Harvey raised the cuff on his shirtsleeve and pointed to the watch, then studied Leonardo's face as he thought about it and wavered for a moment before succumbing to temptation.

"Sounds doable," he said finally. "How soon do you need all this to happen?"

"ASAP."

"Okey-dokey," Leonardo said. "If you're going any distance south of the border, you'll need a visa. Where do you plan to cross over?"

"Calexico," Harvey replied after a moment's thought. He figured crossing there would have him off the beaten path. He had often gone four-wheeling in the dunes west of Yuma, and the All-American Canal nearby would be the perfect place to stage his fake suicide.

"You got a driver's license on you right now?" Leonardo asked.

Harvey nodded.

"Hand it over, then, and I'll see what I can do."

Harvey passed his license to Leonardo. "I'll probably need transportation from Mexicali down into Baja."

"That's going to cost ya, too."

"Whatever," Harvey replied with a casual shrug. "The watch should cover it."

When he left the bar later that night, he wasn't as drunk as usual. He drove to Walmart, found a parking place, went inside to use the facilities, then climbed into the back of his truck to go to sleep under the canopy. He was grateful for the presence of his mattress. He was also glad that by sleeping there, he wasn't risking having the cops roust him out of a good night's sleep like they would have had he tried sleeping in his former office.

Ali Reynolds might have won the battle, but she sure as hell hadn't won the war, Harvey thought as he drifted off to sleep. In a way his mother had gotten off easy. Ida Mae had died, and that was the end of it. She hadn't had time to think about what she'd done to deserve what happened to her. That arrogant Reynolds bitch wouldn't get off nearly that lightly. She'd have to spend the remainder of her life living with and regretting the fact that she was the one ultimately responsible for the death of Princess Prius.

What could be better than that?

|CHAPTER 24|

SEDONA, ARIZONA

When Ali and B. arrived at Chris and Athena's house for dinner that evening, they didn't come empty-handed. Thanks to Alonzo's talented efforts, they came with a dinner-to-go care package of meatloaf, the twins' all-time favorite mac and cheese, and a mixed salad, along with a freshly baked rhubarb pie, the whole spread happily received and happily consumed. They had visited for a time after dinner, careful not to overstay their welcome. Athena seemed to be recovering well from her C-section. Logan's big sister, Colleen, couldn't get enough of her newborn brother, holding him and cooing over him much of the time. Colin, on the other hand, was far more interested in his latest video game.

"Did I ever mention I really like being a grandpa?" B. asked as they headed back home.

"You might have said that a time or two before," Ali replied, "but it's one of those things that bears repeating."

Back at home, in the library, they poured glasses of

wine and settled in to discuss their day. By mutual agreement there was no further discussion of the situation with Ali's parents. Instead they turned their attention to High Noon, where the vandalism at Cami's house had been uppermost on the list as a topic of concern.

"Who do you suppose has it in for Cami?" B. asked. "Wrecking all four tires at once and doing it the way it was done took time and effort. Is there maybe a love triangle of some kind going on?"

Ali shook her head. "Not that I know of," she said. "As far as I can tell, she has no romantic entanglements of any kind. Cami comes to work, she goes to Krav Maga workouts, she hangs out at the shooting range, and then she goes home. I've never heard a hint about any boyfriend. Believe me, if she had one, Lance and Stu would tease her unmercifully."

"Which might be a good reason for keeping it quiet," B. offered.

"Maybe," Ali agreed, but she wasn't entirely sold on the idea.

"And what do you think of Mateo?"

"I think he'll be a good team player," Ali suggested. "The fact that he was willing to go out to Cami's place this afternoon along with everybody else to help install her new surveillance system really impressed me. He didn't have to do that, especially considering he'd only just met her."

The whole crew had been able to pitch in on that and make quick work of it because B. had been in the office to cover the bases in their absence.

Ali paused and took a thoughtful sip of her wine before she spoke again. "What if he really didn't do it?" she asked finally. "What if Mateo didn't kill that girl and just spent seventeen years of his life in prison for no reason?"

"What makes you say that?" B. asked.

"Something you mentioned earlier," Ali answered.

"What?"

"The fact that for all those years of parole hearings he kept right on telling the same story," Ali said. "I wasn't a cop for long, but I learned a thing or two while I was. Liars screw up. They tell lies, and then they can't remember what they said earlier. That's why it's so easy to trip up the bad guys—they can't keep their stories straight from one interview to the next. In contrast, Mateo's story never wavered, even though sticking to his original story precluded an early release."

"You really think he might have been wrongly convicted?"

"Maybe," Ali answered. "It sounds to me as though his original defense attorney might have sold him down the river by getting him to accept that plea deal. Those aren't appealable. Once you take a plea, you have to live with it no matter what, and that's what he did. He didn't get sentenced to life in prison. He got out after sixteen years, plus the one spent awaiting trial, but those are seventeen years taken from his life that he'll never get back. If Mateo didn't kill that girl, he should have been pardoned rather than being let out on parole."

"Are you suggesting we go to something like the Innocence Project?" B. asked.

Ali shook her head. "They tend to concentrate on death-penalty cases or instances where people have received life without parole. Maybe I should ask Dave and see what he suggests."

Dave Holman was a longtime Yavapai County homi-

cide cop. For a while, before B. had come along, Ali and
Dave had carried on a brief fling that ended amicably on
both sides. They remained on good terms even now, not
only with each other but with each other's current spouse
as well. The previous fall Gordon Maxwell, who'd been
the Yavapai County sheriff for decades, had retired. To
no one's great surprise, Dave had been elected to the
office of sheriff.

"It can't hurt to ask," B. said. "Now, what's the deal
with this McCluskey character? I want the whole story."

So she told him the story again, in more detail this
time than she'd been able to include in their long-
distance discussions.

"You really thought he was going to take a swing at
you in the bar?"

"I did, and so did Shirley," Ali answered.

"Does he have any record of violent behavior?"

Ali shook her head. "Not that I know of, but I suppose
that's a possibility. I doubt we need to worry about him all
that much, though," she added. "According to our newly
installed video-surveillance system, he spent most of the
day moving his goods out of the office. My guess is now
that he's no longer able to sleep there overnight, he's just
going to walk rather than wait around for us to launch
eviction proceedings. And that's fine with me. Throwing
him out that way would take time and effort, and I don't
want to be bothered. The amount of back rent he owes
us isn't worth it. Besides, based on what Chris had to say
about him earlier, I'm happy to be shuck of him."

"What did Chris say?" B. asked.

"Earlier this week he asked me about work, and I
mentioned Harvey McCluskey's name. A few months
ago Chris told me that friends of theirs bought a house

where McCluskey did the home inspection. After they moved in, they discovered there were termite issues that he never mentioned in his inspection. The problem was serious enough that had they known about it in advance, they never would have gone through with the transaction."

"So the guy's both a bully and a cheat," B. observed, "and I can't help but wonder what else. Maybe we should have Frigg do a deep dive on him just for the hell of it. He may not be our problem any longer, but if someone comes asking for a reference, I'd like to know the full story, wouldn't you?"

"It can't hurt," Ali said. "I'll ask Stu to have Frigg do one in the morning, but isn't it about time we called it a night?"

With that she gathered up the wineglasses and took them to the kitchen. Then, after letting Bella out for one last walk, they all hit the hay.

|CHAPTER 25|

OAK CREEK VILLAGE, ARIZONA

Mateo Vega awakened on Sunday morning to a splash of blue sky and bright sunlight outside his window and to the surprising reality that he was in someone's guest room—not as a prisoner in a cell, not as a roomer with drunken housemates snoring in bedrooms nearby, but as a guest. Not only that, he was a guest with a job where he would be using his brain and his tech skills rather than duking it out on a loading dock in summer's humid heat and winter's chilling rains. No, he'd be working in a computer lab again after what was close to a twenty-year absence.

When the aroma of coffee permeated the room, Mateo rolled over, sat up, and surveyed his surroundings. The room was spacious and comfortably furnished with a large dresser, a small desk with a rolling chair, an easy chair, and a pair of bedside tables. The room also came with its own separate bath. Mateo got out of bed, treated himself to a long hot shower, and then dressed in the clothing he'd planned to wear home on the plane today. Except now he wasn't going home. He was staying here—

in Arizona. It still seemed more like a dream than reality, but the room was real enough, and so was the mug of coffee Stu handed Mateo when he entered the kitchen.

The night before, Stu had driven into the two-car garage at one end of what, to Mateo, seemed like an enormous house. They had walked in through a room lined with CPUs. There'd probably been twice that number earlier in the day at High Noon when Stu had given him a tour of the office, but Mateo was astonished to find so much computer power in a private residence. When he'd made a comment to that effect, Stu had shrugged.

"That's Frigg," he said, "Frigg with two g's, by the way. She's my AI."

"AI?" Mateo repeated. "You have your own private AI? How did that happen?"

"It's a long story," Stu had told him. "I'll tell you about her sometime, but for right now let's get you settled."

Mateo took his coffee to the kitchen table and sat down.

"I hope you like Frosted Flakes," Stu said, bringing an enormous box of cereal and a gallon of milk to the table. "This is what I usually have for breakfast. You're welcome to join me, but don't tell Cami. She thinks presweetened cereal is evil."

Mateo didn't think presweetened cereal was evil. As far as he was concerned, it was expensive, and he seldom treated himself to that kind of extravagance.

"My lips are sealed," he said.

Stu brought bowls and silverware to the table along with his iPad. "I was just talking to Sid, the guy who manages the Mingus Mountain RV park across the street from High Noon. Given the distance from here to the office and the fact that you currently don't have a vehicle, your staying here with me long-term doesn't make sense. The RV park is well within walking distance of work. According to Sid, April is when most of his snowbirds head home, and several of them are willing to offer their RVs as short-term rentals. If you're interested, that might be a good place to settle in temporarily until you find something permanent. Would you like his number?"

"Please," Mateo said.

Stu, busy pouring cereal into his bowl, nodded. Once he had added milk, he texted the phone number to Mateo, and Mateo sat there for a long moment staring at it.

"I still can't quite believe all this is happening," he said finally.

"Believe it," Stu told him.

"The only thing that would make it any better would be if I could tell my mother the good news," Mateo said ruefully.

"Why don't you?" Stu asked.

"I don't have her number," Mateo replied. "When I've tried sending letters, they come back marked 'RETURN TO SENDER.' For all I know, she died and no one bothered to tell me."

"Your mother's not dead," Stu said.

"She's not?"

Stu shook his head.

"How do you know that?"

"Before I ever sent you those hack simulations, I had Frigg do a deep dive into your background. Your mother is living in Walla Walla with people named Delfina and Ron Orozco."

"Delfina is one of my older sister's daughters," Mateo said. "She's probably helping out with Delfina's kids, but I had no idea they lived in Walla Walla."

"Would you like your mother's cell-phone number so you could call her?"

"You have her number?" Mateo asked uncertainly.

"I don't have it on me," Stu answered, "but I can get it." He paused and pulled the iPad closer to his cereal bowl. "Frigg, are you there?"

"Good morning, Stuart," a woman's computerized voice said. "I hope you're having a pleasant day."

"I am," he replied. "Would you please text Olivia Vega's cell-phone number to Mateo Vega's cell phone?"

"Of course," Frigg said. "Will there be anything else?"

"That's all, thank you."

As a second ding announced the arrival of another text, a dumbstruck Mateo sat there with his loaded spoon halfway between the bowl and his mouth. "That's Frigg?"

Stu nodded.

"And she had both my mother's number and mine available, just like that?"

Stu nodded again.

"But how . . . ? "

Stu sighed. "As I said last night, it's a very long story, and I'll be happy to tell you all about her sometime, but first why don't you give your mom a call? I'm pretty sure she'll be delighted to hear from you."

Leaving behind the rest of his Frosted Flakes, Mateo started back toward his room but then stopped and turned back to Stu. "If I have my landlord ship things to me, should they come here or to the office?" he asked.

"Until we get you settled somewhere else, here would be fine," Stu answered. "I'll text you the exact address."

"And one more thing," Mateo said. "Is there a dress code at work?"

Stu laughed outright. "If you're asking whether we all

wear suits and ties, that would be a definite no. Wear what's comfortable. What you have on now is fine."

Nodding, and with that in mind, Mateo returned to the guest room, dialing Randy Wasson's number as he went.

"How'd it go?" Randy asked. "And when do you need a ride home from the airport?"

"I don't need a ride because I got the job," Mateo answered. "I start tomorrow."

"Good for you and bad for me," Randy grumbled. "As I said, you're the best roomer I've ever had."

"But could you do me a couple of favors?"

"What kind of favors?"

"There are some books in my room that need to go back to the library. And then, if you wouldn't mind packing up my computer and clothes and shipping them to me? Oh, and my Bose earphones, too. Everything else can stay. You can check to see if the other guys want any of my stuff. If not, just toss it."

"I'll be glad to," Randy said. "Where do you want things shipped?"

"To the place where I'm staying right now. I'll text you the address. Once you know what the shipping costs come to, I can reimburse you."

"Not to worry," Randy said. "Your rent is paid to the end of the month. I'll take it out of your security deposit. That will more than cover it. In the meantime, man, I'm glad things are working out for you. You deserve it."

"Thank you," Mateo murmured. "You've been a lifesaver. I'm grateful for everything you did for me."

When the call ended, Mateo sat down on the side of his bed and stared at what he knew to be his mother's phone number. It was just after nine on a Sunday morning. He didn't know anything about Walla Walla, but if there was a Catholic church anywhere nearby, and he was sure there was, his mother would be getting ready to go to Mass. She answered after the second ring.

"Hello?" she asked warily. Her voice sounded much older than Mateo remembered, and obviously she didn't recognize the phone number.

"It's me, Mom," Mateo croaked, forcing his voice past the lump in his throat. "It's Mateo."

He heard a gasp from the other end of the line. "Mateo, really?"

"Really."

"Where are you? Eddie told me you'd broken your parole and taken off. When I didn't hear from you, I thought you were dead."

"I'm not dead. When I tried calling, your phone was disconnected," Mateo said. "And when I sent you letters, they came back unopened and marked 'RETURN TO SENDER.'"

"I never saw them," Olivia said. "But where are you?"

"In Arizona."

"But what about being on parole? Are you allowed to go out of state?"

"I came for a job interview, Mom, and I got it. The people I worked for before I went to prison gave me a job and a second chance. I start tomorrow. They'll notify my parole officer about where I am and what I'm doing."

There was a long pause before his mother spoke again. "I'm so happy you're okay," Olivia murmured at last, "so happy to know you're alive. It's an answer to my prayers."

"What's going on with you?"

"After your dad died, I had to move out of the foreman's house. I lived with Eddie and Maria for a while. Then, after Delfina had twins, she had her hands full, so I moved here to help out."

"You have my number now," Mateo told her. "Call me whenever you want."

"I will, son," Olivia declared. "I surely will."

|CHAPTER 26|

COTTONWOOD, ARIZONA

Harvey spent Sunday morning at the Busy Bee Laundromat. He always washed his clothes on Sundays, more out of spite for his mother than for any other reason. As far as Ida Mae had been concerned, Sundays were meant for church and nothing else. She wouldn't have been caught dead with laundry hanging on her clothesline on a Sunday.

Maybe most of the rest of the world agreed with her, because Laundromats were hardly ever crowded before noon on Sundays. Sometimes Harvey thumbed through Sunday-morning papers left behind by customers who'd preceded him. Today, however, no newspapers were available, so he spent most of the time brooding about Princess Prius.

When he had started to go after her and Ali Reynolds in his office, most people—most sensible people—would have taken a step backward, but neither of them had retreated an inch. Come to think of it, that little black-haired Asian bitch had actually taken a step toward him, as if daring him to make a move. What an annoying pipsqueak! How dare she?

Harvey's phone buzzed in his shirt with Leonardo Bianchi's number showing on caller ID. "When are you coming by with my watch?" he wanted to know.

Harvey was surprised. "You've already got what I need?" he asked.

Leonardo chuckled. "You think my guys work Monday through Friday, nine to five? When somebody needs something fast, it's generally not during standard business hours. Besides, they owe me a favor or two."

"Where are you?" Harvey asked.

"The Cowpoke," came the reply. "Where do you think?"

When Harvey's clothes finished drying, he put on a clean but wrinkled shirt and headed for the bar. The gym opened late on Sundays, so he'd missed his morning shower. When he showed up at the bar half an hour later, Leonardo was in his customary spot. He turned and raised his glass in Harvey's direction.

"Top of the morning to you," he said with a grin, although it was already early afternoon.

"Same to you," Harvey muttered, settling onto the stool next to Bianchi.

Joe the bartender caught Harvey's eye. "The usual?" he asked.

Harvey nodded. As he sat there waiting for his beer to show up, he stared regretfully at his watch. The Rolex was the last remaining vestige of a different existence—the last time his life had been going in the right direction—and he was sorry to lose it. But wearing a Rolex on the beach in Mexico wouldn't be doing himself any favors. It would only attract unwanted attention—the worst kind of unwanted attention. After a moment he unfastened the clasp and pushed the watch down the bar until it came to a stop next to Leonardo's almost empty glass. The Big Dude was a serious drinker whose beverage of choice was generally vodka on the rocks.

He returned the favor by shoving a manila envelope in Harvey's direction. Opening it, Harvey examined the contents. His old driver's license was there, as was a new one with his photo and a new name—Harold Wilson McBride. A surprisingly legitimate-looking U.S. passport, also in that name, was accompanied by a properly stamped visa that would allow him to travel into the Mexican interior. Included in the packet was a sizable roll of Mexican pesos. Given the current value of the peso, that much paper money probably didn't amount to much, but it was enough to give Harvey a starting point.

"Looks good," he said. "Thanks."

"When are you planning on taking off?"

"Sometime soon," Harvey said.

He left the Cowpoke a little over an hour later, drove to Cornville, and took up his bird-watching station. Harvey had done his homework. He knew that a bird called the elegant trogon occasionally but rarely made appearances in central Arizona. He was prepared to tell anyone who asked that he'd heard one had been sighted in the area and he was hoping to spot it—but no one ever asked.

And nothing much else happened either. All afternoon there was no sign of movement inside or outside Princess Prius's home on Tuff Cody Trail. Toward evening, when Harvey was about to give up and call it a day, the front door opened and his target stepped outside.

|CHAPTER 27|

CORNVILLE, ARIZONA

Camille Lee's mother would have been deeply offended by how her daughter spent that Sunday. She devoted two hours in the morning to acing target practice at the shooting range—Sue Lee was opposed to guns of all kinds and in every circumstance. She spent the late morning putting in an hour at the Krav Maga gym—her mother didn't know a thing about Krav Maga, but Cami was pretty sure she wouldn't approve of that either. It came dangerously close to turning human bodies into deadly weapons. In the afternoon she cooked up a Crock Pot full of Kung Pao chicken and a batch of pork fried rice, using recipes her grandfather had taught her. Once the food was cooked, she sorted it into small containers so she could take them to work the next day and use them to stock the fridge in the break room.

Sue Lee wanted her daughter to marry and have kids, and when they spoke on the phone, she never failed to ask if Cami had a boyfriend. Cami had male friends, yes. Boyfriends? No, and she was perfectly happy with her social life just the way it was. She enjoyed the people she met at the gym and the shooting range, and she liked the people at work. The fact that Stu, Lance, and even the new guy, Mateo, had pitched in to help install her home's surveillance system meant a lot to her.

Getting the bases of those individual units pounded into the rock-hard ground in the yard and assembling the individual units had taken a lot of physical effort. So although the solar-powered lights and cameras were in place, the system was not yet functional. Since the vandalism attack that had wrecked her tires had happened overnight, Cami waited until late afternoon before going out to work on the system. She wanted to fine-tune things at a time of day when she'd be able to adjust the camera angles to cover the largest areas in and around her yard with the best amount of nighttime focus.

Once fully operational, the cameras would send data to the cloud through Cami's home Wi-Fi hub, which would then automatically forward the resulting videos to her workstation at High Noon. Unfortunately, getting things up and running wasn't exactly duck soup. Having twelve individual devices located at various locations on her property was probably surveillance overkill, but better to be safe than sorry. However, unlike the slick system she'd just installed at High Noon's office complex, none of these components were designed to be refocused and adjusted remotely. Instead each one had to be focused not only by hand but by trial and error as well.

The solar-powered, motion-activated devices were considered to be state-of-the-art technology. Because this was all brand-new, however, it wasn't surprising that two of the twelve devices suffered from infant mortality. Once connected, they refused to come online at all. The problems could have been due to a failure in the solar battery pack, a difficulty in either the Wi-Fi connection or the camera, or all of the above. Whatever the issue, Cami was unable to successfully troubleshoot the problem on the spot in either of the malfunctioning units, and she was left muttering under her breath that the quality-control people at the Sunlight Surveillance manufacturing plant in Albuquerque, New Mexico, weren't doing their jobs.

Unfortunately, the two DOA devices happened to be mission critical. One was meant to be focused on the driveway approaching her house. The other was supposed to cover the carport. That meant the two duds, as well as two working units, had to be yanked out of the ground so the latter two could be replanted to focus on the driveway and carport. All that revision amounted to time-consuming physical labor.

Once the sun went down and darkness settled in, Cami had to resort to using a battery-powered lantern as a work light. By then, with all the remaining devices hooked up to her Wi-Fi, her next challenge was fine-tuning the focus on each of the cameras. IPad in hand, she examined the video feeds from each separate unit, leaving the one nearest the street for last. To adjust that one, she pulled her car out of the carport, then drove past the house several times, stopping after each pass and checking the resulting video in order to ascertain that license-plate details were in focus and readable. If any potential intruders thought they could drive a vehicle up to her house without being noticed and/or identified, Cami was pretty sure they would be dead wrong.

|CHAPTER 28|

CORNVILLE, ARIZONA

Harvey had been watching Princess's activity for more than an hour when he finally tumbled to what she was doing. What he'd originally thought was nothing but a batch of outdoor lighting was, more than likely, some kind of high-end surveillance! Okay, so puncturing her tires had been a stupid move on his part. She'd gotten with the program and hired someone to install a security system, but was it already up and running, or was she still working on it as he watched?

Someone less stubborn than Harvey McCluskey might simply have decided that at this point targeting Princess was too risky a proposition. But Harvey was who he was and exactly the same as he'd always been. Ida Mae had often told her son that he was too pig-headed for his own good, and her assessment still held true. The more he watched Princess work, the more he saw her bend over and straighten up, the more he studied her sweet little butt, the more he wanted her. She was totally focused on what she was doing and totally unaware that she was in mortal danger. That realization excited him, aroused him. He was sitting here just out of her line of vision and holding the power of life and death in his hands. Because that's exactly what he intended to do—wrap his hands around that fine little neck of hers and squeeze the life out of it.

To make that happen, Harvey needed to act soon. If he waited too long, he might miss the opportunity to take her by surprise. Still, waiting for the cover of darkness, he planned his attack. The other houses on Tuff Cody weren't that close to hers, but he would need to capture her in a way that kept whatever noises might escape her lips from attracting attention. That meant putting her out of commission instantly. The brass knuckles he'd used on Ida Mae had belonged to someone else, but Harvey owned his own pair now and kept them in his glove box, just in case. The thing was, he didn't want to kill Princess right off the bat. He wanted to have some fun with her first, so that initial blow had to be enough to knock her senseless without being deadly.

As the sun set, he retrieved his bedroll from his truck and unzipped it so it would be fully open when he used it to engulf her. Among the miscellaneous bits of junk in the back of his truck, Harvey located a roll of duct tape. He pulled off several long strips and hung them from the ceiling of the cab-high canopy. When it came time to secure his captive, he'd need to act fast. He wouldn't have the luxury of struggling to pry pieces of sticky tape loose from the roll.

It was full dark when Harvey's preparations were complete. Then, without turning on his headlights, he moved the truck across Cornville Road and into position, parking on the shoulder of Tuff Cody Trail, just short of Princess's driveway.

He had turned off the engine when, much to his dismay, the Prius suddenly backed out into the street. Harvey's heart sank. If she was leaving now, he'd missed his chance and she'd most likely spot his truck. Much to his relief, she didn't leave. Instead she backed a few yards into the street and then returned to the driveway. Stopping a few yards in, she left the Prius idling and got out of the vehicle. Approaching the nearest yard lamp, she messed with it for a time. After repeating the process twice more, she must have achieved what she regarded as a satisfactory result.

Pulling back into the driveway, she cut both the engine and the lights. By then Harvey was already on the move, sprinting toward her, bedroll in hand. If she had exited the vehicle immediately, things might have been different. Instead she stayed in the driver's seat for a few moments with her head bent over what he supposed was the iPad she'd been using all afternoon. Whatever the cause, that small delay gave Harvey a chance to cover the distance between them without her becoming aware of her danger.

By the time she opened her door, Harvey was already in position. As she emerged and began to straighten up, he threw the opened bedroll over her body, completely enveloping her. Lifting her off her feet with one arm, he punched her hard with his brass-knuckled fist before she could let out a cry of alarm. With her head covered and invisible, he missed his target. The blow intended for the side of her skull landed instead on the cushioning flesh of her ear. Still, it was enough to do the job, and she immediately fell limp in his arms.

As a heavily burdened Harvey struggled, he was dismayed to hear an invisible dog barking like crazy from a nearby house. That was the last thing he needed—a damned dog alerting the whole neighborhood that something was amiss. Not only that, Princess was heavier than he'd expected her to be, certainly heavier than she'd looked from a distance. By the time they reached the truck, he was panting and out of breath. With the dog still making a racket, Harvey needed to be gone in a hurry.

Afraid of being caught, he hefted Princess over the tailgate and rolled her onto the still-inflated mattress. Spooked by the dog's continued barking, Harvey rushed through the process of securing his captive. Even so, she was beginning to stir as he finished the job. To be on the safe side, once he removed the bed roll, he slapped a layer of duct tape across her mouth, then slammed the door on the canopy shut, locking it for good measure.

Harvey had planned to go into the house in search of any ready cash or valuable jewelry, but the stupid dog put an end to that idea. Instead he started the engine and drove past Princess's driveway in a reasonably sedate fashion before making a slow U-turn in front of the house on the far side of hers. Only when he turned right off Tuff Cody Trail and onto Cornville Road did he hit the gas pedal and speed away.

Harvey didn't turn back toward Cottonwood. Instead he drove east, aiming for I-17. He knew he was headed first for the All-American Canal, with the border crossing in Calexico his eventual destination. Those were both several hundred miles to the south and west, but before going there, Harvey and Princess had a date somewhere to the north of that—maybe in some empty corner of Arizona desert on the far side of Seligman or Kingman.

Somewhere out there, Harvey told himself, *I'll find a place that will fit the bill just fine.*

At about the same time, however, he happened to glance at his gas gauge and realized with a start that he'd made a terrible tactical error. He had been so caught up in stalking his prey and taking her captive that he'd neglected to fill up before launching his attack. With the gauge sitting at only half-full, he couldn't travel nearly as far as originally intended, and stopping for gas with her in the back of the truck was out of the question. If she somehow came around and started yelling or pounding for help, Harvey would be in deep trouble.

No, he decided, he'd need to find a suitable spot much closer to hand. During the time he'd lived in Prescott, he'd palled around with a guy who liked to go prospecting in the wilderness area south of Mayer. Harvey had accompanied him on some of those expeditions where they'd used a tangle of primitive forest roads for both coming and going. No doubt somewhere off one of those dirt tracks he would find a location isolated enough to serve his purpose. With that in mind, when Harvey reached the southbound merge onto I-17— that's the direction he headed all right, but only as far as Cordes Junction. There he turned off the freeway and drove west.

|CHAPTER 29|

PRESCOTT NATIONAL FOREST, ARIZONA

When Cami's eyes blinked open and she found her-self imprisoned in the back of a moving pickup truck, she had no idea that her next-door neighbor's dog, an obnoxious corgi named Lizzy who was usually the bane of Cami's existence, would make all the difference in whether she lived or died.

Helen Wilson, an eighty-something longtime widow and Cami's next-door neighbor, was an Anglophile of the first order. Every flat surface in her home served as a shrine to the primary heroine of Helen's existence, Her Majesty Queen Elizabeth II. Helen's walls contained visual displays of all things queen-related. The collection of slightly faded posters and yellow-tinged photos chronicled Queen Eliz-abeth's public life. She was pictured wearing her World War II uniforms, her wedding dress, and her coronation robe. There were pictures of her standing straight-backed and grim during Princess Diana's funeral and happier, newer ones that featured her with her great-grandchildren. Helen Wilson's home contained a motherlode of Queen

Elizabeth memorabilia—from commemorative teacups to ceramic dolls to salt and pepper shakers. Helen's holiday visitors were often surprised to find that her Christmas tree was decorated with an amazing assortment of Queen Elizabeth–themed ornaments.

That Sunday evening Lizzy—Helen's corgi named after the queen herself—barked steadily for the better part of half an hour. Harvey need not have worried or rushed. It turns out Helen was a believer in that old adage about "early to bed, early to rise." She had taken to bed at her usual time—seven thirty—and once she removed her hearing aids, Helen Wilson didn't hear a thing, Lizzy's perpetual barking included.

When Cami awakened, however, a noisy corgi was the last thing on her mind. As she slowly regained consciousness and struggled to find her way through a debilitating mental fog, she tried in vain to sort out where she was and how she'd gotten there. Her head throbbed. The whole right side of her face felt as though it were about to explode, and the intensity of the pain made thinking challenging. She seemed to remember that she'd been out in the yard or maybe in her car, but she wasn't clear on exactly why she'd been there or what she'd been doing. All of that was a complete blur. Someone must have attacked her while she was outside, but she had no idea who it was or how it had happened. Besides, who would have done that? Who did she know who bore her this kind of animosity? Why was she in the back of a strange moving vehicle with no idea of how she'd gotten there or where she was heading?

Gradually Cami's senses cleared, and the first thing that registered was the smell—a sweet, slightly musky odor that she knew she'd encountered before, but where? When?

Closing her eyes in concentration, the answer came to

her at last: Harvey McCluskey's cologne! She was lying on a bed of some kind in the back of his pickup, and the bedding reeked of the same cologne that had wafted from his office when Cami and Ali had gone to roust him out of bed. So was that what this was—revenge for being evicted?

With her head still pounding, it hurt too much to move, so Cami lay motionless for a time in total darkness broken only by the passing of occasional headlights. Rather than struggle with the unknowable, Cami tried to focus on what was real. There was a gag of some kind over her mouth. Her hands and legs were tightly bound, although she couldn't be sure how those restraints had been constructed. Were her mind clearer, Cami might have realized sooner that in his frantic hurry her captor had made another strategic error. Rather than fastening her hands behind her back, he'd bound them in front of her.

Once that reality dawned on her, Cami took immediate action, using her bound hands to rip what turned out to be several layers of duct tape off her mouth. With the gag gone, she opted for maintaining her silence. No one was around, so screaming for help would do nothing but alert her captor to the fact that she was awake and coming to her senses. Cami might not have made any noise with her mouth uncovered, but she put that new reality to good use. Using her teeth, she peeled away the layers of duct tape that had been wrapped around her wrists. Every motion of her head made her want to scream with pain, but she kept on, because she knew that freeing her hands was the only way to save her life.

Cami had no idea how long that cumbersome process took. With her hands finally free, she used her fingers to explore the damage to the side of her head. The bloodied flesh of her ear was swollen to twice its usual size, and it was still seeping in spots, but there didn't seem to be any gaping wounds on her ear or her scalp. Next she turned to the task of removing the tape from her legs. Working mostly in the dark, that wasn't easy either. She was still involved in that task when the truck veered to the right and came to a stop. Once it lurched forward again, everything in the truck bed shifted to one side, including Cami. Caught off guard, she tumbled off the mattress and blundered into what felt like a collection of loose boxes, slamming into one of them with her damaged ear. It took every bit of grit she could muster to keep from howling in agony. As the truck got under way again, Cami noticed that now there was far more traffic than before. She suspected that they had just merged onto a freeway, most likely I-17. Considering the right-hand turn, she thought they were heading south toward Phoenix.

While working on the tape, she'd tried to come up with some kind of game plan. Her two choices were simple— fight or flight. McCluskey had most likely overcome her earlier because he'd taken her by surprise from behind. In the gym Cami had managed to deck more than one surprised opponent Harvey's size or even larger, but that was with all her faculties intact. There was a possibility that her head wound might have compromised her balance and reaction times. In other words, flight was it, and to make that happen, she needed to get the hell out of the truck, something that had to be accomplished before he came looking for her. The only way for that to work would be to throw herself out of the truck while it was still moving.

Once Cami's legs were free, she crawled to the truck's tailgate. On the way, she encountered the roll of duct tape. Thinking it might prove useful, she stuck it on her wrist like an oversize bracelet so as not to lose track of it. At the tailgate, she quickly found the latch. Unfortunately, when she tried turning the handle, it was locked, most likely from the outside. In other words, her only means of escape would be to break the window—but how?

Turning back to the interior of the truck bed, she searched for a suitable implement. With no toolbox to be found, Cami decided McCluskey evidently wasn't a DIY kind of guy. First she dug through the loose junk littering the truck bed. Then she searched through the contents of the various banker's boxes. Most of those were filled with articles of clothing, but finally, when one of the boxes rattled, she opened it and hit pay dirt.

The first thing her searching fingers encountered was a small pocketknife. The blade wasn't big enough to serve as a real weapon, but she snatched it up anyway. When she shook the box a second time, she was rewarded with another rattle. This time her fingers closed around something metal—a wooden-based trophy of some kind. Cami had no idea how sturdy it would be, but it was the best thing she'd found so far.

Thinking that the middle of the slightly curved back window would be the weakest part, she grabbed the top of the trophy and threw it with all her might. To her ears the noise as the tempered glass shattered into hundreds of pieces sounded as loud as the crack of a firearm. She held her breath for several moments. If Harvey had heard the sound or felt the blow, he'd pull over and come to check on her, but the truck kept right on moving.

Feeling through the layer of broken glass on the floor, Cami finally located what was left of the trophy. It had broken into two parts, with the wooden base separated from the metal. She left the wooden piece where it was and stuffed what remained of the metal part into another pocket. It wasn't much of a weapon, but it was better than nothing.

Cami's next problem was figuring out the best way to exit a moving vehicle without ending up dead in the process. She would need as much cushioning as possible, so she crawled back to the boxes and went straight for the clothing. She dug through several boxes until she found a pair of sweats. They were huge. She had to use duct tape to fasten the pants around her waist, and it took two more strips of duct tape around each ankle to turn the sweats into pantaloons that wouldn't trip her up when she tried to move. She was performing the same operation on the shirtsleeves when the truck did in fact slow down.

Lights from buildings as well as streetlamps told her they'd entered a town of some kind, but she had no idea which one. The problem was, her preparations weren't quite complete when Harvey executed a quick left turn followed almost immediately by a second one before Cami could make it as far as the tailgate. She was on her way there, crawling across the mattress, when the truck veered again, this time to the right. With clouds of dust pouring in through the broken window, Cami realized they were now on a dirt road, hurtling through the night at a speed far too rapid for her to risk jumping. Determined to be ready the next time the truck slowed, Cami worked her way back toward the tailgate once more. As she crawled across the mattress, the thick bedroll clumped up under her, and that gave her an idea. Here was a whole other layer of cushioning.

Dragging the bedroll with her to the back of the truck, she wiggled inside and zipped it up around her. Minutes later, when she felt the truck begin to slow once more, she pulled the bedroll as tightly as possible around her body before easing her way up and over the empty window frame. At the next curve, rather than leaping, she oozed her way out of the truck.

Tuck and roll, she reminded herself as she fell. *Tuck and roll.*

And that's exactly what she did. She hit the ground hard, temporarily knocking the wind out of herself and sending herself rolling over and over, away from the departing truck. She came to an abrupt halt moments later when her lower right leg slammed hard into something solid on the shoulder of the road—the post of a guardrail as it turned out. The sharp pain that shot through her body took away what little breath she'd regained, and her first agonizing attempt to move the newly injured limb told her it was broken.

Lying still in the darkness, she listened, hearing the rumbling sound of the pickup fade into the distance. That was a relief. It meant he hadn't figured out she was gone—at least not yet. As soon as he did, however, Cami knew he'd come back looking for her. And if he found her—if she was still here . . .

Some way or other, broken leg or not, Cami knew she had to put as much distance as she could between herself and the road.

Escaping the confines of the bedroll with her injured leg was absolute agony. Standing up and walking was impossible. Her only remaining option was to crawl on her hands and one good knee, dragging the useless leg behind her. She was tempted to abandon the bedroll, but at the last minute she didn't. Instead, with every agonizing movement, she pulled it along behind her. If McCluskey came back looking for her, the bedroll's khaki-colored outer layer might provide some measure of camouflage.

The rising moon gradually lightened the desert landscape around her. The ground at hand was mostly filled with winter-dead grass that provided almost no cover. As

Cami inched past a scrawny mesquite tree, she heard the sound of an approaching vehicle. Barely fifty feet from the road and still out in the open, she threw the bedroll over the top of her body and then lay deathly still beneath it, holding her breath, with the sound of her thumping heart in the foreground and the noise of the approaching truck in the background. After what seemed forever, the vehicle sped by without slowing. Once it went past, Cami let out her breath and gasped for air. Since it hadn't slowed, maybe that meant it had been someone else's vehicle, but Cami doubted that was the case. It seemed far more likely that McCluskey had discovered she was gone but with no idea of where or when, he'd doubled back looking for her. He might have missed seeing her this time past, but that didn't mean she was safe.

As soon as Cami's pounding heart stilled, she caught her breath and resumed her desperate life-or-death flight. Every movement was excruciating. The rough ground pulverized her bare hands. Every creep forward threatened to dislodge the makeshift duct-tape belt anchoring Harvey's oversize pants to her body, and after every tiny advance she had to pause long enough to pull up the pants and drag along the bedroll. By now, however, she realized that bringing the bedroll with her was an absolute necessity. It may have been early April, but here in the high desert, it was bitingly cold.

Once more she heard a vehicle coming her way. This time it seemed to be traveling more slowly. She froze in her tracks and again pulled the bedroll over her body. Forcing herself to lie perfectly still beneath it, she held her breath and listened for what she feared most—the dreaded sound of a closing car door, because if Harvey McCluskey found her here, Cami Lee knew she was dead.

|CHAPTER 30|

PRESCOTT NATIONAL FOREST, ARIZONA

As Harvey McCluskey drove along, he was pleased with himself. He had bagged the snotty little bitch with no trouble at all. If it hadn't been for that blasted dog, the whole thing would have been perfect, but even so he'd made it work. He took I-17 south and then turned off at Cordes Junction. At Mayer he turned south again before merging onto Pine Flat Road.

He was confident that at this hour of the night no one would be out and about on this lonely stretch of roadway, giving him plenty of time and plenty of privacy to do whatever he wanted to that feisty little piece of cargo he had trapped in the bed of his truck. Sheer anticipation at being able to wring the breath out of her tiny body physically aroused him, and it made him almost giddy to know there was life in the old guy yet.

It turned out the road was worse now than he remembered, making for slower going in several places than he'd expected. Finally, several miles into the wilderness, he pulled off at a wide spot in the road, cut the lights, and climbed out of the cab.

"Come-to-Daddy time," he muttered under his breath as he walked toward the tailgate. When he saw the broken window, he stared at it in shocked amazement. With a sinking heart, he searched inside the canopy. When Princess was nowhere to be found, he was furious. Where the hell did she go? How long had she been gone? How did she get out?

Racing back to the cab, Harvey jumped inside, started the engine, and pulled an immediate U-turn. He would find Princess if it was the last thing he did, and once he found her, he would by God make her pay—in spades.

|CHAPTER 31|

PRESCOTT NATIONAL FOREST, ARIZONA

As Cami inched along, each foot of forward movement required supreme physical effort. Each squirm of her body sent new waves of pain shooting through her injured leg. She worried she might go into shock before finding shelter, but she struggled on. Beads of perspiration poured down her forehead and stung her eyes, but still she endured, dragging the now impossibly cumbersome bedroll behind her. She understood that once she stopped moving, her sweat-dampened clothing would instantly turn to ice. At that point she'd need the bedroll more than ever. She'd been cold just riding under the unheated canopy. Out here in the open, it was infinitely worse.

When Cami heard another approaching vehicle, she glanced back over her shoulder. The headlights were moving much more slowly. This time she was sure it was McCluskey, searching for her. Once again she pulled the bedroll over her and dropped to the ground, only this time when she stretched out, her bleeding fingers encountered something hard and round in the dirt next to her—a branch of some kind. Closing her hand around it, she pulled it close and felt a tiny glimmer of hope. Maybe she could use the stick to create a makeshift splint that would help stabilize her leg.

McCluskey went past without stopping. Perhaps he thought she would stick close to the roadway in hopes of covering more ground. When he was gone once more, Cami emerged from under the bedroll and examined her new prize—a slightly crooked hunk of dry mesquite.

All through this agonizing ordeal, the roll of duct tape had remained on her wrist, and now was the time to use it. Feeling along the length of her lower leg, she found a distinct bow that indicated the location of the break. Suspecting she needed to straighten it in order to keep from further damaging the leg, Cami gritted her teeth and pulled it as straight as she could manage. Despite her best effort to remain silent, a howl of agony escaped her lips. Fortunately for her, only nearby forest creatures heard the racket.

Once Cami could breathe again, she set about creating the splint. Fastening it directly to her leg wasn't an option. Instead she positioned the branch against the leg of the sweats and then used strips of duct tape to lock it in place. Being relatively still for the time it took to make the splint had chilled her. Now both hands shook with the cold, and her teeth chattered. She needed to get moving again. Once she did, with the splint in place, it was marginally easier than before.

The moonlight was brighter now. Just ahead of her she spotted a thicket of low-growing shrubbery. As the sound of the approaching pickup assailed her ears once more, she made for the undergrowth. It turned out to be a thick clump of manzanita that looked as though it might provide reasonably good cover. There was just enough room between the bottom branches and the ground for her to scramble underneath. As she did so, some small creature—a bunny, most likely—scampered past her and out into the open.

With the very last of her strength, Cami managed to encase herself in the bedroll. The ground might have been cold and rock hard beneath her, but for the first time since tumbling out of the truck she felt sheltered and somewhat safe. Cocooned in the welcome warmth of the down-filled bedroll, Camille Lee surprised herself and immediately fell into an exhausted and dreamless sleep.

|CHAPTER 32|

PRESCOTT NATIONAL FOREST, ARIZONA

As the night wore on, Harvey grew increasingly angry, to say nothing of desperate. He had to find Princess. If she somehow made it back to civilization and could identify him before he made good his escape, he was in deep trouble. An hour into his search, he drove into Mayer and located an all-night minimart, where he filled the gas tank. Inside he picked up a cup of coffee, a couple of premade sandwiches, some chips, and a flashlight.

Then he drove back out to Pine Flat Road and searched some more. The rough gravel surface of the road didn't lend itself to leaving behind any kind of prints. Several times he stopped the truck and went tramping off through the woods to search some more, but it was no good. Princess had vanished into thin air.

Finally, about two o'clock in the morning, Harvey was forced to give up. It was a good four-hour trip from here to the All-American Canal. He needed to drive there and ditch his truck before daylight. Once he'd staged his suicide, he'd hitchhike as far as Calexico and be across the border before anyone knew he was gone.

With that in mind, Harvey turned his back on the Prescott National Forest and headed east toward I-17. He was beyond angry, but he was scared as well. That tiny demon of a girl had outsmarted him and gotten away, and that made Harvey McCluskey mad as hell.

|CHAPTER 33|

SEDONA, ARIZONA

B. and Ali enjoyed a wonderfully quiet Sunday. Alonzo had taken the day off to visit friends and family in Phoenix, which meant they had the house completely to themselves, and they reveled in it. Late in the afternoon, B. had fired up the Weber and barbecued a pair of rib eyes. In the evening they had settled in to watch a few episodes of *Longmire* on Netflix. By the time the day was over, they felt as though they'd been on a tiny vacation.

They were both still asleep early Monday morning when B.'s phone rang on his bedside table. "Stu," he said as he picked it up. "Whatever's wrong?" After a slight pause, he added, "Yes, Ali's right here. I'll put the phone on speaker. Now, what's going on?"

Stu's anxious voice came through the phone. "Cami was supposed to relieve Lance at six o'clock this morning. She didn't show up, didn't call in, and isn't responding to calls or texts. Lauren was on duty, so Lance asked her to stop by Cami's place and do a welfare check."

Everyone at High Noon Enterprises knew that Yavapai County deputy Lauren Harper was now Lance Tucker's main squeeze. Lauren was Sedona born and bred, and she credited Ali's daughter-in-law, Athena, with inspiring her and getting her back on track during her high school years. Shortly after signing on with the Yavapai County Sheriff's Department under the old administration, Deputy Harper had gotten crosswise with her first partner, Tom Doyle, a chauvinistic old-school guy who specialized in sexually objectionable hazing and bullying. When Lauren pushed back, Doyle succeeded in having her sidelined to a lowly desk job at the Oak Creek Village Substation. That was where Ali had first encountered Lauren, when she'd provided invaluable help in handling fingerprint evidence from a break-in attempt at High Noon.

Unfortunately for Deputy Doyle, once Dave Holman took over as sheriff, he knew where all the Doyle bodies were buried. Dave had more or less coerced the man into taking his retirement and going away while Lauren ended up back on patrol. How she and Lance had become an item was open to conjecture at High Noon, but Lance wasn't talking about it, and neither was Lauren.

"So?" B. was saying urgently into the phone. "What happened? Did Lauren locate her?"

"She did not," Stu replied. "Cami's car's there in the carport with the driver's-side door open and the key fob still in the cup holder. Cami's iPad and cell phone were both found inside the vehicle. The house is unlocked. She isn't there, but her purse is."

Alarmed now, Ali sat bolt upright in bed. "I can't imagine Cami going anywhere without her phone. Were there any signs of a struggle?" she asked.

"The open car door is suspicious," Stu answered, "but other than that the answer is no."

"So what's the situation on the ground right now?" B. wanted to know.

"Deputy Harper notified her supervisor of her findings, and they're apparently treating this as a possible kidnapping. My understanding is that detectives are on their way to Cornville right now. So is Sheriff Holman."

"And so are we," Ali asserted. "As soon as we're dressed, we'll be headed there, too."

"What about you?" B. asked.

"Mateo and I are on our way to Cottonwood to relieve Lance."

"Okay," B. said. "Be safe."

Ali and B. were out of the house in five minutes flat. With Alonzo not due home until much later in the day, they brought Bella along for the ride.

"What about all of Cami's Krav Maga training?" B. remarked as they exited their driveway onto Manzanita Hills Road. "I would have thought she'd be able to defend herself."

"Not if someone caught her completely off guard," Ali said grimly. "I'm guessing she was overwhelmed before she had a chance to fight back."

"But who would do such a thing?" B. wondered.

Ali shook her head. "I have no idea."

On the trip to Cornville, B. disregarded all suggested speed limits. They arrived at Tuff Cody Trail far sooner than they should have, pulling up next to a cordon of emergency vehicles at the same time newly elected Sheriff Holman arrived in his Interceptor.

Ali was about to begin threading her way through the

parked vehicles when Dave stopped her. "This is a crime scene, Ali," he said. "You can't go in there."

"But . . ." she began.

B. and Ali had supported Dave in his run for office, but at that moment their participation counted for nothing. "No buts," he told them firmly. "I said no, and I mean no!"

"But someone needs to get a look at Cami's iPad and cell phone," Ali argued. "According to Deputy Harper, both were found inside her vehicle. There's a good chance one or the other may contain important evidence."

The flash of annoyance on Dave's face made it clear that he didn't like hearing information on the case from someone outside his department. "What kind of evidence?" he wanted to know.

"Cami's car tires were damaged while her vehicle was parked in her carport the night before last, and installing a surveillance system seemed like the prudent thing to do," Ali explained. "The hardware was installed but not connected on Saturday. We believe she might've been working on completing the installation at the time she disappeared. If the system happened to be up and running, it's possible it may have picked up something. If so, the resulting video might be stored on her iPad."

"Nobody's going anywhere near Cami's vehicle or her iPad until my crime-scene people are done with them," Dave declared. "Is that clear?"

Ali nodded reluctantly. With that, Sheriff Holman turned his back on them and stalked off. When a frustrated Ali glanced in B.'s direction, however, she saw a thoughtful expression on his face.

"What about her cloud account?" B. asked. "Is

there a chance her surveillance video might be stored there?"

Everyone at High Noon was encouraged to have both their work and private computers and devices set to back up automatically on a daily basis. Nodding her understanding, Ali reached for her phone and dialed Stu's number.

"What's happening?" he asked.

"We're at the scene," Ali said. "Naturally, they won't let us anywhere near the action, which means we can't lay hands on Cami's iPad. Is it possible for you to access her cloud account to see if any surveillance footage turns up there?"

"I can't," Stu said at once, "but I'm pretty sure I know someone who can."

"I think I do, too," Ali agreed, "and it's about time Frigg earned her keep."

A worried and very tired Lance showed up at the crime scene. He was every bit as anxious as B. and Ali, and even more upset than they were about not being allowed closer to the action. They were in the process of bringing him up-to-date when Ali's phone rang with Stu's face showing on caller ID.

His voice was nothing short of exuberant. "Frigg can't access the cloud right now," he said. "That's going to take some time, but it turns out Cami's laptop is still at home, and Frigg was able to hack into that."

"And?" Ali asked breathlessly.

"Cami was working on the surveillance system Sunday afternoon and evening, focusing each of the individual cameras and setting them to automatically upload video files to both her home computer and the cloud."

Holding her breath, Ali could barely speak. "And?" Ali repeated.

"And several of them got a clear shot of Cami's attacker," Stu answered. "He threw what looked like a bedroll over her and then whacked her upside the head, knocking her out cold. Then he picked her up and packed her off."

"Could you identify him?" Ali asked.

"I sure as hell could," Stu growled in reply, "and it's someone we know all too well. Harvey McCluskey."

Ali sucked in her breath. "Is this because of the eviction?"

No one replied to that question because no one had to. For everyone within earshot—Lance, B., and Stu—the answer was painfully obvious. Of course it was.

"The next order of business," Ali said, "is to have Frigg go to work on a background check on McCluskey."

"Ordinary or complete?" Stu asked.

"Both," Ali replied, "and the sooner the better."

"Will do," Stu said. "I'm on it."

When the call ended, Ali started toward the barrier of police cars.

"Wait," B. said. "Where are you going?"

"To tell Sheriff Holman that we've identified his suspect." She repeated the same sentence to the hapless deputy who attempted to halt her progress. Something in the set of her jaw must have gotten through to him, because he stepped aside and let her pass.

Dave, catching sight of her as she marched through the parked vehicles, hurried toward her with a thunderous look on his face. "I thought I told you—"

"We've identified your suspect," Ali said.

He stopped in his tracks. "You have?"

She nodded. "We were able to access Cami's computer files directly, including her uploaded surveillance footage. We have the attack itself on video. The guy you're looking for is named Harvey McCluskey. He's been renting an office from us for the last year or so, but he quit paying rent a couple of months ago. We're in the process of starting eviction proceedings."

"So that's his motive, then?"

"Most likely," Ali answered, nodding again. "At least that's how it looks to me."

"Okay," Dave said. "We'll get right on it. I'll get his vehicle information and post a BOLO. If he's driving around Arizona, somebody's LPR is bound to nail him sooner or later."

Ali knew enough copspeak to understand that LPR stood for "license-plate recognition," a camera system installed in all police vehicles that registers plate information for every passing vehicle.

"And about earlier," Dave added after a moment. "I'm sorry."

"Not to worry," Ali assured him. "You were only doing your job."

|CHAPTER 34|

Mateo Vega was sound asleep well before seven when Stu pounded on the door. "Wake up, Mateo," he said urgently. "We've got to go."

Mateo pulled on yesterday's clothes and hurried out into the hallway. "What's wrong?"

"Cami didn't show up for work this morning. She may have been kidnapped."

Minutes later, when Mateo scrambled into Stu's idling pickup, there were two travel mugs full of coffee waiting in the cup holders. "Hope you like it black," Stu said. "If you're a cream-and-sugar guy, you're out of luck."

"Black is fine," Mateo said. "Thank you."

He was in the truck when Stu placed a call to B. Simpson and Ali Reynolds, bringing them both up-to-date about what was going on with Cami. Mateo listened in silence to both that phone call and to Stu's subsequent communication with Frigg.

"Where do you want me to send the dossiers?" Frigg asked.

"Send them to my computer at High Noon," Stu told her. "That's where I'm headed."

"Very well," Frigg said. "I'll get right on it."

Mateo was astonished by what he'd just heard and by the easy conversational way the AI's computerized voice spoke. He didn't say anything about that until Stu ended the call.

"Frigg almost sounds like a real person," he ventured.

Stu nodded. "Yes, she does," he agreed.

"So what's the difference?" Mateo asked after a pause.

"The difference between what?"

"You told Frigg Ali wanted two dossiers—one ordinary and one complete. What's the difference?"

"Ordinary dossiers are squeaky clean and can be shared with law enforcement. Complete ones may contain pieces of unauthorized information and are for internal use only," Stu replied.

"What kind of background check did Frigg do on me?" Mateo asked after another pause.

"Both," Stu answered at once.

"And what did you find out?"

"You mean other than the fact that you've just spent sixteen years in prison for second-degree murder?" Stu asked with a grin. "That appeared in both dossiers," he added. "In case you're interested, your mother's private information including her current address and phone number came from the complete one."

Mateo was stunned. *Has Stu Ramey just cracked a joke?* he wondered. The Stuart he had known in the past never would have. And was that the way things were going to work at High Noon? People were just going to mention Mateo's time in prison in passing as though it were nothing more than an ordinary piece of someone's personal history?

"You make it sound like being in prison is some kind of everyday occurrence," Mateo said finally, "as though it's no big deal."

"Maybe it isn't," Stu replied. "Are you under the impression that you're the only ex-con in the bunch? You might have a heart-to-heart chat with Lance Tucker one of these days. B. plucked him out of a juvenile detention center in Texas, and he found me holed up in a homeless shelter. What counts with B. Simpson is technical skill, and we've all got that in spades—you included."

"What about Cami?"

Stu shrugged. "She's the exception to the rule—born with a silver spoon in her mouth, got straight As all through school, and has never been in trouble a day in her life. Except for . . ."

Except for right now.

After a lengthy silence, Mateo changed the subject. "So Frigg's a hacker, then?"

Stu nodded. "The best one you've never met," he said. "She was created by a brilliant but incredibly misguided computer genius named Owen Hansen. Hansen's fondest desire was to be a serial killer when he grew up, and he built Frigg to work with him in that regard. She was his strategic planner, playing Bonnie to Hansen's Clyde."

"What happened?" Mateo asked.

Stu hesitated before he answered. "Hansen killed my best friend," he said finally. "I went after him for it, and in the end I brought them down."

"Them," Mateo repeated. "You mean you brought down both Hansen and Frigg?"

"More or less," Stu said. "Rather than go to jail, Hansen threw himself off a cliff on Mingus Mountain—that peak you see right up there on the far side of Cottonwood," he added, pointing through the windshield. "I figured once he was gone, so was Frigg, but that assumption turned out to be premature. As Hansen grew more and more unhinged and unpredictable, he quit following Frigg's strategic advice. Somehow she must have deduced that if he ended up out of the picture, she would be shut down as well, so she took steps to keep that from happening."

"That sounds like self-awareness," a stunned Mateo observed.

Stu nodded again. "It does indeed."

"But is that even possible?"

"At the time I didn't think so," Stu replied, "but she put a number of complex measures in place so that if Hansen disappeared, she was guaranteed to end up in my custody. I guess she decided that if I was smart enough to take Hansen down, I was smart enough to handle her."

"Are you?" Mateo asked.

Stuart Ramey shook his head. "I'm not sure," he said dubiously, "but so far, so good."

|CHAPTER 35|

On Saturday afternoon Stu had given Mateo a brief tour of the building and equipment, but the tour on Monday morning was far more comprehensive. At this point nothing had been done to set up a workstation for Mateo, something Cami had been expected to handle. With her currently AWOL, Mateo was left as a floater, shadowing Stu as he went from place to place, observing along the way. Things might have gone to hell in a handbasket at the home office here in Cottonwood, but according to the monitors all was well as far as the company's far-flung customers were concerned.

When Stu finally took a seat at his workstation, Mateo moved a rolling desk chair next to his. An instant later one of the wall-mounted monitors over Stu's desk began flashing bright red. Alarmed, Mateo immediately assumed it was an incursion alert of some kind.

"Not to worry," Stu explained quickly. "It's only a Howler from Frigg." He tapped out several keystrokes that turned on the audio connection.

"A Howler?" Mateo repeated blankly. "What's that?"

"Haven't you ever read the Harry Potter books?"

"Of course I've read the Harry Potter books," Frigg interjected. "Is there a particular passage you'd like me to find?"

"I wasn't talking to you," Stu told her. "I was asking Mateo Vega, High Noon's newest employee. He was hired on Saturday."

"Good morning, Mr. Vega," Frigg said politely. "So happy to meet you. I hope you're having a pleasant day."

Mateo squirmed uncomfortably in his seat. This computer program with a female voice probably knew more about him than he knew himself, but since Frigg was apparently waiting for an answer, he finally managed to utter a reply. "Glad to meet you, too," he mumbled.

"So what's up?" Stu asked.

"Are you aware that Ms. Lee is using a device called Tru Fit tracker to record her physical activity?"

"Yes," Stu said. "It's the only one that takes all her physical activity into consideration, including her Krav Maga workouts. Why?"

"Once I located Ms. Lee's password file, I was able to access her tracker program. Through its GPS system, I've now been able to locate Ms. Lee."

Frigg's delivery was calm and businesslike. Stu's response was not. "You have?" he shouted. "Where is she?"

"Six and a half miles southwest of a town called Mayer, Arizona, and approximately fifty yards north of Pine Flat Road."

Stu was almost rigid with excitement. "Is she alive?" he demanded.

"Absolutely," Frigg replied. "When I got that first hit on her location, her heartbeat and respiration indicated she was sleeping. In the last few minutes, her vitals have started indicating that she's awake now, although her body temperature appears to be much lower than normal."

"Send me the exact location, and I'll get the sheriff's department to dispatch Search and Rescue."

"I'm sending the coordinates now, but I can actually do better than that. The Tru Fit comes complete with a third-person tracking program for situations like this. Where should I send that?"

"Send it to Ali's cell along with any activation instructions."

"Will do," Frigg said. "Now, about those McCluskey dossiers," she added. "Information is starting to come in. Where do you want me to send it?"

"Ordinary to Ali," Stu said at once, "and complete to me."

"On it," Frigg said, and signed off.

As Stu dialed another number, an astonished Mateo was left shaking his head. "Frigg can do all that?" he asked under his breath.

"That and a whole lot more," Stu confirmed before speaking into his phone. "Ali? Frigg just located Cami. She's somewhere south of Mayer, about fifty yards north of Pine Flat Road. We've got a device-locating app working on her fitness tracker. Frigg is sending that to your phone."

"What terrific news!" Ali exclaimed. "I'll go let Sheriff Holman know."

When the call ended, Stu turned to Mateo. "Well," he said, "what are you staring at?"

"This is amazing," Mateo muttered, "absolutely amazing."

"It is," Stu agreed. "Any questions?"

"Only one," Mateo said. "What's a Howler?"

|CHAPTER 36|

PRESCOTT NATIONAL FOREST,
ARIZONA

This time as Ali marched through the vehicle cordon, the deputy in charge made no effort to stop her. Even Sheriff Holman seemed glad to see her. "Any news?" he asked.

Ali paused and held up her phone. "We've managed to locate Cami's fitness tracker," she told him, keying something into the screen. "I'm sending you the coordinates. What the numbers won't tell you in plain English is that she's north of Pine Flat Road, somewhere southwest of Mayer."

"Alive or dead?"

"Definitely alive," Ali responded. "The tracker records her temperature, respiration, and heart rate. She's been asleep, but now she's awake."

"I'll dispatch officers there immediately," Dave said.

"Not without me, you won't," Ali said. "I'm the one who happens to have the Tru Fit locator system up and running on my phone."

"But . . ." Dave began.

"As you said earlier, no buts," Ali countered.

"What if McCluskey's still there?" Dave asked. "What if he's armed?"

"So am I," Ali told him. "I have my Glock, and if the guy comes after me, I'm fully prepared to use it."

Dave Holman sighed in resignation. "What about a vest?" he asked.

"Not with me," she conceded.

"Will B. be coming along?"

"Of course," she said. "We're a matched set, and Cami works for both of us."

"All right, all right," Dave relented. "I've got a couple of spare vests in the back of my Interceptor. I can lend you two of those. Stop by and pick them up on your way past, and let the deputy know I gave you permission. I'll be right behind you."

|CHAPTER 37|

PRESCOTT NATIONAL FOREST, ARIZONA

When Cami's eyes blinked open, she was stiff and sore. Her injured ear throbbed like crazy, and her fractured leg ached from the inside out. She was cold, hungry, and thirsty, and she desperately needed to pee. But she was alive. Harvey McCluskey hadn't succeeded in finding her, and since she wasn't dead, she now needed to make her way back to civilization. She had no idea where she was, and neither did anyone else.

Slowly she wormed her way out from under the manzanita. Once outside the protective covering of the bedroll, she was instantly chilled to the bone, and that made the urge to urinate all the more intense. There was no way she could stand to undress or squat to do the job. Instead she had no choice but to simply let nature take its course. At first the liquid dribbling out between her legs was surprisingly warm on her flesh, but all too soon it turned frigid.

Once in full daylight and dreading what lay ahead,

she examined her lacerated hands. Crawling as she'd done the night before was the only option for getting back to the road and finding help, but her mutilated hands were nowhere near up to the task. Not only that, the material covering her one functional leg was so shredded that the skin underneath the ragged cloth was scraped raw. As Cami examined her daunting injuries, despair flooded through her. Finally, though, she shook it off. Since there was no one there to save her, Cami would have to save herself. If she could crawl, that's what had to be done.

But then, in a moment of inspiration, she glanced down at her duct-tape bracelet and realized there might be a solution. Reaching back into the manzanita thicket, she pulled out the bedroll. Dragging it behind her once more, she inched over to a nearby low outcropping of rocks. With some difficulty she raised herself into a sitting position and leaned against them. After extracting Harvey McCluskey's puny pocketknife from her pants, she went to work on the bedroll. Last night the down-filled canvas-like material had saved her life twice over, not only from the fall but also from the cold. This morning it would protect her hands and knees as she crawled back to the road.

First she sawed off a large triangular piece and used that to create a long shawl that she threw over her shoulders and fastened around her neck. As soon as that was in place, Cami felt instantly warmer. Next she created a sturdy knee pad for her good knee, securing that with a few more strips of duct tape. The roll was close to empty now, but she was almost done. With the knee pad in place, she tackled two of the corners, cutting them off so she could place her hands inside and on top of both the down filling and the outside casing. She fastened the makeshift mitten on her left hand with no difficulty. Doing the same thing with her already wrapped and less capable left hand was a ten-minute ordeal. By the time the job was done, the cardboard roll of duct tape on her wrist was completely empty. She could have discarded it on the spot, but she didn't.

Assuming she survived, in no small way that roll of duct tape had saved her life. Rather than tossing it away, she returned the empty cardboard bracelet to her wrist. Someday, she thought, I'll have it put in a shadow box and frame it. And then, for good measure, she realized she'd need to put a scrap of the bedroll in that shadow box as well. After all, Harvey McCluskey had used both the bedroll and the tape against her. Now, with their help, she was hoping to turn the tables.

|CHAPTER 38|

MAYER, ARIZONA

Lance had been off talking to Lauren when Ali slipped away to speak to Dave Holman. He returned to where B. and Ali stood, next to the Audi, slipping into borrowed Kevlar vests.

"What's going on?" he asked.

"Frigg just used the GPS on Cami's exercise tracker to locate her," Ali replied.

"She's still alive?"

Ali nodded.

"Where is she?"

"Somewhere off Pine Flat Road south of Mayer," B. answered. "We've got a device-location app running on Ali's phone. We're headed there now."

"I'm coming, too," Lance said.

"No you're not," B. said, shaking his head and placing a cautionary palm on Lance's shoulder. "You've already been up all night. We're going to be shorthanded at work for the next little while, and you're going to need all the sleep you can get. I want you to go back home and get some rest. We'll go look for Cami."

It looked for a moment as though Lance would object to being sidelined. Instead he nodded. "You're right," he agreed finally. "On my way. Let me know how she is, okay?"

"We will," Ali said. "We promise."

In the car and heading east on Cornville toward I-17, Ali keyed Pine Flat Road into the Audi's GPS system. Moments later a tinny voice announced that the trip would take fifty-five minutes. A glance at the speedometer told Ali that at their current speed the trip wouldn't take nearly that long.

For a time neither of them spoke. B. finally broke the silence. "So what's up?" he asked. "You're thinking something. I can smell the smoke from here."

"This is all my fault," Ali said. "If I hadn't taken Cami with me when I went after Harvey McCluskey, none of this would have happened."

"It might not have happened to Cami," B. conceded, "but it might well have happened to someone else. Because of the surveillance system, we now know who the culprit is, and we also know she's still alive."

"So far," Ali murmured, "but what if she's hurt?"

"If she is, we'll deal with it," B. said.

They were merging onto the freeway when Ali's phone rang. "It's Stu," she told B. "You're on speaker, Stu. What's up?"

"We think Cami's hurt," he answered.

"Why?" Ali demanded. "What's going on?"

"She's currently on the move," Stu said, "but Frigg believes she's crawling rather than walking."

"Are you kidding?" Ali asked.

"Not kidding," Stu replied. "Frigg compared Cami's customary steps per minute to her current movements. She appears to be moving only a few inches at a time."

"Let me call you back, Stu," Ali interjected. "I need to bring Sheriff Holman up to speed."

Moments later she had Dave on the phone and reported in.

"Okay," he said in response. "I'll have an ambulance and EMTs dispatched to the scene as well. Where are you right now?"

"We just turned southbound on I-17."

"I'm a couple of miles behind you because I'm just now approaching the intersection. I'm moving full out, complete with lights and siren. Once I pass you, tuck in behind me. I'm pretty sure B.'s Audi will be able to keep up with my Interceptor."

B. smiled and nodded. "I'm pretty sure it will," he agreed.

A minute or so later, Dave Holman's vehicle overtook them. Once he flew past, B. sped up until the Audi was directly behind the patrol car.

As they approached Mayer, Dave slowed to the posted speed limit. When they turned off Highway 89, an ambulance fell in behind the Audi, but with Ali's eyes focused on the red dot on her cell phone's screen she barely noticed. She looked up only as they turned onto South Jefferson Street. That's when Dave Holman pulled over and waved them past, allowing the Audi to assume the lead.

|CHAPTER 39|

PRESCOTT NATIONAL FOREST, ARIZONA

Inching along on the ground, Cami was aware of every tortured ache and pain. The fall from the back of the truck seemed to have done more damage than she'd realized, and there wasn't a spot on her body that didn't hurt. Her lips were parched. Her strength was flagging. Each bit of forward movement had to be followed by a period of rest. During one of those, she heard a flurry of vehicular traffic coming from the road. There was no way anyone in those passing cars could see her, but knowing there were people out there gave her hope that Harvey McCluskey wouldn't be among them. The last thing he'd want would be for his truck to be spotted anywhere on Pine Flat Road.

Then, to Cami's amazement, she heard a car door slam as a man's voice began calling her name. "Cami— Cami Lee, are you here? Can you hear me?"

Holding her breath, Cami froze to the ground. She couldn't tell for sure if it was Harvey's voice, but the caller knew her name? The only person who could possibly know she was here was her kidnapper himself, and if he was within hearing range right now, how long before he found her?

Krav Maga training or not, Cami knew that in her current physical condition there was almost nothing she could do to defend herself. Still, almost nothing was better than nothing at all. Desperately tearing off one of her makeshift mittens, she felt around until she located a sizable rock. With that gripped tightly in her bloodied fist, she prepared to resist to the best of her ability. Then she lay still and waited. A moment later the man called out again.

"Cami, it's Deputy Tommy Morales with the Yavapai County Sheriff's Department. Are you here?"

Could this be real? Cami wondered. Was a rescuer really at hand, or was this Harvey trying to trick her into revealing her location? Believing it to be the latter, she didn't respond or move. The speaker was near enough now that she could actually make out his footsteps, coming closer and closer. Yards away they stopped.

When the deputy spoke again, he wasn't speaking to her but shouting into his radio. "Deputy Morales here! I've got her! Repeat, victim is found, due south of my patrol car. Appears to be in rough shape. Send EMTs!"

Suddenly Cami felt a hand close around her wrist, the gentle fingers probing for her pulse. "Yes, she's alive," Deputy Morales continued into his radio. "She appears to be seriously injured but definitely alive." Then, suddenly, the hand that had checked her pulse moved to her shoulder.

"Hold on, Cami," he said quietly. "I've got you now. Help is on the way, and the EMTs should be here any minute."

With that, Cami opened her bloodied fingers and let the rock she was holding slip harmlessly from her grasp. She might have been parched, but there was enough moisture left in her body to allow tears of gratitude to flow from her eyes and drip down into the dirt.

Somehow help had found her, and she really was safe.

|CHAPTER 40|

PRESCOTT NATIONAL FOREST, ARIZONA

Outside of Mayer, South Jefferson Street became Pine Flat Road, a stretch of primitive roadway that was in actuality little more than a Forest Service road. B.'s Audi was in the lead, but due to the rough, washboarded surface of the street, the sedan was forced to move at a crawl. Ali glanced away from her phone screen long enough to notice that sheriff's department patrol cars were parked here and there along the shoulder. In other words, Dave Holman had done more about deploying assets to the scene than just summoning an ambulance.

Behind them a siren wailed. On a straight stretch of roadway, the ambulance surged past them, leaving the Audi in a swirl of dust. At the same time, Ali's phone rang. Sheriff Holman's photo was on the caller ID, so Ali switched over to speaker.

"Hello?"

"One of my deputies found her," Dave said. "That's where the ambulance is going."

"How far?"

"A little ways up and on the right. It sounds like she's in pretty rough shape."

Minutes later they pulled up behind the flashing lights of the now-stopped ambulance. Ali could see a group of men clustered together off the road to their right. As soon as the tires stopped moving, she was out of the car and running in that direction. Dave pulled over and leaped out of the Interceptor. He pounded after her, but he didn't bother telling her to stop. It would have been a waste of breath.

Ali didn't ask for permission to join the group of EMTs surrounding a loaded gurney. She simply pushed her way through. Cami lay faceup with her bloodied and swollen hands resting on a foil-topped warming blanket while someone attached an IV drip to one arm. Her eyes were closed, and her scraped and battered face was barely recognizable. One ear was swollen to twice its normal size.

"Cami," Ali breathed. "Are you all right?"

Dark eyes flashed open, and Cami looked up at Ali with her usual self-deprecating grin. "Not exactly," she whispered, "but I'm better now than I was a little while ago."

An EMT was speaking into a radio. "We're giving her liquids," he reported. "One leg's broken and may need surgery. Her hands look like she's been in a prizefight. We'll be transporting her to Prescott Community shortly."

"Harvey McCluskey, right?" Ali asked.

Cami simply nodded.

"Do you want me to call your folks?" Ali asked.

"Not really," Cami replied. "They'll be pissed. But

you'd better call them anyway. I'd do it myself, but I lost my phone."

And very nearly your life, Ali thought. "Your phone isn't lost," Ali said reassuringly. "I'll reach out to your parents."

"Excuse me, ma'am," one of the EMTs said, shoving Ali aside. "We need to get her out of here."

It wasn't a question of rolling the gurney over the rough ground. Several people simply stepped forward and carried it. B. appeared at Ali's side as the group headed for the ambulance.

"How is she?" he asked.

Rather than answering, Ali turned to him and melted against his shoulder. Then, after a moment, she held up her phone, dialed Stu's number, put the phone on speaker, and replied to B.'s question over that.

"Cami's alive and on her way by ambulance to Prescott Community Hospital. She's got a broken leg and some other injuries, I'm not sure how serious. But you know our Cami. She's pretty tough."

"Thank God," Stu murmured, "although I don't think the word 'tough' quite covers it."

"She asked me to call her folks. Could you have Frigg forward their numbers to me from her contacts list?"

"Will do."

"And please call Lance to let him know."

"No need to call him," Stu told her. "He came back to the office and is grabbing some z's on the daybed out back. He was pretty beat. I'll tell him as soon as he wakes up."

With that, Ali and B. headed for the Audi. Soon a series of texts came in from Frigg supplying the contact information Ali had requested, but she wasn't ready to make those difficult calls immediately. She needed some time to gather herself.

"Cami's parents are going to be fit to be tied," Ali told B. "I know from things she's said in the past that both of them disapprove of her taking the job with us. This will make the situation that much worse."

B. nodded. "Even so, you need to call them."

"But what should I say?"

"Tell them as much as we know," B. replied.

Ali tried the landline home number first, but no one answered. On a weekday morning, that made perfect sense. Next she tried Cami's father's office and cell phones. Cheng Lee didn't answer either, but when Ali dialed Sue Lee's office number, someone picked up after only one ring.

"Professor Lee," came the stiff, off-putting greeting.

"This is Ali Reynolds from Cottonwood," Ali said into the phone. "I'm Cami's boss."

"I know who you are," Sue Lee snapped. "Why are you calling me? What's happened?"

"There was an incident at Cami's home last night," Ali said. "She was kidnapped but somehow managed to escape. We've only just now found her. She's suffered some injuries and is currently in an ambulance on her way to Prescott Community Hospital in Prescott, Arizona."

"How badly is she hurt?" Sue Lee asked curtly.

"At least one broken leg," Ali said. "She was evidently severely dehydrated and has lots of cuts, scrapes, and bruises. She could have some internal injuries as well."

"Does this have anything to do with that job of hers?" The sneering disapproval in Sue's voice was obvious. And the question cut right to the heart of the problem.

"Probably," Ali answered after a pause. "Her attacker has been identified as a man named Harvey McCluskey. He's a former tenant in our office complex. I was in the process of initiating eviction proceedings against him."

"So this is your fault."

Ali sighed. "Probably," she admitted. "Cami wanted me to let you know what's happened. But, Mrs. Lee, if you're flying into Phoenix and need to be picked up at the airport, I'll be glad to come collect you and bring you to the hospital, or if you prefer, I can send someone else. Just let me know which flight."

"That's Professor Lee," Sue insisted, "not Mrs. As far as Camille is concerned, whatever has happened to my daughter is due entirely to her own foolishness. I have classes to teach and office hours to keep. I'm not going to disrupt my life to go flying off to Arizona just because she's gotten herself into some kind of trouble. You might check with my husband, though. Cheng has always coddled her. He may be interested in coming to her rescue, but I am not."

With that, Professor Lee hung up.

Almost unable to believe her ears, Ali stared at her phone for a moment before turning to her husband. "Did you hear that?"

"I certainly did," B. said. "I think now we have a pretty good idea why Cami is working for us here in Arizona rather than for someone closer to home in Silicon Valley."

"Yes we do," Ali agreed, "in spades! She needed to put some distance between herself and an extremely toxic mother."

Just then there was a sharp tap on the window behind Ali's head. When she turned to look, Dave Holman was standing outside the Audi. Ali buzzed down the window. "What's up?" she asked.

"That BOLO paid off big time," he announced.

"You caught him?"

"No, but we've located Harvey McCluskey's vehicle. It was sitting partially submerged in the All-American Canal west of Yuma just off I-10. A suicide note was found inside, but so far no body has been located."

"Do you really think he's dead?" Ali asked.

"I do not," Dave replied grimly. "I believe he faked the whole thing. I've asked the Imperial County Sheriff's Office to bring in tracking dogs to see if they can pick up his trail after leaving the vehicle. My best guess is that he's on his way to Mexico. I've contacted Border Patrol. They've alerted all sectors and are distributing his photograph to all personnel and posting it on their facial-rec systems. If McCluskey tries to escape U.S. jurisdiction by crossing the border, you'd better believe someone will grab him."

Dave walked away then, and Ali closed the window.

"Where to?" B. asked.

"Prescott Community Hospital," Ali replied. "On the way we'll pick up a Burger King Whopper Jr. patty for Bella. She won't mind waiting in the car."

|CHAPTER 41|

COTTONWOOD, ARIZONA

When Shirley arrived at the office on Monday morning, Stu introduced her to Mateo and then quickly brought her up to speed on everything that had happened overnight. Calm in the face of the ongoing crisis, Shirley spent some time helping Mateo negotiate the stack of employee-intake paperwork required to bring someone new onboard. When that was finished, she came into the lab area and worked with Stu and Mateo to create a new workstation. That's what they were doing when Ali's call came in telling them that Cami had been found alive but injured and was being transported to the hospital.

An hour later they were in the process of reallocating computer keyboards and reinstalling wall monitors for Mateo's use when Lance emerged from the back room smoothing his sleep-rumpled hair.

"What's happening?" he asked.

Stu told him, and Lance gave Mateo an appraising look. "If Cami's on the disabled list for the time being, we'd better get you up and running in one hell of a hurry."

"That's the whole idea," Stu said.

Once Mateo's hardware was in place, Lance, claiming he had rested long enough, took over the responsibility of showing Mateo the ropes, acquainting him with the various monitoring procedures, schooling him on how to respond to alarms indicating actual breaches or possible incursion attempts, and giving him brief introductions to the many arrows in High Noon's tech quiver that could be used to successfully counter such events.

During their practice sessions, Stu went back to performing the actual monitoring. In the meantime he kept an ear tuned to his police scanner. If anything turned up in the search for Harvey McCluskey, he wanted to be the first to know.

|CHAPTER 42|

Adelina Muñoz Padilla, a widow, was born in Mexicali and had lived there all her life. She had two sons: Alfredo, the older one, and Gabriel, the younger. Alfredo was a police officer with the Mexicali Police Department, and Adelina lived with him, his wife, Lupe, and their three kids.

Fredo had always been on the beefy side. In school he'd played rugby, while Gabe, smaller in build and much faster on his feet, had preferred soccer. In high school he was recruited—possibly illegally—to come to the United States on a full scholarship to a private high school to play on their team. Thinking her son would have access to both a better education and better opportunities in the States, Adelina had been only too happy to send him along.

What she hadn't seen coming was that while Gabe was in the United States on a student visa, he would fall in love with an American girl, Melinda, who would end up getting pregnant. They had married soon after the birth of their first child and had two more after that. While Melinda went back to school to earn a teaching degree, Gabe had been hired on with the U.S. Border Patrol to support the family. Once Melinda had her degree in hand, she'd been recruited to teach English at Calexico High School. After a couple of years of fighting red tape and to Adelina's great joy, Gabe had managed to be transferred to Calexico as well.

No one made homemade tamales the way Adelina did, and all her kids and grandkids adored Nana's tamales. Every Sunday afternoon, either Lupe or Fredo would drive her to the border, where she would walk across, dragging a small Rollaboard behind her. Inside the Rollaboard was everything needed for an overnight stay, along with a plastic bag filled with freshly made tamales. Once across the border, either Gabe or Melinda would pick her up and take her to their home. On Monday mornings the process was reversed, sans tamales.

Adelina's crossings were uneventful because everyone on both sides of the border knew her. They always smiled and waved her through. In fact, she was treated as something of a local celebrity. In all of Mexicali, she was the only woman who had sons working on both sides of the border fence—Fredo with the municipal police on the Mexican side and Gabe with Border Patrol on the U.S. side. Once upon a time, they might have checked the contents of her bag whenever she crossed the border, but not anymore.

That week was spring break in the Calexico school district, so rather than wake up early to ride with Gabe in the morning, Adelina was able to sleep in and get a lift back to the border from Melinda. Paying no attention to the surveillance cameras aimed in her direction, Adelina crossed over the traffic lanes and entered the guard shack to chat briefly with Gabe, who was stationed inside.

She hadn't even noticed that a man was following close on her heels as she approached the border, but the surveillance equipment overhead did. Suddenly an audible alarm chirped inside the shack. Gabe, realizing that someone suspicious had just registered on their facial-rec software, swung into action, pushing his mother aside.

"Hey, you!" he shouted at the man hurrying by. "Stop!"

But the man didn't stop. In fact, he broke into a run, which was a stupid thing to do, because not ten yards away and just on the far side of the official line Alfredo Padilla stood waiting. He'd been expecting his mother and watching for her arrival so he could call Lupe to come pick her up. He heard Gabe order the man to stop and then saw the guy make a break for it.

Fredo was seven years older than Gabe. He had started in the police force years before Gabe joined the Border Patrol, but Gabe was already a step or two up the ladder in terms of rank. For Fredo, however, there was good reason he stayed right where he was, content to be assigned to the border detail. And what was that reason? More than anything Alfredo hated paperwork with an abiding passion, and in this instance he understood exactly what was at stake.

If someone from the United States actually succeeded in making it across the border, the paperwork required of whoever had the misfortune of taking him into custody was an absolute nightmare, so Fredo decided on another course of action. He was just as burly and every bit as tough as he'd been in high school, so when the fleeing suspect came racing in his direction, Fredo did what rugby players do—he stepped forward, planted his feet, and stood firm.

When the suspect slammed into him at full speed, the force of the collision was enough to send the guy flying backward across that invisible line in the sand that Alfredo knew full well was there. Meanwhile Gabe raced forward to take the stunned suspect into custody.

Much later surveillance video would reveal that both Harvey McCluskey and Gabe Padilla were still on the U.S. side of the line when Gabe snapped a pair of handcuffs on his wrist, while Fredo stood smiling on the Mexican side with his arms folded across his chest.

A kid in the back seat of a passing vehicle happened to capture all the action on his cell phone, and the resulting video went viral on both sides of the border.

As for Adelina Padilla? From then on she was even more of a local celebrity than she'd been before.

|CHAPTER 43|

PRESCOTT, ARIZONA

At the hospital Ali and B. learned that Cami had been taken into surgery. Because Cami had put Ali's name on the necessary HIPAA form, the ER doc who tended to her initially was allowed to give them information.

"Ms. Lee is one gutsy girl," he said wonderingly. "First she wrapped herself up in a bedroll and then dove out of the back of a moving vehicle to escape her captor. That's how she broke her leg. Then she used a hunk of dead mesquite to create a splint. She attempted to set the bone herself, which must have hurt like hell. Unfortunately, it's not a clean break. Our X-rays indicate that several splinters of bone fragments remain near the break, and those must be surgically removed. That's why she's in the OR. Depending on what her surgeon finds, she may need a rod and screws to repair the damage. She also has a couple of cracked ribs and serious cuts and abrasions on both hands and legs from crawling on the ground to get away from the guy. In other words, she's going to be off work for a time and off that leg for even longer."

"What about her ear?" Ali asked. "That looked awful."

"It's badly swollen all right, but there's no permanent damage. That's where the guy hit her. If he'd landed that blow straight to her skull, she'd have a concussion for sure. All things considered, she's lucky to be alive."

When the doctor left, Ali and B. decamped to the waiting room outside the surgical pavilion. "Cami threw herself out of the back of a moving pickup?" Ali murmured. "'Gutsy' hardly covers it."

Her phone rang with a California area code showing. After the shocking conversation with Sue Lee, Ali had called Cami's father's numbers and left messages on both. She was glad it had taken Cheng Lee this long to return her call, because at least now she had some solid information to pass along to him.

Naturally he was dismayed to hear the news, but he was much less confrontational about it than his wife had been. He thanked Ali for the information, assured her that he would immediately make arrangements to fly into Phoenix, and yes, he would greatly appreciate being transported from the airport to wherever his daughter was at the time of his arrival.

"That's a relief," B. said when the conversation ended. "At least Cami's got one parent who gives a damn about her."

A few minutes later, B.'s phone rang with Alonzo on the line. Since there was no one else in the waiting room, B. put the call on speaker. "I'm about to leave Phoenix," Alonzo said. "Is there anything you need me to pick up on the way?"

"As a matter of fact, there is," B. said. "I'll need you

to drop by Prescott Community Hospital and pick up Bella."

"The hospital," Alonzo yelped. "What's going on?"

As B. began recounting the long story of everything that had happened, Ali leaned back in her chair and closed her eyes. Eventually the morning's emotional turmoil caught up with her. Feeling exhausted, she did the very best thing you can do in a hospital waiting room—she fell asleep. She was still sleeping when the ringing of her own phone, still resting in her hand, awakened her. When she looked at the screen, she saw Sheriff Holman's name and photo.

"Hello?"

"We got him!"

Ali could barely believe her ears. "McCluskey? You did? Where?"

"He was trying to cross into Mexico at the Calexico port of entry. He's been arrested and is being held in the Imperial County Jail in El Centro. We're in the process of putting together the paperwork to extradite him from California to Arizona. With any kind of luck, we'll be able to send someone to bring him back here tomorrow or the next day."

Ali was relieved. "Good," she murmured.

"And how's our girl doing?"

"Still in surgery."

"I've got to hand it to you guys," Dave added after a moment. "Without that surveillance video, McCluskey might have gotten away. He had a high-quality fake passport that had already passed muster. Knowing who the suspect was, we were able to provide Border Patrol with his driver's-license photo. Their facial-recognition program is what nailed him. So thank you for that, and please consider this my apology for giving you so much guff about your needing access to her iPad and cell phone."

Fortunately, we had Frigg for a work-around, Ali thought, but what she said aloud was, "Apology accepted."

"I just wish we knew what else McCluskey's been up to," Dave added. "There was duct-tape debris found in the back of the truck. When someone shows up at a crime scene with duct tape in hand, it's like he's driving around with a rape kit at the ready. I doubt this is McCluskey's first rodeo, so maybe when we run his DNA through CODIS, we'll get a hit."

Ali was struck by that chilling thought. Was it possible that Harvey McCluskey had been a serial rapist all along and nobody knew?

"They caught him?" B. asked when Ali hung up.

"Yup, he's in jail in El Centro. Dave's people are putting together the necessary paperwork to have him brought back here."

"Good," B. said. "I think I'll hitch a ride home with Alonzo and Bella. I'll leave the Audi here with you and take the Cayenne over to the office. With Cami out of commission, we're going to need Mateo up and running a whole lot faster than I anticipated. Since Stu and Lance will be handling their jobs and Cami's, too, the least I can do is take over Mateo's training."

Ali nodded. "Makes sense to me," she said.

Alonzo arrived sometime later. Once he and B. took off, Ali was left alone in the waiting room, thinking about what Dave Holman had said. Maybe this wasn't Harvey McCluskey's first venture into sexual assault. Frigg had created a detailed dossier on the man's life and times, but up to now life had been too hectic for Ali to read it. She was about to call Frigg and ask to review the material when a man in surgical scrubs entered the room.

"Ms. Reynolds?" he asked.

"Yes," Ali replied.

"I'm Dr. Harrison, Cami's surgeon. She came through the surgery just fine. It's a serious break, however, and she won't be able to put any weight on the leg for some time. She's in the recovery room right now. Did the people at the front desk give you a buzzer?"

Ali nodded.

"Good," the doctor said. "Someone will summon you once she's moved to her own room."

"Thank you for letting me know."

When the doctor left, Ali dialed Frigg. "Good afternoon, Ali," Frigg said. "I hope you're having a pleasant day."

"Not exactly," Ali responded. "I'm in a waiting room at the hospital where Cami just underwent surgery, but I need your help. I know you already sent me a complete dossier on Harvey McCluskey, but it's gone now."

That was Frigg's best trick. Once she sent a message, read or not, after a certain period of time it simply vanished from the recipient's device, leaving behind no digital trace for anyone else to follow.

"Could you please resend it? Since I'm going to be stuck here for the next several hours, I could just as well make myself useful."

"Would you like me to send an audio version?"

"As I said, I'm in a public place right now. Send a text version for the time being, and please start from the beginning. I want to know his whole history."

"Will do," Frigg replied. "Happy to be of service."

|CHAPTER 44|

PRESCOTT, ARIZONA

Once Cami was transferred from recovery into the ICU, Ali moved to a different waiting room, where a family waited for news about a teenage daughter who'd been seriously injured in a car crash. While they all struggled with a storm of emotions—fear, anger, and disbelief—Ali kept her nose buried in her iPad, reading the information Frigg forwarded to her and then scrubbed away again once Ali finished reading.

When the weeping parents emerged from the daughter's ICU room, with the father gravely shaking his head, family members waiting there exploded in sobs and wails of grief. Wanting to allow the stricken family some privacy, Ali left the room, only to run into Gordon Maxwell, the former sheriff of Yavapai County, out in the hallway.

He greeted her with a broad grin. "Just the lady I was looking for. How's your girl doing in there?"

"Cami's made it through surgery, and now she's in the ICU. How did you hear about it?"

"I may be out of the game, but Dave still keeps me

in the loop. I understand congratulations are in order to your people for IDing the suspect."

"Cami herself deserves most of the credit for that," Ali said. "If she hadn't spent her after-work hours fine-tuning that new surveillance system, we wouldn't have had a clue. So what are you doing here?"

Maxwell beamed at her. "My granddaughter just had a baby girl, which makes me a great-grandfather. Came by the hospital to meet her for the first time. Care for a cigar?"

The cigar in question was wrapped in pink cellophane.

"Congratulations, but no thanks on the cigar," Ali said with a smile. "I never touch the stuff. But how are you? Have you been keeping busy?"

"I've hooked up with an outfit called TLC—The Last Chance. It's a volunteer cold-case squad made up of a bunch of old geezers just like me—retired cops, DAs, and forensic folks from all over the country—who might have been put out to pasture but haven't found a way to get the job out of their systems. We work mostly very cold cases, even ones where some of that newfangled genetic stuff comes into play. We've also helped get a guy or two exonerated, which is only fair, I suppose."

The grieving family burst out of the ICU waiting room behind them, bringing their tumult of sorrow down the corridor with them.

"I should go," Maxwell said hurriedly. "Sure I can't interest you in a cigar?"

"No thanks."

"When Cami's up to it, you be sure to tell her I said hello."

"I will," Ali promised.

Just then her phone rang. This time she recognized Cheng Lee's number.

"How's Camille?" he asked as soon as Ali answered.

She told him what she knew, after which he moved straight into logistics. "I'll be coming in on a Southwest flight that arrives in Phoenix at ten past six. Can someone be there to meet me?"

"Of course," Ali said. "I will be. Can you text me the flight information?"

"Is Prescott big enough that I'll be able to rent a car if I decide I need one later?"

His unstated but nonetheless implied snobbery was all too clear. It seemed Cheng Lee doubted that intelligent life existed on the far side of the Colorado River. He probably considered Arizona to be a vast desert wasteland populated by cowboys and Indians and lacking in modern conveniences such as indoor plumbing and running water.

"There are several car-rental agencies here," Ali assured him. "Prescott Community Hospital is actually located in the Prescott Valley area, with a Hilton Garden Inn within walking distance."

"What about Uber?" he asked. "Do they have that?"

"I'm not sure," Ali answered. "If they do, I've never used one, but I'm pretty sure taxis are available."

"All right, then," he said. "I should be fine. I'll see you sometime after six. How will I know who you are?"

Ali looked down at her clothing. She was still wearing what she'd thrown on that morning when she and B. had raced out of the house for Cornville. Her worn jeans and tennis shoes topped by a faded Sedona High School sweatshirt probably weren't going to go over very well with someone accustomed to living in the rarefied groves of Silicon Valley.

"I'm tall and blond," Ali said, "with more than a hint of gray. I'll be holding an iPad with your name on it." *And I won't be wearing a Stetson or cowboy boots*, she added to herself.

"Okay," he said. "See you then."

Ali glanced at her watch. It was after two. She didn't need to leave for Phoenix right that minute, but she'd have to take rush-hour traffic into consideration as she headed for Sky Harbor.

Returning to the now-deserted ICU waiting room, Ali checked on Cami. She seemed to be sleeping, so Ali stayed where she was. Thinking of Cami's parents, Ali could only shake her head. No wonder Cami was so intent on putting down roots far from home, and Ali for one was glad she'd done so.

ICU visitors were only allowed in patients' rooms for ten minutes each hour, so Ali set the timer on her iPad and continued perusing Harvey McCluskey's history as reconstructed by Frigg. Public records revealed that he'd been born in Butte, Montana, in 1966. Both of his parents, Ida Mae Collins McCluskey and Leo Ray McCluskey, were deceased. The dates on their death certificates indicated they had died weeks apart in 1981. Ida Mae's manner of death was listed as homicidal violence and Leo's as suicide. Property records revealed their property on German Gulch Road had passed to their son, Harvey, upon Leo's death. It was sold to new owners in 1983, with proceeds from the sale held in trust for their son once he reached his twenty-first birthday.

Other than public records, Frigg had been unable to uncover much about Harvey's early life. It wasn't until the local newspaper, the *Butte Mountaineer*, began digitizing its content as opposed to microfiching it that the

AI was able to begin putting flesh on the bones of the story. Ida Mae had disappeared without a trace in the winter of 1981. Police investigators had focused their efforts on only one suspect—her surviving spouse, Leo. When he committed suicide weeks after his wife's disappearance, the case went cold. Once Ida Mae's remains were located and identified years later during an EPA-mandated cleanup of mine waste, the case was marked closed.

Despite having lost both his parents at such an early age, young Harvey seemed to have thrived. He graduated from high school with good, if not stellar, grades and excelled in both football and wrestling. During his senior year, he became the state wrestling champ. After graduation he joined the military and did a number of tours of duty, serving as an MP. After leaving the army, he moved to Las Vegas, where he'd worked for a number of years on casino security teams. So far, so good, but then Frigg had hit a content bonanza—the media storm surrounding the 2004 death of Harvey's wife, Maureen (Marnie) Richards, a nurse at Sunrise Hospital in Las Vegas.

Reading accounts of Maureen's fatal plunge into the depths of the Grand Canyon made the hair on the back of Ali's neck stand on end. Harvey and his bride of one day had been hiking down into the canyon when she tumbled to her death. The autopsy had shown no indication of foul play. A re-creation of the incident had suggested that her injuries were consistent with a fall rather than being pushed or propelled off the trail's edge. Marnie's death was quickly declared accidental, and no further investigation was deemed necessary. Reading about the incident, Ali wasn't so sure. With the waiting room currently empty, she felt free to summon Frigg.

"I hope you're finding my material helpful," the AI said.

"I am," Ali answered, "but I'm curious. Did Harvey receive any kind of financial benefit from Maureen's death?"

"Yes, he did," Frigg responded. "She had group life insurance through work. Six months after she died, an insurance payment in the amount of one hundred thousand dollars was paid to her surviving spouse—fifty thousand for the death itself plus a fifty-thousand-dollar accidental-death benefit."

"Thank you," Ali said.

"Will there be anything else?"

"I'll let you know. I'm still reading."

Just then Ali's alarm went off. Turning off her iPad, she hurried into Cami's room and was relieved to find her awake.

"How are you doing?" Ali asked.

Cami gave her a weak smile. "I'm not sure," she said. "How about if you tell me?"

"Let's see," Ali replied. "Your leg is broken. They had to install a rod to hold it in place. You've got some broken ribs. Your one ear looks like a prizewinning boxer's after a major bout, and there are enough scrapes and bruises on your body to go head-to-head with any self-respecting motorcycle rider in terms of road rash."

"But I'm not going to die?"

"Evidently not."

"What about McCluskey?"

"Thanks to your surveillance system, he's been taken into custody in California. Sheriff Holman is working on having him extradited back to Arizona."

Cami sighed in obvious relief. Just then a nurse came

in to check her vitals. Ali offered to step outside, but Cami asked her to stay.

"How are we doing?" the nurse asked.

Ali felt herself bristling at the question. It sounded like something a pretentious kindergarten teacher might use to address one of her students. Fortunately, Ali managed to stifle.

"I'm feeling hungry," Cami murmered.

"I'll see about bringing you something—maybe some chicken noodle soup," the nurse answered. "How does that sound?"

The kindergarten-teacher voice was back, but Cami nodded gratefully. "Yes, please," she said. "Sounds good."

Cami and Ali stayed silent until the nurse left the room. Once she was gone, Cami spoke first. "Did you call my parents?"

Ali nodded and glanced at her watch. "Your dad's flying in this afternoon. In fact, I'll need to take off in a few minutes to go pick him up from Sky Harbor."

"And my mom?"

Not wanting to answer that question directly and say outright that Sue Lee couldn't be bothered, Ali fudged. "She won't be coming."

"Big surprise there," Cami snorted. "She disapproves of me."

"I can't imagine why."

"Because I don't do things her way," Cami replied, "which means, according to what my grandfather always told me, I'm just like her."

"Having to look in the mirror can be very disturbing at times," Ali said.

The nurse returned with a tray far sooner than either Cami or Ali had expected. While the nurse adjusted the bed, Ali realized that with Cami's hands swathed in bandages eating was going to be a challenge. The nurse must have realized the same thing, because she said, "Don't worry. I'll help you eat."

The woman's tone of voice might have been grating, but her caring was very real. Wanting to spare Cami the embarrassment of being observed while having to be fed like a baby, Ali took her leave.

Once in the silence of the car, she had plenty of time to think. When Maureen, aka Marnie, McCluskey had taken that fatal dive into the Grand Canyon, it had been easy for everyone to give Harvey the benefit of the doubt. At the time it probably hadn't occurred to anyone that there was at least one—maybe even two—unexplained deaths hiding in his background. His mother had clearly been murdered, but what were the chances that his father's suicide had been faked? By virtue of inheriting the family home, Harvey had profited from his parents' deaths just as he had from his bride's. The money from the sale of the couple's property hadn't come to Harvey immediately, but it had eventually.

As Ali merged onto southbound I-17 at Cordes Junction, she summoned Siri to dial Dave Holman's cell phone rather than his office number. She wasn't interested in fighting her way through the obligatory screening process.

"How's Cami?" Dave asked at once.

"Doing well, I think," Ali replied. "She's out of surgery and awake. She was actually sitting up and eating when I left a little while ago."

"That's a relief. So what's going on?"

"I've been looking into Harvey McCluskey's background. According to public records, he's either one very unlucky guy or, as you pointed out this morning, this isn't his first rodeo."

"How so?"

"When he was fifteen, his mother disappeared. Her remains weren't located until years later when autopsy findings determined she'd been murdered. Her husband, Harvey's father, was evidently the only suspect in her disappearance, which eventually turned into a homicide. He was never officially charged, tried, and convicted because he supposedly committed suicide within weeks of his wife's disappearance."

"You say 'supposedly,'" Dave said. "What makes you think the cops got that wrong?"

"Because years later on a honeymoon to the Grand Canyon, Harvey's bride of one day slipped off a hiking trail and died. A few months later, he had a hundred-thousand-dollar payday from her group life-insurance policy."

"I can see where you're going with this," Dave said. "So either he's incredibly unlucky or he's a stone-cold killer. How old was he when his mother died?"

"Fifteen, but two years later he took first place in the state wrestling championship, so even as a kid he was no ninety-pound weakling."

"Has he ever been arrested in any jurisdiction?"

"Not that I can tell, but you'd be able to ascertain that more easily than I can."

That, of course, was a little white lie, but Dave Holman knew nothing about Frigg, and Ali wasn't planning to tell him.

"This is all interesting," Dave murmured, more to himself than to Ali. "Very interesting."

"Would you like me to send you the links I used?"

"No thanks," Dave replied. "That's not necessary. I've got people here who can look into this, but thanks for the heads-up. I appreciate it."

"You're welcome," she said.

Having put the issue of Harvey McCluskey's questionable history squarely in Dave Holman's lap, Ali settled in to pay attention to her driving.

|CHAPTER 45|

PRESCOTT, ARIZONA

O nce Harvey McCluskey had waived an extradition hearing late that evening, all that was needed to complete the process was for someone from Dave's department to go pick him up. The assignment fell to the two detectives assigned to Cami Lee's case—Dan Morris and Rick Rojo. The drive from Prescott to El Centro was four and a half hours long, give or take. With pit stops for food, fuel, and other necessities along the way, it would probably be closer to six.

Sheriff Holman had deemed that driving back and forth would be more effective than flying. For one thing, during an hours-long ride in the backseat of an unmarked patrol car, there would be plenty of time for idle chitchat. Since McCluskey was clearly the sole suspect in Cami's kidnapping, he would have to be Mirandized if he hadn't been already, but that was case-specific. After talking with Ali, Dave suspected there were several other cases in need of examination and maybe a bit of casual discussion.

After a moment or two of consideration, Dave picked up his phone and dialed his chief deputy. "Have Morris and Rojo taken off yet?"

"Not so far."

"Ask one of them to stop by and talk to me before they leave," Dave said.

Twenty minutes later Danny Morris popped his head into the room. "You wanted to see me, boss?"

"I did," Dave said. "Before you take off, I'd like you to stop by the equipment room and use a pair of latex gloves to put a brand-new set of cuffs into an evidence bag. When you clap those cuffs on McCluskey's wrists and later when you remove them, wear gloves again. Once they're off, the cuffs need to go straight back into the evidence bag so we can send them down to the Arizona Public Safety Department Crime Lab in Phoenix."

Danny frowned. "You're hoping to grab his DNA?"

"I am indeed," Dave answered. "I've had Records looking for a rap sheet on McCluskey, and they came up empty. Near as I can tell, he's never been arrested for any serious offense."

"Which means most likely his DNA isn't in CODIS?"

"Exactly, and I want a profile on him there ASAP," Dave said. "When McCluskey attacked Cami Lee, he showed up with a rape kit in hand. That suggests she may not be his first victim."

"Okay," Detective Morris replied. "We're heading out and plan to drive straight through. We'll switch off at the wheel. Believe me, if McCluskey happens to discard a paper cup or a straw along the way, we'll grab that, too."

With that he started for the door, but Dave stopped him. "One more thing."

"What's that?"

"I'd like you to chat him up as you go. Not about the kidnapping, of course. Anything he says about that at this point wouldn't be admissible. Just talk about life in general. I had Deputy Harper pull some info about the guy off the Internet. I'll have her e-mail what she found to you. I understand McCluskey grew up in Butte, Montana. Detective Rojo grew up in Morenci. Being from dying mining towns might work as a conversation starter."

"So just general chitchat, then?"

"Yes, but if you happen to have the recorders on your body cams running during the course of all that idle conversation," Holman added with a grin, "it wouldn't hurt my feelings one bit."

"Gotcha," Detective Morris said.

"As you're headed home, once you're about an hour and a half out, give me a call on my cell. When it's time to book Harvey McCluskey into our county jail, I plan to be here in person as part of his welcoming committee."

|CHAPTER 46|

SEDONA, ARIZONA

"So how was it?" B. asked as he and Ali were getting ready for bed. Bella was already burrowed under the covers.

"Let's just say when Mr. Lee and I showed up in Cami's hospital room, she wasn't exactly overjoyed to see him."

"Really?" B. said with a frown. "What's he like?"

"Dour," Ali answered after a moment's thought. "No discernible sense of humor, and he made it quite clear that he regards everything connected to Arizona with utter disdain."

"If that's the case, what does he think of his daughter?"

"He's completely mystified as to why Cami would choose to live here instead of somewhere closer to home in California. By the way, as far as he's concerned, her name is Camille. None of this Cami stuff for either her father or mother. They both clearly disapprove."

"I'll stick with Cami, then," B. said. "But having grown

up in what sounds like a very dysfunctional family, how did Cami turn out to be as normal as she is?"

"Beats me," Ali responded, "but I'm glad she did."

"And how's she doing physically?"

"Progressing," Ali answered. "When it came time for her to eat something, the nurse had to feed her because of the bandages on her hands. They had already moved her out of the ICU and into a regular room by the time Mr. Lee and I arrived at the hospital this evening, but I'm afraid it's going to be a long road back for her."

"Will she be able to manage on her own at home?" B. wondered.

Ali actually smiled at that. "Who says she'll be on her own? Don't forget, Shirley and her mother live right down the road. Once Cami is out of the hospital and back home, unless I miss my guess, Shirley will rally neighbors to do whatever needs doing." Then, after settling into bed, Ali added, "How are things at work?"

"I've canceled all of this week's meetings, including that job interview on Friday. That way I can concentrate on bringing Mateo up to speed. He's a quick study, but there's a lot to learn. I'm doing most of the actual training while Lance and Stu cover both their own parts of the operation and Cami's, too. What about you? Are you coming in tomorrow or heading to Prescott?"

"Prescott," Ali answered at once. "With Cami's dad there, I think she'll need all the emotional backup she can get."

"Fair enough," B. said.

That was the plan, but it disintegrated when Ali's cell phone rang at six forty-five the next morning and she saw her mother's face on caller ID. It was odd for Edie to be calling this early.

"Hey, Mom," Ali said, holding the phone to her ear and sitting up in bed. "What's up?"

"It's your father," Edie Larson wailed into the phone.

That brought Ali to full attention. "Dad? What happened? Did he take off again? Have you notified the police?"

"The police are already here," Edie croaked, her voice barely audible. "Bobby didn't just run away, Ali. He's dead!"

A chill of shocked disbelief shot through Ali's body. "Dead?" she repeated blankly. "How can that be?"

"Please come," Edie pleaded urgently through broken sobs without any further explanation. "I need you here with me—now!"

"Coming, Mom," Ali said, leaping out of bed. "I'll be there as soon as I can."

When B. emerged from his shower, he was surprised to see that not only was Ali out of bed, she was also half-dressed. "What's going on?" he wanted to know.

"That was Mom on the phone," Ali said through gritted teeth, trying to keep her emotions in check. "She says Dad's dead. I've got to go."

"Dead?" B. echoed. "Oh, Ali, I'm so sorry. Do you want me to drive you?"

Ali ran a brush through her hair and pulled it back into a ponytail, shaking her head all the while. "No, thanks," she said. "I'm better off driving myself. Whatever's going on, I'll need my own transportation."

Alonzo was in the kitchen as Ali raced through on her way to the garage. "What's wrong?" he asked as she dashed past.

"It's my dad," she told him. "I've got to go."

She knew that saying anything more right then would

cause her to burst into tears, and she couldn't risk that. Her mother was clearly in pieces. That meant Ali had to hold it together. On the drive from the house to her folks' place, she might have managed to bite back tears, but that didn't keep her limbs from shaking or calm the racing of her heart.

Blocks away from Sedona Shadows, she could see that the road ahead was blocked by a cordon of emergency vehicles parked across the street. Behind the line of flashing lights, a double-tanked gasoline truck stood jackknifed, partially on the sidewalk and partially across the road. Knowing she wouldn't be able to get any closer, Ali pulled over and parked. Getting out of the car, she dialed her mother's number as she walked. Betsy Peterson answered.

"Edie Larson's phone," she said.

"Where's my mom?" Ali demanded.

"She's in the other room talking to two police officers. She left her phone out here with me."

"Has she been to the scene, to wherever it happened?"

"Not yet. She tried, but officers kept her back from it."

"Then how does she know Dad is involved?"

"Harriet, one of the dining room servers here at Sedona Shadows, was just coming on shift. She saw the whole thing firsthand. She recognized Bob and came rushing in to tell your mother. By then Edie had figured out Bob was gone. She was just getting ready to go find him."

"But how can you say for certain he's dead?"

There was a part of Ali that still refused to believe it was true, to accept the idea that her father was gone.

"Jack, our security guard, had to drive past the scene

to go home when he got off work. He called back and said he saw someone covered with a blanket lying on the ground and that all the EMTs were just standing around doing nothing."

Ali's throat clenched. That was it, then—it really was true. Her father was no more.

"All right," she managed to say aloud. "I had to park and walk. Tell Mom I'll be there as soon as I can."

Outside the front door to Sedona Shadows, Ali had to pause for a moment and take a few deep breaths in order to prepare for the emotional onslaught that was about to engulf her. The moment the doors slid open, she found herself in a lobby full of upset and anxious people, some older than her parents and some younger. They stood and sat around in shocked dismay, speaking in low undertones. When Ali entered, utter silence fell over the room. No one said a word to her or to one another as she made her way through them.

Ali was in the corridor approaching her parents' unit when the door opened and two people emerged, a man and a woman. She recognized the man as a detective for Sedona PD, but in that moment she couldn't summon his name.

"Ali?" he said.

When she nodded, he must have understood her current state of bewilderment. "Detective Cox with Sedona PD," he supplied kindly. "Wally Cox, and this is Detective Andrea Delgado. I'm so sorry for your loss."

"Thank you," Ali answered numbly. "How's my mother?"

Detective Cox shook his head. "Not very well," he said. "She should probably be under a doctor's care. This has come as a terrible shock to her, especially considering her age."

Ali brushed aside the age issue. What was wrong with her mother right then had nothing at all to do with age and everything to do with despair.

"What happened?" she asked. "Was it an accident?"

"We can't say definitively at this moment. We're in the process of securing some video surveillance footage that should tell us exactly what happened, but for right now we're treating your father's death as a possible suicide."

"But . . ." Ali began.

"Mr. Larson left your mother a note," Detective Cox said. "She found it on the kitchen counter when she got up."

"He left a suicide note?" Ali asked in disbelief. "What did it say?"

Detective Cox glanced in his partner's direction and nodded. Detective Delgado was carrying a file folder. She opened it and held it up for Ali to see. The file contained a single piece of notebook paper, no doubt torn out of the small spiral notebook her parents kept on their kitchen counter to jot down shopping lists and various reminders. The writing was sloppy. Even so, Ali recognized her father's somewhat erratic penmanship:

> *Edie, This is for the best. I'm sorry. I love you.*
>
> *Bobby*

"Your father's handwriting?" Detective Delgado asked. Before Ali could nod in confirmation, her knees began to buckle. Detective Cox took hold of her elbow and steadied her for a bit, then guided her to a chair.

"Maybe you should just sit for a moment," he suggested.

"No," Ali insisted, shaking off his hand. "I'm all right. I need to be with my mom."

"You do understand that the note is evidence," Detective Cox explained. "We need to take it with us for now, but we'll return it to your mother when it's no longer needed for our investigation."

Ali watched in silence as Detective Delgado returned the letter to the file and closed it. Meanwhile Detective Cox reached into a pocket and withdrew a business card, which he handed to Ali.

"Here's my contact information in case you have any questions, and again, sorry for your loss."

Ali nodded but still said nothing. Once the two cops walked away, she rose to her feet, walked to the closed door of her parents' apartment, and then raised her hand to knock, but somehow she couldn't quite bring herself to do so immediately. Instead she stood frozen in place for the better part of a minute because she knew that once the door opened, she would have to come face-to-face with the rest of her life—a life without her father in it.

Finally, after taking a deep breath, she knocked. When Betsy opened the door, Ali stepped inside. Her mother, still wearing her nightgown and robe, was seated at the tiny kitchen table. She seemed utterly shattered and appeared to have aged decades overnight. No longer capable of shedding tears, Edie Larson sat staring dry-eyed at the floor with a look of utter desolation on her face. She glanced up only when Ali's feet entered her line of vision.

"This is my fault," she whispered. "I'm the one who killed Bobby. I should have told the front desk that he wasn't allowed to go out on his own. And what about the poor man who was driving the truck? He's going to have to live with this for the rest of his life."

"You're wrong, Mom," Ali asserted. "None of this is your fault."

"But it is," Edie insisted, "and a lot of it was pride on my part. I didn't want people around us to know how bad things were. I didn't want everyone here sticking their noses in our business. I wanted to keep what was going on with Bobby just between the two of us. I didn't want other people involved."

Ali rested a hand on her mother's shoulder. "You did the best you could," she said. "You made decisions you thought were right at the time, and second-guessing them now isn't going to help. Dad left on his own terms, Mom. He did what he did in order to spare you from suffering, probably more than to spare himself. Yes, we don't like it, but the decision was his and nobody else's."

"But what am I going to do now?" Edie whispered brokenly.

Ali remembered a time when she herself had asked that same question. The words were still engraved on her heart. She'd uttered them that dreadful long-ago night in the hospital in Chicago—the night Dean Reynolds died. Seven months pregnant with Chris, Ali had fled Dean's hospital room only after he breathed his last. The line on the machine had gone flat, the pumping on the respirator quieted, and there was nothing else to be done. In the waiting room, she'd fallen into her mother's arms.

"What am I going to do now?" Ali had wailed. Remembering her mother's words from back then, she repeated them now verbatim.

"You'll do what you have to do," Ali said softly.

"But . . ." Edie objected.

"No buts," Ali replied. "First you need to go shower and dress. Then you need to comb your hair and put on some makeup. You'll be talking to lots of people today. You owe it to yourself and to Dad to look and be your best. It's what he would want you to do."

"Really?" Edie asked.

Ali nodded. "Really."

"All right, then," Edie Larson said, hoisting herself to her feet. "I'll go get dressed."

|CHAPTER 47|

PRESCOTT, ARIZONA

It was four in the morning when a call from Detective Morris came in on Dave's cell. He grabbed the phone, silenced the ringer, and then hurried into the bathroom, closing the door before he answered. He needn't have bothered. His wife, Priscilla, had long since learned to deal with overnight phone calls by wearing a superb set of earplugs to bed. She didn't stir.

"Sorry we took so long," Morris said. "The guys at the jail in El Centro couldn't get their act together. What should have been an easy-peasy handover turned into a bureaucratic shitstorm. We didn't leave the jail until almost midnight."

"But you got him?" Dave asked.

"We did."

"Where are you now?"

"The GPS says we're an hour and a half out. Our ETA is six a.m."

"All right," Dave replied. "I'm on my way, too. I'll meet you at the sally port."

And he did. After driving from Sedona to Prescott, Dave was there waiting when Morris's unmarked car pulled inside. Sheriff Holman himself opened the back passenger door. When the prisoner stepped out, he was wearing an orange Imperial County Jail jumpsuit. He was also wearing handcuffs and a set of shackles, most likely compliments of Imperial County.

"Welcome back home to Arizona, Mr. McCluskey," Dave said pleasantly. "I'm the Yavapai County sheriff. I hope you had an uneventful journey."

"Screw you," McCluskey snarled. "I've needed to take a leak for the past hour and a half, and jerkface over there wouldn't stop so I could relieve myself."

"I'm sorry you feel that Detective Morris's customer-service skills are lacking," Dave observed. "When you fill out your satisfaction survey, be sure to mention that. In the meantime what say we get you booked into your new digs?"

Detective Morris came around the back of the vehicle, suppressing a grin as he took hold of the prisoner's arm. "Right this way, Mr. McCluskey," he said. "I'll get those cuffs off you now so you can visit the restroom."

While Morris escorted the prisoner into the building through a series of locked doors, Detective Rojo opened the trunk and removed two items. One appeared to be a dark leather gym bag. The other could have been a white plastic shopping bag, except for the logo printed on the outside—Imperial County Jail.

"His personal effects?" Dave asked.

Detective Rojo nodded.

"Great," Dave said. "I can hardly wait to take a look. Did he say anything?"

"Hardly a word," Rick replied. "He's not exactly the

conversational type. Grew up in Butte. Both his parents are deceased."

"Did he say how?"

"Nope."

"We asked if he was married. He said he was once but not anymore. Just for the record, he didn't bother mentioning that said wife died on their honeymoon the day after they tied the knot. Based on what Lauren's paper trail told us, his not saying anything about that strikes me as a red flag."

"Me, too," Dave agreed. "You're probably worn out, but if you're not too tired, once McCluskey's in a cell, I want the three of us to go into an interview room and turn on a camera while we inventory his property. We need to have a video record of everything we find."

At that hour of the morning, the booking area was fairly quiet. Most of that night's drunks were already locked up and sleeping things off in their own cells. While escorting McCluskey over to the intake clerk, Detective Morris passed an evidence bag to Sheriff Holman. Inside was a shiny pair of handcuffs.

Holman dialed the desk sergeant. "Who's on duty right now? I've got something that needs to be driven to the crime lab in Phoenix within the next couple of hours."

"Deputy Hawkins is available," the sergeant replied.

"Good," Dave replied. "Send Merrilee to the booking room right away."

Merrilee Hawkins might have been new to the department, but she certainly wasn't new to law enforcement. She had transferred in from Baltimore because as a black single mom she wanted to raise her two young sons far from what some people liked to call the murder capital of the world. She was able to do shift work because her mother had moved to Yavapai County with her. Merrilee was fair, tough, and smart, and Dave Holman expected her to go far.

"What do you need, sir?" Deputy Hawkins asked when she turned up a few minutes later.

Dave handed her the evidence bag. "Do you know where the crime lab is in Phoenix?"

"No, but I'm pretty sure I can find it."

"This needs to be handed over directly to a criminalist named Barbara Lemon," he said. "She should be at work by the time you get there, and she knows it's coming. She also knows this is a rush job."

"Got it," Deputy Hawkins said, and off she went.

As the booking process wrapped up, McCluskey seemed to become more and more agitated. "What about all my stuff?" he wanted to know. "Isn't it supposed to be turned over to a property room or something?"

"It is, and it will be," Dave assured him, "once we finish inventorying it."

"But . . ." McCluskey began.

Sheriff Holman cut him off midsentence. "We need to evaluate whatever was found on your person at the time of your arrest in order to determine whether items in your possession have any bearing on our case. The folks in California wouldn't have had any idea about what might or might not be pertinent. The inventory process will be conducted under video surveillance. Once it's finished, you'll be presented with a complete list of what's been taken into evidence and what will be sent along to the property room."

Clearly McCluskey wasn't thrilled with that answer,

but as a jailer led him away, there wasn't much he could do about it.

In the interview room, Dave turned on the video equipment. He started the process by announcing the time and date as well as who was in attendance. They began with the gym bag. The contents in that consisted mostly of clothes, and the officers kept track of each individual item as they sorted through them. At the bottom of the bag, they came across a sizable roll of Mexican pesos along with a file folder.

While his partner counted the cash, Detective Rojo opened the file and removed what turned out to be a wedding photo. "Looks like the bride's a lot younger than the groom." Still holding the photograph, he picked up a second item. When he realized what he was holding, the detective's eyes bulged.

"Look what we have here," he said, passing both items to Dave. "A wedding picture and a death certificate, both in the same file folder."

Taking the documents in hand, Dave examined them in silence. In the photo, McCluskey was much younger than he was now—probably in his midthirties. The radiantly smiling woman at his side was at least a decade younger. "It says here that Maureen Annette Richards died in 2004. Obviously they hadn't been married long enough for her to change her name."

"Because she just happened to take a fatal plunge into the Grand Canyon the day after he married her," Morris growled. "Dollars to doughnuts the asshole killed her."

"And got away with it, too," Rojo added.

"Until now, maybe," Dave said, "but we've got him in our sights, and there's no statute of limitations on homicide."

It occurred to Dave that in terms of their being recorded at the time, they all could have been a bit more discreet, but even cops are entitled to their opinions.

When the three men finished with the contents of the gym bag, they turned their joint attention to the plastic tote from the Imperial County Jail, where they removed one item at a time. On top was a collection of clothing, most likely consisting of the things McCluskey had been wearing at the time of his arrest. It was only at the bottom of the bag that they found anything of any real interest.

First out was a worn leather belt. Next came a fake passport, already stamped with a visa allowing him to travel into the interior of Mexico. It was an amazingly well-done forgery that featured McCluskey's photograph but bore the name Harold Wilson McBride. A faded leather wallet came next. It held a little folding money and a driver's license in McBride's name. Behind a small flap at the back of the wallet was another driver's license—this one in Harvey's own name. There were no credit cards and no photos of any kind. The roll of pesos Harvey carried in his gym bag was apparently all the money he had.

The only remaining item was a small see-through evidence bag. In it was a gold chain—an expensive-looking one at that—with three items strung on it—two rings and a larger gold circle of some kind. Emptying the bag onto the table, Dave unclasped the chain and removed the three baubles so they could be examined individually. One appeared to be a gold wedding ring with a minuscule diamond embedded into the metal. After studying the ring for a moment, Dave passed it along to Detective Morris. Next up was something that appeared to be nothing more than a hoop of gold.

"What's this?" Dave asked with a puzzled frown as he held it up so the others could see it more clearly.

"Looks like one of my wife's earrings," Morris answered. "She loves those hoopy things, the bigger the better."

The final item was clearly a class ring, complete with a blue stone at the center. On one side of the stone were the letters THS and on the other a D, a G, and the year 2007. As Dave handed the ring over to Morris, Detective Rojo suddenly lurched from his chair and hurried toward the door.

"Where are you going?" Dave asked.

"To find a damned magnifying glass," Rick Rojo responded. "I think there's something engraved on the inside of the wedding band."

While Rick was gone, both Dave and Dan took a crack at studying the ring. Yes, there was something written there, but neither of them could make it out.

Rick returned a few moments later, magnifying glass in hand. "Luckily our crime lab had one," he said.

By then Dave was holding the ring, so Rick passed the magnifying glass over to him. With the lens trained on the inside of the ring, two different sets of initials jumped out at him—IMM and MAR.

"Well, my, my, my," Dave muttered under his breath. "What do we have here? Unless I'm mistaken, IMM stands for Harvey's mother, Ida Mae McCluskey. The MAR would be for Maureen Annette Richards. Good spotting, Rick," Dave added, handing both the ring and the magnifying glass back to the detective.

Once the inventory was complete, Dave could see

that both detectives were exhausted. "You two go home and get some sleep," he told them. "When you're both back on duty, we'll be taking a look at a couple of cold cases—two in Montana and the other a lot closer to home, right here in Arizona. We may not have any direct proof about those, but it looks to me as though we're sitting on a whole slew of circumstantial evidence. We've got Harvey McCluskey in jail on a kidnapping charge at the moment, but I'd much rather see him go down for murder. Let's see what we can do to make that happen."

It was breakfast time by then. Once Detectives Morris and Rojo went home, Sheriff Holman left the department as well, walking a couple of blocks to his favorite diner, the Chuck Wagon on Whiskey Row. It was just after 8:00 a.m. The bar at the back had some of Whiskey Row's regular denizens on hand for their morning dose of hair of the dog, but Dave was there for food only, his customary breakfast order—eggs over easy with crisp bacon, well-done hash browns, and whole-wheat toast. Tina, his usual waitress, had delivered a cup of coffee to his favorite spot on the counter by the time he finished stepping through the entrance.

"How's it going?" she asked with a smile.

"It's going," he said. "As to how well? That's currently up for grabs."

While Dave tucked into his breakfast, he was thinking about Barbara Lemon. He'd dealt with her on several occasions during his years as a homicide cop, and she was by far his favorite criminalist. He knew that the state's crime lab had recently come into possession of the latest in DNA technology. Years earlier creating a profile had been an expensive, time-consuming process. Now all that had changed. These days a profile could be obtained in a matter of hours, but demands on the new system were overwhelming. Dave was well aware that he had used his longtime relationship with Barbara to jump the line. Still, he was hopeful. His gut was telling him he and his investigators were onto something important.

After breakfast he went back to the office and tried to turn his hand to his usual administrative duties, but his heart just wasn't in it. He kept watching the clock— watching and waiting.

Finally, a little before eleven, his cell phone rang with Barbara Lemon's name on caller ID.

"I'm holding my breath," Dave said into the phone. "What do you have for me?"

"The big kahuna," she replied. "Not only do I have a profile, I have a hit on CODIS!"

Sheriff Dave Holman felt a wave of gooseflesh sweep down his leg. "Are you serious?"

"Absolutely. I'll be sending an official notification in a few minutes, but I wanted to give you a heads-up. Harvey McCluskey's DNA matches that found at the scene of an unsolved homicide in Nye County, Nevada, from August 2007."

"What's the victim's name?" Dave asked.

"Dawna Marie Giles," Barbara said. "She was a seventeen-year-old runaway who disappeared from her parents' home in Tonopah. She was last seen alive on Saturday, August fourth, 2007. Her partial remains were found later that same day, two miles off Highway 95, twenty miles south of Beatty."

"Does the sheriff there know you got a hit?"

"He's not yet been informed," Barbara replied, "and I'd appreciate it if you'd wait to contact him until after you both receive the official notification. I'll be sending one to him and to you at the same time."

"Don't worry," Dave said. "I won't blow your cover on this, Barbara, but I owe you big."

Before Dave did anything else, he located the non-emergency phone number of Nye County Sheriff's Department. Then, for the next ten minutes, he paced the floor in his office, waiting for an incoming e-mail notification. When it arrived, Dave picked up the receiver on his landline and dialed.

Eventually someone answered. "Nye County Sheriff's Office, may I help you?"

"I'd like to speak to your sheriff."

"May I say who's calling?"

"Sheriff Dave Holman of Yavapai County, Arizona," he replied. "I'm calling about the 2007 homicide of Dawna Marie Giles. I'm currently holding a suspect in my jail whose DNA matches your crime scene."

|CHAPTER 48|

Once Nye County sheriff Bill Longren came on the line, it turned out the whole thing was a big surprise to him. Before Dave called, Longren had been tied up in a board of supervisors meeting and had not yet seen Barbara's e-mail. As soon as he realized what was going on, he asked to put Dave on hold.

"Let me get my cold-case gal in here," he said. "Mike Priest, the original investigator, passed away from cancer two years ago. Detective Susan Moore is the one currently assigned to the case. Dawna Marie's murder may be cold as ice, but it sure as hell ain't forgotten!" he added.

Once Detective Moore was in Longren's office and the phone on speaker, what followed was an hour-long three-way conversation. With the full agreement of both sides, the entire call was taped. Dave broke the ice by telling the Nevada-based officers exactly what he knew about Harvey McCluskey—how he'd been taken into custody in the kidnapping case, how they'd used handcuffs to gather his DNA, and how the state crime lab in Phoenix had discovered the CODIS connection to their case. He finished off by supplying the last piece of the puzzle—the class ring taken from McCluskey's gold chain—a ring with the initials DG built into the design.

Then it was Susan Moore's turn. She got straight into it. "Dawna Marie was last seen leaving a friend's home in the early hours of Saturday morning, August fourth, 2007. After a serious altercation with her mother over underage drinking and breaking a midnight curfew, she spent the remainder of the night with her best friend, Brianna Lester, who reported that when Dawna Marie left her house that morning, she was on her way to Vegas to hook up with her boyfriend, Jason Tuttle. He was later interviewed and eliminated from the investigation due to the fact that he had a rock-solid alibi—he was cooling his heels in the Clark County Jail on a DUI arrest that whole weekend. No other viable suspects were ever identified.

"After Dawna left Brianna's house, she was never seen alive again. Late on Saturday afternoon, a guy named Joseph Rawls flagged down a passing deputy and told him he'd found a dead body three miles off Highway 95. Rawls was a character, an old-time prospector who supported himself by finding and selling geodes and the occasional arrowhead. That's what he was doing at the time he found the body—searching the desert south of Beatty for geodes. He and his dog were camped out in the desert minding their own business when Rawls spotted smoke. Worried about the possibility of a wildfire, he cranked up his RV and went to check it out. He found the body while it was still burning. Rawls was a dry camper who always carried plenty of water with him, so he used some to douse the flames."

"But Rawls wasn't involved?"

"No," Susan said. "DNA ruled him out, same as it did the boyfriend."

"I believe you used the word 'was.' Does that mean Rawls is no longer with us?"

"That's correct," Susan replied. "Mr. Rawls is now deceased. He died of natural causes a year or so after finding the body, but because he was there so fast with gallons of water, he was able to extinguish the fire before the body was entirely consumed. That's the reason we ended up with DNA. The autopsy revealed that Dawna Marie had been strangled as well as sexually assaulted."

"What about electronic devices?" Dave asked.

"The victim didn't have a phone with her," Susan said. "That was part of the fight with her mother. Mrs. Giles was paying the monthly charges for Dawna's iPhone. Since her daughter wasn't willing to play by her mother's rules, Mama Giles confiscated the phone."

"Which meant there was no way to track her movements electronically?"

"Correct. We've continued to work the case ever since without generating any new leads. Mike Priest handled the case for years. After he passed away, it was handed over to me. Dawna's mom calls me every month without fail to see if we've made any progress."

"I'm guessing you're the one who'll be doing the calling today," Dave suggested.

"I won't be calling her," Susan Moore replied. "The moment I'm off the phone with you, I'll be going to speak to her in person, but first, what do you see as our next step?"

Susan's use of the word "our" let Dave know the Nye

County Sheriff's Office was in this fight right along with him.

"Detectives Morris and Rojo, the guys who brought McCluskey back from California, will be in touch. They know more about the other case than anyone else, and they can bring your team up to speed. But before we sign off, there's something else you need to know."

"What's that?" Sheriff Longren asked.

"Dawna Marie Giles may be just the tip of the iceberg. We've learned that Harvey McCluskey's mother disappeared and was presumed murdered while he was still in high school. Her husband, Harvey's father, was the prime suspect in the mother's disappearance. He died, allegedly of suicide, a few weeks after his wife's disappearance. Her body wasn't found until years later, and her manner of death was determined to be homicide. Cause of death was blunt-force trauma."

"You said the father allegedly committed suicide," Susan noted. "Is that in question?"

"At this point I think the matter bears looking into. In 2004 Harvey McCluskey married a nurse in Las Vegas. She died the day after their wedding ceremony on a honeymoon hike in the Grand Canyon. She just happened to fall to her death. Since there were no witnesses present, her death ended up being ruled accidental. McCluskey was the sole beneficiary of an insurance payout of a hundred thousand dollars."

"Not bad for a one-day marriage," Susan observed, "but it sounds like you're saying you think Harvey's good for all these homicides."

"I think it's possible," Dave replied.

"How come?"

"Because when Harvey was taken into custody, he

was wearing a gold chain with a few items strung on it. One of them was Dawna Marie's class ring. We also found a wedding ring there engraved with two sets of initials—his mother's and his late wife's."

"Anything else on the chain?" Sheriff Longren asked.

"A gold hoop of some kind. One of my detectives thinks it may be part of a pair of earrings."

"So three victims for sure," Susan said, "maybe four counting the father, and five counting the earring."

"That's how I see it," Dave told them.

"How long can you hold him on the kidnapping charge?"

"Should the judge grant bail, which is doubtful, I doubt McCluskey will be able to post it. As far as I know, the guy's flat broke."

"Just in case," Susan said, "I want to get to work on all this right away. Please send us your detectives' contact info."

"Will do," Dave replied, "and you do the same."

When that call ended, he made a second one—this time to Sheriff Tom Hickok of Coconino County. Because their counties happened to be next-door neighbors, Dave and Tom were on a better-than-first-name basis.

"How's it going, Davey my man?" Sheriff Hickok asked.

"Things are a bit complicated around here at the moment. I'm calling about an old case, one that happened on your patch back in 2004."

"That's a little before this patch ended up becoming my patch," Hickok said. "What's the deal?"

"A woman named Maureen Annette Richards was on her honeymoon when she died falling from a hiking trail in the Grand Canyon. Her death was determined to be accidental at the time, but I've stumbled across information that indicates she might have been the victim of a homicide."

Hickok sucked in his breath. "Okay," he said. "When it comes to cold cases, Detective Jana Davis is my go-to gal. I'll have her track down the file and give you a call so you can speak to her directly. Will that work?"

"Does for me. Thanks, Tommy. Appreciate it."

|CHAPTER 49|

SEDONA, ARIZONA

Soon after Edie disappeared into the bedroom, Betsy excused herself to return to her own apartment, leaving Ali alone with overwhelming feelings of grief and loss. After a few moments, however, she realized that she had to switch gears from being a grieving daughter to being a concerned mother. Knowing she didn't want her grandkids to find out about this from someone else, she called Chris at school and asked for him to be summoned to the office.

"Grandpa committed suicide?" Chris asked in disbelief when he heard the news. "How can that be?"

Ali's mother had kept a tight lid on her husband's looming mental-health crisis, and Ali realized now that she had, to a lesser degree, done the same thing—at least as far as bringing Chris and Athena into the loop. Now it was her responsibility to tell them.

"He was developing dementia," Ali explained. "Mom hadn't told anyone, not even me. I only just found out about it a few days ago, and with everything that was going on with Athena and the baby, I didn't want to heap anything more onto your plate."

"What do I tell the twins?" Chris asked bleakly.

Ali wrestled with that. Was disingenuousness about Bob Larson's health situation going to be passed along to another generation by dodging the realities concerning the circumstances of his death?

"Tell them he stepped in front of a truck," Ali advised at last. "You don't have to go into any further details about whether it was accidental or deliberate. They're kids. Let Colin and Colleen draw their own conclusions for the time being and plan on giving them the whole story years from now when they're older."

"As soon as I can get a sub, I'll pick them up from school," Chris said. "Are you at Grandma's?"

"Yes."

"Do you want me to bring them there?"

Ali glanced around the tiny space that passed for a living room. "Probably not," she said. "I have a feeling that any minute now the dam is going to break and your grandmother's unit will be flooded with people. I'll try to bring her by your place later on today if that's all right."

"Okay," Chris said, "but what about you, Mom? How are you doing?"

"Hanging in," she replied, "but just barely."

She called B. and was still on the phone with him, bringing him up to date, when Edie emerged from the bedroom. As she stepped through the door, Ali was struck by her mother's transformation. Totally put together and seemingly in control, she clutched a file folder in one hand.

"It's what your father used to call his game plan," Edie explained, nodding toward the folder in response to Ali's unasked question. "His final wishes. I need to go by Smithson's. I called them and told Althea I was coming. Will you drive me there, or should I drive myself?"

Smithson's Family Mortuary was a Sedona institution. Started by a local pioneer named Al Smithson in the early 1900s, the business had been known as Smithson's and Sons for generations. Once the current proprietor, Al's great-great-granddaughter Althea, took control from her father, the name had been changed to reflect that new reality.

"Of course I'll drive you," Ali said, but then she realized her car was still parked several blocks away.

"No matter," Edie said, once Ali explained. "We can take the Buick."

They avoided the crowd in the front lobby by leaving through a back entrance that led directly to the tenant parking area. "What's this about a game plan?" Ali asked as she eased her mother's sedan out of its reserved and numbered spot.

"Bobby and I did this right after we sold the restaurant and moved here," Edie said. "In the process of making sure our affairs were in order, we planned our own funerals—music, Scripture, the whole shebang—and paid for them in advance, so there shouldn't be any surprises on that score. By the way, your father wanted you to give his eulogy."

"Me?" Ali echoed in dismay.

"He figured that after all those years in the news business you were probably better at public speaking than anyone else in the family."

There was nothing Ali could say in response to that. Besides, if that was her father's wish, it was exactly what would happen.

As she pulled out of the parking lot, she saw that the highway in front of Sedona Shadows was still closed and traffic was being diverted onto side streets. Police vehicles were parked at odd angles everywhere. Ali understood the grim reality that investigations of fatal traffic incidents were complex and time-consuming.

"How long will this take?" Edie wanted to know.

"To get the highway open again?" Ali asked.

Edie shook her head. "No, how long will it take before they release Bobby's body to the mortuary?"

Ali sighed. "No telling," she said. "They'll need to do an autopsy first."

"There has to be an autopsy?"

"Has to be," Ali answered.

"All right, then." Edie sounded resigned. "I suppose I'll just have to live with that, won't I?"

Ali's phone rang as they pulled in to the mortuary parking lot. A glance at the screen told her Dave Holman was on the line. Without answering, she switched the phone's ringer to silent. Once inside Smithson's, Ali and her mother were greeted by a woman Ali had never met before. Edie introduced her as Althea Smithson.

"So sorry for your loss," Althea murmured to Ali. "Won't you please come this way?"

As they followed Althea into a tastefully decorated office, Ali noted that although the woman was wearing a wedding ring, she had obviously kept her maiden name. She motioned Edie and Ali into chairs.

"I have Mr. Larson's file right here," she said, opening a folder of her own and examining the documents inside. "Has anything changed?"

Edie shook her head. "I have my own copy. Nothing's changed except for the fact that we have another great-grandson now—Logan James. You'll need to add his name to the list of survivors."

"As for prepaid cremation, is that still the plan?"

"Yes, please," Edie answered. "He always wanted his ashes scattered up on the rim."

"And you still prefer a pine box as opposed to an urn?"

Edie actually smiled at that. "That's correct. Bobby liked to say that a pine box was good enough for him, and biodegradable, too."

Ali looked at her mother in amazement. The shattered woman she'd seen earlier that morning when she first entered her parents' apartment no longer existed. Edie Larson was back in control. It was as though while showering and getting dressed her mother had also outfitted herself in a suit of emotional armor.

"You'll need to let the ME know that when they're ready to release the body, we'll be the ones taking charge," Althea explained. "We won't be able to set a time frame or schedule a service until after that happens."

"I understand," Edie said. "Is there anything else?"

"No," Althea said. "I have everything I need."

———

"Have you told Chris and Athena?" Edie asked once they were back in her Buick.

"I called Chris," Ali said. "He was going to pick up the kids and take them home."

"Then that's where I'd like to go next," Edie said. "I need to speak to all of them, face-to-face. In the meantime I need you to do me a favor."

"What's that?"

"I know you have lots of connections inside law enforcement," Edie said. "I'd like to have the name and address of the man who was driving that truck. I want to go see him and offer my condolences."

Ali was shocked. "Are you sure about speaking to the driver directly, Mom?" she hedged. "Maybe you should consult an attorney first. He'd most likely advise against your making any kind of direct personal contact. What if the driver decides to sue the estate?"

"I don't care if he sues me for every last dime," Edie said determinedly. "Telling him I'm sorry for what happened is the right thing to do."

Ali could see that arguing the point would get her nowhere. "Yes, ma'am," she agreed meekly.

By then they had arrived at Chris and Athena's place. "If you don't mind," Edie said, putting a restraining hand on her daughter's arm. "I'd rather talk to them alone. I haven't been straight with them up to now, and I owe them all an explanation."

Ali didn't argue with that either. "Okay," she said. "I'll see about getting the driver's contact information."

Watching her silver-haired mother approach Chris and Athena's door with her back ramrod straight, Ali couldn't help but marvel at her appearance. She didn't look like a distraught widow. She walked with the firm determination of someone who was six feet tall and bulletproof.

Once the door opened and Edie disappeared inside, Ali didn't bother calling anyone at Sedona PD for information concerning the truck driver. She dialed up Frigg instead. Under the circumstances that was less complicated all the way around.

|CHAPTER 50|

SEDONA, ARIZONA

By early afternoon Ali was still cooling her heels in the car, waiting for her mom to return. Left with some time to herself, she remembered to check her silenced phone. In addition to Dave's earlier call, there were three more—two of them with blocked numbers. Neither of those left messages. Given the circumstances, Ali assumed they were most likely media outlets looking for a comment. The third one was from her good friend and Sister of Providence, Sister Anselm Becker, calling from her convent in Jerome. She did leave a message.

"Everyone here at St. Bernadette's is praying for you and your family. Call if you can, but I'll understand if that's not possible."

Ali decided to return Dave's call first. "I heard what happened to your dad," Dave said when he answered. "I'm so very sorry. I also heard that the investigating officers don't believe it was an accident."

"It wasn't," Ali answered grimly. "Dad stepped into the path of that truck on purpose."

"But why?" Dave asked. "What would make someone like Bob Larson go off the rails like that?"

In that moment, having watched her mother maintain a tight grip on her emotions helped Ali control her own.

"Dad was drifting into dementia, although he still had some lucid moments. He took advantage of one of those this morning and removed himself from the equation. He knew that what was coming would be hell on my mom, and I believe he wanted to spare her."

"I'm pretty sure she wouldn't have agreed with that assessment."

"You're right, she didn't, and that's why he didn't discuss it with her beforehand. He took off while she was still asleep."

"How are you doing?" Dave asked pointedly.

"I'm trying to help my mom hold it together, and that's helping me do the same thing."

"If there's something Priscilla and I can do . . ."

"No, Dave," Ali said quickly. "Not right now, but thank you for offering. Was there anything else?"

"I wanted to update you on the McCluskey case. He waived an extradition hearing, so we've brought him back. He's being held in the jail here in Prescott, but his arrest has set off a firestorm of homicide investigations in three different states—Arizona, Montana, and Nevada."

Ali knew what a compliment this bit of conversation was. Prohibitions against law-enforcement officers discussing active cases with outsiders were universal, and the fact that Dave trusted her enough to do so meant a lot.

"Three states?" she echoed. "I thought there were only two—Arizona and Montana."

"This morning the crime lab down in Phoenix used CODIS to connect McCluskey to an unsolved rape/homicide in Nye County, Nevada, dating from 2007. Thanks to all the background information you provided, we're now in possession of enough physical evidence to justify reopening two officially closed cases—the death of Harvey's mother, Ida Mae, and the supposedly accidental death of his wife, Maureen Annette Richards, who fell to her death in the Grand Canyon in 2004.

"I just got off a call where I introduced myself to Detective Jana Davis, the Coconino County investigator who'll be looking into that case. Butte, Montana, has been put on alert as well. Right now we've got McCluskey dead to rights on the kidnapping charge, but sending him up for murder in one of those other cases would be a lot more to my liking."

"Mine, too," Ali agreed.

Just then a call came in from B., so Ali hung up with Dave and switched lines. "Where are you?" B. asked.

"Waiting outside Chris and Athena's house. Mom wanted to talk to them on her own, so I'm giving her some space. What's happening there?"

"Shirley's on her way to Prescott to pick up Cami and bring her home."

Ali was astonished. "They're releasing her this soon?"

"On the condition that she'll have someone in the household to look after her. Her father evidently wanted her to come back to California with him. She said absolutely not, and they got in a huge row over it. I suggested that she come stay at our place. She said no to that as well. Since she's dead set on going home, Shirley volunteered to help out. She says she lives close enough that she can look after Cami while keeping an eye on her mom at the same time. I also said you and I will pitch in as needed, and Alonzo, too, if necessary."

"Cami actually agreed to that kind of arrangement?"

"Evidently. When it came to choosing between her dad and Shirley, there was no contest. As far as I know, Mr. Lee is on his way back to California with his nose permanently out of joint. How are things on your end?"

"Once Mom finishes talking to the kids, she wants to go speak to the truck driver who hit Dad."

"Is that a good idea?"

"I don't think so, and it sounds as though you don't either. But *she's* bound and determined."

"Do you know who he is and where he lives?"

"His name is Milton Albright, and he lives in Camp Verde."

"I'm surprised the cops let that leak."

"They didn't. That nugget of information came straight from Frigg."

B. sighed. "Figures," he said, but he made no further comment on that score. "Just so you know, without Cami we're so shorthanded that I'll probably end up staying here at the office tonight. You can bring me a change of clothing in the morning, or I'll have Alonzo drop some off. Unless you need me to be there with you. If you do, just say so."

Ali's first choice would have been to have B. at home that night, but these were tough circumstances all the way around. She was tempted to tell him what Dave had told her about the McCluskey case, but she didn't. That information would come out in due time, and when it did, she'd need to be as shocked and surprised as everyone else.

"Don't worry about me," Ali said. "I'm looking after Mom right now, and you're looking after the shop. We're both doing jobs that need to be done. By the way, how's Mateo working out?"

"I'd say surprisingly well, except it's not so surprising. He's exceptional. He's too new to turn loose unsupervised, but he's catching on faster than anyone expected."

Ali's phone vibrated in her hand, and the caller ID screen said Sister Anselm.

"Sister Anselm is calling. I've got to go."

"Let me know what happens with the truck driver. I'm predicting wholesale disaster."

"So am I," Ali whispered.

She hung up with B. and picked up Sister Anselm's call. "Sorry I didn't get back to you earlier."

"I'm sure you've been busy."

"I have been." Over the next few minutes, Ali brought her friend up-to-date on everything that was going on. When she got to the part about Shirley volunteering to look after Cami, Sister Anselm called a halt.

"What are Shirley Malone's qualifications for that kind of duty?" the nun demanded hotly. "Is she a trained nurse? Is she a patient advocate? Of course not, but you just happen to know someone who is, and I'm available. So text me the address of Cami's home in Cornville. Let Shirley know I'll be there to take over once they arrive."

Ali didn't bother arguing. There was no point. "Yes, ma'am," she said for the second time that day. She no longer had the strength or energy to put up a fight.

Just as she hung up, Edie emerged from the house

and opened the passenger door. Ali turned her phone back to silent and put it away.

"Did you get the address for me?" her mother asked.

Ali nodded. "It's already in the GPS."

"Let's go, then," Edie said. "I want to get this over with before I lose my nerve."

|CHAPTER 51|

COTTONWOOD, ARIZONA

Halfway through his second full day at High Noon Enterprises, Mateo Vega was afraid his head was going to explode. He had arrived on Saturday expecting a job interview and nothing more. Instead he'd been hired on the spot. Then, due to the crisis with Cami, he'd been put straight to work.

In the intervening time, he'd learned so much new stuff he could hardly believe it. In the joint he'd learned at his own pace, but the speed of that had been determined by the availability of materials accessible through interlibrary loans. He wanted to send Mrs. Ancell a note to tell her about this wonderful stroke of good fortune, but there was literally no time. Very soon now someone from High Noon would need to let his parole officer know that Mateo was staying on in Arizona because he had a JOB! But that would have to wait as well, because there was too much happening.

Earlier that morning Stu had told Mateo to take a break and walk across the street to the RV park and check in with the manager. Sid had shown him the unit in question. Someone else might have found the tiny space lacking, but for someone who'd spent more than a decade and a half in an eight-by-ten cell, the place was downright luxurious. His cell hadn't had a kitchen. The RV did. It might have been minuscule, but it included a two-burner stove, a microwave, and a one-drawer dishwasher. His cell had had a stainless-steel toilet but no shower. The RV had a bathroom with a shower and a door that could be opened, closed, and even locked from the inside if necessary. Showers in the Monroe Correctional Facility were public and notoriously dangerous. There'd been no television set in his cell. This one had a forty-inch flat-screen attached to one wall of the tiny living room, and both cable TV and a Wi-Fi connection were included in the monthly rent.

Compared to what Mateo had known before, he would be living in the lap of luxury. And when Sid told him the sum total for the first and last month's rent as well as the security deposit, Mateo didn't have to pause. High Noon's signing bonus had already been electronically deposited into his bank account, and he knew he had enough to cover it.

"I didn't bring along any checks, and they'd be from out of state anyway, so why don't you use this for my upfront costs," Mateo suggested, handing Sid his Visa. Moments later the charge went through, and suddenly Mateo Vega had his own place to live—a private one with no drunken roommates!

Yes, life in Arizona was very good indeed.

|CHAPTER 52|

CAMP VERDE, ARIZONA

During the drive from Sedona to Camp Verde, Edie Larson maintained complete radio silence. Ali meanwhile wrestled with a growing sense of dread. She couldn't imagine that the driver of the truck would be happy to have them show up on his doorstep, much less be interested in hearing what her mother had to say. And if this ended up turning into some kind of litigious situation, her mother's in-person visit could have dire consequences. Once lawyers and insurance companies got involved, Ali feared that whatever nest egg Edie and Bob had set aside for their retirement would be completely wiped out. Even so, despite the possibility of impending lawsuits, Edie remained determined to say her piece.

As they turned onto South Third, both sides of the street were lined with cars. Since the Albrights' home was smack in the middle of the block, it seemed likely a crowd was gathered there. Ali pulled over and parked behind the last car.

"Are you sure you want to do this?" she asked.

Edie nodded. "I'm sure," she answered, "but this time I'd like you to come along."

Clearly relegated to a backup role, Ali followed her mother down the street, up the Albrights' front walk, and onto their porch. When Edie knocked on the door, a man wearing a clerical collar answered.

"Is Mr. Albright available?" Edie asked.

"I'm Matthew Grogan, Mr. Albright's pastor. Can I help you?"

"My name is Edie Larson," she replied. "Robert was my husband. I'd like to have a word with Mr. Albright if it's at all possible."

Grogan gave Edie a long, assessing look before making up his mind. "All right," he said, "one moment, please. I'll see what I can do." He closed the door then, leaving Edie and Ali waiting on the small wooden porch for what felt like an eternity. Eventually, however, the door opened again.

The man standing before them now was stocky and solidly built. He was somewhere in his mid-forties and dressed in workaday khakis. His eyes were red, as though he'd been crying, and the look of devastation on his face was the same one Ali had seen on her mother's when she'd first arrived at Sedona Shadows earlier that morning.

For several seconds Milton and Edie simply stood staring at each other in silence. "I'm Milton," he said at last. "What do you want?"

Edie took a deep breath. "I came to tell you that my husband had been having mental issues—dementia issues. I was asleep when he left and had no idea he'd gone out on his own. I came to tell you that what happened isn't your fault and that I'm so sorry."

Another long silence followed. Then, to Ali's utter astonishment, the two of them—the grieving truck driver and the grieving widow—simply fell into each other's arms and wept. It was, as Ali told B. later, a moment of pure grace.

When they parted at last, Milton wiped the tears from his face and said, "Thank you for telling me. Would you care to come inside?"

"I'd better not," Edie replied. "I've said what I came to say. We'll be going now."

With that she turned and retraced her steps, Ali once again following behind.

Back in the car, silence returned. Ali couldn't help but feel slightly ashamed of herself. Clearly her mother's kind gesture had meant the world to a man shattered by having taken someone else's life through no fault of his own, and Ali had done her best to dissuade her mother from taking that course of action.

"Where do you want to go now?" Ali asked.

"Back home," Edie said. "I need to start facing up to the folks at Sedona Shadows. They're our neighbors. They're all going to want to say how sorry they are, and I need to let them do it—the same way Milton Albright did for me."

Back to Sedona Shadows they went. This time Edie insisted on walking in through the lobby while Ali went around back to park. When she entered the lobby several minutes later, she found Edie in the midst of a crowd of concerned and sympathetic residents. Eventually Ali and Edie returned to the unit, where Betsy, using her own key, had made herself useful in the interim. With the help of the staff in the facility's kitchen, she had organized a small buffet on the kitchen counter, complete with finger sandwiches, cheese and crackers, and a variety of cookies.

For the remainder of the afternoon, Ali stayed with Edie as a steady stream of visitors filed through the unit. Other than Betsy, who kept cups filled with either tea or coffee, no one stayed long. They came, spoke briefly to Edie, had some refreshments, and left. Even so, by five o'clock in the afternoon Ali could tell that her mother's emotional capacity was completely depleted.

"I think we need to shut this down for now," Ali announced. She found a Post-it Note, wrote the words "NO VISITORS, PLEASE," and stuck it on the outside of the door before she closed it. Then she turned to her mother. "I think you should rest."

Edie nodded her agreement.

"Would you like me to bring you a tray from the dining room?" Betsy asked.

"No thank you," Edie said. "I'm not hungry. I'm going to undress and lie down for a while, although I doubt I'll sleep." She reached into her pocket, pulled out her phone, and turned it on. Until that minute Ali had no idea the phone had been on her mother's person.

"Fifty-three calls," Edie said after a moment, "but I'm not going to try to return any of them right now."

"Good idea, Mom," Ali agreed. "Just leave them be for the time being. Tomorrow you can return them or not at your leisure."

For an instant Ali considered offering to stay over, but then she thought better of it. She had no doubt that her mother needed some time and space to grieve on her own. After planting a good-bye kiss on her cheek and giving her a quick hug, Ali left.

All day long, Ali's phone, too, had been silently blowing up. On the walk back to her car, she discovered she had forty-six missed calls and eighteen voice messages. Most likely there would have been more of the latter, but by now her voice-mail box was probably completely full. She also had seventy-three new e-mails and dozens of text messages. At that point Ali decided to take a little of her own advice. She returned B.'s call and let him know she was on her way home. She left everyone else's for later.

In the house Ali found Bella in the kitchen eagerly awaiting her arrival. There was a note from Alonzo saying there was homemade Senate bean soup in the fridge if she wanted to heat up some of that in the microwave. Right that moment Ali wasn't hungry, any more than her mother had been.

Once in the bedroom, she put her almost-dead phone on the charger. Then she undressed and slipped into the shower. There, standing under a cascade of steamy water, she finally gave way to the storm of tears she'd held in abeyance all day long. Her father's note had made it clear that he'd done what he felt was best for him and what he thought best for his wife, but had he understood how much it would hurt everyone he left behind? How could he go off and leave them without giving any of them a chance to say good-bye? How could he do that?

Ali stood there crying until she ran out of both tears and hot water at the same time. Once she'd dried off and donned her robe, she padded out to the kitchen.

She hadn't been wrong in trying to encourage her
mother to eat, so she took that bit of her own advice to
heart as well. Fortified by some soup, she returned to
the bedroom. There, seated on the love seat with Bella
cuddled next to her and with both her phone and computer within easy reach, Ali set about returning all those
calls and messages.

|CHAPTER 53|

PRESCOTT, ARIZONA

By five o'clock that evening, Sheriff Holman was on the phone with Detective Jana Davis of the Coconino County Sheriff's Office.

"I've spent the whole afternoon reviewing everything we have on the Maureen Richards case," she told him. "The witness interviews are all on VHS tapes, so there's really no way to share them, but I can summarize what they said. Maureen's family members have always believed that Harvey McCluskey killed her. Her sister, Rochelle, reported that when Marnie was little, she and two of her brothers had spent several hours trapped at the top of a stalled Ferris wheel. The brothers had both walked away from the experience unscathed, but Marnie had been left permanently traumatized. Since she'd been terrified of heights, Rochelle maintained that the idea that Marnie would willingly take a hike into the Grand Canyon was completely out of the question. McCluskey's response had been something to the effect that Marnie had been excited about starting her new life with him and had wanted the two of them to do something daring together."

"It was daring, all right," Dave muttered under his breath. "It was downright deadly."

"That's what the investigators thought at the time," Jana agreed, "but with no signs of foul play, no physical evidence, no questionable bruising, and no apparent defensive wounds, the prosecutor wasn't willing to take the case to court. In his opinion investigators didn't have enough. Maybe we still don't, but I'd like to come have a chat with him about it."

"Be my guest," Dave said. "Have at it."

"Thanks," Detective Davis said. "I believe I will. As a matter of fact, I'm already on my way. I should be there in just under an hour."

By then Dave's early-morning serving of over-easy eggs was in the distant past. After winning the election, he and Priscilla had talked about moving to the county seat in Prescott, some eighty miles away, but Priscilla's thriving nail-salon business was based in Sedona and Cottonwood. Besides, they both loved their home in Sedona. So he had rented a studio apartment where he batched it during the week unless he felt like making the long commute home. As it happened, this was a night Priscilla had invited friends over for dinner. Late as it was, he called to let her know what she'd probably already figured out—that he wouldn't be there to greet their guests.

"What else is new?" she asked resignedly. "I'm pretty much used to it by now."

For the second time that day, Dave hiked over to Whiskey Row's Chuck Wagon. The bar in the back was doing land-office business with an entirely different demographic—the evening drunks as opposed to morning ones. Once again Dave's beverage of choice was black coffee. For food he ordered a bowl of chili.

As he ate his solitary meal, he couldn't help but consider that if Harvey McCluskey had just left Cami alone and if Ali hadn't gone digging into the guy's background, none of the rest of this would have come to light. The man appeared to have gotten away with multiple murders for decades. In the absence of the failed kidnapping, he might have kept right on doing so.

————

An hour and a half later, Dave was sitting on the other side of the two-way mirror as Detective Jana Davis entered the interview room where Harvey McCluskey and Detective Morris were already seated and waiting.

"Who's this?" McCluskey asked when she entered.

He directed his question at Danny, but Jana was the one who answered. "I'm Detective Davis of the Coconino County Sheriff's Office. I'm here to talk to you about the death of your wife, Maureen Annette Richards."

There was an abrupt change in McCluskey's demeanor once he realized this was going to be a far different conversation from the one he'd expected. "Oh, that," he said with a dismissive shrug. "Everybody knows that what happened to Marnie was an accident."

"Do we?" Jana asked. "How is it you both ended up on that steep hiking trail that morning?"

"It was all Marnie's idea," McCluskey said at once. "She loved hiking."

"Like hell she did," Dave muttered under his breath. "And the first lie doesn't stand a chance. You've got him, Jana. Now take him down."

Clearly McCluskey had forgotten the story he'd told

investigators all those years earlier about the hike being a breakfast-time honeymoon surprise, but Detective Davis allowed his remark to go unchallenged.

"Did she ever mention anything to you about being stuck on a Ferris wheel?"

There was a pause before he answered. "A Ferris wheel?" Harvey asked with a frown. "Not that I remember."

Detective Davis turned her attention from Harvey to Danny. "Did you happen to bring that evidence bag with you?"

"I certainly did," he replied, reaching into his pocket and producing the clear evidence bag that contained not only McCluskey's heavy gold chain but also the three trinkets that had once dangled from it. Morris set the bag on the table and pushed it purposefully in Harvey's direction.

"Why don't you tell us about the items in this bag?" Jana asked. "They obviously hold a good deal of significance for you."

There was another long pause as Harvey looked first at the bag and then back into Jana Davis's intense, inquiring gaze. "I think I want an attorney now," he said finally. "I don't want to talk anymore."

"I'm sure you don't, Mr. McCluskey," Jana agreed with a tight smile. "But you'd better hope to hell that you get a good public defender, because I believe you're going to need one."

|CHAPTER 54|

SEDONA, ARIZONA

Ali tackled the voice-mail messages first. Those were all from people who knew her and her parents well enough to have Ali's cell-phone number, and the messages left behind were more or less of a piece. The earliest ones came from people who'd heard that something bad had happened at Sedona Shadows and that Bob Larson might have been involved. Those callers simply wanted to know what was going on. Callers from later in the day had access to more details. They knew that Bob was gone and wanted to express their condolences. They asked how Edie was doing and wondered what they could do to help.

Once Ali had responded to the voice messages, she continued working her way through the missed calls, returning them as she went. These folks now knew that Bob was deceased and asked about when and where services would be held. As Ali continued returning those calls, a process interrupted more than once by yet another incoming one, she answered questions to the best of her ability. The truth was, it was impossible to predict when the funeral service could be held.

Along the way Ali began feeling relieved when someone didn't answer and she was able to leave a voice mail. That usually cut short the conversation by ten to fifteen minutes.

When Ali finally turned to her computer, she had over a hundred e-mails and literally dozens of text messages. She quickly formulated a short message that included what most people seemingly wanted to know.

Thank you so much for your concern about my dad. As you can imagine, both my mother and I are a bit overwhelmed at the moment, but Mom is doing as well as can be expected, considering what's happened.

Because of the circumstances surrounding Dad's death, we're unable to determine exactly when we'll be able to schedule a funeral service, but once we can, we'll do our best to let everyone know about it in a timely manner.

With that one-size-fits-all message saved and ready to copy and paste, Ali started responding to the well-wishers. As she went along, she was able to slip in personal messages over that standard response. That made the going much faster. And when she encountered messages that were clearly from media outlets following the story and hoping for an interview, she sent two words without any further elucidation: "NO COMMENT!"

It was hours later and she was close to seeing light at the end of the tunnel when her recharged phone rang again with a call from Dave Holman.

"How are you doing?" he asked when Ali answered.

"I feel like I've been run through a wringer. How about you?"

"The same," he said. "We were expecting company tonight. I was supposed to be home in Sedona, and I'm not."

"Is Priscilla pissed?" Ali wondered.

"I don't think so," Dave replied with a chuckle, "but only because the woman's a saint. With everything that was going on, I couldn't very well walk away from the department. In fact, I just this minute got off the phone with Howard Clifton, chief of police in Butte, Montana. Turns out he was new on the job and working patrol when Ida Mae McCluskey went missing, so the case was hardly unfamiliar to him. He remembered it well. Once I told him what we were looking at, he sent one of his investigators looking for Ida Mae's murder book.

"There wasn't a whole lot there. At the time of her disappearance, her husband, Leo, was the prime suspect. Harvey McCluskey, 'Broomy' as he was called back then, was interviewed. He claimed he was at a party at a friend's house and had been there all night. The friend in question—Anthony DeLuca—and several other boys who were also there that night backed him up. When Ida Mae's remains were discovered years later, her husband was already dead, so Butte PD called it a job and marked the case closed with no further investigation.

"However, it turns out Anthony DeLuca stayed on in Butte. He still lives there, running a small construction outfit. So Chief Clifton sent someone out to talk to him earlier this afternoon. Guess what? It turns out, back then, he and his buddies weren't exactly straight with the cops. At the time they admitted there was some underage drinking going on at the party, but they didn't mention how much—both beer and tequila. Before the night was over, they were all passed out cold."

"But maybe not McCluskey?" Ali asked.

"Maybe not," Dave agreed. "It's possible he could have snuck out of the house without anybody knowing he was gone. But here's the real kicker: Anthony DeLuca claims Harvey McCluskey flat-out hated his mother— absolutely despised the woman."

"If he could come and go that night without anyone being the wiser, his alibi for his mother's disappearance has just been blown to smithereens," Ali offered.

"Correct," Dave replied. "His alibi for that night is out the window."

"What about what happened to his father?"

"That's suicide for sure," Dave said, "no doubt about it. But Clifton said he'll have one of his detectives follow up with some of the other guys from the party. With Ida Mae's ring as evidence, he's willing to look into building a circumstantial case."

"Amazing," Ali breathed.

"And ditto for Maureen Richards," Dave said. "When Detective Davis from Coconino County brought up Marnie's name, you could see it left McCluskey stunned. And first rattle out of the box, she nailed him in a lie. At the time Maureen died, he said the hike into the canyon was some kind of honeymoon breakfast surprise. This afternoon he said the whole thing was Maureen's idea, even though she was well known for being afraid of heights. It's easy to remember the truth because it's the truth—that's what happened. When you're lying, it's a lot harder to remember what you said in previous interviews, especially years later. Once a suspect's story starts shifting, you can be damn sure the guy's got something to hide, and one way or another we're going to find out what it is."

Once that phone call ended, Ali closed her computer, took Bella out one last time, and headed for bed, but as it developed, not for sleep.

Considering all that had happened that day, it wasn't so surprising that Ali would end up tossing and turning, but amazingly enough what kept her awake was that last phone call with Dave and what he'd told her about guilty suspects not being able to keep their stories straight. What if someone's story never changed? Did that mean that person was telling the truth?

Bella endured Ali's restlessness for a time, but she finally abandoned Ali's side of the king-size bed in favor of B.'s. At last Ali switched on the light and bailed on the bed altogether. Earlier she'd scanned through the dossier that Frigg had created on Mateo Vega, but that was all she'd done—scan it. And once the decision had been made to hire him, she hadn't bothered to go into it in any depth.

But now something else was going through her head and nagging at her. Harvey McCluskey had walked around as a free man for decades after possibly murdering his own mother. What if Mateo Vega had spent the better part of two decades in prison, locked up for something he hadn't done?

Back on the love seat, Ali opened her computer and summoned Frigg.

"Good evening, Ms. Reynolds," the AI said. "You're up rather late. Can I be of any assistance?"

"Yes, you can," Ali said. "I'd like you to send me the transcripts for each of Mateo Vega's parole hearings."

"All of them?"

"Yes, please."

"Will there be anything else?"

"No, that's all I need."

Within a surprisingly short time, the transcripts started arriving. Ali scrolled through the proceedings one by one until she located each of Mateo's statements. Year after year what he said was the same, almost word for word: that he'd taken the plea deal at the urging of his defense counsel in hopes of receiving a lesser sentence; that he and Emily Tarrant had had sex before going to the party; that during the party he had interrupted her getting it on with someone else; that they had quarreled and left the party together but that on the way home she'd gotten out of the car. He claimed that was the last time he saw her. And each time his statement concluded the same way: "Even though we fought, I cared about Emily. I'm very sorry she's dead, but I didn't kill her."

By the time Ali finished reading the last of the transcripts, she was reasonably sure of one thing: Mateo Vega was innocent and had spent sixteen years of his life locked up for a homicide he hadn't committed.

|CHAPTER 55|

BELLINGHAM, WASHINGTON

As J.P. Beaumont, a homicide cop, I was seldom bored. As a retired homicide cop, I'm frequently bored to tears, and that was certainly the case on a blustery April morning in Bellingham, Washington. With a chill wind blowing in off the bay, I should probably have been out walking and might well have been if I still had a dog, but Lucy, the rescued Irish wolfhound that my wife, Mel Soames, and I had fostered for a time, had gone off to live in her forever home in Jasper, Texas, with my newly discovered granddaughter. But that's a whole other story.

So what was I doing that morning? I was halfheartedly scrolling through Irish wolfhound rescue sites looking for a Lucy replacement, but I wasn't having much luck. And that's when my cell phone rang. Had it been the landline, I for sure wouldn't have answered. But this was on my cell, and caller ID told me the call was coming from a place called Prescott, Arizona. I was intrigued, but with more and more junk callers spoofing different locations these days, I almost didn't answer. On ring number three, I gave in.

"Beaumont here," I said.

"Jonas Beaumont?" an unfamiliar male voice asked.

That was not a good sign. I had abandoned both my given names—Jonas Piedmont—at the first possible opportunity. People I know call me Beau, J.P., or Asshole, take your pick. The people who call me Jonas are usually selling something.

"Who's calling?" I demanded icily.

"My name's Gordon Maxwell," the man replied. "I'm the former sheriff of Yavapai County, Arizona. I retired last year. You're with TLC now, right?"

TLC—aka The Last Chance. Now the call started to make sense. TLC is an all-volunteer cold-case outfit made up of retired law-enforcement officers, forensic folks, CSIs, and prosecutors. We're the kind of driven people who might have been put out to pasture but who find it impossible to stay that way. If people won't pay us to do the job we love, then guess what? We'll do it for free.

A couple of years ago, a good friend of mine, Ralph Ames, saw how miserable I was in retirement and put me in touch with TLC. At my first TLC gathering, I sat in a room with twenty-five other people. Adding up all our years of service, we discovered we had a combined total of eight hundred and sixty-one years of law-enforcement experience. If you ask me, that's a hell of a lot of talent to leave withering on the vine.

"You've got me," I said in a less confrontational tone. "Most people call me Beau. What do people call you?"

"Gordy," he replied. "At any rate, TLC may be where

I got your name and number, but this isn't necessarily a TLC case—I mean, not officially anyway. But the original crime occurred in your neck of the woods, and I thought you might be able to do some digging on it."

"What do you mean by 'isn't necessarily'?" I asked.

"This isn't really a cold case. It was closed years ago but maybe not solved, if you get my drift. A friend of mine named Ali Reynolds brought it to my attention. Would you mind if I passed along your number and had her give you a call? She's good people," he added. "I think you'll like her."

"All right, then," I said agreeably. "The least I can do is talk to her."

"Thanks," Gordy said. "I appreciate it."

He hung up then, leaving me sitting there with a phone in my hand, waiting to see if it would ring.

|CHAPTER 56|

SEDONA, ARIZONA

Having slept so little the night before, Ali awakened late, but since she and B. had already decided she wouldn't be going to work that day, it hardly mattered. Once she had her first cup of coffee in hand, she'd called Gordon Maxwell. After giving him a brief overview of the situation with Mateo Vega, she asked if he thought this was something that might interest TLC. He promised he'd look into it.

Shortly after getting off the phone with him, she heard from her mother, calling to say that the medical examiner had notified her that Bob Larson's body would be released to the funeral home later that morning and would Ali mind driving her to Smithson's to drop off some of her father's clothing and then take Edie to the beauty shop for a cut and perm? Naturally Ali said yes on both counts.

After the meeting at Smithson's, where they finalized plans for the funeral, now scheduled for Friday afternoon at two, Ali had been in the car waiting for the end of her mother's beauty-shop appointment when Gordon called her back.

"I've located an investigator in Washington State who might be willing to look into the Mateo Vega situation," Gordon said. "His name's J.P. Beaumont, but he calls himself Beau. He lives in a town called Bellingham up near the Canadian border. Here's his number."

Ali hadn't mentioned a word to B. or anyone else about contacting TLC. If it all came to nothing, that would be the end of it, and no one other than Ali herself would be disappointed. By five to twelve, after dropping Edie at Sedona Shadows, Ali was back home and sitting in the library when she finally picked up her phone. "Here goes nothing," she told herself as she dialed the number Gordon had given her.

The phone was answered almost immediately. "J.P. Beaumont here," a male voice said.

"I'm Ali Reynolds from down in Sedona. I believe Gordon Maxwell might have told you about me."

"As a matter of fact, he did," came the reply. "According to what he said, you believe there may have been a miscarriage of justice somewhere along the way. Why don't you tell me about it?"

For the next little while, Ali related everything she knew about Mateo Vega and his connection to Emily Tarrant's homicide back in 2001, stressing the idea that in all the years Mateo had been in prison, his story about the homicide had never changed, nor did he accept any responsibility.

"What's your interest in all this?" Beau asked when Ali finished.

Ali thought for a moment before she answered. "Mateo was fresh out of college and working for my husband's previous company at the time of his arrest. After being released from prison almost a year ago, he's been working at a minimum-wage job. Despite the fact that he's a very smart guy as far as computer science is concerned, with his record no one would give him a job doing anything other than working on a loading dock. Once my husband learned what was going on, we reached out, and we've now hired Mateo to work for us at our company here in Cottonwood, Arizona. He strikes me as a nice man. Not a young man any longer, but a nice one, and I can't help but think something has gone haywire here."

"JDLR," Beau said, and Ali laughed aloud at that bit of law-enforcement jargon.

"Yes," she agreed, "it just doesn't look right."

Ali expected Beau to tell her that he'd think it over and get back to her with an answer. Instead he surprised her.

"Okay," he said. "I was jotting down details as you went along. Let me see what I can find out on this end. Is it all right to call you back on this number?"

"Yes, that's fine."

"Talk to you soon, then," Beau finished, and then he hung up.

Ali sat holding the phone for a long moment after the call ended. Whether or not anything came of this, she had at least taken a stab at it. Now it was time for her to face up to her next task. With an aching heart, she opened her laptop determined to set about doing one of the toughest writing assignments she'd ever undertaken—composing her father's obituary.

|CHAPTER 57|

BELLINGHAM, WASHINGTON

No one was more surprised than I was when I told Ali Reynolds I'd look into the Mateo Vega situation. Initially, before we connected, I thought she was most likely just another empty-headed do-gooder messing around with something that was none of her business. But when it became clear that she was truly concerned about what had happened to Mateo Vega and that she'd done her homework, that changed. When I mentioned the JDLR shorthand, I didn't mean to say it aloud. It just popped out of my mouth, but the fact that she instantly understood that that bit of copspeak meant "just doesn't look right" sucked me in.

But there were other reasons I said yes. The first TLC case I ever worked was one that had ties to both Arizona and Washington State. A guy named John Lassiter had languished in an Arizona prison for decades over a crime he didn't commit, put there by a gang of corrupt law-enforcement officers and prosecutors. What right-thinking good cop wouldn't jump at the chance to take down some bad ones? And once TLC's investigation into Lassiter's situation helped find the answers to a long-unsolved Seattle-area homicide, I became a true believer—in like Flynn, as the saying goes.

Based on what Ali Reynolds had told me, Mateo Vega's situation seemed to be vaguely similar to Big Bad John's. I was impressed that she'd gone to the trouble of obtaining the guy's parole-hearing statements, and the fact that they never varied over the years carried a lot of weight with me, just as it did with her. But unfortunately, out in the real world, there are plenty of prosecutors who prefer encouraging suspects to accept plea deals over having to undertake thorough investigations. In other words, from what I was hearing, enough "there" was there to make me want to know more.

I may be retired, but Mel, my wife, as the somewhat newly appointed chief of police in Bellingham, Washington, is definitely not in that same boat. When I opened my computer earlier that morning, a reminder had appeared on my calendar saying Mel and I were due to attend a soiree of some kind that evening. The party would be chock-full of local dignitaries. They and all their significant others were expected to get cleaned up, put on their best bib and tucker, and show up on time.

As the spouse of a local police chief, I do my best to perform my husbandly duties when called upon to do so. However, tonight's gathering was one of those recurring events that happen every year, and I'd had the misfortune of attending the previous one.

I'm one of those guys who's given up drinking on a permanent basis. Having to stand around for a couple of hours making idle conversation with a bunch of strangers isn't my idea of a good time. At such events I usually walk around with a glass of ginger ale in hand so I'm not required to explain why I'm not drinking. There are lots of reasons for that, by the way, but most party guests don't want to hear about them.

After a minimal amount of thought, I decided to use Mateo Vega's case as my get-out-of-jail-free card for the evening. I called Mel's office. For a change I got through to her without having to wait on hold.

"What's up?"

"A guy from TLC just called," I told her. "I've got a case and need to head down to Seattle ASAP."

"Do you really have a case, or are you just trying to weasel out of having to go to the shindig tonight?" she asked.

"Would I try to pull a dumb stunt like that?" I asked, playing a card I knew in advance wouldn't work.

She laughed. "Case or not, you're excused, but on one condition."

"What's that?"

"You have to make an effort to see the kids before you come back home."

These days my "kid" situation is a little complicated. First on the list would be my son and daughter-in-law, Scott and Cherisse, and their son, JonJon. They named the poor kid Jonas in my honor. Thankfully, they started calling him JonJon almost from day one.

Next up on the "kid" roster is my relatively new daughter, Naomi, and Athena, the granddaughter who lives in Texas. Although Naomi is now in her thirties, she's been a part of my life for only a matter of months. She came about as the unintended consequence of a drunken one-night stand back in the eighties. I believe I already mentioned there are reasons I gave up drinking, and having occasional one-night stands is very close to the top of that list.

The next part of Naomi's story is tragically all too familiar for too many families. She was a smart kid who fell in with a bad crowd in high school. Naomi ran away from home and ended up in Seattle, where she took up with a fellow druggie who turned up dead months before Athena was born—murdered, surprisingly enough, by something that had nothing to do with either narcotics or drug trafficking.

Distraught and homeless, Naomi abandoned her newborn baby at a local hospital, and Athena's other grandpa, hoping to keep the baby out of foster care, showed up on my doorstep asking for help in his quest to be appointed Athena's legal guardian. That's what brought me into the picture.

You'll be happy to know that at this point Naomi is in a good place. She has successfully completed a residential drug-treatment program. For now she has decided to leave Athena in her father's—her *other* father's—care while she goes back to school to work on an associate's degree.

There's also my other daughter, Kelly, who lives in southern Oregon. Kelly got knocked up in high school and took off with her musician boyfriend. Where are they now? Happily married with two kids. But since they live the better part of two states south of us, adding them to this trip's agenda wasn't necessary.

"I'll do my best to see both Scott and Naomi," I promised Mel, "as long as they're not too busy."

"Okay, then," she said, giving me her blessing. "Have fun, but you owe me one."

"I certainly do," I told her.

Before heading out the door, I did a quick Internet search on the Emily Anne Tarrant homicide and learned that although the beach in question appeared to be located in Edmonds, for some reason the case had been investigated by the King County Sheriff's Department. The lead investigator on the case had been a guy named Henry Norton. Wonder of wonders, Hank Norton happened to be someone I knew personally back in the day, and not in a good way. Even while I was still at Seattle PD, he'd had a reputation in local law-enforcement circles for cutting corners and pushing envelopes. And while Mel and I worked at the Washington State Special Homicide Investigation Team, or SHIT yes, I realize those initials add up to a very unfortunate acronym, but it's a name we all wore with pride, and without it I might never have met my wife—we'd run up against several of Detective Norton's sloppily handled cases.

With only the barest outline of Emily Tarrant's case in mind, I headed down I-5, knowing exactly where I had to go to flesh out the story.

For the record, evidence boxes take up lots of room. When a case is deemed closed, the evidence involved doesn't disappear in a puff of smoke. It has to be kept and maintained in an orderly fashion. As downtown Seattle real estate has become more and more expensive, local cop shops including King County have gone looking for warehouse space in less pricey parts of the city—in this case a nondescript warehouse just south of CenturyLink Field.

When I arrived, I used my private-investigator ID to gain admittance to the building. The guy behind the counter, a kid who looked to be barely out of junior high, took my information, copied my ID, made a note of the case I was interested in, and then sat me down in a cubicle to wait. Much to my surprise, he was back with the banker's box in question in very short order.

Since the Tarrant case was closed, there was no prohibition against my examining or photographing any of the evidence I found there. Even so, every move I made was under the watchful eye of a surveillance camera. After dusting off the top of the box and peeling away the red tape that had held it shut, I went through everything inside, copying material as needed with the scanning app on my iPhone, but the truth of the matter is, there wasn't much there.

Emily Tarrant's autopsy listed manual strangulation as the cause of death. There were lots of postmortem scratches and contusions on the body due to its having been tossed into a blackberry patch shortly after death. The autopsy reported that a rape kit had been performed. DNA evidence had been obtained from that as well as from Emily's clothing. Those samples had been submitted to the Washington State Crime Lab for processing.

As for the murder book itself? For a homicide case, it was very sparse indeed. Other attendees at the beach party had been interviewed without much enthusiasm or with any apparent follow-up. They all agreed that both Mateo and Emily had been at the party. The couple had arrived together and left together. As they were leaving, they were reportedly involved in a heated argument, although no one seemed to know the exact cause of the disagreement.

It was clear to me that Mateo had been the focus of Hank Norton's investigation from the very beginning. No other suspects were ever identified or brought in for questioning. Part of the problem owed to the fact that once Mateo left the party, there was no one who could verify his movements between then and the following afternoon when he reported his girlfriend missing. From that moment on, as far as the lead investigator was concerned, Mateo was the prime suspect.

I could have requested to watch the videos of Hank Norton's interviews with Mr. Vega right away, but I didn't bother. I'd seen him in action before, and at the moment I didn't need to sit through hours of watching him bullying a suspect to convince myself he was a bad cop.

The Emily Anne Tarrant case was declared officially closed some fifteen months later when Mateo Vega appeared in a King County courtroom and pled guilty to second-degree homicide. Had the investigator involved been anyone other than Hank Norton, I might have let it go at that. As it was, I was obliged to dig deeper.

DNA profiling is both expensive and time-consuming, although it's a hell of a lot faster these days than it used to be. Statewide, the Washington State Patrol Crime Lab is the entity that does DNA processing for all Washington-based jurisdictions—it tests the evidence, obtains the DNA samples, creates the profiles, and submits them to CODIS. I worked more closely with the crime lab during my time with SHIT than I did while working for Seattle PD, and the special homicide stint of my policing career was a lot more recent. As a result, when I got to the crime lab and asked who was on duty in the DNA section, I was delighted to learn that Gretchen Walther was holding down the fort. She's someone I know.

Several minutes later she came down to reception.

After an effusive greeting, she escorted me upstairs. By the way, no one gets a free pass into the crime lab. Either you have an escort with you or you don't go. On the way to the lab, I told Gretchen what I was looking for—profiles obtained from the Emily Anne Tarrant homicide. Once back at her computer station, she quickly typed the information I had provided into her computer. When the first results came back, she studied them for a long time, frowning.

"That's odd," she muttered at last.

"What's odd?"

"These profiles were obtained within a month of the day the homicide occurred. As far as I can tell, the results were forwarded to the King County prosecutor's office, but there's nothing here to indicate that either of those original profiles was ever entered into CODIS."

That was a serious admission, and Gretchen probably shouldn't have said it aloud, but the cat was out of the bag.

"Can you enter them now?" I asked.

Another period of frowning silence was accompanied by warp-speed keyboarding while I stood there waiting, shifting from one foot to the other and forcing myself to remain absolutely quiet.

"Okay," she said finally, "the one from the rape kit was rejected because it leads back to Juan Mateo Vega and is a duplicate of one submitted by the Monroe Correctional Facility upon his arrival there some fifteen months after the initial profile was obtained."

"That means the one from the crime scene never arrived?" I asked.

"Correct," Gretchen replied. "Now I'll run the profiles taken from the victim's clothing."

After more swift keyboarding, Gretchen finished typing and pressed Send. Very little time passed   not more than thirty seconds—before a whole new set of material appeared on her screen. This one included a mug shot of a man whose face was covered with tattoos. Moments later Gretchen printed it out.

"There you go," she said, handing the page to me. "Meet Mr. Josiah Young. He's currently serving three consecutive life terms at the Monroe Correctional Facility for three counts of forcible rape and murder."

And that's when I knew for sure that Ali Reynolds was right. Mateo Vega had just spent sixteen years of his life locked up for a crime he didn't commit.

Feeling invigorated and excited, I left the crime lab. By then it was after six. My intention was to go straight to our condo at Belltown Terrace and start boning up on the life and times of one Josiah Alvin Young, but once in the car I realized I had totally missed lunch, and I was starving.

Driving north toward downtown, I did the only thing any self-respecting cop of my generation would do—I pulled in to the drive-thru at Krispy Kreme and ordered a dozen doughnuts, enough to cover both dinner and breakfast, with maybe some left over for lunch.

As I drove away from the window with the sweet-smelling box sitting on the front seat beside me, I couldn't help but feel a tiny bit sorry for Mel. Whatever version of rubber chicken she was having for dinner tonight couldn't possibly measure up to those doughnuts.

|CHAPTER 58|

SEATTLE, WASHINGTON

Upstairs in our Belltown Terrace penthouse, I made coffee—coffee has never kept me awake—and downed three of the doughnuts—plain-glazed and scrumptious. Then I turned on the gas-log fireplace in the study and settled in with my computer. When Gretchen mentioned the name Josiah Young, I had recognized it as one of the interviewees from Emily's murder box. He'd been one of the individuals at the beach party and someone Hank Norton had interviewed in the course of his lightweight investigation.

With the information obtained from Gretchen in hand, I now knew that Young had been nineteen years old at the time of the murder and living with his parents in Boise, Idaho. He'd been in Seattle that weekend, visiting his stepbrother, Andrew Little, one of Mateo's best friends from the U Dub. Since Josiah had been at the party, I had reason to believe he was the guy Emily Tarrant had been making out with when Mateo caught up with them down on the beach. In other words, Hank

Norton hadn't noticed the killer hiding in plain sight because he'd been totally focused on the boyfriend.

At the time of the homicide, Josiah was a kid barely out of high school and with no prior history of juvenile offenses. Six years later, by age twenty-five, he was serving life in prison, convicted of three separate rape/murders. His preferred hunting grounds were out of town—two in Spokane and one in Pullman. His victims, all coeds, were invariably petite blondes. From the photos provided, those three girls might well have been Emily Tarrant's sisters. In addition, Young was the prime suspect in the rape/murder of a University of Idaho student in Moscow, Idaho. Once Washington nailed him with three consecutive life without parole sentences, prosecutors in Idaho decided to let their case slide. They didn't see any need to go to the time, trouble, and expense of putting him on trial.

Emily might have been Josiah Young's introduction to bloodlust, but Mateo Vega had been the one who paid the price.

When I finished my dive into Josiah's ugly history, it was time to figure out what to do about it. In the past, as a sworn law-enforcement officer, I wouldn't have had to wonder. I'd have taken my findings up the chain of command—but as an independent operative for The Last Chance, I was part of no chain of command. I had uncovered a whole lot of damning evidence, but as a member of TLC's loose-knit community of volunteers, I couldn't do a whole hell of a lot with it. Fortunately, I knew people who could.

The Lassiter case in Arizona had introduced me to an organization called Justice for All. Think of JFA as a stealth version of the Innocence Project, small but effective, as in "speak softly and carry a big stick." My only question was this. Would anyone there be interested in Mateo Vega?

There are any number of reasons that outfits like TLC keep us old geezers on their rosters. We're handy as hell because, as I mentioned earlier, not only do we have decades of experience, we come complete with long-standing networks of connections. In this instance, after a single call to Brandon Walker down in Tucson, I was referred to JFA's local Seattle-area contact, Chloe Bannerman in Redmond, Washington.

I called her at home just after eight, and her initial response to me was every bit as frosty as mine had been to Gordy Maxwell earlier in the day. "Who the hell are you?" and "How did you get this number?" Dropping Brandon Walker's name into the conversation and saying this was all about JFA quickly smoothed Chloe's ruffled feathers.

"All right, then," she said. "What do you need?"

So I told her, and not in twenty-five words or less. By the time I finished, she was on her game. She wanted all pertinent details, names, and phone numbers, and I could hear her making detailed notes as we went along. When our conversation was coming to a close, she asked if I had discussed the matter with anyone other than her.

"Nope," I said. "I asked Brandon for a local JFA contact, but I didn't mention any of the details to him."

"I see here that you didn't include any direct contact information for Mr. Vega."

"That's because I don't have it," I told her. "My involvement came strictly from that earlier conversation with Ali Reynolds."

"In that case," Chloe said, "I'll start with her, but would you do me a favor?"

"What's that?"

"Call her and let her know I'll be in touch. After that I'd appreciate it if you'd keep a low profile. If JFA ends up taking any kind of action on this, I'd like to be in charge of controlling the media narrative."

"Yes, ma'am," I agreed. "Some of my past involvements with the media have been problematic at best."

When I finally got off the phone, I had no clue what Chloe would do, but I was pretty sure she was going to do something. By then it was nine thirty. Was that too late to call Ali back? After a moment's hesitation, I decided it wasn't. She answered after only one ring.

"Sorry to be calling so late," I said after identifying myself, "but I've managed to unearth some pretty important evidence that may be enough to exonerate Mateo Vega."

I heard a sharp intake of breath. "Are you serious?"

"Deadly serious," I told her. "Someone named Chloe Bannerman will be calling you. She's with a wrongful-conviction organization called Justice for All. Years ago I worked with JFA, although not with Chloe herself, on another case. When she asked for Mateo's contact information, I advised her she'd need to go through you."

"Thank you so much, Mr. Beaumont," Ali said. "I'll look forward to her call."

"Call me Beau," I said. "That's what my friends call me."

By the time that call ended, it was getting on toward ten and time to make good on my promise to Mel—to no avail. I tried Scotty first. It turned out JonJon had an ear infection, so seeing them the next day was out. As for Naomi? She was tied up with midterms. So what did I do? I headed home to Bellingham. The penthouse at Belltown Terrace is nice as far as it goes, but without Mel it's just . . . well . . . a penthouse.

The good thing about traveling on I-5 at that hour of the night was zero traffic. And despite my not having seen the kids, I was pretty sure Mel would be happy to see me, to say nothing of the rest of those Krispy Kreme doughnuts.

|CHAPTER 59|

SEDONA, ARIZONA

Writing usually came easily for Ali, but not that afternoon. She struggled with her father's obituary for more than two hours before she'd finally refined it to the point where she was willing to share it with her mother. Once Edie heard it and gave her stamp of approval, Ali sent it along to Althea at the mortuary.

The whole time Ali had been working on the obituary, her phone and computer had continued to explode with a brand-new round of incoming texts and e-mails. Before facing her next writing assignment—her father's eulogy—she decided to tackle at least some of that electronic correspondence. The number of messages alone was downright daunting—almost the same-size deluge as the day before, but once Ali started reading them, she found subtle differences from the ones that had come in the previous day.

She'd known all along that her father was generous in nature, but it wasn't until that afternoon, reading through the countless e-mails expressing both condolences and gratitude, that Ali began to understand the full extent of it.

First came the individuals from the group of vets in the homeless encampment up on the Mogollon Rim. Ali knew about them because she had often been involved in delivering holiday meals, warm clothing, and blankets to the unfortunate folks living there. But Ali hadn't known about any of the three separate women who wrote to say that when they were struggling single mothers, Bob Larson had stepped up to do extensive repairs on the broken-down vehicles that had been their only means of transportation, at a time when the repairs in question would have been totally beyond their means. Several people described the loads of wood he had dropped off to fuel the wood-burning stoves that were their only source of winter heat. And any number of middle-agers told how, as kids, their damaged bicycles had been rehabbed in Bob Larson's backyard workshop.

The message that really struck Ali was from a woman, a single mom, whose home had been washed away during a sudden winter flash flood shortly before Christmas. With her whole existence wiped out, someone had found her a place to live in what was mostly an empty shell of a mobile home. On Christmas Eve, Bob organized a group of his pals. They showed up at her new place with a pre-decorated Christmas tree, along with trucks and cars loaded with furniture and household goods, to say nothing of toys and clothing for her three young children.

Bob had always been the public face in these efforts—delivering various goods and services—but Ali realized now that he hadn't done it all on his own. Those acts of kindness had been made possible with the full cooperation and understanding of her mother, Bob's partner in both life and work.

After answering some of those touching notes, Ali took a step back. Rather than simply replying, she printed off each of the missives as well as her responses. Once transformed into hard copies, these were no longer ephemeral messages that came in and disappeared into cyberspace. Watching the stack grow, Ali decided she would use them to create a small chapbook—something physical that long after the funeral her mother would be able to read at her leisure.

Ali was still at work on that at six o'clock in the evening when she heard the garage door open. Surprised, she and Bella headed for the kitchen, where they met up with B. as he entered.

"What are you doing here?" Ali asked. "I thought you were going to stay over."

"So did I," B. said, "but I was outvoted. Under the circumstances Lance and Stu both thought my place was here with you. Either we can stay home or, if you want, we can drive over to Cornville and check on Cami."

Ali was more than ready to get out of the house. "Alonzo made a batch of lasagna for her today," she said. "I was planning on dropping it off tomorrow, but why don't we go now? At this point we know way more about Harvey McCluskey than we did before, and I doubt Cami has heard any of it."

With that decided, they packed up the lasagna and Bella and headed out. On the drive over, Ali told B. about the ongoing investigations surrounding Harvey McCluskey, but she didn't mention her conversation with J.P. Beaumont concerning Mateo. Why get someone's hopes up if nothing ever came of it? Instead she spent the remainder of their drive time regaling B. with all the things she'd learned about her father in the course of the afternoon.

When they arrived at Cami's house in Cornville, Sister Anselm answered the door. "How's the patient?" Ali asked.

"Grumpy," was the nun's glum answer, "but come on in. Cami doesn't seem to think she's in need of my assistance, but until those bandages come off her hands and she can use a pair of crutches, I'm afraid she's stuck with me and that wheelchair. The damage on her hands is close to what you'd get from second- or third-degree burns. Those aren't going to miraculously heal themselves overnight, and the bandages must be changed on a daily basis."

Sister Anselm's face brightened when she caught sight of the foil-topped baking dish B. was carrying. "From Alonzo?" she asked.

B. nodded. "Lasagna."

"Good," Sister Anselm said, taking the dish and leading the way inside. "When it comes to cooking, I can manage, but I'm not in Alonzo's league."

Furniture had been pushed aside to make room for maneuvering Cami's wheelchair. Dressed in a pair of shorts and a loose-fitting sweatshirt, she sat with her leg extended straight out in front of her. Her cast stretched from halfway up her thigh to the tips of her toes. The bandages on her hands looked like white boxing gloves. Her face was still bruised and battered, but her swollen ear had shrunk back to almost its normal size. As advertised, she was not a happy camper.

"I hate this," Cami grumbled. "I can't stand having people fussing over me."

"At least we brought food," B. said cheerfully. "Alonzo sent along some lasagna."

Cami held up her bandaged hands. "Great," she said, "but how am I supposed to eat it?"

"The same way you ate your lunch," Sister Anselm growled. "I'll feed it to you—like it or lump it."

Had there been a door available, Sister Anselm probably would have slammed it behind her as she stomped her way over to the kitchen area. In Cami's newly designed open floor plan, however, her only option was to disappear around a corner with the baking dish in hand.

"How are you?" Ali asked.

"Better, I guess," Cami replied. "But I have no idea how long it'll be before I can come back to work."

"Going back to work is the least of your worries right now," B. assured her. "For the time being, we're all pitching in and holding things together."

"How's Mateo working out?"

"Better than expected," B. answered.

"Have you two eaten?" Sister Anselm called from the kitchen.

"No," Ali said, "but—"

"There's plenty here. I'll heat it up, and we'll all have some."

"I never knew she was so bossy," Cami muttered under her breath.

"Yes," Ali said. "It's her way or the highway, so you'd better get used to it. Now, if you're up to it, we'd like to fill you in on what we've managed to learn about Harvey McCluskey while you've been lounging around in a hospital bed and generally taking life easy."

That comment elicited the slightest hint of a smile on Cami's face. "By all means," she said. "Tell me."

Back home in Sedona, Ali handed B. the stack of condolence messages she'd received, answered, and printed out.

"There must be over a hundred of these," he said, shaking his head.

Ali nodded. "And these are only the ones I worked on today. Almost as many came in yesterday."

"How big is Smithson's funeral chapel?" B. asked.

"I'm not sure. Why?"

"Because if all these people turn up for the service, a lot of them will end up being sent away."

"What do you suggest?"

"Find a bigger venue."

"Like what?" Ali wondered.

"What about the high school auditorium?" B. responded. "That holds six hundred or so, and I'm guessing Chris and Athena would have some pull on that score."

"Okay," Ali agreed. "I'll look into it first thing tomorrow morning."

Later, as they were about to head to bed, Ali's phone rang. "Just let it go to voice mail," B. advised. "You can deal with it in the morning."

With the 206 area-code number showing on caller ID, however, Ali went ahead and answered. "Sorry to be calling so late," said a now-familiar voice, "but I've managed to unearth some pretty important evidence that may be enough to exonerate Mateo Vega."

Ali caught her breath. "Are you serious?" she whispered, barely believing her ears. By the time the call ended, B. was frowning at her.

"Beau?" he asked. "Who's that?"

"Someone calling with some very good news," Ali

answered, but before she could go into any more detail, the phone rang again.

"Is this Ali Reynolds?" a woman asked.

"Yes."

"My name's Chloe Bannerman. I hope it isn't too late to call."

"Not at all," Ali said, "but do you mind if I put the phone on speaker? My husband is here, and I'd like him to hear what you have to say."

"Your husband would be Mr. Simpson, the man who hired Mr. Vega?"

"That's correct."

"Then by all means put him on speaker. That way I won't have to say this more than once. I work with an organization called Justice for All. JFA's sole focus is sorting out wrongful convictions," Chloe explained. "Due to the evidence Mr. Beaumont has supplied, I believe there's a good chance that if we were to take on Mateo Vega's case, we might be able to achieve a satisfactory outcome. Do you think Mr. Vega would be interested in speaking with me?"

"Absolutely," Ali said.

"Can you give me his number?"

"I can, but he's not available right now. Could I have him call you sometime tomorrow?"

"Of course," Chloe said. "Have him do so at his convenience."

By the time that conversation ended some twenty minutes later, B. might have been every bit as thrilled as Ali, but he was still in the dark about a lot of it.

"Lucy," he said, as she put the phone back on its charger, "I think you have some 'splaining to do!"

|CHAPTER 60|

COTTONWOOD, ARIZONA

Even though it was past midnight when Mateo got into bed, he awakened long before his alarm went off. He lay there for a moment, savoring the idea that he had a queen-size bed with clean sheets and blankets all to himself. When he got out of bed, he walked barefoot to the bathroom, where there was a toilet that wasn't stained with someone else's dribbles. He took a shower that was long and hot and totally private, without a drunken roommate pounding on the door and yelling at him to hurry the hell up. Then he went a couple of steps—that's all it took—to cover the distance to his tiny kitchen, where he started the coffee. The RV came totally furnished with linens, a toaster, dishes, silverware, and a well-used Mr. Coffee.

Late the previous afternoon, Stu had given Mateo a lift to Walmart, where he purchased a couple changes of clothing and some food—coffee, bread, milk, tortillas, peanut butter, eggs. The tortillas were a disappointment. His mother's tortillas had been so thin that you could almost see through them. These were much thicker and stiffer, but they were his, and with a generous layer of peanut butter they worked just fine. The real miracle of all this food was that he could put it away and not have someone else steal it.

He ate his breakfast in front of the flat-screen TV, watching local news programming and switching channels with wild abandon. When breakfast was over, he slid his utensils and coffee cup into the single-drawer dishwasher, filled the proper container with detergent, and turned it on. That was pretty amazing, too. The house in Renton had a dishwasher all right, but it didn't work, and, to a man, his roommates never in their lives bothered to clean up after themselves. The kitchen had always been a filthy mess. This one wouldn't be.

With that, Mateo set out to walk to work, a spring in his step. He'd walked to work in Renton, but this was different. This was in the desert with a clear blue sky overhead—a sky that reminded him of growing up in Yakima. In Renton the sodden gray skies for days and weeks on end had always left him feeling sad. And then there was the job—this job—doing something that was challenging and exciting. Sorting through other people's discarded junk on the thrift store's loading dock had been necessary work and vitally important for the impoverished people who shopped there, but it had never been very satisfying.

Mateo understood that he'd arrived at High Noon when the company was in crisis mode. With Cami currently absent, he'd been put on a fast track to responsibility that was being delivered in a matter of hours rather than weeks or months. But he knew, too, that he was catching on, doing what was needed, and being paid more than he'd ever imagined possible. When he went shopping the day before, he'd been able to do so without worrying about having enough money to cover his purchases. Even after paying for the RV rental, his signing bonus was still serving him well.

He approached the door to High Noon in good spirits and let himself in with the expectation of a busy day at work. Shirley greeted him with a warm smile. "Before you go back to the lab," she said, "B. and Ali would like to have a word with you in Mr. Simpson's office."

Mateo's heart fell. In his experience, someone wanting to have "a word with you" was never a good thing. It reminded him of the grade school principal who'd wanted to have a word after a misfired baseball broke a classroom window or Detective Norton showing up on his doorstep in Lynnwood all those years ago saying he wanted to have a word with him and would Mateo mind riding along to police headquarters in downtown Seattle. Back then Mateo *had* minded, but he didn't have any choice, and he didn't have any choice now either. Had he done something wrong? Was he about to be sent packing?

With a curtain of despair descending around him, Mateo started down the hallway. The door to B.'s office was open. When he poked his head inside, B. and Ali were clearly discussing Ali's father's upcoming funeral. "So the auditorium's a go, then?" B. was asking.

"Yes, it is. With both Chris and Athena teaching there, it was pretty much a done deal," Ali replied. "And I've already let the mortuary know about the change in venue. They'll be getting the word out, and so will I."

Just then B. noticed Mateo standing in the doorway.

"Oh, there you are," he said. "Come in and have a seat. Ali has some things she'd like to discuss with you."

The last thing Mateo wanted to do was sit. If someone was coming at you with a shank, you needed to be on your feet, ready to either take off or fight back. But Mateo sat anyway. What else could he do?

He studied Ali. She was older and attractive, but it occurred to him that under the present circumstances she was probably dangerous as well. And the first words out of her mouth made his heart freeze.

"We've been looking into your situation," she said.

This is it, Mateo thought. *They've decided having an ex-con on the payroll is a bad idea after all.* Knowing what was coming, he sat stock-still and waited.

"Have you ever heard of an organization called Justice for All?"

Stunned, Mateo had to think for a moment and regroup before he could answer. "No," he said at last, shaking his head. "I don't think so. Why?"

"Before we hired you," Ali explained, "we did a deep dive into your background. As part of that, Frigg obtained transcripts of all your parole-board hearings. The thing that stood out to me was that you always said the same thing. Your story never changed."

"That's because what I was saying was true," Mateo said defensively.

"That's what occurred to me as well," Ali replied. "A friend of mine referred me to a guy named J.P. Beaumont from Washington State, who works with a group called TLC—The Last Chance. They're an all-volunteer organization devoted to solving cold cases. Yesterday Beau uncovered information indicating discrepancies in how evidence from the Emily Tarrant crime scene was handled."

"What discrepancies?" Mateo asked.

"We'll go into details in a moment," Ali said. "Armed with what he'd learned, Mr. Beaumont then reached out to a woman named Chloe Bannerman, JFA's point person in the state of Washington. Ms. Bannerman would very much like to speak to you, and I told her I'd have you give her a call this morning."

Unsure of what was being said or where this was going, Mateo shifted in his seat. "Who is this woman?" he asked. "And why exactly does she want to speak to me?"

"As I said, JFA specializes in overturning wrongful convictions," Ali said. "She'd like very much to discuss your case."

Mateo's heart thumped. For a moment he could think of nothing to say. "Someone wants to discuss my case?" he stammered stupidly.

"Would you like me to give her a call?" Ali offered. "I'd be happy to put her on speaker."

Mateo's head was spinning. "Sure," he said at last. "See if you can reach her."

Moments later Chloe Bannerman's cheerful voice filled the room. "Good morning, Mr. Vega," she said. "I'm happy to meet you."

"Me, too," Mateo mumbled.

"I assume Ms. Reynolds has told you that after some back-and-forth discussion with the executive committee Justice for All may be interested in looking into your case."

"Yes, ma'am," Mateo said. "She told me that."

"So let me ask you a question, Mr. Vega. Does the name Josiah Young ring any bells?"

Mateo had to think about that before he answered.

"Sure," he said finally. "He's a lifer in the joint. I didn't know him personally, but I remember him. He's the asshole everybody inside calls Tattoo Man. He has ink all over his body. Why?"

"I believe Mr. Young's stepbrother, one Andrew Little, was a friend of yours."

Mateo's head went back to those long-ago times. He hadn't thought about Andy in years. The party on the beach was the last time he'd seen or spoken to his one-time best friend.

"Right," he said. "Andy and I were friends back then, but I had no idea he and Josiah are related."

"Would it surprise you if I told you that Mr. Young was a guest at the same beach party you and Emily attended on the night she disappeared?"

"He was there?" Mateo croaked, tumbling at last to the implications.

"He was," Chloe Bannerman confirmed. "You might have seen him at the party, but without the inked face. That came later."

"How can you be sure?" Mateo asked.

"Because Mr. Young's DNA was found on the clothing Emily was wearing at the time she was murdered. The crime lab obtained two separate profiles, but for some reason no DNA samples obtained from that crime scene—his or yours—were ever entered into CODIS. If Mr. Young's had been, and if he'd been connected to Emily's homicide in a timely manner, four other young women might well be alive today and you most likely would never have gone to prison."

Mateo sat frozen in stunned silence, barely able to breathe.

"Are you there, Mr. Vega?"

"Yes, I'm here," he managed.

"Mr. Young's presence at the Tarrant crime scene and his subsequent criminal behavior cast grave doubts on the validity of your conviction, so I'm wondering if you would be interested in having JFA look into this matter for you."

"How much would it cost?"

"Nothing at all up front," Chloe assured him. "If JFA were to end up winning a wrongful-imprisonment judgment against the state of Washington, we would of course receive a portion of any resulting settlement. The details of that arrangement would be laid out in the retainer paperwork required in order for us to represent you—if you're interested, that is."

"I'm interested," Mateo croaked.

"Very well," Chloe said. "I can overnight the documents or I could e-mail a set via DocuSign. Which do you prefer?"

"Why don't you e-mail the DocuSign material to him here at the office?" Ali suggested. "That will speed up the process, if that's okay with you, Mateo."

"It's okay," Mateo answered, speaking barely above a hoarse whisper. "Thank you."

With that he fled—first B.'s office, then the building, and finally the office park itself. He managed to hold himself in check long enough to make it back to the privacy of his RV. There he fell onto the bed and buried his face in the pillow. Only then did he finally let a torrent of tears spill out—tears of gratitude. After all those years of his trying to tell people he hadn't murdered Emily, someone somewhere finally believed him.

|CHAPTER 61|

SEATTLE, WASHINGTON

As expected, Mel was more than happy to have me back home that night. The next afternoon I was once again prowling Irish wolfhound rescue sites on the Internet when Chloe Bannerman called.

"Mateo Vega just put JFA on retainer," she said. "He was completely gobsmacked by the idea that Josiah Young might be responsible for Emily Tarrant's murder. He remembered him from his time in prison—mostly because of his tattoos, but the two of them had no direct interactions. Mateo never connected the guy called Tattoo Man with someone who attended that long-ago beach party. For one thing, as a teen, I doubt that Josiah Young's face was covered with all that ink."

"Probably not," I agreed, "so what's the next step?"

"JFA will be doing a full-scale investigation into the case—not only about the state's failure of oversight in regard to uploading the DNA but also into the investigation itself."

So much for Hank Norton, I thought.

"With Young already in prison," Chloe continued, "there's no reason to be hush-hush about it. I'll probably launch a media campaign to see if we can suss out anyone who might be able to offer additional information."

"Will you be mentioning me by name?"

"Not if you don't want me to."

"That would be my first choice," I told her.

"I don't blame you," Chloe agreed with a laugh. "This case is going to rattle a bunch of law-enforcement cages. I wouldn't want to do anything that might make things difficult for Bellingham's chief of police."

So Chloe Bannerman knew about Mel and me? Obviously not much got past her.

"How long before the media bomb goes off?" I asked.

"If I have anything to do with it, that will happen sooner rather than later," she replied.

That made me smile. I like it when karma finally gets around to biting bad people in the butt, and in my book Hank Norton definitely qualified as bad people.

|CHAPTER 62|

At two on Friday afternoon, the auditorium at Sedona High School was packed to the gills. The principal had actually dismissed school an hour early that day in order to avoid having a traffic jam in the parking lot. Reverend Dennis Duncan, pastor of Sedona's Faith Lutheran Church, would be officiating. Although Bob and Edie had been lifelong members of the congregation, they'd attended church services irregularly during their working years and faithfully in retirement.

The high school band room, located near the auditorium, was designated as the pre-service gathering place for family members. Smithson's had made arrangements for a limo to pick Edie and Betsy up from Sedona Shadows and return them there afterward. Everyone else was expected to make their own travel arrangements.

When B. and Ali showed up at one thirty, Chris, Athena, and the kids were already in attendance. Baby Logan's first public appearance would be in honor of his great-grandfather's passing. Colin and Colleen, decked out in their Sunday best, were amazingly subdued. As soon as the two greats (as Edie and Betsy were routinely called) arrived, the twins gravitated in their direction and then stuck to the two women like glue. Observing that from the sidelines, Ali was pleased. All four of them were grieving, and it occurred to Ali that sharing grief was somehow less devastating than facing it alone.

At ten minutes to two, Althea Smithson, dressed in suitably somber attire, marshaled the family members into a line and escorted them into the auditorium through a side entrance. Once inside they were directed to sit in the front row. As they filed into their places, Ali noticed that the auditorium was full, with every seat taken. A standing-room-only crowd lined the rear of the auditorium. Ali hoped no one would alert the fire department.

Once she was seated, Ali's eyes filled with tears when she saw the myriad flower arrangements covering the stage. In the middle of that collection of flowers stood a small table draped with a black cloth. The tabletop held only two items, the first a poster-size photo of Bob Larson dressed in a tux for some shipboard occasion on one of the cruises he and Edie had taken together. In accordance with Bob's wishes, the second item was a highly polished pine box. Ali was glad Edie had resisted any suggestions that she consider switching over to an urn.

This was a service rather than a show, so the lights in the auditorium remained up throughout. Someone seated at a keyboard onstage was playing a grim classical piece Ali didn't recognize. She doubted that that particular bit of introductory music would have been her father's first choice.

When Reverend Duncan stepped up to the lectern, a

hushed silence fell over the room. "The opening hymn, 'Morning Has Broken,' was always one of Bob Larson's favorites," he announced. "You'll find the words to three verses printed in the program. You may remain seated."

The singing started sporadically enough, but eventually the voices joined in a full-throated chorus. Ali didn't have to read the words from the program, because she knew them by heart. She'd heard her father singing them often enough, uttering them almost under his breath as he wielded spatulas over the hot breakfast grill at the Sugarloaf Café. Ali did her best to sing along: "Morning has broken like the first morning . . ."

But a few lines in, her singing voice faltered. As her own vocal cords stopped functioning, she glanced in her mother's direction, only to see that Edie, too, had fallen silent. The twins kept right on singing.

Ali sat through the invocation and Scripture reading, hearing very little of it. She was lost in her own world, battling a surprisingly serious case of nerves. At last Reverend Duncan nodded in her direction. "Bob's daughter, Ali Reynolds, will now share a few words."

With that, Ali rose from her seat and walked up the stairs and onto the stage. Once behind the lectern, she took in the room, trying to wrap her mind around the number of people in attendance. Her father hadn't been famous. He wasn't a local politician or a fallen law-enforcement officer. He might have been an ordinary man, but the crowd was here nonetheless. She suspected that many of those gathered to honor Bob Larson were people who'd benefited from his kindness over the years and had sent some of those countless messages of appreciation in the last few days.

In the second row, just behind the family, Ali caught

sight of several familiar faces, including Stu Ramey's. That wasn't surprising. Her father had lent his beloved Bronco to Stu when he'd needed access to a standard-transmission vehicle while learning to drive. At the very end of that row, Cami sat with her cast-clad leg sticking out into the aisle. Across from her, also in the second row, Sister Anselm rode herd on Cami's wheel-chair.

As Ali paused momentarily, gathering herself, Sister Anselm caught her eye and sent her an encouraging smile. That small gesture was enough to spur Ali forward. Taking a deep breath, she began.

"Looking around the room," she said, "I see people who come from all the different facets of my father's life. Bob Larson was a large man who made an impact on a number of people, many of whom are here today. Some showed up to honor my dad's cooking, because Bob Larson made some of the best corned-beef hash ever served in Sedona."

That remark was greeted with a few chuckles and a bit of nervous laughter.

"Others are here," Ali continued, "because my father gathered firewood and clothing and food for them in times of need. They know that my father was an honorable man whose word was his bond. If Bob Larson made a promise, he kept it. That was simply the way he was."

A number of people in the standing-room-only section applauded at that and let out a few loud whoops. Yes, those homeless vets were there to be seen and heard.

"I'm here," Ali resumed, "because Bob Larson was a good and loyal husband and partner to my mother for sixty-five-plus years. I'm here because he was an excellent father who taught me the honor to be found in hard work and in doing whatever job you choose to the best of your ability.

"Bob Larson wasn't a guy who measured his success by the kind of car he drove—I'm sure many of you remember him tooling around in that old Bronco of his, which, unlike the grandfather clock in that old poem, has somehow managed to outlive him—or the house in which he lived. My parents spent most of their married life together in a humble two-bedroom house out behind the Sugarloaf Café. No, my father's success is reflected in the number of lifelong friendships he made along the way and in the people he reached out a hand to help.

"So yes, I'm sorry he's gone, but he lived a good and honorable life. And I'm grateful we had him for as long as we did."

When Ali returned to her spot in the pew, she saw Colleen, snuggled at her great-grandmother's side, Edie weeping quietly into the child's carefully braided hair. It was the first time since that day on Milton Albright's front porch that Ali had seen her mother shed tears.

As she sat down, B. leaned over to her and whispered, "Good job."

She nodded gratefully. "Thank you," she mouthed back.

The closing hymn was another one of Bob's favorites, "In the Garden." Following that and just before the benediction, Reverend Duncan suggested that after the service people go to the school cafeteria, where refreshments would be provided by the Ladies' Auxiliary of Sedona Faith Lutheran.

For two cents Ali would have gone straight home, but that wasn't an option. She was Bob Larson's daughter, and that afternoon her place was at her mother's side in Sedona High School's cafeteria, visiting with her father's mourners.

|CHAPTER 63|

MONROE, WASHINGTON

At two o'clock on Friday afternoon, Chloe Bannerman sat in a locked interview room in the Monroe Correctional Facility awaiting the arrival of Josiah Young. Dressed in a gray pinstripe suit with a spotlessly white high-necked blouse, she looked the part of what she had once been—a no-nonsense high school English teacher who had always worn her long hair in a thick coil at the base of her neck. Once black, her hair was now gunmetal gray, and because it was much thinner now, the coil wasn't nearly as large as it used to be.

Chloe was now seventy-three years old. She had come of age at a time when college-bound girls were encouraged to become either teachers or nurses, which was exactly what her trial-lawyer father had expected her to do. She'd complied initially, mostly because she'd always tried to be a dutiful daughter and because her father was paying her way through college, but after two years of teaching she'd called it quits, gone back to school on her own, and become the lawyer she'd always wanted to be. Her father had never forgiven her for that—and vice versa.

She sat upright with her hands folded calmly on the metal-topped table in front of her. She wasn't worried about what she would say because she fully expected to let Josiah Young do most of the talking.

When a guard escorted a heavily shackled Tattoo Man into the room, Chloe knew enough about him that she wasn't taken aback by either his appearance or the smug expression on his face. He would have swaggered as he entered, but unfortunately the shackles on his legs made swaggering pretty much a nonstarter. Every visible inch of Josiah's body was covered with a dense layer of tattoos. Even the flesh of his ears and the skin of his shaved skull were inked to the max. In the artificial light of the interview room, Josiah looked as though he had simply turned blue from the inside out.

Chloe waited patiently while the guard seated the prisoner and secured his handcuffs to the rings welded to the middle of the table.

"Who exactly are you?" he demanded.

His arrogant tone told Chloe everything she needed to know about who Josiah was—an insecure adult who had never escaped the misery of being an objectionable, know-it-all teenager. Back in her teaching years, she'd been barely four years older than some of the seniors assigned to her classrooms. Despite the proximity in age, she'd still managed to take some of the worst hotshots down a peg or two. Ironically, it was those in particular—the toughest nuts—who after outgrowing their youthful obnoxiousness had actively sought her out years later to thank her for being strict with them back in high school. Josiah Young, however, hadn't outgrown being a teenage jerk, and he never would.

"My name's Chloe Bannerman," she answered. "I represent an organization called Justice for All. I'm here to discuss the death of a young woman named Emily Anne Tarrant."

Josiah didn't so much as blink when Chloe mentioned the victim's name. Instead he lounged back in the chair as far as the handcuffs allowed and shrugged his shoulders. "Be my guest," he said. Then, with a grin, he added, "Oh, wait, you came all the way out here to see me, so I guess you already *are* my guest."

Chloe knew that anything said in the interview room would be duly recorded on the prison's surveillance system, but she wanted an audio copy of her own. She pulled out her cell phone and set it on the table next to her. "I hope you don't mind if I record this conversation."

Josiah grinned again. "Not at all. I'm already a three-time loser. How much worse could it be? Feel free to record away."

"Very well. This recording is being made at 2:06 p.m. on Friday, April thirteenth, 2018, in the Monroe Correctional Facility, Monroe, Washington. Present in the room are Josiah Alvin Young and Chloe A. Bannerman. Now, tell me, what do you know about Emily Tarrant?"

"The name doesn't ring a bell."

"That strikes me as strange," Chloe said, "but allow me to bring you up to speed. Emily Anne Tarrant was murdered in July 2001 after attending a beach party outside Edmonds, Washington. I believe you attended that same party as a guest of your brother Andrew."

"My stepbrother," Josiah corrected, "not my brother."

"So you do remember the party?"

"Vaguely."

"What were you doing in the Seattle area that summer?"

For the first time, a hint of anger surfaced through Josiah's blue-inked features. "My mother's husband thought spending some time with that goody-goody asshole son of his would get me to shape up." Then, glancing around the interview room and holding up his cuffed hands, he grinned again. "I guess it didn't quite work out that way."

"Your stepbrother would be Andrew Little."

"Yup."

"Did you strangle Emily Tarrant to death?" Chloe asked.

That did catch Josiah off guard, and he shot her a piercing look. "What makes you think I did?"

"Your DNA was found on her clothing."

"So? I was down on the beach smoking some grass when she came looking for a hit."

"Then you *do* remember the party?"

"I suppose, but that's all that happened. We were sitting there on a dead log smoking a joint when her boyfriend showed up and raised holy hell."

"That would be Mateo Vega, a friend of Andrew's?"

"I guess."

"Maybe you and Emily were doing more than just smoking," Chloe suggested.

Another shrug. "Maybe," he agreed.

"And after Emily and her boyfriend left the party, did she come back and ask you for a ride home?"

"Maybe," he said again. He was playing coy, but Chloe knew she was homing in on him.

"What happened then? Did you ask her for sex in exchange for the ride and she turned you down?"

Suddenly Josiah's anger exploded. "She didn't just turn me down. She started screaming her head off. Grabbing her by the throat was the only way I could shut her up. Otherwise everybody still at the party would have heard her."

"What did you do then?"

"Once she finally quieted down, I threw her body in a blackberry patch."

"Once she was dead, you mean," Chloe said. "Thank you so much, Mr. Young. I believe that's all I need."

"Did you know Emily's boyfriend ended up in here, too?" Josiah asked. Now he was actually smiling.

"Really?" Chloe asked. It was her turn to play coy.

"I never had any dealings with him," Josiah said. "There was no need, but I always thought it was funny as hell that he got sent up for Emily's murder and I didn't."

"Mr. Vega served sixteen years in prison for a crime he didn't commit. He doesn't think it's funny, Mr. Young, and neither do I," Chloe replied. "But again, thank you. You've been most helpful."

"What are you going to do about it?" he sneered.

"You'd be surprised," Chloe said.

With that she turned off her phone, stuffed it into her pocket, and picked up her briefcase. At the door she gave it a loud tap. "We're done here," she announced to the guard waiting outside. "I'm ready to go."

|CHAPTER 64|

COTTONWOOD, ARIZONA

On Saturday afternoon, a week after the initial job interview, Mateo was working his first-ever solo shift. Stu had said he should call if anything turned up that he couldn't handle, but so far that hadn't happened. He was so engrossed in making sure he followed all the procedures exactly that when his phone rang in his pocket, the sound startled him.

When he pulled it out and saw the 425 area code, he assumed it was most likely his parole officer calling from a home number rather than his office. On Monday, Mateo had called to check in and had been told that if he was now working out of state, his employer would need to send a written verification so that suitable parole supervision could be set up in that location. Mateo had asked B. to send the notice, but with everything that had been going on during the week, he doubted that had happened.

"Hello?"

"Mr. Vega?"

He recognized Chloe Bannerman's voice at once.
"Yes," he said. "It's me."

"I wanted to let you know that I interviewed Josiah
Young yesterday afternoon. While we were talking, he
admitted on tape to having strangled Emily Tarrant."

Mateo's heart seemed to stop beating. Was it possible
that his almost twenty-year nightmare was coming to an
end?

"He did?" Mateo managed at last. "Seriously?"

"Yes, seriously. Based on the paperwork I submitted,
including your signed retainer agreement, JFA's executive committee has voted unanimously in favor of taking
on your case. That means we're totally behind you, Mr.
Vega, and we'll be going to war with the King County
prosecutor's office on this as early as Monday morning. I
wanted to give you a heads-up. In case any media people
try tracking you down, please refer all of them to me."

Mateo finally found a way to breathe again. "Thank
you," he choked. "I'll be sure to do that."

"You're very welcome," Chloe said. "It's not a done
deal yet by any means, but we've taken the first steps."

"I don't know how to express my gratitude."

"You don't have to," Chloe said. "This isn't a job for
me. It's my passion."

For a few moments after the call ended, Mateo sat
there with the phone in his hand, not quite knowing
what to do next. But then he did the only thing that made
sense. He dialed his mother's number in Walla Walla and
told her. Mateo was the first person outside of Justice
for All to hear what Chloe Bannerman had learned from
Josiah Young. Olivia Ortega Vega was number two.

|CHAPTER 65|

BELLINGHAM, WASHINGTON

Mel is an early riser, even on weekends. I'm not. Now that I can sleep in, I do. When I came out to the kitchen that Sunday morning, she was already up, dressed, and had read the Sunday papers, both the *Bellingham Review* and the *Seattle Times*.

"Did the bombshell wake you up?" she asked, handing me a cup of coffee.

"What bombshell?" I wondered.

"Chloe Bannerman's," she answered, handing me the front section of the *Times*. The headline said it all:

GROUP SEEKS TO OVERTURN
2002 HOMICIDE CONVICTION

Justice for All, a nationally known wrongful-conviction group, has agreed to fight what they call a botched investigation and mishandled evidence that erroneously sent an innocent man to prison for sixteen years for a homicide he did not commit.

According to JFA spokeswoman and attorney Chloe Bannerman, Mr. Juan Mateo Vega, on the advice of his original public defender, pled guilty to a charge of second-degree murder in 2002 in order to avoid the possibility of a far longer prison sentence had the case gone to trial.

Mr. Vega served a total of sixteen years for the murder of Emily Anne Tarrant, whose body was found in a blackberry bush near the scene of a beach party outside the community of Edmonds, Washington.

Mr. Vega and the victim had both attended the party and were observed having an acrimonious quarrel while there. Mr. Vega said that the argument continued as they left for home. Shortly thereafter the victim exited his vehicle and was never seen alive again. When she didn't return home, Mr. Vega reported her missing the following day.

Ms. Tarrant's body was located two days later. The ensuing investigation into her death was led by Detective Henry Norton, then the King County Sheriff's Office's lead investigator, who has since retired.

Ms. Bannerman maintains that tunnel vision on the part of investigators led them to focus completely on Mr. Vega without looking at any other viable suspects. She claims that DNA evidence that might have exonerated her client was mishandled by the Washington State Patrol Crime Lab.

"DNA evidence from the Emily Tarrant crime scene was never uploaded to CODIS, the national database that maintains the DNA profiles of criminal offenders, as well as unidentified ones taken from crime scenes. Had the DNA been properly uploaded at the time, it would have led investigators to Josiah Alvin Young, who has recently admitted to strangling Ms. Tarrant.

"Mr. Young is currently incarcerated in the Monroe Correctional Facility, where he is serving three consecutive life sentences on three separate convictions of forcible rape and murder. Mr. Young is also the prime suspect in a fourth homicide case currently pending in Idaho.

"Since Mr. Young was also in attendance at that 2001 beach party, a more thorough investigation from King County investigators might have led to his arrest, thus preventing the subsequent homicides of at least four other innocent young women."

Ms. Bannerman went on to say that the state's failure to properly upload the DNA profiles to CODIS in a timely fashion most likely contributed to those other deaths.

Mr. Vega was released on parole in May 2017, having served sixteen years in prison, and he remains on parole today. Ms. Bannerman says she fully expects Justice for All to file a wrongful-conviction suit against the state of Washington, seeking financial restitution for all the years Mr. Vega spent in prison.

"I remember Hank Norton from our days with SHIT," Mel observed when I looked up after finishing the article. "I thought he was a worm the first time I met him, and clearly I wasn't wrong. Chloe Bannerman sounds like a pretty awesome sort."

"She is," I agreed. "She most certainly is."

With that I took my coffee and headed for the family room.

"Where are you going?" Mel asked. "Don't you want some breakfast?"

"Eventually yes," I said. "But first I'm going to fire up my computer and send that article to Ali Reynolds so she can pass it along to Mateo."

"I doubt she'll need to," Mel replied. "Unless I miss my guess, Chloe Bannerman will have sent the news to her client long before she contacted the *Seattle Times*."

It turns out Mel was right on that score. Mateo already knew, and so did Ali Reynolds. I was the one who was late to the party.

|CHAPTER 66|

MONROE, WASHINGTON

On Sunday mornings the mess hall at the Monroe Correctional Facility was as quiet as it ever got—which is to say not very. But on this particular morning, there was an unidentifiable buzz in the air that was intense enough to penetrate through Pop Johnson's single-minded concentration as he sat at a table reading Brad Thor's most recent thriller.

In his previous life, Henry Mansfield Johnson hadn't been into reading. Mateo Vega had changed all that. For the five years they were cellmates, Mateo had spent every waking moment reading the thick technical volumes he dragged in from the prison library. Then one day he had tossed a worn paperback onto Pop's cot—*Radigan* by Louis L'Amour. Within the matter of a few chapters, Pop was hooked. The story took him to places he'd never been and now would never go. Almost magically, they transported him beyond the walls of his cell, and suddenly Pop Johnson became something he'd never expected to be—a reader.

Because Mateo worked in the prison library, he was able to lay hands on new books long before anyone else could. By the time Mateo was paroled, Pop, too, was working in Mrs. Ancell's library, where he found that the fastest way to the woman's heart was to be a devoted reader. In Mateo's absence Pop still had first dibs on new books. He much preferred hardbacks to paperbacks, but not for reasons Mrs. Ancell would have found endearing. Over time Pop became something of a legend because he always had a book with him wherever he went—and that included the mess hall.

One of the reasons Mateo and Pop had gotten along as cellmates was that neither of them made waves. They steered clear of troublemakers, but they weren't to be trifled with either. If someone tried to push one of them around, they had each other's back.

There was a definite hierarchy in the seating arrangements in the mess hall, and Pop always gravitated to the least popular table in the room—the one farthest from the serving line. He had finished the powdered-egg slop that passed for breakfast and had his head buried in the book when the tension in the room finally broke through his concentration.

"What's going on?" he asked the guy next to him.

"Didn't you hear? It was all over TV news this morning. Some hotshot woman lawyer is coming after Tattoo Man—says he's the one who killed the girl your old roomie, Mateo, got sent up for."

"No shit?"

"No shit."

Pop looked around the large, noisy room. Tattoo Man always sat at the very best table, the one closest to the end of the serving line. The people seated there could just as well have been put out with a rubber stamp—a blue rubber stamp at that. They were all inked from head to toe, but it was clear from Josiah Young's superior attitude that he considered himself to be the leader of that particular pack.

The fury Pop Johnson felt in that moment left him shaken. Emily Tarrant's real killer had been here in the same prison with Mateo for years without anyone knowing the truth? A young man—a good man—had been robbed of a big chunk of his life due to a crime committed by that tattoo-covered pile of crap? Pop remembered what Mateo had said before he left—that he was going to find a job, yes, but that his primary goal was to find Emily's real killer. And all the while the murderer in question had been right here in the same prison.

Pop didn't have to think about what he was going to do next. It wasn't as though his actions were premeditated. He tucked Brad Thor's book under his arm, picked up his tray, and headed for the dishwashing stand and the line of garbage cans that just happened to be on the far side of Tattoo Man's reserved table.

Once Mateo was released and Pop had been left to his own devices, he'd set about fashioning what he expected to be a defensive weapon, using a discarded toothbrush as the base. One end had been sharpened to form a stiff, three-inch-long plastic needle. The other end had been cross-filed to create a rough surface. And that shank was the reason Pop Johnson only read hardback books these days, preferably brand-new hardbacks.

A queer old guy dragging a steady stream of books around didn't appear to be much of a threat. Initially guards had thumbed through the pages to make sure

Pop wasn't using the books to transport some kind of contraband. Eventually they got tired of looking and just left him alone.

The problem was, all the guards ever checked were the pages themselves. They never delved into the spines, and new-book spines were still stiff enough that Pop could shove the shank inside, concealing it completely. The rough, cross-filed surface acted as a piece of hard plastic Velcro, hanging up on the bound pages under the cover. Pop could pull the weapon out easily enough, but it never fell out of its own accord.

He walked slowly and carefully as befitting his age. He'd read enough books that he knew exactly where his weapon would do the most damage—at the top of Tattoo Man's neck, just at the base of his skull. A single upward thrust into Josiah Young's medulla would take him out. Lacking the brain function necessary to control breathing, Tattoo Man would be dead in a matter of seconds, and justice would finally be served right there in the mess hall.

Had any evidence at all against Josiah Young been presented in a court of law? No. Had he been found guilty by a jury of his peers? No, but in this case Pop Johnson was prepared to function as judge, jury, and executioner all at once, with no plea deals available.

Pop was sure his wouldn't be the only weapon at the scene, but that hardly deterred him. He had served more than forty years of his two life sentences. This was his forever get-out-of-jail-free card.

Pausing after emptying his tray into the trash, he kept his back turned to the room long enough to extract his shank from the book binding. When he turned around, he was less than five quick steps from Tattoo Man's back. He covered the ground quickly, before anyone even noticed he was moving in that direction. And as soon as the shank plunged deep into the unprotected flesh at the base of Josiah Young's skull, Pop knew he'd hit his target.

For a moment the room seemed to freeze in place, and then all hell broke loose. Josiah's seatmates and henchmen rose up in fury as their dead leader fell face-first into his empty serving tray. They came after Pop, but he didn't bother trying to run, because he knew that not escaping was his best hope for escape.

Someone else's shank cut into him, slicing open his abdomen. It hurt like hell, but all Pop could do was laugh. The jackass might be killing him, but he was giving him a way out, and that was the only thing that mattered.

Alarms sounded as guards poured into the room, using batons and tasers to break up the melee. Eventually one of them knelt over Pop. "Hang on, old-timer," he said. "Help is coming."

"Is he dead?" Pop whispered back.

"Yes," the guard replied. "I think so."

"Good," Pop said. "I just finished me some unfinished business."

|CHAPTER 67|

SEDONA, ARIZONA

After an amazingly tough week, B. and Ali had spent the weekend resting and regrouping. Monday found them both back at work. Sister Anselm assured them that Cami's hands had recovered enough that they'd been able to remove the bandages. By the end of the week, she expected that their temporarily wheelchair-bound employee could be back on the job on a limited basis, although she would still need some help getting around, both at home and at work.

With Cami's expected return in mind, B. set about rearranging his scrubbed appointments from the previous week. As for Ali? With tax returns due today, she was glad she and the accountant had ironed out all the details weeks earlier. Thankfully, there would be no last-minute filings today. As she started on the accumulated mess on her desk, an anxious Shirley appeared in her doorway.

"An investigator from the Arizona Department of Public Safety, a Detective William Margate, is out at the reception desk," Shirley said. "He wants to talk to Mateo. I asked him what it's about. He said it's confidential. What should I do?"

"Bring him here to my office," Ali said. "Is Mateo in the lab?"

Shirley nodded.

"Ask him to come here, too."

When Shirley ushered the detective into Ali's office, she rose to greet him. "I'm Ali Reynolds, Mateo Vega's employer. If I may ask, what does this concern?"

"As I told the lady out front, this is a private matter that needs to be discussed with Mr. Vega himself."

Mateo appeared in the doorway. "Whatever it is, you can talk about it with Ali here in the room. What's this all about?"

The detective, seated in front of Ali's desk, looked uneasy. "I believe you're acquainted with a gentleman named Henry Johnson, sometimes known as Pop."

Mateo nodded.

"I regret to say that I'm here to deliver some bad news," Detective Margate said. "Mr. Johnson died early today. He was badly injured yesterday morning in a riot at the Monroe Correctional Facility. He was airlifted to Harborview Medical Center in Seattle, where he underwent emergency surgery for a stab wound to the abdomen. Unfortunately, he did not survive. Prison records list you as his next of kin, so I'm here on official business. We located you by contacting your parole officer."

"What kind of a riot?" Mateo wondered. "Pop wasn't the kind to get himself into any kind of trouble."

"From what I've been told, Mr. Johnson was the instigator of the violence. He attacked a fellow inmate from behind and fatally stabbed him."

"Which inmate?" an ashen-faced Mateo asked.

Margate pulled out a notebook and examined his notes. "One Josiah Young," he answered.

Mateo's knees buckled under him. He staggered forward and dropped heavily onto the nearest chair. At last he got a grip on himself.

"Are you saying they think I had something to do with it?"

Margate seemed genuinely surprised at that. "Why, no," he said. "Did you?"

"No," Mateo said. "Pop and I were friends. Once I was released on parole, I started sending him money every month for his commissary account, but that's all. We've not been in touch otherwise."

"Very well," said Margate, rising to his feet. "Sorry for your loss," he added. "I'll show myself out."

Once the detective was gone, Mateo remained where he was for a long moment. When he came to himself, he saw that Ali was studying him intently.

"Pop was my friend," Matco said. "We were cellmates for five years. He must have heard about Josiah's confession to Emily's murder and—" He broke off, unable to continue.

"If I were you," Ali said kindly, "I believe I'd give Chloe Bannerman a call."

|CHAPTER 68|

SEDONA, ARIZONA

Ali and B. were at home that night and sorting out their day when Ali's mom called.

"I know you need to work," Edie said, "and if this is too much to ask, please tell me, but I was wondering if you could do me a favor tomorrow?"

"Of course, Mom," Ali said, "whatever you need. Where and when?"

"Could you pick me up tomorrow morning around ten? I need you to drive me somewhere. It'll probably take a couple of hours—three, maybe four."

"Happy to, Mom," Ali said. "See you in the morning at ten o'clock sharp."

Ali arrived at the appointed hour, pulled up under the Sedona Shadows portico, and then texted her mother to say she was there waiting. It was the first time Ali had seen Edie since the day of the funeral. When she came through the double doors, she walked with a firm step, carrying a shopping bag in one hand, with the polished pine box tucked under her other arm.

As soon as Ali saw the box, she knew where they were going.

"Up to the rim?" she asked as her mother climbed into the Cayenne and fastened her seat belt.

Edie said nothing. She simply nodded.

Once Edie was inside the vehicle, Ali identified what was in the bag, because the spicy aroma of a Sugarloaf Café sweet roll soon filled the air. While Ali was growing up, that scent had been an integral part of her existence. Happily, the café's new owners continued to use Edie's standout recipe.

"I take it we're having a picnic?" Ali asked.

Edie nodded again.

As they pulled away from Sedona Shadows and turned onto the highway, Edie seemed disinclined to speak, so Ali kept quiet as well. That didn't mean it was a lighthearted drive, however. There was something heavy looming in that lengthening silence, and Ali worried about what it would be.

It wasn't until after they turned north on I-17 that Edie finally spoke. "I understand why Bobby did what he did," she said, "but I'm not sure I can forgive him for it. I believe he wanted to spare me, but he never bothered to ask if I wanted to be spared. I wanted more time with him, Ali. That's all I wanted—more time."

Ali considered saying something about quality of life or self-determination. Since those weren't words that would soothe her mother's aching heart right then, she didn't mention them.

"Dad loved you, Mom," Ali said simply. "And he thought that what he was doing was a reflection of that."

"Well, he was wrong," Edie asserted.

The same brooding silence settled back over them.

"I liked what you said about him in your eulogy," Edie said after another long pause. "Bobby was a good man. I'm going to miss him terribly, even though he could be incredibly annoying at times—for all the reasons you mentioned. He was always looking out for others and not necessarily looking out for us."

Ali nodded. "In the past few days, I've found out more about that than I ever imagined."

"So I'm proud of him and mad at him at the same time," Edie said. "Does that make any sense?"

"It makes perfect sense."

"He always said that if he went first, he wanted me to go on living," Edie continued. "So that's why we're scattering his ashes today. If he'd been buried instead of cremated, they would have taken him straight from the funeral to the cemetery. So it seems to me the sooner the better, right?"

"Mom, what's important in this moment is doing what's right for you as opposed to what might have been right for him or anybody else."

"Thank you for saying that," Edie said. "It's almost the same thing Betsy said to me this morning at breakfast. And in terms of moving on, she's my role model."

No argument there, Ali thought. Athena's grandmother was the poster child for reinventing herself in the aftermath of a spouse's death.

"And why the sweet roll?" Ali asked.

"The two best things Dad and I ever did were having you and inventing that sweet-roll recipe. I wanted you here with me so we could toast him with a sweet roll before we open the box."

"If that's what you want, that's exactly what we'll do."

Again quiet settled into the vehicle, only this time it

wasn't quite as heavy. Minutes later, when Ali glanced toward the passenger seat, she realized her mother had quietly nodded off. Ali didn't awaken her. She didn't know for sure that her mother wasn't sleeping well, but she guessed that to be the case. As the Cayenne turned off I-17 at the exit to Schnebly Hill Road, Edie jerked awake.

"I didn't mean to fall asleep," she said.

"It's fine, Mom. Don't worry about it."

Half an hour later, after threading their way through the homeless encampment, they pulled over to a spot where Edie said she knew there was a path out to the edge of the rim. Ali kept her mouth shut and let her mother lead the way to their intended destination. It was a small clearing with a breathtaking view over the edge into the Verde Valley far below. Obviously, other people had found this spot to be enchanting, too, because someone had gone to the trouble of constructing a rustic split-log bench. That's where they sat.

Edie opened the bag and pulled out a pair of paper plates, napkins, some plastic knives, and a small disposable container filled with butter.

"Bobby always said it was criminal to eat one of these without butter."

"Agreed," Ali said.

She sat quietly while her mother sliced the single roll in half and then placed one of the pieces on the plate she passed to Ali, who immediately slathered on a layer of butter.

"Bobby and I worked on this recipe for weeks," Edie remarked. "When we finally had two candidates we thought would work, we left it up to Evie to decide, and this is the one she chose."

Evie had been Edie's twin sister, and she, too, had been a partner in the restaurant.

"Good choice," Ali said.

"I always thought so."

They sat in silence, this time savoring the sweetness.

"Thank you for driving me up here. I could have done it on my own, I suppose, but I was afraid I would have cried the whole way."

"You didn't," Ali observed.

"No, I didn't," Edie agreed.

By the time they finished their snack, a stiff wind was blowing out of the east. As they cleaned up their mess, both women were feeling the chill, but Edie was determined to forge ahead. Taking a deep breath, she reached for the box. Ali was surprised to see that it was more of a freestanding drawer than it was a box. A push on the top caused the drawer to slide out into the open. Seeing the gray contents inside, Ali swallowed hard, but Edie was determined.

Extracting the drawer from its frame, she straightened up and walked toward the cliff. Following behind, Ali couldn't help herself. "Careful," she warned.

"Don't worry," Edie replied, suddenly sounding more like her old self. "I wouldn't want you to lose both your father and me at the same time."

As they stood on the edge of the precipice, a steady breeze continued to blow behind them.

"Are you ready?" Edie asked.

"Ready," Ali said.

"Good-bye, Bobby," Edie said after a pause. "I miss you so much."

With that, Edie Larson heaved the contents of the drawer into the air. Mother and daughter stood side by side watching as the cloud of ashes, borne on the breeze, drifted out of sight, disappearing into the distance far below.

When Edie finally turned to face Ali, they both burst into tears and then retreated to the bench together.

Eventually, when their tears abated, Edie fit the loose drawer back into its frame. Then, picking up both the box and the bag, she led the way back to the car.

"What are you going to do with the box?" Ali asked once they were back inside the Cayenne with their seat belts fastened.

"Reuse it, of course," Edie said. "These things don't grow on trees, you know." Then, after a pause, she added, "Come to think of it, I guess wood does grow on trees. But there's no reason to spend just for the sake of spending. I looked these up on the Internet. It turns out a box like this is way more expensive than one of those tacky urns. When it's my time to go, you can reuse the same box, and I want my ashes scattered in the same place. Got it?"

This was so like Ali's parents—so like both of them—and in that moment she felt bathed in their love.

"Got it," Ali replied. "I hear you loud and clear."